"This series go ⟨✓⟩ W9-CJY-858 ndersen is a must read for m⋯.
— #1 *New York Times* bestselling author J. R. Ward

Storm Kissed

"A superb thriller . . . fast-paced and character-driven. . . . Fans will relish this exhilarating tale."
— Genre Go Round Reviews

"Thrilling. . . . With this tale of prophecy and curses, Andersen really shakes up her series. Love, loss, passion, and drama are all here. You won't be able to put this one down."
— *Romantic Times*

Blood Spells

"For readers with a hankering for a fascinating and intricate foray into the Mayan world, the Nightkeeper series is just perfect."
— The Romance Readers Connection

"Andersen has created a compelling cast of characters whose personal travails add richness to these highly entertaining novels. Another excellent job."
— *Romantic Times*

Demonkeepers

"Andersen ramps up the danger . . . mix[ing] action and elements of Mayan myth—from a voyage to the underworld to a fantastic high-stakes ball game—with soul-searching, lust, and romance. Jade's inner journey is particularly engaging, and while the background makes more sense to returning fans, even new readers will find plenty to latch onto."
— *Publishers Weekly*

"Intense . . . thrilling . . . a world that fans of any genre will enjoy."
— The Romance Readers Connection

"Fabulous . . . will have the audience appreciating the skills of master magician Jessica Andersen."
— *Midwest Book Review*

continued . . .

The Novels of the Nightkeepers

Nightkeepers
Dawnkeepers
Skykeepers
Demonkeepers
Blood Spells
Storm Kissed

MAGIC UNCHAINED

A NOVEL OF THE NIGHTKEEPERS

JESSICA ANDERSEN

A SIGNET ECLIPSE BOOK

SIGNET ECLIPSE
Published by New American Library, a division of
Penguin Group (USA) Inc., 375 Hudson Street,
New York, New York 10014, USA
Penguin Group (Canada), 90 Eglinton Avenue East, Suite 700, Toronto,
Ontario M4P 2Y3, Canada (a division of Pearson Penguin Canada Inc.)
Penguin Books Ltd., 80 Strand, London WC2R 0RL, England
Penguin Ireland, 25 St. Stephen's Green, Dublin 2,
Ireland (a division of Penguin Books Ltd.)
Penguin Group (Australia), 250 Camberwell Road, Camberwell, Victoria 3124,
Australia (a division of Pearson Australia Group Pty. Ltd.)
Penguin Books India Pvt. Ltd., 11 Community Centre, Panchsheel Park,
New Delhi - 110 017, India
Penguin Group (NZ), 67 Apollo Drive, Rosedale, Auckland 0632,
New Zealand (a division of Pearson New Zealand Ltd.)
Penguin Books (South Africa) (Pty.) Ltd., 24 Sturdee Avenue,
Rosebank, Johannesburg 2196, South Africa

Penguin Books Ltd., Registered Offices:
80 Strand, London WC2R 0RL, England

First published by Signet Eclipse, an imprint of New American Library,
a division of Penguin Group (USA) Inc.

First Printing, April 2012
10 9 8 7 6 5 4 3 2 1

This book is dedicated to Paula R. Happy birthday to a dear friend, fan, teacher, poet, and occasional lead foot. This one's for you!

AUTHOR'S NOTE AND ACKNOWLEDGMENTS

I'll admit it: I'm a sucker for a handsome daredevil, especially one with a soft spot for animals. Enter Sven, a former wreck-diving, hard-partying adrenaline junkie who has become the Nightkeepers' best tracker, thanks to his coyote familiar, Mac. Sven is a loner, though, a wanderer who, sharklike, suffocates if he's in one place for too long. And Cara Liu, who's known him all her life and loved him just as long, knows he won't always be there when she needs him . . . so she's learned not to need him. Or anyone, really—she's a powerful leader in her own right, and does just fine on her own. So when the two of them are thrown together in the final months before the doomsday war, and tasked with turning four dozen former rebels into a magic-wielding army, fur flies.

Please join me now as Sven and Cara snarl and snap, and try not to fall for each other all over again while the doomsday clock counts down, friends turn against friends, and the promise of a powerful ally means cheating death itself.

To explore the Nightkeepers' online world and sign up for my newsletter, please visit www.JessicaAndersen.com. Also, please become a fan on Facebook to get a look at my oh so Freudian typos and other authorial misadventures!

My heartfelt thanks go to Deidre Knight, Claire Zion, Kara Welsh, and Kerry Donovan, and others too numerous to name for helping me bring these books to life; to J. R. Ward for being my sounding board; and to my family, friends, and many e-friends for always being there for a laugh or (cyber)hug. And most of all to my husband, Greg, for showing me that soul mates, spontaneous combustion, and true love do exist, and that they're so very worth waiting for.

Finally, thank you, dear reader, for picking up Sven and Cara's story. I hope you love it as much as I do—this one is very special to me.

Jessica (aka Doc Jess)

Bound by blood and magic, the Nightkeepers must defend mankind from the rise of terrible demons as the end date of 12-21-2012 approaches. Although most of the magi must find and bond with their gods-destined mates to reach their full powers, one among them draws his magic from another source and wanders free, unmated and alone, save for his coyote familiar.

Testing the barrier between the earth and underworld, the demons have sent a dark-magic scourge—the *xombi* virus—to infect the Nightkeepers' human allies and build an army of the damned. After months of battling the *xombis*, the coyote mage returns to the Nightkeepers' home, little suspecting what he's going to find when he gets there . . .

CHAPTER ONE

September 10
T-minus three months and
eleven days to the foretold doomsday
Skywatch
Near Chaco Canyon, New Mexico

Cara Liu figured it didn't matter whether it was a Catholic mass or a bloodletting ritual; funerals just flat-out sucked. More, the grief of losing Aaron—who had been a good guy, always ready with a laugh, a beer, or an ass kicking, depending on the situation—came with an equal amount of fear, because the men and women gathered around the pyre knew damn well that it could've been any one of them.

Aaron might've been the first *winikin* to lose his life fighting alongside the Nightkeepers, but it was a sure bet he wouldn't be the last. With the earth's magic-wielding guardians decimated and the end-time approaching fast, their new leader, Mendez, hadn't had a choice. Within a month of Cara's persuading fifty rebellious *winikin* to return to the training compound that they and their parents had fled nearly three decades earlier, Dez had "promoted" the traditional servants on to Nightkeeper-led fighting teams and put them through a crash course in killing demons and protecting their own asses, roughly in that order.

Sure, the *winikin* had voted in favor of fighting ... but given that the alternative was an apocalypse that would turn mankind into an undead army, what other choice was there?

As the last of them passed by the pyre, thunder grumbled in the distance, warning that the darkening horizon meant business. It had been a dry desert summer, but it looked like the autumn rains were coming sooner rather than later.

Like now.

"That's just freaking great," Cara muttered to nobody in particular, using irritation to blunt the knowledge that Aaron wouldn't be dead if it hadn't been for her. She had tracked him to a small town in upstate New York, where he'd been teaching high school English and coaching basketball, and she'd persuaded him to come to New Mexico. *The world needs you,* she'd said. And now, nine months later, he was dead, killed down in central Mexico when it had turned out that the extermination team hadn't taken care of all of the infected villagers after all. There had been one left, and it had gotten Aaron before any of the others had had a chance to react.

When Cara's eyes prickled, she scrubbed at them on the pretext of shoving her black, skunk-striped hair out of her face. She stood apart from the others, halfway up a flight of stone steps that led from the packed earth of the ball court. Wearing slim black pants and a matching blazer punked out with chains and zippers, with her weapons belt conspicuously absent in deference to the ritual, she thought—hoped—she looked calm, controlled, and capable. Nobody else needed to know that her insides were churning with anger and grief, along with the unease that had been dogging her for days now, weeks.

Don't think about it, she told herself. *It's nothing.*

Only it didn't feel like nothing.

If she had been a true Nightkeeper, she would've thought it was prescience, a foretelling of some dire threat. She was a *winikin*, though, which meant that the nerves were probably just nerves, brought on by the knowledge that the zero date was almost on top of them and her people weren't the united force they needed to be. Far from it, in fact.

Don't think about it, she repeated inwardly, and forced herself to look at the intricately tied funerary bundle that rested atop the pyre. But it was like trying not to think about a big white wolf, because the moment she thought it, *boom,* there the big furry bastard was, smack in the middle of her brain, along with all the other stuff she was trying to ignore. It wasn't like she was playing ostrich, either. In fact, she was emulating the Nightkeeper warriors and their ability to prioritize their goals and put the needs of the many over those of the few, even if those few were teammates or even their families and loved ones.

Love . . . Now, there was a concept. As was family.

She glanced over at her father, Carlos, who was a stocky bull of an ex-rancher in his fifties. His hair was silver-shot and his face was showing its age now, where before he'd looked a good decade younger than his calendar years. As she gazed at him, his shoulders went suddenly very square beneath his dark suit jacket, letting her know he'd caught her look, though he didn't respond, didn't even meet her eyes. The fiercest of the traditionalists, he hadn't forgiven her for leaving Skywatch in the first place, never mind everything that had happened since circumstances had forced her to return.

Jamming her hands in her jacket pockets, she rocked back on the worn heels of her black cowboy boots. Holdovers from her old life in Montana, they were as much a comfort to her as chocolate might be to another woman. They reminded her of green meadows, endless gallops, and family dinners, all long gone.

She sighed and glanced again at the horizon. "The winds are changing," she said, pitching her voice so it would carry to her second in command, who stood below her on the ball court.

Zane nodded without taking his eyes off the pyre. "We should move this along if we want to beat the rain." The ex-marine was at parade rest, though she wasn't sure whether he was standing guard, awaiting orders, or a little bit of both.

He had been one of her first recruits, and although he had carried serious rank out in the human world, he had zero problem taking orders from an inexperienced, pintsize woman ten years his junior. Rather than joining the others in complaining about how she'd wound up as their leader, he had done his damnedest to squelch the discontent and help level things off among the rebels, traditionalists, and Nightkeepers. And thank the gods for that, because she didn't know how she could have gained even a semblance of control without him.

Touching the high-tech bracelet she wore on her right wrist, over the place where she had once been marked with the glyphs that tagged her as a servant to the coyote bloodline, she murmured into the bracelet's audio pickup, "Rabbit? It's time."

The magi had paid their respects already, leaving the *winikin* to conduct their own ceremony, as was proper. Cara had decided to break with tradition, though, in having the Nightkeepers' sole surviving fire starter light Aaron's funerary bundle—both for the symbolism and because it would ensure a complete burn.

To her surprise there hadn't been much of a protest, even from the trads. Then again, it wasn't the first change she'd made, and it sure as heck wouldn't be the last. Her predecessor, the royal *winikin* Jox, hadn't chosen her to do more of the same; he'd picked her precisely because of who and what she was: a half human, half *winikin* who had been born after the massacre that wiped out their numbers and been raised by one of the most traditional of the trads, but who had no interest in serving the bloodline as Carlos did.

I want someone to shake things up, Jox had written in the sealed letter that named her the *winikin*'s new leader, and she had done plenty of that. But the countdown to the end date was down to its last three months and a few days now, which meant there wasn't much shaking room left. At some point they were going to have to go with what they had.

"Here he comes." Zane tipped his head toward the open end of the ball court nearest to the mansion.

Rabbit approached at a ground-eating jog. Although at twenty-three he was the youngest of the magi by nearly a decade, he looked to be in his late twenties or early thirties, having been aged prematurely by the strange and powerful hybrid magic given to him by his mixed heritage. Pale eyed, sharp featured, and back to sporting a short Mohawk, Rabbit could've stepped right out of central casting for *Last of the Mohicans,* even though his jeans, black tee, Goth-chained boots, and MAC-10 machine pistol were thoroughly modern.

Many of the *winikin*—and not just the newcomers—were wary of Rabbit, who was a mind-bender and telekine in addition to being a fire starter. Cara, though, felt a certain nonconformists' kinship. They were both half-bloods, both prone to making waves. He had the advantage, though—he had more magic than all the other Nightkeepers put together. She just had herself, and the illusion of control.

She came down the steps while he took his place at the foot of the pyre. And, as she hit the ground, she pretended not to see Zane's outstretched hand. Guilt stung, though, along with a fleeting wish that things were different between them.

Zane was a good man, clean-cut and handsome in a blocky, bench-pressed sort of way, and it would've made practical and political sense for them to get together. But two days ago, when he'd surprised the hell out of her by showing up at the door of her suite with a bouquet of cactus blooms and feelings she hadn't realized he'd been percolating, he'd put it exactly like that: Their pairing would be practical, politically advantageous, and stable. That wasn't exactly the protestation of undying love she would've been hoping for ... if she'd been hoping for one. Which she hadn't been, because although destiny, or whatever you wanted to call it, might have forced her back to Skywatch, she'd be damned if she let herself fall into a relationship because it was practical or con-freaking-venient.

She wanted more than practicality, more than a lover

who was her lover because he was right down the hall. No, she wanted sparks, fireworks, affection, trust. A guy who turned her on, adored her, would be there for her no matter what . . . and in her experience, that combination was about as common as a whale watch in the desert.

Besides, she thought, stifling a sigh as Zane fell in beside her and they crossed the short distance to the pyre together, it wasn't like she had the time or energy to start something right now. Not even close. She had an army within an army to lead, dissidents to soothe, battles to fight . . . all in the hopes of making it through to December twenty-second intact and moving on with her life.

That was her promise to herself, the four words that kept her going day after day: *I'll do it after.*

After the final battle, when—please, gods—Skywatch disbanded and they all went their separate ways, she would throw herself into the hunt and find a job she loved, a man she loved, a life she loved. Sparks, fireworks, volcanic eruptions . . . She would go for broke and live the life she hadn't managed to find before Skywatch reopened, when she'd been young and sheltered, or after she'd gone off on her own, little realizing that her restlessness and chronic poor health had been the magic's way of saying, "Get back where you belong."

Well, she was back at Skywatch, all right, but she still didn't belong. She was determined, though, to live long enough to rejoin the world, and do her part to make sure there was a world worth escaping into. And if that meant falling asleep some nights with her pillow clutched to her chest and her insides so hollow they ached, then that was a sacrifice she was willing to make. That was what she'd told Zane—more or less—the other night, and it was what she reminded herself of now as she had to fight a brief and unfair desire to lean into his solid bulk.

Instead, taking a deep, settling breath, she moved into the circle on Rabbit's right side, which put her next to Natalie, the pretty blond archaeologist who had become her closest friend at Skywatch. The women exchanged a look, but said nothing. Now wasn't the time.

When Zane stepped up to complete the circle on Natalie's other side, face set, Cara nodded to Rabbit. "Go ahead."

The big, tough-looking mage hesitated, though, and took a long look around at the the *winikin*. The pause lasted so long that she wondered what he saw. Did he notice that he was taller than any of them by at least a head, heavier by a good fifty pounds? Did he ask himself what the hell Mendez was up to, trying to make the members of the servant class into a fighting force? Or was he thinking about something else entirely?

It was hard to tell with Rabbit.

Finally he said, "For what it's worth, I think it sucks that the First Father's magic has trapped you the way it has. It's not fair that you don't have a choice whether to serve or not, and, well . . ." He scanned their faces, though she didn't know what he was looking for, still didn't know what he saw. "Anyway. I'm sorry for your loss."

He said something else, but Cara couldn't hear him over the sudden rushing in her ears as his words kicked up memories of one of the things she was seriously trying not to think about: the last funeral she attended.

I'm sorry for your loss, the priest had told her, and most of the people who filed past the grave had spouted a variation on the theme. She had made the right noises, forcing herself to act the hostess because there was nobody else left to carry the burden. Her mother was in that fresh-turned grave, her father just standing there beside her, staring through the people who stopped to shake his hand and murmur something they thought would comfort. And the fourth member of their strange little family—her so-called foster brother, Sven, who hadn't been any sort of brother at all—hadn't even shown up. He was off diving the Great Barrier Reef, he'd said by way of a voice mail, and couldn't get there in time. So he hadn't even tried.

That wasn't the first time Sven had let her down, but it had been the final proof that he cared far more about his adventures than the people who loved him.

Shit. Don't go there. And for gods' sake, focus. This wasn't about her and Zane, wasn't about her and Sven, wasn't about her at all. It was about completing the ritual and showing the *winikin* that she wasn't dumping all of the traditions. Just the ones that didn't make modern-day sense.

Realizing that Rabbit had started the funerary rite, she winced and made herself dial back in.

"We ask the First Father, the Hero Twins, and the gods themselves to take the *winikin* Aaron Rockwell up into the sky to be reborn," he said, reciting from memory, though she'd told him he could read it. "Since what has happened before will happen again, we will see you anew, brother, in the next cycle of life." He lifted an oblong bundle wrapped in gray cloth, which he opened to reveal a thin, narrow stone spike that had been carved to resemble the barb of a stingray's tail and sharpened to a deadly point. He turned and handed it to Cara.

Her stomach churned as she took the smooth, thin stone, but there was adrenaline alongside the nerves now. The funeral ceremony was one of the very few rituals that called on the *winikin* to make their own blood sacrifice, bringing it very close to an actual spell. And there were recent hints that the *winikin* could do magic, after all. But although Dez had lifted the stricture forbidding the *winikin* from working magic—he too had been put in place to shake things up—none of them had been able to manage even the simplest spell. More, a search of the Nightkeepers' vast library had failed to turn up any hint of how a *winikin* was supposed to work magic, or even whether it was possible. She kept hoping, though. And given the nature of the magic and its dependence on blood sacrifice, it was tempting to think that Aaron's death might open the floodgates.

As she slid her fingers along the spine, all other thoughts fell away, leaving only her awareness of the pyre and the others gathered around her, the sudden tension in the air. *Please, gods,* she whispered inwardly. Then, steeling herself, she set the spine to the tip of her tongue, then closed her eyes and, with a quick, jerky move, drove the bloodletter deep and yanked it free again.

Pain flashed and her stomach lurched as blood filled her mouth, making her want to gag at the salty tang. Instead, she let the blood pool in her mouth, then stepped forward and spit out the mouthful of mingled saliva and blood—both sacred to the gods, who had given their blood to create mankind in a land where water was scarce.

Optimism flared for a nanosecond . . . and then died. Because when her offering hit the pyre there were none of the red-gold sparkles the Nightkeepers talked about seeing when they dialed into their magic, no buzzing hum in the air. All she got was a throbbing tongue, a gnarly case of muck-mouth, and a solid reminder that none of the prophecies ever even mentioned anyone besides the Nightkeepers fighting in the final battle, never mind using magic to do it.

Exhaling, she passed the spike to Zane, who took it without comment and made his sacrifice in grim silence. The others did the same, all the way around the circle until the bloodletter returned to Rabbit, who touched it to his lips and then tossed it on the pyre. Overhead, the storm clouds had blotted out the sun, turning the scene dark and gloomy, though the air didn't really smell of rain.

Rabbit looked around the circle again, as if he wanted to say something else. But then he shook his head, focused on the funerary bundle, spread his fingers, and called fire in the old tongue with a whisper of *"Kaak."*

Energy crackled and a gout of flames erupted from the base of the pyre. The fire geysered upward in a blaze that rose ten, then twenty feet, and the air went suddenly scorching, burning Cara's skin. *Whoa!* She stumbled back, shielding her face with her arm as the churning in her stomach suddenly increased a thousandfold. "Rabbit, dial it down!"

"I can't!" His eyes were wide, his face ashen as he tried to beckon the power back into him. "It's not working! The magic is—"

Crack! A huge lightning bolt lashed up from the fiery pillar and speared into one of the black storm clouds. Cara screamed, heart clutching as the cloud freaking *detonated*, fragmenting into dark chunks that plummeted toward the earth, trailing vapor. The missiles hit in a circular spray around them, impacting meteor-fast, shaking the earth beneath her feet and digging huge craters that spewed dirt and broken stone.

"Form up!" Zane shouted over the roar of the fire and the aerial cannonade. Some of the *winikin* responded instantly, scrambling into the four fighting teams; others stood and gaped.

"Get close together," Rabbit yelled. "I'll shield!"

Cara went for her wristband, hit the panic button that would broadcast on every available channel and trigger the alarms back at the main mansion, and shouted, "Mayday! Mayday! The funeral is under attack!"

"Come on!" Natalie grabbed her arm and dragged her into a stumbling run toward the others as Rabbit started casting his fiery orange shield spell around them.

Catching sight of movement, Cara missed a step, and the churning in her gut suddenly condensed to a hard, cold pit of terror. "The craters! Look!"

Shiny black shadows writhed within each pit, and then boiled up and over to become dark creatures, huge animals that had been twisted into hideous monsters. *Gods!* What *were* they? How had they gotten inside Skywatch's shields? She saw jaguars, foxes, eagles, owls, all black and slick, their pelts glued together into slimy spikes by a sticky coating, as if they had just been born, fully formed, from the underworld itself.

Gods!

The demons screeched and roared as they materialized, a dozen of them and then more, landing with earth-shuddering thuds and casting around momentarily before they oriented on the *winikin* and began to move. They were slow at first, uncoordinated, as if learning to use their bodies. But that didn't last long.

Rabbit shouted, "Cara, move! Come on!" He waved

to the single gap that remained in the fiery shield, left open for her and Natalie.

Heart pounding, Cara bolted the short distance remaining and shoved Natalie through. "Is everyone—" She turned back and broke off with a gasp as she caught sight of two stumbling figures lagging behind, recognized them. *"Zane!"*

He was coming toward them half carrying, half dragging Lora, who had been a decorated cop in the outside world, but now was limp and sobbing.

Cara's breath froze as a shadow rose up behind them: a huge eagle with a minivan wingspan and a talon spread the size of a human head, coordinated now and flying with fiendish intent, its coal red eyes locked on its prey. It was maybe a thousand feet from Zane. Eight hundred. Seven.

He wasn't going to make it.

Her heart went *thudda-thudda*, but she didn't let her voice shake as she said to Rabbit, "Give me your gun."

His eyes blazed. "No fucking way. I'll go."

"You need to protect the others." The demons were homing in on the *winikin* huddled within his glowing shield.

"I— Shit. Here." He tossed the MAC-10. *"Go!"*

She caught it, fumbled it, then got it in a two-handed grip. The machine pistol still felt strange in her hands even after all the training she'd had, as if her body knew on the DNA level that she wasn't made for fighting. But she hung on to the weapon, fingers slipping with the cold sweat that suddenly bathed her as she wheeled and bolted toward the stragglers.

The demon eagle was very close to Zane. A few hundred feet, if that. *Do it,* she told herself. *Just do it!* Heart thundering in her ears, she fired over his head, wasting the first burst and then sending a wobbly line of bullets stitching across the creature's torso and left wing. The beast screeched and its wing beats faltered, but it stayed in the air, locking onto her with blazing crimson eyes. The fury in them—the pure *evil*—froze her momentarily in place. This was the enemy they were going to be fighting during the war, she realized with sudden sharp horror. Not the *xombis* or any other sort of possessed human, but the demons themselves. And these were the smallest of them.

Oh, gods. She couldn't do this. *They* couldn't do it. There was no way a dozen magi and fifty-some *winikin* could fight an army of these things and win.

"Cara, no!" Zane waved her off with his free hand, his expression going wild. "Get back!"

Snapping from her paralysis, she bolted toward him, toward the demon, her legs moving while her brain screeched, *Wrong way!* But she skidded and got to Lora's other side. Imagining the demon's hot breath on her neck, she screamed, *"Move!"*

They ran for the shield, legs pumping, but Lora was deadweight, dragging them down. Rabbit extended a tendril of the shield, trying to meet them halfway, but it wasn't enough.

Hearing the snap of feathers, Cara twisted around and muffled a cry of terror at seeing the creature nearly on top of them. She fired off a burst of jade-tipped bullets into its gaping mouth, but this time the bullets just seemed to piss it off more. It screamed and reached for her, claws spreading into a ring of wickedly curved blades.

"Down!" Rabbit bellowed.

Zane yanked Lora to the ground and Cara hit the

deck a nanosecond behind them as the mage unleashed a huge fireball. A crackling roar seared over them and then the fiery missile slammed into the raptor, driving it back and away. The eagle was instantly ablaze. It screamed and flailed its flaming wings, then fell with a sickening thud that jarred the ground beneath them.

Cara and Zane lunged to their feet and dragged Lora up, but from within the shield, Natalie screamed, "Look out!"

Whipping around, Cara let out an, "Oh, *shit*," at the sight of a huge, rangy, doglike creature bearing down on them. Its fur was mottled black and stuck up in spikes fouled by the ropy saliva that slicked its jaws and chest, coming from a mouth that showed huge fangs and barbed ivory teeth.

Throat closing with bitter panic, she yanked away and shoved Lora and Zane toward the shield. "Move!"

"No, damn it." Zane spun back, eyes fierce. "Let me—"

"Go. That's an order." She got between them and the oncoming beast, heart thundering in her ears as she told herself, *You've just got to slow it down long enough for Rabbit's magic to recharge.* They had trained on scenarios like this. Now it was time to put that training to use. Aware that Zane had followed orders—whatever he might feel for her, he was a soldier at heart—she aimed for the dog-creature's legs and fired.

She got two shots off and then heard a sour *clunk* as the machine pistol freaking jammed.

"No!" She yanked at the receiver arm that had come loose, locking the bolt, but it didn't budge. The huge dog—wolf?—seemed to understand what had happened. Its gleaming red eyes lit and it accelerated, jaws gaping.

"Run!" Natalie screamed.

Cara spun and bolted. The shield was farther away than she thought, the demon closing fast. Panic spurted, along with a thought of, *Oh, gods, this is it.* And then the world did a weird slow-motion thing around her.

She saw Zane shove Lora into the shield and turn back for her, but the beast was too close, too fast. She could hear it right behind her, could feel the jarring thud of its feet through the worn soles of her boots and smell its rotting stench. Her body tensed for pain, for fear, and incredulity flared at the knowledge that she wasn't going to make it. She was going to be the second *winikin* to die in battle, wasn't ever going to get the chance to live the life she wanted after the war. Her breath sobbed. *Please, no.*

She glanced back just in time to see the huge creature rock onto its haunches, preparing to spring, and—

"Cara, get down!" The words came from the other side of her, in a deep voice that jolted her like lightning and sped the world back up to normal once more.

Before she could react, a gray-and-buff blur raced past with a bloodcurdling howl of rage, and the hard, heavy weight of a man's body slammed into her, knocking her out of the demon's path and taking her to the ground. Her rescuer wrapped his arms around her and rolled them as they hit, so he took the brunt and cushioned her fall.

There was sudden warmth, solid muscle, and the yielding, unfamiliar press of a man's body. And not just any man: She caught rapid-fire impressions of sun-bleached hair against deeply tanned skin, stormy blue eyes, and an air of wildness that defied the high-tech armband and warrior's garb. Their legs tangled, and when they stopped rolling, he was on top of her with his hips planted firmly between her thighs. Instead of untangling himself, he reared up over her on one arm and lifted the other to summon first a shield and then a huge fireball, and although her brain was struggling to catch up, her soul already knew exactly what was going on.

"Sven," she whispered, frozen with the shock of seeing her foster nonbrother again after so long, though her body reacted to the way his magic spit and sparked, prickling awareness across her skin.

He looked grimmer and more tired than he had a few months earlier, when he'd taken off for the south. There were new stress lines cut alongside his aristocratic nose and wide, slashing cheekbones, and his old trademark surfer's ponytail was a grown-out military brush cut now, gone shaggy and adding to the sense of some wild creature contained within human form. He wore close-fitting armor and the Kevlar-impregnated black-on-black of a Nightkeeper, and he was all warrior as his eyes went to where an enormous gray-and-buff coyote—his bonded familiar, Mac—was fighting with the huge black demon.

"Leave it!" he ordered. Mac quickly tore away and leaped back, and Sven unleashed his deadly fireball with a heave that rippled through his body and into Cara's.

Hiss-boom! Instantly engulfed in flames, the demon-dog reared back with a horrible, unearthly howl. A terrible stench filled the air as it struggled in its death throes. The other animals too were dead and dying, making Cara suddenly aware that the rest of the magi had arrived and were tightening around the *winikin* in a protective ring as the creatures melted to stinking black puddles. After a moment, even those faded and disappeared, leaving silence behind.

Dead. Silence.

As her pulse pounded in her ears, she thought crazily that it was the kind of utter quiet that came in the aftermath of a disaster that didn't cause any actual casualties but had come damn close, to the point where everyone sort of sat there for a second, thinking, *What the fuck just happened?* Because that was what had to be going through the minds of the other *winikin*. It was undoubtedly what the magi were thinking as they watched the last of the creatures puff to greasy smoke. And it was what she ought to be thinking too. Because although the Nightkeepers' former nemesis, the Xibalban mage Iago, had tricked his way into Skywatch twice, no demon had entered the compound in nearly thirty years. Not since the Solstice Massacre.

But although those were the questions she knew ought to be going through her head, her mind had blanked. All she could do was stare at Sven as he levered himself off her and rose to his feet with a loose-limbed grace that sharply defined the muscles under his tight black clothing, making her entirely aware of his body, and the imprint it had left on her own.

Don't think about it, she told herself, but the familiar refrain barely registered.

There was a low whine and the scuff of paws on dirt as Mac trotted over to stand beside him, then looked at her with his pale green, human-seeming eyes gleaming, his ears pricked and his plumed tail wagging in wide sweeps. Sven and the coyote made a formidable pair, and the sight tightened her throat. It had been a long six months since they had gone down to Mexico to head up the Nightkeepers' efforts to contain the spread of the *xombi* virus — an infection that was part magic, part disease, and thoroughly vile. She had worried about them, especially when the reports back from the southern front had grown increasingly grim. But her relief that they were home safe caromed off resentment that she hadn't gotten any word beyond the official reports, nothing personal, nothing that acknowledged her and Sven's connection or the fact that he'd been the one to bring her back to Skywatch to take on a job she hadn't wanted. He'd promised to help her with the *winikin* . . . and then he'd taken off without a word. Which was just Sven, and shouldn't have surprised her.

It had, though, and that was why, as irritation won out over relief, she summoned a flip smile she knew would piss him off, and said, "Hey, welcome back. Did you miss me?"

That was a laugh, of course, because he'd always made it his business never to miss anyone.

CHAPTER TWO

Sven had braced himself to see Cara, thinking through what he wanted to say to her . . . but as he stared down at her now, caught between the desire to haul her into his arms and the nearly overwhelming urge to shake her until her damn fool teeth rattled, he was floundering because they were way the fuck off his script.

He had planned on getting her in private and talking to her—really *talking* to her, for the first time in years. He sure as shit *hadn't* been prepared to show up just as the alarms went nuts, and to get out to the ball court just in time to see her trying to outrun some godsdamned hellbeast—a demon inside *Skywatch,* for fuck's sake!—armed with a jammed MAC-10 and more guts than common sense. He hadn't been braced to find himself planted on top of her as he'd pulled the magic necessary to take the creature down. And he sure as shit wasn't ready to be this close to her while his pulse thudded off rhythm with those urges, along with knowledge that he'd just come damn close to losing her.

He rolled off of her, stood, and hauled her to her feet,

though the distance didn't do nearly enough to cool him off. His rehearsed scene had started something along the lines of, *I know this is a couple of decades too late, but I owe you an apology....* Instead, he found himself leaning down to roar, "What in the *hell* were you thinking? You nearly got yourself killed!"

Mac moved to his side, ruff bristling, but then subsided and settled to his haunches with his eyes fixed on Cara. *Friend,* he sent in the thought-glyphs that were his main way of communicating. *Missed friend.* But that wasn't enough to cool the fury riding high in Sven's blood. Mac existed in the moment—the demon was gone *now*; he was happy to see Cara *now*; he was hungry *now*. Humans, though, had to deal with the past-present-future stuff. That meant that when Sven looked at her, he didn't see a petite woman with a striking white forelock and exotic deep brown eyes, wearing curve-hugging black pants, an edgy black jacket, and an air of, *You and what army?* Well, yeah, he saw that. But he also saw the girl she'd been.

He saw her at ten, galloping bareback on her fat spotted pony, with her hair streaming out behind her like a white-striped black banner.

He saw her at fifteen, returning to the ranch battered and bloody, cradling a broken wrist and defending the chestnut filly who had tossed her, seeming unaware that his heart had stopped at the sight of her injuries.

He saw her at seventeen, propositioning him in the back barn with the sweetly inexpert kiss he'd never forgotten, saw her eyes fill when he turned her down and rode away, not knowing it was one of the hardest things he'd ever done.

He saw her at twenty-one, when she tracked him

down in a crappy one-room apartment to drag him to Skywatch, overriding his protests with three words: "You owe me." And he sure as shit *had* owed her. He'd broken her heart that day in the barn, and he hadn't done it gently, because he'd been feeling none too gentle himself.

He saw her a few months later, when he told her to leave Skywatch, claiming that she didn't fit in and he didn't need her, trying to make the break a clean one for both their sakes, because those not-so-gentle feelings had come back like gangbusters, only to come up against roles, rituals, and the end of the damned world.

He saw her at twenty-three, when she had come back to Skywatch to lead the rebel *winikin,* looking confident, capable, dead sexy, and nothing like the girl she had been, yet somehow exactly like that girl.

He saw her just now, facing down a hellhound with no armor, no shield, and no backup. And because unlike Mac he could imagine the future, he also saw what would have happened if he hadn't gotten there when he did. It wasn't tough to picture—gods knew he'd seen plenty of bodies over the past six months. And he'd be damned if he added hers to the list.

Her eyes narrowed. "Back off, Nightkeeper. I was just doing my job."

"It's not your job to get yourself killed," he grated, then leaned in closer to make his point, putting them nose-to-nose. He could feel the soft warmth coming off her skin, smell the faintest hint of flowers and spice turned sharp by the scents of battle. And he was all too aware of the magic riding high in his bloodstream, making him want to do things he had long ago filed under Bad Idea. Gritting his teeth and willing the images away, he ground out, "The *winikin* can't afford to lose their leader."

She scowled. "I know what I'm doing."

"Bullshit. If Mac and I hadn't just rolled in when your mayday came through—"

"One of the others would've saved my ass," she interrupted. "And there's no way I was going to hide behind the shield and watch Zane and Lora die."

"Zane. Right." If he'd had fur it would've bristled. "Any reason he didn't send you and Lora ahead and cover you?"

"Because I ordered him to get his ass moving, and it wasn't like we had time to stand around and rock-paper-scissors it."

"Sven!" Dez called. "Get over here."

Growling under his breath, Sven looked to where the other Nightkeepers were gathered beside the charred, smoking pyre, no doubt in the first stages of a "what the hell were those things, and how the fuck did they get inside Skywatch?" conversation. "We need five minutes," he called.

"No, we don't." Cara took a big step back, creating a gap between them that felt far greater than a few feet of space.

"We're not finished."

"Oh, yes, we are." She held up a hand. "Look, we had a deal. You do your thing and I do mine, and we leave the past in the past. Remember?"

Yeah, he remembered, all right. It had sounded good at the time, back when she'd first returned to Skywatch and they had been trying to find a way to coexist without things getting personal. Now, though, he wanted to get personal, to a degree. He needed to make things right—or at least own up to what he'd done wrong. The past six months had changed him, he hoped for the better.

He exhaled through his nose. "Look, Cara, I— "

"Something's wrong," she interrupted, attention fixed on the others, where there was a sudden flurry of activity, a few shouts. "Come on." She was in motion before he could call her back, beelining for where JT was suddenly faced off opposite Carlos, both of them red faced and furious.

Sven cursed and strode after her, knowing she was right. Duty called. And wasn't that a bitch?

As Cara headed toward the others, she was too aware of Sven walking beside her, Mac dogtrotting at his heels. The two moved alike, making her think of wide-open spaces and the kind of freedom she was suddenly dying for, because she was raw from the funeral, shaky from the attack, and churned up over Sven's unexpected return, which could spell trouble. The rebel members of the *winikin* mistrusted her old connection to the coyote mage, thinking it put her closer to the traditionalists or, worse, the Nightkeepers themselves. That meant she needed to watch not just her own step, but their perceptions, as well.

Sure enough, as she drew nearer, a couple of the rebels shot her dark looks that accused her of fraternizing. Or maybe the accusation was inside her, coming from the heat that was still vibrating through her body, singing a familiar inner refrain of, *He's back, he's back, he's back,* just as it had when she was younger. Back then she'd thought each time he came home that he'd finally be ready to settle down, stick around, be there for the people who needed him.

Focus, she told herself, shoving aside the lingering heat and the churning excitement that belonged to the too-optimistic girl she couldn't afford to be anymore.

"What's wrong?" she asked as she reached the *winikin*. They gave way, muttering and shifting, letting her into the group and then closing around her, shutting Sven on the outside.

As she reached the center, JT snarled, "Fuck this," and spun and stalked away in the opposite direction, shoulder-checking a couple of guys who didn't get clear fast enough.

Out of the corner of her eye, she saw Dez shaking his head as if to say, *Typical,* but she knew that JT might have a temper and a major shoulder chip when it came to the Nightkeepers, but the fiery rebel wasn't irrational. If he was in a mood, there was a reason.

Just as she turned to ask her father what the hell was going on, another of the newer *winikin,* Sebastian, caught her arm. "You going to show us yours?" He was a hard-edged fiftyish man who had lost his wife and child in the massacre and made no secret of his hatred for the magi ... and right now, he was looking at her like she was the enemy. His eyes were hard and harsh, his grip rough enough to put a stir of fear in her belly, though she didn't—couldn't—let it show.

"Godsdamn it, Sebastian." She yanked her arm away. "What the hell are you—"

She broke off as he shoved back his right sleeve to bare his forearm ... which now wore a black, tattoolike mark of two interconnected ovals, along with eyes and a gaping beak, and the hint of feathers. Cara froze as her heart *thudda-thudda*ed in her chest, kicked off rhythm by shock.

Oh, holy shit. It was the mark of the owl bloodline.

And it hadn't been there before the funeral.

Cloth rustled and a few more of the rebels pushed up

their sleeves to bare their forearms, which now bore their bloodline marks. She saw an eagle, an ax, a curl of smoke, and two others she didn't recognize. But she sure as hell recognized the despair in their eyes. She'd seen it in her own right after Carlos had forced her marks on her, indenturing her to Sven and putting her under Nightkeeper law whether she liked it or not. Because where the Nightkeepers' forearm marks were the symbols of status and power, the marks of the *winikin* made them into servants, pairing the *aj winikin* "I serve" glyph with smaller bloodline glyphs.

The rebels hadn't chosen to have their souls linked to those of specific Nightkeeper children, and they hadn't been through the marking ceremony. . . . Yet they were suddenly wearing bloodline marks, as if the gods themselves had commanded it.

"Well?" Sebastian demanded. "Where's yours?"

Oh, shit. Her stomach clutched and she reflexively clasped her right wrist beneath her jacket, which suddenly felt heavy and too hot. The coyote and the *aj winikin* had faded when Sven sent her away from Skywatch, leaving her with a chronic low-grade malaise that hadn't cleared up until she returned to the compound. Still, though, she hadn't gotten her marks back when she returned, and she'd been damned grateful to have that freedom. Now, though . . .

She took a deep breath and pushed back her sleeve, then hissed out a long, slow breath. Because her arm was bare, and she didn't have a clue whether that was a good thing or not.

By later that afternoon, as Sven's debriefing with Dez in the royal quarters headed into its second hour, the

Nightkeepers knew three things about the attack: One, the blood-ward surrounding the compound hadn't been deactivated to let the creatures through; two, there was no evidence of a magical hot spot within Skywatch that might've been used as a conduit to bring the creatures up from the underworld; and three, there hadn't been any detectable power surges suggesting a spell other than Rabbit's fire magic.

In other words, they didn't have a fucking clue how the things had gotten in.

More, the brain trust—aka Jade, Lucius, and the Night-keepers' ancestral library—couldn't figure out exactly what the attackers had been. They didn't seem to have been true demons—too easy to kill; they were too big to have been demon-possessed animals of earthly origin; and they didn't match up to anything else in the records.

So for the moment, Skywatch was sporting some serious motion and magic detectors, and everyone was staying armed, indoors and out, while trying to get back to business as usual.

"Sorry," Dez said as he hung up the house phone after yet another update. "Where were we?"

The Nightkeepers' leader was sleekly bald—a characteristic of the strongest magi of the serpent bloodline—and he wore a muscle shirt that showed off the *hunab ku* king's glyph on his bulging upper biceps. With his black leather jacket slung over the back of a fussy sofa—a holdover from when the former rulers, Strike and Leah, had lived in the royal suite—and wearing ripped jeans and a studded belt, he looked more like a rocker than a king, but his eyes were piercing and intelligent, and his questions had made it clear that he'd studied all the reports Sven had e-mailed back over the past six months.

"I think we got through most of it," Sven said, keeping his voice dead level and his face set, because that was the only way he could talk about the things he'd seen and done down south. A low whine came from the floor behind his chair, though, where Mac had finally settled.

Dez crooked a finger. "Let's finish it, then."

"After Sasha and Rabbit confirmed that the human hosts died during the very first stages of the *xombi* infection and the virus allowed the *Banol Kax* to control the body from that point on, we didn't have a choice. We spent the next few weeks hunting and exterminating the infected villagers." Sven paused, wishing he could spit the bitter taste from his mouth, swallowed it instead. "It's been a month since the last report of a new infection. Rabbit's friends down there will keep their ears to the ground and let us know if and when a new outbreak occurs ... or something else happens."

Dez nodded. "The demons need to get a foothold here on earth. With the *xombis* knocked back, they'll regroup and try something else."

"I'll head back down south in a few days," Sven said. "Between Mac's nose and my magic, we'll have a better chance of picking up on whatever they try next." And he'd be out and moving, away from the hemmed-in box canyon and the training compound that might've been built to accommodate hundreds, even thousands, but somehow felt overcrowded with only seventy or eighty people rubbing elbows.

"Actually, I'd like you to stick around for a while."

Sven smothered the wince that came when his bone-deep need to keep moving bumped up against the fealty oath he had sworn to his king. "You and Reese headed north?" The two were Denver natives, and had set up an urban center of ops in an old warehouse in their former 'hood. Sven had Skywatch-sat once or twice when the king and his mate had gone up to the city, keeping a Nightkeeper presence at the compound while the others were on assignment.

"Actually, I've got something else in mind." Dez paused. "How are you getting on with Carlos and Cara these days?"

"Fine." Or they would be fine once he had a chance to sit down with them. Yelling at Cara hadn't been part of the plan, but he could fix it. He *would* fix it, all of it. He'd made that promise to himself.

Dez nodded. "Good, because I need someone on the inside."

"Whoa." Sven held up a hand. "Wait. On the inside of what?"

"The *winikin*," Dez said flatly. "Those creatures came in during Aaron's funeral, and it sure as hell looked like they were after the *winikin*, not us. I want to think it's another sign that there's some sort of *winikin* magic waking up, but the cynical side of me says there might be something more . . . as in, maybe one of them already found his—or her—magic and is using it against us."

"Hang on. You think what happened today was sabotage?" Sven shook his head. "No way. Not a *winikin*." Even the rebels admitted that the Nightkeepers were humanity's best chance of surviving the war.

"Rabbit said it didn't feel like any magic he recognized. And they all got their bloodline marks, even without the ceremony. That says magic to me."

"But . . . shit." His brain raced even as his instincts kept saying, *No way.* "The First Father turned the slaves who escaped with him from Egypt into the *winikin*, right around when they came to this continent. That was way before the magic split into its light and dark halves. So whatever power they've got—if anything—would be related to the ancestral magic, which Rabbit would recognize." He paused. "And even if you're right and a *winikin* could summon those creatures, what would be the point? You said it yourself—they seemed to be targeting the *winikin*. Besides, if they were supposed to attack the Nightkeepers, why go after us this close to the end date? Are you saying you think one of the *winikin* is in league with the *Banol Kax?*" Because, shit, that was a hell of an accusation. One that, if it got out, would fuck any hope of solidarity.

"Not necessarily." Dez was silent for a moment, no doubt deciding how much more to say. He and his mate, Reese, were as tight-lipped as they were brilliant strategists, and they formed a closed unit at the top of the hierarchy—some thought too closed at times. After a moment, though, he said, "Look at the history. A thousand years ago, the Xibalban sect split from the Nightkeepers and took the dark magic with them because they believed the Nightkeepers had it wrong, that the sky gods were the ones who wanted to take over the earth and the *Banol Kax* were the good guys, right?"

"So Rabbit would have us believe." Ever since a run-in with a dying Xibalban shaman the year before, Rabbit had been trying to get the Nightkeepers to seriously consider that their long-ago ancestors had been tricked into believing in the sky gods. "You don't think he's been experimenting with dark magic again, do you?"

Dez shook his head. "No. My gut says he's toeing the line. But who's to say there's not another group of Xibalbans out there? We went from thinking they all died out in the fifteen hundreds to thinking Iago and his red robes were the last of them . . . only to discover that Iago's people were a nasty offshoot of an original, relatively peaceful sect. What if there's another offshoot out there? And what if they got to one of the rebels?"

"I don't see how that could be possible. Rabbit scoured the area a couple of years ago looking for information about his mother, and then did the rounds again when the *xombi* virus hit, trying to find a cure. If there were other magic users out there, he would've ID'd them by now."

"We're not in the highlands." Dez gestured to the compound surrounding them. "What if there's another group like us, more peaceful than Iago's crowd, but that believes in the underworld as strongly as we believe in the sky gods?"

"We would've seen something by now, and you know it." Sven paused. "So why are you hearing horses and trying to talk yourself into zebras?"

The king exhaled heavily. "Because we know how to fight the Xibalbans, and we could even handle a traitor or two . . . but the *Banol Kax* scare the crap out of me. If that's what broke through here today, we're in deep shit. So right now, yeah, I'm hoping for stripes."

Sven wished he had a joke at the ready, one of the quick toss-off lines that used to come so easily for him. But those days were gone. Now he could only shake his head and say, "Better not let the others hear you talking like that. You're our crazy-brave king who's not afraid of anything."

"Unless we get some more weapons in our arsenal, crazy-brave isn't going to be enough." Dez's expression fell back into its usual resolute lines. "But we'll soldier on and keep pushing the boundaries. It's all we *can* do, right now." He paused. "Which brings things back to you. Are you willing to lean on Carlos and Cara for intel on the *winikin*—especially the newcomers—without letting them know what you're up to?"

Shit. He didn't want to . . . but he could see the king's point. "You're not making it an order?"

Dez shook his head. "The way I see it, they're the only family you've ever known, so I don't want to force you to spy on them." His lips quirked. "Besides, the last time I gave you a *winikin*-related order, things didn't go exactly the way I had planned."

After telling Cara that she was Jox's chosen successor, Sven had given her the opportunity to bolt and she'd taken it. Then, a few weeks later, she showed up at Sky-watch with the rebels . . . on her own terms.

Sven shrugged and pointed out, "She got here eventually."

"Yes, she did, and I'm far better off with her willing cooperation than I would've been if I had forced her into the position. That's why you're getting a choice now."

"What happens if I say no?"

"I'll use Rabbit to eavesdrop. I don't want to, though."

"Christ," Sven muttered, though Carlos had boxed his ears more than once early on for calling on the son of the Christians' God. "It'd be a fucking train wreck if they figured out you mind-bent them to get information." Bad enough if they caught wind that the king suspected them of treason. If they realized Rabbit was using his magical talents to spy on them telepathically . . . *Shit.* Twenty times worse. A hundred.

"Like I said, I don't want to do it. But we can't afford to have this blow up."

Then don't ask me to do it, Sven almost said, because gods knew he'd fucked up major assignments before, like the time he'd fumbled a translocation spell during a museum heist and Patience had wound up hurt. He'd gotten steadier since bonding with Mac, but he hadn't been given any really sensitive tasks since then, either. Most of his assignments had been of the slash-and-burn variety. Or tracking. He and Mac together were hell on wheels finding shit, and it kept them on the move. But spying? And using Cara and Carlos to do it? He didn't know about that.

"Why not ask someone else? There are plenty of others who are closer to their *winikin* than I am." *Hello, understatement.*

"Because you also worked with JT down south, and you got along with him as well as anyone outside of the rebels has, which gives you connections in both camps. And besides"—a ghost of a smile touched Dez's lips— "Reese and I agree that if Rabbit is our loose cannon, you're our wild card. We have this feeling that you haven't gotten to the bottom of yourself yet, and that if and when you do, big things could happen."

"Big good, or big bad?"

The smile got real. "That's the 'wild' part." The king paused. "Do you gamble?"

Sven thought of winter nights, a fire in the hearth, and an ancient wagering game spread out on the kitchen table: the *patolli,* which was an ancestor of the modern Parcheesi, with rolls of the dice, figures moving around the board, and strategies of defense and offense. Carlos had used it to teach him war games; Cara had used it to win her way out of chores; and her mom, Essie, had just liked having the four of them together in one place.

When the memory threatened to hit the nostalgia button, he set it firmly aside and shook his head. "Not for a long time."

"Well, maybe it's time to give it a shot." The king stood. "Think about it and let me know."

But as Sven strode away from the royal suite, with Mac at his heels and no real destination other than "away," he didn't know what the hell he was going to do. If there was a problem—or worse, a traitor—it needed to be dealt with, and fast . . . but if there wasn't, and it came out that he'd been getting close to Cara and Carlos to spy on the *winikin,* it wouldn't be worth trying to fix those relationships. In fact, if that happened he might as well just hit the road and keep on going, because they—and especially *she*—would never speak to him again.

CHAPTER THREE

"Lame, lame, boring, meh, lame ..." Near dusk on the day of the funeral gone awry, in a dark corner at the rear of the long, narrow stone room that housed the library, Rabbit rifled through yet another box of carefully labeled artifacts. The brain trust had culled the pieces as being more or less related to the boar bloodline, so he was going over them in the hopes that he'd get a vibe. So far, though, there was a whole lot of nothing going on.

Okay, the artifacts themselves were pretty cool—he had come across a set of spear-thrower missiles that were made out of intricately carved peccary-tusk ivory and weighted with slivers of stone, and he had been tempted to swap out the ceremonial knife he wore on his belt for a longer, thinner blade made of pale green stone and carved with repeating boar motifs. But a MAC-10 loaded with jade tips—or better yet a fireball—kicked ass over a spear-thrower any day, and the knife he wore had been his old man's. And although Red-Boar had been a miserable son of a bitch, tradition said you used the weapon that got handed down, like it or lump it. Besides, he wasn't browsing for some "ooh, shiny" shit to take with him just because it appealed. The magi all had boxes to go through, because the Nightkeepers badly needed some new tricks.

"Boring, boring . . ." He paused to pick up a weird-ass clay statue that was about the length of his forearm and covered with a red pigment that had faded to Pepto pink. Although the glyph incised on the bottom was a boar, the thing itself looked like some sort of waterbird. Eyeballing it, he muttered, "Shit, glad you're not giving me any tingles." He could just picture himself going up against the dark lords wielding a Death Flamingo, or whatever the fuck it was. *No frigging thank you.* He shook his head and put it back down. "Sissy, boring, lame, lame . . ."

Gods, there was a ton of stuff from the boar bloodline. Then again, the boars had been the royal bloodline prior to the jaguars, reigning during the first millennium, when the library was established, so he guessed it made sense they would figure heavily in the archived material. And he didn't mind some quiet time alone in the library, really. It was peaceful, and he'd been pretty damn short on peace lately.

The cluster-fuck with the *xombi* virus had taken something out of him, plain and simple. He had gone down there thinking he, Sven, and the others would be able to handle the outbreak, save the villagers, and block the magical pipeline that was causing the problem. Instead, he'd found himself razing the very villages he'd gone there intending to protect, then helping Sven track and kill the *xombis,* napalming dozens of them, hundreds.

He still woke up pretty much every morning with the stink of it lodged in his sinuses.

"No buzz, no buzz, boring, boring . . ." He moved to a

nearby rack, stopping at a carved bone miniature of five warriors wearing ceremonial garb, toting spear chuckers and stalking a wild peccary. Beside that was an incense burner painted to show a boar-bloodline warrior offering his heart to a woman who turned her face away.

That one pinged, though not because of any magic.

Damn it. He rubbed the heel of his hand over the center of his chest, which had suddenly gone hollow and achy because of how things had been between him and his human girlfriend, Myrinne, lately. He loved her one hundred percent—he'd kill for her, die for her, and anything in between—but he wished he could get her to stop pressuring him to experiment with the other half of his magic. More, he wished that it didn't feel like more and more that when she said, *I love you,* it really meant, *I love you when you do what I want.* Especially when what she wanted him to do went against the king's orders.

Last year, a dying Xibalban shaman had named Rabbit the "crossover" and said that his mingled blood made him the key to winning the war using both the light magic of the Nightkeepers and the dark powers of his Xibalban half. But not long after that, their enemy Iago had managed to break Rabbit's connection to the dark magic—and since then, pretty much every time he'd tried to make a real impact he'd just wound up making things worse, until Dez had finally ordered him to stop trying to reconnect with his darker side. These days he was doing his damnedest to follow orders and be a good mage, a good soldier. And that was driving Myrinne up a freaking wall.

"Shit." Letting go of the big, weighted-down box he'd just been about to open, he launched to his feet, suddenly needing to pace off the restless energy that came from inside the hollow place in his chest, along with the sly inner voice that said he was a lucky son of a bitch to have her and he'd better do whatever it took not to fuck it up. Once he was on his feet, though, he swayed and had to slap a hand out to steady himself against the nearest wall. "Whoa. Vertigo."

Sweat popped on his forehead and crawled down his spine, and a rush of nausea filled the hollows. He swallowed hard, then blinked to clear his eyes when they threatened to fog.

Shit, maybe that third chili dog had been a bad idea. He'd needed to recharge his batteries, but maybe he should've gone with nice, safe pasta instead of five-alarm pig by-products and extra pepper jack.

Except ... His head whipped up as logic made it through the spins, reminding him that the magi didn't usually get pukey from stuff like food poisoning. Which meant this was something else.

Like something in that box, maybe?

Backtracking, he dropped to his heels and tugged on the cross-folded flaps to open the box. It was more than half full of flat stones that had been carved into all sorts of weird shapes. The inner flap was labeled in Lucius's crabbed writing: *Eccentrics for our favorite eccentric.*

"Nice," Rabbit muttered. Lucius—the Nightkeepers' head researcher and an ass kicker in his own right— might've rolled his eyes a little at his request and grumbled about needles in haystacks, but he'd come through and collected a shit ton of eccentrics.

The small, flat pieces of stone were all different shapes, from abstract geometrics to detailed images of people, animals, glyphs, gods ... it was all fair game. In ancient times, they had been worn as pendants or symbols of office, tucked into pockets as charms, or even busted up as sacrifices. The small stone artifacts were as common as arrowheads farther north, and hadn't been thought to have any real magic . . . until the dying shaman had given one to Rabbit and named him as its wielder, suggesting that some eccentrics, at any rate, could be important.

But although Rabbit had been able to sense power in the small black flint carving, he'd never managed to trigger any sort of magic. Which was why he had asked Lucius to cull others for him, thinking he might need a full set, or a Nightkeeper half to go with the Xibalban piece.

And now, sure enough, as he spread his fingers and let his hands hover above the collection, hot, sparkling magic rose up, feathered along his palms, and flowed into his veins, sweeping along to pool at a point on his upper right thigh, where he carried the black eccentric in his pocket.

Holy shit, he thought, pulse suddenly thundering in his ears. *Holy, holy shit.* He had known. Somehow, he had known it would work like this.

Dipping into his pocket, he wrapped his fingers around the eccentric, which was all curves and points and looked a little like a flame frozen in stone. Normally it was cool and a little greasy to the touch; now it was blood-warm, echoing the heat coming from the box. And when he pulled it out, he saw that a faint skim of magic slicked the surface of the stone, picking up silver glints in the light.

Silver! His breath hissed out as excitement kicked in. That wasn't dark magic; it was *muk*—the light and dark powers joined together. Of the Nightkeepers, only Michael could wield the silver power, and he commanded solely its killing aspect, not its other facets.

But if the magi could harness *muk,* they could win the war.

Rabbit's heart pounded. It wasn't the first time he'd wondered if he could be the guy to rebuild the bridge—the crossover—between the light and dark magic, reuniting the halves. But it was the first time he thought it might actually happen, there and then.

Please, gods. He wasn't sure if he sent the prayer to the sky or the underworld; he knew only that he meant it with every fiber of his being.

Pulse thudding, he shoved his free hand into the box and started sifting through. Pain stung his fingers and palm as the sharp edges bit in, but he didn't stop, instead letting his blood smear the stones and mingle with the magic as he searched for the source of the heat.

The spinning in his head shifted his perceptions, making things seem very surreal, like he was standing outside and watching himself pick through stone shapes of white, black, green, gray, with a few flashes of yellow and orange. There was even a single piece of deep, vibrant crimson stone that practically glowed from within, gorgeous and powerful, and seemed so out of place that he picked it up, cradled it in his palm, and stared at it for a long moment before he noticed that his fucking hand was burning.

"Ow! Shit." Instinct had him juggling the thing to his other hand.

Power roared the second the two eccentrics touched. Brilliant, blinding light flashed from the pieces, so bright and searingly hot that he dropped the stones. They fell, fused together in a twisted shape of black and red. He didn't hear them land, though, didn't hear anything except the *wham-bam* of his heart and the scrape of his boots as he stumbled and went to his knees. He hit the box on the way down, overturning it with a rattling crash.

Light. Heat. *Gods.*

He shielded his eyes with his arm, which felt naked and singed beneath his shirt. And then, thank fuck, the heat flatlined, then faded to a glow. Rabbit gaped as the glow coalesced into a shape that got bigger—first dog size, then man. "What the fuck?"

Within moments, he was staring at a woman's white-cloaked figure. And oh, holy shit, he could see right *through* her.

She was dark haired, fine featured and somehow ageless, rendered even more otherworldly by her eyes, which were a cloudy, opaque white that gleamed from within. She was wearing a feather-worked, embroidered ceremonial robe and a crackling aura of power like he'd never seen before. This wasn't the greasy brown roil of dark magic, the sparkling red-gold of Nightkeeper power, or even the sliver gleam of *muk*; it was translucent. It wasn't anything he knew, but suddenly it was *everything,* awe inspiring and overwhelming.

If he hadn't already been on his knees, he would've ended up there now. His legs were shaking; his whole body was shaking. "Are you one of the creators?" His voice cracked on the question.

Those luminous eyes widened. Then, to his surprise, she smiled. "No, I'm not. Though in a sense, I suppose I am, from your perspective." Her voice was soft, feminine and singular, with none of the chorus effect that came from the ancestral beings known as the *nahwal.* So what was she? A ghost? A goddess?

His heart pounded even faster, though he couldn't

have said why his fight-or-flight was kicking in. Maybe it was the way the bones of her face suddenly seemed familiar, as if he'd seen them in another time and place. Or maybe it was flat-out awe. He didn't know. He only knew that it felt like he was on the edge of something huge. And that he, who had rarely—if ever—done humility, all of a sudden felt pretty fucking humble.

Voice dropping to a strangled whisper, he forced out: "Who are you? Why are you here?"

"Don't you recognize me, Rabbie?"

"I don't . . ." He swallowed hard and, then, when that didn't move the lump in his throat, hacked a hairball clearer of a cough. "My name is Rabbit. Nobody calls me 'Rabbie.'"

The nickname—a shortened version of the already weird-ass name his old man had hung on him—had always made him twitch. He hated it even more than he'd hated "bunny-boy," "Playboy," and all the others his high school tormentors had used put together, hated the way it made him feel incomplete, alone, and very, very young.

"No, Rabbit was your nickname. Your birth name was Rabbie."

"My . . ." A crushing pressure vised his chest, stealing his breath and putting him on his hands and knees, gasping for air. A humming whine grated in his ears, a gathering darkness crept in on his vision, and incredulity washed through what was left of his brain as he realized that he was about to fucking faint.

Rabbie. My Rabbie. My baby boy. The memory came out of nowhere, singsong words that reached inside him, grabbed his heart, and squeezed.

"No," he grated in between wretched gulps of air. "No fucking way. That's not . . . you're not . . . no way."

No. Impossible.

"Rabbie." The word was a sigh that prickled his skin.

But was it impossible? No, not really. The shaman had said his mother had probably been one of the handful of his village's women who had joined—either willingly or by abduction—Iago's dark, vicious sect of Xibalbans.

"You're her." It burned to say, agonized to think, yet when he lifted his head to look at her, he saw his own face. "You're my mother."

"*Yes*." Her colorless eyes glittered. "You didn't forget."

He had, though; his memories began entirely with the strange blended family he'd grown up in. Red-Boar might not have given him affection, acceptance, or even the fucking time of day, but he'd had the good sense to eventually go live with Jox, Strike, and Anna. Even then, Rabbit had grown up a little wild and a lot rebellious, outcast and unhappy until the magic came along and gave him a reason to grow the hell up. It wasn't until after his old man was killed, though, that he had gone looking for his mother, trying to understand the other half of his magic, the other half of himself.

And now she was here . . . only she wasn't. She was see-through and wreathed in magic, clearly not a creature of this plane anymore. He couldn't breathe, couldn't think, could only say, like a dumb ass, "You're a projection, aren't you? A spirit from the dark barrier." The barrier, like the magic itself, had long ago been split into its light and dark aspects. Where the Nightkeepers could visit the light barrier to gain wisdom—and occasionally confusion—from their ancestors, the Xibalbans could do the same with its dark, shadowy half. His eyes went to the eccentrics, which were locked together in a shimmering swirl of red and black. "Those things summoned you."

"I'm sending my image through them, but yes, they're the catalyst." Her voice went soft. "And, yes, I reside in the dark barrier. We both do."

"You and Red-Boar?" Rabbit frowned, because it didn't play. His father had been firmly entrenched in the light magic, and he had always and forever mourned the Nightkeeper wife and sons he had lost in the massacre. As far as Rabbit knew, he hadn't wanted another family, certainly hadn't wanted his half-blood son. Then again, it had never been clear how he'd wound up siring Rabbit with a Xibalban in the first place. Which meant . . . Shit, he didn't know what it meant. Only that he'd been waiting for this for a long, long time. A million questions raced through him, but beneath the roil was a huge, excited warmth. Because while his cynical, battle-hardened self said this could be a trick, the image a fake, he knew, deep down inside, that she was real.

"I speak of Tristan. Your brother."

"I don't . . ." Rabbit trailed off, eyes widening, then filling as the singsong memory came again, this time caroling, *Trisss-tan and Rabbie climbing in the trees. Laughing and playing, and chasing honeybees . . .* "Gods," he whispered, forcing the syllable past a surge of nausea. "Tristan. Turtle. You called him Turtle." He couldn't see faces, only the outlines of a woman and a little boy who wasn't him, but was so very familiar that it hurt, deep down inside.

"Yes, Tristan. Turtle. He was so cautious, where you were always on the move, hopping from place to place."

She paused, face going achingly tender and heart-rendingly sad. "You two were—"

"Twins," he whispered, knowing it with the same bone-deep certainty that recognized her. *I had a twin.* Not just a brother, but another half of himself—not identical, but rather complementary, filling in the gaps and making a perfect, powerful whole.

Harsh noise roared in his brain and then downward to fill his throat and chest, tearing him with a single wrenching sob. *No. Gods, no. Please. It hurts.* But he couldn't escape the memories now; they crowded him, banging against a barrier he hadn't even realized existed in his mind. He'd had a brother. A twin. And Red-Boar had never told him. Never even hinted that there might be a reason that he'd so often felt jagged and incomplete, like he was missing part of himself.

Son of a bitch.

Rabbit hung his head, trying to fight the nausea, the dizziness, the blackness that took on the shadowy shape of a face very like his own, only not. Something cool touched the back of his neck, a gentle, feathery brush of ghostly fingertips that telescoped time, turning him once more into a child. Pain ripped through his soul as memory broke through. He sagged and cried out, dry-heaving as she touched him again, freeing the last of the long-ago pain, and sending him into the memories. And into a vision that wasn't his own.

The small house tucked amid the trees, glittering with leaf-dappled sunlight, might've been made of the same wood and thatch the native Mayan villagers used, but with its blocky construction, framed windows, and silly flower boxes, it looked more like a starter home in the 'burbs.

Which in a way it was, Phee thought as she followed the hidden path leading home.

The house and the family inside it were a fresh start, a do-over for both of them after her imprisonment, his bad luck, and the miracle of her and Red-Boar finding each other, healing each other to the point of moving on.

Alerted somehow of her arrival—maybe by a change in the birdsong overhead, or some residue of the mindbender's talent he had once wielded—he came through the front door, eyes locking on her instantly. As it always did, her heart missed a beat at the sight of him. Tall and layered with lean muscle that popped beneath nut brown skin, with his skull shaved and his shirt off, he was a fantasy she hadn't dared dream when she'd hung, naked and shackled, in the Xibalbans' ritual chamber of horrors. Now, though, she was free to look at him, free to run her hands over him.

Simply and wonderfully free.

He didn't smile when he saw her; he rarely ever relaxed the fierce scowl that had grooved deep lines beside his mouth, and his eyes would probably always carry shadows, no matter how much time separated them from the massacre that had taken his first family. But Phee had learned to look beneath his fierce exterior and see the subtle easing of tension that said, "I'm glad you're back."

Those small signs were all she needed. That, and the sight of two small faces popping out behind their father, the sound of their voices saying, "Mommy's home!"

Her heart lifted as the boys—both miniature versions of their father, but with her gray eyes, one light haired, the other dark—scrambled through the door and raced toward her, arms outstretched. They whumped into her knee-high and wrapped around her as if she'd been gone for days on a supply run rather than just the couple of hours she had taken to walk the perimeter of their safe zone.

Slinging her rifle over one shoulder, she crouched down and hugged them back.

"All clear?" Red-Boar asked.

"You've said it yourself—at this point, checking for footprints is as much a habit as anything."

It had been four years since she had escaped, three and a half since Red-Boar had found her lying almost dead at the edge of a ruined Mayan pyramid. And it had been more than two years since the last rumor that men wearing the bloodred quatrefoil of the Werigo's vicious Xibalban sect were searching the highlands for her. Still, though, they stayed vigilant. They had the boys to worry about now.

Oblivious to his mother's thought process, Rabbie— aka Mr. Short Attention Span—pulled away from her and bounced back to his father, talking animatedly and so fast that only every third word was really intelligible.

Tristan wound his arms around her neck and grinned. "Rabbit and turtle?"

"Again?" she asked, laughing past the sudden tightness in her throat. "You've already heard it a zillion times." The story had been the boys' favorite even before she and Red-Boar had started using the all-too-apt nicknames.

"Rabbit and turtle!"

"Okay, okay. Let me get a drink first." She stood, taking Triss with her and feeling the strain of his good, solid weight in her arms. As she headed for the house, a flock of parrots burst from the trees high overhead. She stopped and looked up, grinning at the flashes of red and green. "Look!" she said to Tristan. "What do you think the birdies—"

Gunfire split the air, ripping the peace to shreds, and invisible blows slammed into her—thud, thud, thud—*knocking her back and down.*

"Phee!" Red-Boar's anguished bellow roared over the chatter of a second burst of machine-gun fire. A split second later, the underbrush thrashed and six red-robed Xibalbans burst into the clearing.

She didn't know whether she screamed or not, knew only that her heartbeat was hammering in her ears as she fell. She tried to hang on to Tristan, tried to curl around him and then scramble up and away from the attack. But nothing was working right; she couldn't hold on to him, couldn't get up, couldn't do anything but lie there as more shots rang out and one of the boys started crying.

Dear gods, only one. Only . . .

Blackness.

Sometime later she awoke. She knew it was later by the angle of the sun, which was suddenly too bright, making her squint through a haze of tears as she tried to focus on Red-Boar's face. His eyes were swimming with moisture, his face etched as always with grief. But it wasn't old remembered pain right now; this agony was fresh and new, and wholly focused on her.

She was dying. She didn't need to see it in his eyes to know it. Her body was numb and cold, her heart stuttering. "Triss . . . tan?" she asked, forcing her lips to shape the word. "Rabbie?"

A tear broke free and tracked down his face. "Rabbie's fine. And you'll . . ." He swallowed hard. "You'll see Triss soon."

"Noo . . ." She closed her eyes as something broke inside her with utter and devastating finality. There was pain—terrible, rending agony—but there was also a

*strange sort of peace that said soon it wouldn't hurt any-
more. Soon it would be over—the pain, her life, all of it.
Red-Boar, though, would have to live with the agony, not
for his own sake, but for Rabbie's. Her heart broke anew,
because there could be no greater torture for him, she
knew, than to be once more the survivor.*

*"Take him home," she said, knowing that if she hadn't
been chickenshit they would've already been in the States
with their names changed and the last surviving* winikin
*in charge of their anonymity. But she had been too afraid
of the Nightkeepers' high-pressure, high-tech world, clinging instead to the familiar forests she'd grown up in. That
was her mistake, her sin. "Keep him safe and raise him
right. Promise me."*

*His tears were flowing freely now and his eyes were
soul-deep wounds without end. "I promise."*

*She tried to respond, but the only thing that came out
was her final breath as the world went dim. Then dark.*

Then gone.

Rabbit awoke to find himself lying on the stone floor of
the library, cold and stiff, with tears drying on his face
and an aching hole where his heart used to be.

"Hello?" The word came out as a croak, nearly unrecognizable. "Are you still here?"

There was no answer. She was gone.

He rolled onto his side with a groan, then lay there for
a few seconds, gulping for oxygen. His stomach muscles
hurt and his throat was raw, like he'd been retching. And
his whole world felt off balance, like it had gone off the
road and halfway off a cliff, where it teetered, waiting for
a stiff wind to send it crashing down.

His eyes locked on two gleaming pieces of stone lying

nearby, fitted together. Dragging himself to a woozy sort of upright position, he reached for them, then hesitated.

The eccentrics had faded, one to its normal flinty black and the other to a bright white quartz that was shot through with reddish iron streaks. They looked like normal stones now rather than artifacts that had the power to allow a spirit's essence to pass from the dark barrier onto the earthly plane. But that was what they had done.

His mother's ghost had come to him. He had seen her, talked to her.

It almost felt like a dream, except that the eccentrics were there, connected. Just as he felt connected now to her . . . and to the twin brother he'd forgotten. Tristan. *Gods.*

Exhaling softly, he touched the stones, which parted with a soft, almost musical grating sound. He didn't feel anything when he picked them up, didn't get any indication that they were more than plain stones, not even when he fitted them together once more. They aligned perfectly, with the spiky shapes of one fitting into the indentations of the other to create a single whole. But they didn't click into place and there was no heat, no power.

He would have tried putting his own magic into them, but he was too damn woozy. He needed to eat something—*not* more chili dogs—and take some downtime to recharge before he attempted to summon the spirit, or send his own to the dark side of the barrier to speak with her again. And he needed to think things through before he tried any of it.

His gut said she was the real deal, but the things he'd seen in that vision didn't line up with what he knew of his old man. Not by a long shot.

He'd always figured he'd been an accident, something that Red-Boar had kept around as a sort of sacrifice, a penance, just like the brown robes he had worn and the grisly self-sacrifices he had performed on the cardinal days, though he would never say why he was doing penance or what he was praying for. Now, though . . . *Shit.* He didn't know what to think, how to feel.

Even searching for his mother had really been about figuring out the limits of his magic, not finding some sort of model family at the end of the rainbow. But now . . . Gods, he used to be part of something. He'd had a real family once . . . and a brother. A *twin,* for fuck's sake.

All the times he'd felt jagged and unfinished, or turned to say something to someone who wasn't there . . . well, it made sense now, because twins were sacred to the Nightkeepers, powerful.

The hollow place inside him ached—for himself, for his mother, for Tristan . . . and, yeah, even for his old man. Because the guy in that vision sure as shit wasn't the guy he'd grown up with. But at the same time, he knew the past wasn't the most important thing right now, not with the war coming. Sluggish excitement stirred at the realization that if he could learn to use the stones to summon her again, he might be able to pump her for information about the dark barrier, maybe even the plans of the *Banol Kax.* And maybe, possibly, how he was supposed to become the crossover.

Dragging himself upright with a muffled groan, he stuck the stones in separate pockets, righted the box, and used an ancient codex to scoop the other, garden-variety stone chips back into it. He knew darn well that Lucius would have an aneurism if he saw the one-of-a-kind-text-turned-dustpan routine, but his instincts were suddenly telling him he needed to work fast, with his pulse throbbing to a tribal drumbeat of, *Hur-ry, hur-ry, hur-ry!* He was sweating by the time he'd put the box back where it started, stuck the codex back in its folder, and headed for the front of the library, zigzagging like a drunk.

Beyond the racks, the library opened up to a workspace furnished with stone tables and benches. The walls were carved and windowless, and a single wooden door on the short side led out.

As he lurched for the door, it swung open and Myrinne stepped through. He jolted at the sight of her, and at the slash of heat that cut through him—as always—when she came into the room. With her dark hair cut in a sassy, asymmetrical bob and her foxy face bare of makeup, wearing embroidered jeans and a pale yellow shirt that flirted up to show a gleam of jade at her pierced belly button, she looked young and fresh, and so damn beautiful his knees nearly buckled the rest of the way.

Ah, baby.

Longing stabbed, not because he wanted her right then and there—he probably would've passed out right the fuck on top of her if he'd tried anything—but because he wanted things to be back the way they used to be: the two of them against the world. Now they were just . . . different. Tenser, even if he couldn't always put his finger on what was making him tense.

Her face brightened at the sight of him, showing none of that strain. "Hey! I was just coming to— Gods!" She hurried toward him. "What's wrong? What happened?"

"I'm . . . Shit." He took a step toward her, sagged, and slapped out an arm for balance.

"Rabbit!" She got her shoulder under his, and managed to prop him back up. Once he was stabilized, she felt his face, then his forehead, her hand cool on his clammy skin. "You're on fire!"

"Not literally, thank fuck." He let his cheek rest on the top of her head, let himself breathe in the knowledge that even when things weren't quite right between them, she cared for him, worried about him, loved him. Which still seemed like a fucking miracle some days. "I'm okay," he said into her hair. "Just overdid it after pulling so much magic earlier."

It wasn't until the words were out of his mouth that he realized he wasn't going to tell her about the vision.

And what the hell was that about?

She frowned up at him. "You're sure it's just a crash? You didn't get nailed by one of those animals, did you?"

No, he'd been bitten by something else: reluctance. He knew that if he told her about his mother and Tristan, she would start asking questions that he wasn't ready to answer yet. More, she would push him on experimenting with the eccentrics using any means possible, including dark magic. She didn't care that he'd promised Dez he wouldn't try to reawaken the hell-link—as far as she was concerned, he didn't owe the Nightkeepers anything.

Shit, he just wanted some breathing room. He wanted her to keep looking at him like she was right now, with the glint in her eyes that said she was seeing only him, Rabbit the guy, not Rabbit the pyro, telekine, mind-bender, warrior, crossover, or what-the-fuck-ever.

He caught her hands when she would've started patting him down, checking for injuries. "I'll be fine; I promise. I just need some food." And a few hours to process things. Because as his scattered brain cells started checking in for duty, he was realizing that he couldn't tell the Nightkeepers about his vision, either. His mother was Xibalban, after all. The enemy.

Under any other circumstance, keeping this shit all to himself would've felt way wrong. But as Myrinne guided him out of the library and into the passenger seat of one of the compound's ubiquitous Jeeps, clucking and fussing over him as if she too had needed an excuse to let their recent bickering fall aside, it all felt very right. There was a new warmth inside him, singing soft, half-remembered lullabies and letting him know that whatever happened, he wasn't alone anymore, not deep down in his heart. His mother's spirit—and maybe even Tristan's too—was watching him, watching out for him. And thank the gods for that.

CHAPTER FOUR

"Wait up."

Cara winced at the sound of Zane's voice behind her, followed by the heavy tread of his boots catching up to her in the hallway. She stopped, though, and turned back, surreptitiously tucking the package of hot dogs she'd filched from the kitchen into her waistband at the small of her back, beneath her shirt, where they pressed like cold, sweaty fingers.

He had changed out of his funeral garb—she suspected they all had, wanting to put some distance between them and the attack—and was dressed down in fatigue pants and an army green T-shirt, with a blue button-down thrown over it and turned up at the cuffs. On one level she recognized that he looked good, with the button-down deepening the blue of his eyes while the tee showed off the iron-pumping physique beneath. On another level, though, she thought that his eyes were too dark, his muscling too heavy, his face too much on a level with hers, when she would've preferred lighter eyes on a leaner, taller man.

And it was a really, really bad idea comparing him and Sven. Besides, there was no comparison, really. One wanted her, while the other wanted to ride to the rescue when it suited him. And she just wanted to do her job for the next three months or so, and then leave all this—and both of them—behind.

"What's up?" she said, angling her body so he couldn't see the hot-dog bulge.

His eyes searched hers. "I wanted to see how you were doing."

"Fine." Even with him, she didn't dare be anything *but* fine. Not if she wanted the *winikin* to follow her lead. "How are the others?" They had still been muttering over their forearm marks—and her lack of one—when Dez had called her to the royal suite to give her report on the attack.

"They're rattled. Scared. Wondering why the ward didn't stop those things and what the hell else is going to go wrong next."

Was it a good thing or bad that he didn't mention the marks? She tried to tell from his expression, but saw only his concern and a questioning empathy that silently prodded, *Are you sure you're okay?*

"I'm fine," she said again, then realized he hadn't asked the question aloud. *Shit.* Flushing slightly, she added, "Should we do a Bud-'n'-bitch?" The officially unofficial gripe sessions were held once or twice a month in the Nightkeepers' old training hall, which the rebel *winikin* had appropriated and renovated into a rec room. Part town meeting, part drinking game, and with no weapons allowed, the sessions gave the *winikin* an opportunity to blow off steam in no-Nightkeepers-allowed privacy.

He shook his head. "I think you should give it a day or two, see what the brain trust comes up with, and go from there. Besides, tonight might not be the best night to stick everyone in a room and throw alcohol in the mix."

"Yeah. Probably not." Edging back a step, feeling beyond awkward with a pound of hot dogs stuck down her pants, she made a *gotta go* gesture. "Well, I'm going to—"

"He was right, you know," Zane interrupted, and the sudden set of his jaw said that this was what he'd come to tell her.

She stilled. "He who?"

"The coyote mage." That was Zane's name for Sven and was said, as always, with a faint sneer, but the bulk of his anger seemed self-directed as he said, "I should have sent you ahead with Lora. I should have had your back."

"Oh." She hadn't realized he had been close enough to overhear, wondered what else he'd picked up from her and Sven's exchange. Carefully, she said, "I gave you an order and you followed it. You did the right thing."

That squared-off jaw got squarer. "Not this time. And, yeah, I know that following orders isn't optional in the military but this"—his gesture encompassed all of Skywatch—"isn't just an army; it's a community. And you're more than my superior officer, Cara. A hell of a lot more. Which as far as I'm concerned gives me the right—and, hell, the responsibility—to call bullshit on bad orders. I should've done that today. The *winikin* need you. And I . . . Shit." He lifted a hand as if to touch her, but they were too far apart. "I wish I'd been the one. Not him."

A harder, hotter flush hit her and she almost blurted

that it wasn't like that with her and Sven, that he wasn't the one, that *nobody* was. But just in time she caught that he was talking about being the one to rescue her. "You saved Lora and Sven saved me. It was teamwork, Zane, just like we practiced."

"Teamwork." His lips twisted. "Is that what you call it?"

Okay, she thought as a quiver worked its way through her stomach at the sudden heat in his eyes. He wasn't entirely talking about the rescue, after all. "Zane . . ."

"Is it because of him? The coyote?"

"No." *Yes.* "Absolutely not." *Maybe a little.* "It's because of *me.*" Which was true. She wanted more than she'd gotten in her life so far, and she was smart enough, disciplined enough, to know she couldn't go looking for it while struggling to piece the *winikin* together.

He took a step closer, narrowing the gap between them as he searched her eyes. Suddenly she was very aware that they were alone and off duty—or as off it as either of them ever got—and he was close enough to kiss her. Heat stirred, but it came from embarrassment rather than excitement. All she could think was, *Please don't try it.*

He reached out, took her hand, and raised it to press a kiss to her knuckles. His lips were soft, his beard shadow a bristly scrape of contrast, and it was over before she felt anything more than relief that he hadn't tried to kiss her for real.

Without pulling her hand away, she said, "I can't, Zane. I just . . . can't. I didn't ask for this job, but now that I've got it, I need to give it twice as much energy as I have, which means I've got nothing left for anything else, including a relationship, or even a hookup. That's all going to have to wait until I'm done leading the charge." She grimaced. "Then again, given the way the *winikin* are sniping at each other these days, Mendez—or, hell, the gods themselves—might just decide to replace me before then."

Which wasn't something she'd ever said to anyone else before, had barely even acknowledged it herself. And once it was out there, she wished she'd kept it inside, because he hesitated, letting her know that he too had his doubts. But what if that was the right answer? What if she was doing more harm than good? What if—

"You can do this." Zane spaced the words for emphasis, still holding her hand in a grip that felt suddenly warm and solid. "The holdouts are going to get behind you. There's going to come a moment when they're going to rally, not because they'd rather be led by a *winikin*—any *winikin*—than a mage, but because you're the right person for the job." He paused. "That's why you should've been the one hauling ass for the shield today while I stayed behind. And it's part of why I want to be with you. I want to have your back, more than I do now. I want to be there for you, no matter what."

Her chest went tight. "I can't . . . I won't . . . Shit." Breaking off, she pulled her hand away from his and pinched the bridge of her nose, willing back the burn of tears. "I'm sorry. I just can't deal with this right now."

"That's the thing, Cara. Don't you get it? If you let me in then you won't have to deal with things alone anymore. We can work together, be a team. Partners."

Part of her yearned with a fierce intensity she hadn't felt since childhood, when things had been so much simpler, and saying, "I want," hadn't come with all the risks and conditions of adulthood. She wanted to be part of that sort of team; she always had. "I don't think—"

Seeing her waver, he moved in. And kissed her.

At the touch of his lips, she sucked in a breath as a sudden rush of embarrassed heat turned her momentarily light-headed and had her grabbing for his arms. Encouraged, he deepened the kiss, shaping his mouth to hers and sliding in, tongue to tongue. And for a crazy second that went against everything she'd been telling herself for the past two days, ever since he'd revealed his feelings, something inside her said, *What the hell, why not?* His arguments were good ones, and she was so damn tired of being in charge.

So she kissed him back.

His breath hissed out when she softened against him, and he splayed his hands across her back high and low, making her suddenly aware of her own body in a way she hadn't been in a long, long time. Their tongues met and separated with a rhythm that reminded her of the battle strategies that were becoming second nature: probe and retreat, probe and retreat, seeking a weakness in the enemy lines. Only they weren't enemies and this wasn't a battle, and his body was strong and solid, anchoring her. She let herself stay locked there—in his arms, in the moment. And if a small voice in the back of her head said she should pull back, hold off, make sure she knew what she was doing, she ignored it to feel the warm press of his mouth and arms, and the layers of muscle beneath his shirt where she gripped his upper arms.

But that was it, she realized as the kiss went on and her brain kicked back in. She didn't really feel any burning desire to let her hands roam away from his biceps and stroke the rest of him.

No real desire at all, in fact.

At the realization, *What the hell* turned into *Oh, hell*,

and her stomach dropped. What was she doing? She knew this wasn't going to work, had known it the moment he'd bared his feelings and her first reaction had been dismay, her second a profound wish that he'd kept it to himself. And the way her brain was racing as he kissed her now was further proof—as if she'd needed it—that they weren't a match for the short or long term. In the dark depths of the night, she fantasized about a man whose kisses and touch blocked out rational thought and made the world disappear. Not one who made her feel all awkward, like her arms and legs weren't angled quite right as she held on to him.

She must have stiffened or made some sound, because he ended the kiss and drew away, his eyes searching hers. "And for the record, I'm not talking about just a hookup here. I never was. I want us to—"

"Stop," she said in a low, ragged voice. "Please stop."

He hesitated, his expression dimming. "You're seriously not going to give this a chance?" His voice roughened with urgency. "We could be good together. Let me help you. Let me be there for you."

Temptation tugged once more, reminding her of all the times she'd watched the mated magi share a touch or a look, or make a less-than-subtle dash for their quarters hand in hand, and wished she could have what they had. She had tried to imagine what it would be like to be part of a couple—not just a friends-with-benefits thing like she'd had before, but a real couple—and know that there was always going to be someone on her side, ready to back her up if she needed it. Only now that she was being offered exactly that, she found she didn't want it, not the way she had thought. She wasn't sure if it was the timing, the man, or both, but even as her heart cracked a little and her instincts warned that she couldn't risk alienating him, she shook her head. "I'm sorry, Zane, but I can't. I just can't. I need"—*sparks,* she thought, but instead went with—"something different."

His expression flattened. "Something other than a man who cares about you, is attracted to you, and wants to help you succeed?" When she didn't answer, he caught her hands again, his grip warm and sure. "You don't have to answer right away. You can take some time, think it through, be sure you're making the right decision."

"I *am* sure." She reversed so she was the one gripping his hands, the one squeezing to make sure he was paying attention, because she wanted—*needed*—to have this be the end of the discussion. "Please listen to me, and believe me when I say that I'm very sorry—sorrier than I really know how to express—but this isn't going to happen. I said no the other night and I'm saying it now, and I don't need to take time and think it through. This is the right decision for me, and I'm going to have to ask you to respect that." She paused. "I'm sorry, Zane; I really am. Not just because I'm turning you down, but also because now I have to ask you if we're still going to be able to work together after this, or if I should start thinking about rearranging the command structure."

The woman in her knew she was kicking a good man while he was down. The leader she was becoming said she had to know.

Now it was his turn to pull his hands away from their clasp, his turn to take a couple of steps back. He stood with his hands locked behind his back, his chin up, and his eyes looking past her as he said, "Don't worry about me. I know how to soldier up."

Her stomach knotted at his stark tone, and the knowledge that he'd never done anything to make her doubt his professionalism. "I know. I didn't . . . Shit. I'm sorry."

Chin dipping in an almost-nod of acknowledgment that didn't reach his faraway eyes, he said, "Then I guess I'll see you at the morning briefing. If you need me . . . Hell, I'll just see you at the briefing."

She wouldn't have been surprised if he'd saluted or waited for a dismissal, and was almost pathetically grateful he just turned on his heel and strode away, boot steps echoing in the corridor, then fading when he turned the corner for the *winikin*'s wing. Moments later, his door opened and then thunked shut, leaving behind an echoing silence.

Suddenly very tired, as if her exhaustion had just been waiting around for her to notice it, she leaned back against the nearest wall and concentrated on breathing. In and out. In and out. In and . . . *Shit.* How was she going to fix things now? Was it even possible? He might've played it off like they could just go back to business as usual, but there had been real pain in his face just now, real regret, disappointment, maybe even a hint of anger. She knew how it felt to want someone who didn't want her back, and she hated like hell having caused him that pain. He was a good man, had been a good friend.

Freaking sparks, she thought bitterly, swiping a hand across her dry, burning eyes. It would've been so much easier if she could've wanted him.

Sighing, she pushed away from the wall and turned for her suite, only to be brought up by the feeling of a clammy hand on her ass.

Damn it, she had hot dogs tucked into her pants, and an apology to make to the last person she wanted to see right now.

She hesitated, sorely tempted to bag it and head back to her quarters. But that would mean admitting that he still had power over her, which he damn well didn't. So, muttering a curse under her breath, she yanked the wieners out of her waistband and went in search of Sven, determined to get her thanks out of the way and prove that he'd long ago lost whatever spell he'd once cast over her.

Nightkeeper or not, he was just a guy.

CHAPTER FIVE

Despite her determination to just freaking get it over with, Cara almost wimped out twice on the way to Sven's suite: once at the entrance to the mages' wing, and again at his door. Caution said that she was too tired and raw to deal with this now, that she should call it a night and start over in the morning. But the longer she waited, the more important it would seem. A thank-you given in the moment was a toss-off; one twenty-four hours later meant she'd been stewing.

"Don't be a wuss," she muttered. And, clutching the hot dogs in a grip gone slippery with condensation, she knocked hard and fast.

"It's open," he called, voice muffled.

Blowing out a breath, she pushed through the unlocked door, stepped into the main living area of the three-room suite, and let the panel swing shut behind her. She hadn't been inside his quarters since her return to Skywatch, and found that the hang-loose decor the place had sported four years ago—heavy on the surfboards, underwater pics, and treasure maps—had given way to a collection of canyonscapes and coyote motifs.

One of the two bedroom doors was open, and there were sounds of activity within. Through the door, she saw the corner of a bed covered with a rumpled dark blue comforter; a pair of jeans hung off one edge, with a holstered pistol tossed on top. The tableau—a still life done in denim and Glock—threatened to bring a jolt of heat, but she looked away. She had seen plenty of guns over the past nine months; this one wasn't any different, and neither was the man. He was just another mage, fighter, and teammate. She owed him an apology, nothing more. So when she heard him coming out of the bedroom, she took a deep breath and turned back with her thank-you on the tip of her tongue—

And froze at the sight of him.

Wearing sweats that hung low on his hips, with a gray hoodie over his bare torso, unzipped, he wasn't naked, wasn't even showing her anything she hadn't seen before. But it still made a hell of an impact.

Fresh out of the shower, he was using a white towel to rub his hair dry. It blocked his sight and muffled his words as he said, "Thanks for hooking me up with the grub, Carlos." He lowered the towel, started scrubbing at his chest. "I couldn't face going back out to the kitchen and— Oh. Cara. Sorry, I thought . . ." His eyes locked on her and he trailed off, and for a second it was like it had been earlier, with the rest of the world falling away and her perceptions coalescing to the two of them.

Play it cool, she told herself even as her skin prickled. *Don't stare.* But she couldn't stop herself.

His skin was the delicious golden color she remembered from his beach-bum days, when he'd been dead-heading his way through life as a part-time surf instructor, part-time wreck diver, and full-time party animal. Now, though, he was also in fighting form, bulked up through his chest and shoulders, yet still swimmer-lean in the flat planes of his stomach and the ripped lines of the abs that arrowed toward the waistband of the sweats as if deliberately trying to drag her eyes lower.

He made a harsh noise at the back of his throat, then rasped, "What are you doing here?"

For a second her mind blanked. Then she sucked in a breath and said too quickly, "I came to thank you. Tempers got a little hot earlier and I never said how grateful I am for you and Mac rescuing me." Exhaling and telling herself to slow down, relax, not make this into something more than it really was, she lifted the hot dogs. "These are for him." She suddenly felt like an idiot, holding out a ten-pack of wieners as a peace offering.

He nodded, though. "He's nosing around somewhere. I'll give them to him when he gets back, and make sure to tell him they're from you."

"Good. That's good." She wasn't even sure what she was saying, as if one part of her was automatically being polite while the rest of her stared at his chest, caught up in the unexpected intimacy of having him standing there in nothing more than socks and sweatpants, the resentment of knowing that he probably hadn't given it a second thought. She told herself to leave, but instead headed for the kitchen nook, where she put the hot dogs in the fridge. Like the coyote cared if they were warm.

Then, telling herself she would make the gesture and go, she turned back to him and pulled a crinkling bag from her pocket. It was a package of Skittles, a smaller version of the ones they used to plow through during long winter nights, when she, Sven, Carlos, and her mom, Essie, had engaged in cutthroat tournaments of the *patolli*. The ancients had anted up with everything from gemstones and pottery to household furnishings, slaves, and sometimes even their own lives. Her family members had played for chores or a special treat, but most often, they had wagered Skittles.

Giving him the bag was a nod to the past they had agreed to leave behind, but somehow back in her quarters it had seemed like the perfect thank-you. So she held out the Skittles, grateful to see that he'd zipped his sweatshirt to his throat. "These are for you, from my private stash . . . unless you've outgrown crappy candy with one hundred percent artificial everything and zero nutritional value?"

His lips curved. "Hand 'em over."

The almost-smile made him seem far too approachable. His chest might be covered now, but the sweats were worn soft and clung to the lines of his body, putting a twist in her stomach. And, gods, could she be more hormonal? He obviously didn't share her problem—he was just standing there like it was no big deal for them to be alone together in his suite. Then again, for him it *was* nothing. And she needed to pull it together and remember that she wasn't an idiot teenager anymore, or even the girl who had left Skywatch when he told her to go. She had status and responsibilities of her own now, and they had nothing to do with him.

Steeling herself, she resisted the urge to toss the Skittles, and crossed the room instead, putting herself an arm's length away from him as she held out the candy. "Thanks for rescuing my ass today. I would've been in serious trouble if you hadn't been there." She paused, then said softly, "I owe you one, Sven. You saved my life."

He hesitated, then took the bag with a brush of fingertip-on-fingertip contact and moved back to hike a hip on the edge of the sofa in a casual sprawl that put their eyes on the same level for a change. He tossed the Skittles lightly in one hand for a moment, then sighed deeply, and said, "Shit. We're off script again."

"We're . . . what?"

"I was going to come find you, maybe get you to walk out to the back of the canyon with me." Still staring at the Skittles, he tipped his head toward the window. "It's a nice night."

Baffled, she followed his nod. The storm had passed without shedding a drop, leaving a high, dusty haze across the sky. It furred the stars and blurred the outline of the nearly full moon. "We can go if you want."

But Sven shook his head. "Nah. You're here; I'm here. . . ." A sad, tired smile twisted his lips. "Maybe the gods are trying to tell me to stop stalling."

Earlier, she had noticed the new lines between his brows and the seriousness in his storm-sea eyes. Now she saw shadows and an intensity that was nothing like his old chilled-out vibe. It brought a skim of surprise and nerves shivering through her, along with the reminder that she needed to stop thinking of him as the guy he used to be. Like her, he'd been through some serious crap over the past few years—heck, even the past few months. By all accounts, his and Rabbit's efforts to contain and then eradicate the *xombi* virus had been gruesome work, and she had no doubt that he carried new scars, on the inside if nowhere else.

Her inner *winikin* wanted to reach out and soothe him, feed him, take care of him. Her inner warrior, though, had her keeping her distance as she asked, "Are you okay?"

"I don't know if I'm fine or not right now, only that I'm better than I was before. Being down in those jungles, seeing things through Mac's eyes as we tracked the *xombis,* and then making myself cut them down no matter what they said or did . . ." He scrubbed a hand across his face, though the move did nothing to erase the grimness. "Hell, Cara, those nights got long. And lying there, smelling the blood on me and Mac no matter how hard I scrubbed to get it off . . . Shit, it really made me think about my life and the mistakes I've made."

Nerves coiled in her belly, coming from the knowledge that she wasn't in any shape to deal with this. "Okay, now you're scaring me. Do you want me to get someone? Sasha, maybe?"

"I don't need a healer. I need you to listen. You said you owe me, but what happened today doesn't even begin to balance things between us." And the look in his eyes said he wasn't talking about the here and now anymore.

Oh, no. Please don't go there. Face flaming with a blush that pulsed higher with each beat of her thudding heart, she said, "We said we were going to move forward and not worry about the past, remember? A deal's a deal."

But he shook his head. "The deal was a bad idea. And I'm the one who owes an apology."

"I don't want . . ." She trailed off when her throat tightened and her eyes prickled with the threat of tears. "Damn it."

He shifted as if to go to her, but then settled back and offered a hand, eyes darkening with remorse. "Shit, Cara. Please don't cry."

"I'm not. I won't." She waved him off. "Give me a second here." Because the thing was, she *did* want an apology; she always had. She'd just taught herself not to wish for things that weren't likely to happen. And now . . . damn it, she was tired, her defenses low. Swiping at her eyes, she fixed him with a watery glare. "Do me a favor? Don't do this unless you really mean it." Because as much as she didn't want it to matter anymore, it did.

"I mean it, I swear." His words were low and fervent, and carried the force of a blood oath. "I'm sorry, Cara, for all of it. I get it now. I see how I fucked things up, not just with you, but with Carlos too, creating this sort of three-way mess labeled 'shit we don't talk about.'"

Her head spun and her feet felt far, far away from the rest of her, putting her into a very unreal *this-isn't-happening* sort of place. But maybe after all these years it was happening. Maybe he was finally turning into the better man Carlos had always said he could be. "It hurt him badly when you left, you know."

"I know. I was going to go see him first, but . . ."

Her lips twisted on a strange-feeling smile. "I blew the script."

"Yeah. So I'll start with the things I need to say to you, instead." He reached out and took her hand, tugging her closer. The warmth of his skin and the solidity of his grip steadied her, bringing her back to reality as he said, "I'm sorry about what happened that day in the barn, Cara. I should've seen it coming, and I should've handled it better."

Reality screeched to a halt around her. *Wait. What?*

She frowned. "I don't—"

"When you kissed me, my mind . . . I don't know, it blanked. Shock, I guess." His thumb rubbed across her knuckles as his tired-looking eyes softened. "But that's no excuse for breaking your heart and then not saying I'm sorry. And I am. I'm just . . ."

"Sorry," she said dully.

He exhaled. "Yeah."

"You sure are." She wasn't sure whether to laugh, cry, or kick him someplace extremely tender. Really, though, she was the one who deserved a swift kick, because for a minute or so there, she had actually thought he might have changed. And maybe he had, but only a little bit. Only enough to see that he'd played a major role in cracking her family apart, not enough to see that it had been his disappearing act that had done the damage. Instead, he was blaming it on a kiss. One that, although she hadn't consciously remembered it in years, was suddenly there, front and center in her mind.

She was seventeen again, racing for the back barn and bubbling inwardly with the familiar refrain of "Sven's home, yippee!"

The barn was cool with shade and smelled of first-cutting hay, forming a perfect backdrop for the sight of the glossy bay gelding craning around to nudge Sven, who stood at his shoulder, adjusting tack.

Cara stopped just inside the door and let herself stare.

He had his back to her and seemed bigger than he had even a few weeks ago, when he'd come home after his final exams, stayed a few days, and then headed off on a road trip with friends. Now, though, he had changed out of his college clothes—designer jeans and T-shirts adver-

tising places she probably wouldn't ever visit—and into real jeans and a smoky blue, long-sleeved button-down that she and her mom had gotten him because it matched his eyes. Not that he would care about the eye thing. He was a guy, after all, and guys didn't notice stuff like that—or at least not the guys she knew.

Then again, Sven was nothing like those guys. They were goofy and immature, clowning around and trying to impress her and the other girls with their stupid stunts and lame-o jokes. Sven, though ... from the moment he'd come back to the ranch this time around, she had seen right away how he was different, how he was bigger, stronger, smarter, just better *than them, just like her father had always said. He was way cuter than the other boys too, with his stubby pirate's ponytail and the easy grin that said he was good with life and life was good with him. More, there was a vibe of power around him, offset by the gentleness he showed as he stroked the bay's nose, talking softly.*

He'd always had a way with animals. Her father had called it a gift and grinned when he said it; he'd tried to get Sven interested in training the ranch dogs with him, and then the horses. Sven hadn't stuck with either for long, far preferring machines that went fast and far, but he still rode now and then, sometimes loading up with enough gear to spend weeks out in the backcountry ... which, she realized with a jolt, was exactly what the bay was wearing now.

"No!" The soft cry was out before she could call it back.

The gelding snorted as Sven whipped around. His eyes narrowed when he saw her standing there. "I thought you went into town with your mom."

She sauntered across the packed-dirt floor, using the

walk she and a couple of friends had practiced, the one that always got her asked to dance. When she was close enough to inhale the scents of horse and leather, and the hint of his college cologne being overridden by her mom's laundry detergent, she planted her boots on the ground and her hands on her hips. "You were going to take off without even saying hello?"

"I'll be back in a few days."

"Bull. You've packed enough for a week. Longer if you're planning on hunting." And the scabbarded rifle said that was a good bet. Reaching out, she caught his hand and gave it a tug. "Stay. Please. It would mean a lot to Mom."

"Just her?" Suddenly he was looking at her with a strange new intensity.

A hot flush climbed her face, though she wasn't really sure why. "Of course not. I want you to stay too. And Dad—"

"I've already talked to him." He turned away from her and pretended to adjust his rigging.

Of course he'd checked in, and of course her dad had told him it was cool if he took off. What else did she expect? The two of them were thick as thieves. She didn't even bother being annoyed anymore; she was just grateful that she had her mother . . . who didn't look right, wasn't acting like herself, and had a doctor's appointment for next week, though she'd sworn Cara to secrecy. Which was why she didn't dare use it to convince Sven to stick around. Having him in the house, though, would put a gleam in her mom's eyes.

She reached out, hesitated, and then touched his back, first lightly and then harder, splaying her fingers wide to cover the firm muscles beside his spine and absorb the warmth coming through his shirt. He stiffened but didn't turn, and she pressed her cheek to her hand, so she was leaning into him, against him, as she had done when they were younger, before her father had started keeping Sven to himself as much as possible. "Stay," *she whispered, aware that he'd frozen in place and the only sound was the jingle of the bay gelding mouthing his bit, impatient to be off.*

"I can't." The two words came out ragged.

"Why?"

He shrugged her off and turned to face her, his expression thunderous. "I just can't, okay? I promised your father."

Tired of cricking her neck to look up at him, she climbed up on a nearby bale of hay to meet his glare. The moment their gazes connected, though, something strange happened; dark heat in his eyes stopped looking like anger and started looking way more like what she'd seen from the guys she hung out with, the kind of fire that said, I'm getting hot and bothered and I'm wondering if you're going to let me do something about it. *But where with those other boys it was something like a game, coming from Sven, the look seared her to her toes.*

"What promise?" she managed to get out breathlessly.

He hesitated. "I said I would ride out and get a head count on the high pastures, check for signs of any big cats messing with the stock."

Cara barely heard him over the urgent thudding of her pulse and the sudden knowledge that this was her answer. This was how she could convince him to stay. Guys were all the same when it came to the basics, right? God, she hoped so.

She leaned in even as a small, panicked voice inside

her said that this wasn't just any guy. And as that same voice warned that she should stop, back away, and not make a huge mistake, she caught a startled-looking Sven by the collar with her free hand and locked her mouth to his. And kissed him.

Heat flared through her, made of equal parts excitement and the panicked thought of, Oh, shit, what am I doing?

His lips parted on a muffled sound of surprise and his fingers flexed in her grip, but he didn't jerk away. If anything, he yielded against her, not all the way, but enough that she let go of his hand to flatten her palm on his chest, right over his heart. It beat with a quick, jumpy rhythm that sent new, surer heat flaring through her body along with a heady triumph that made her feel suddenly powerful. She—tiny little Cara, with her ranch clothes and weirdly striped hair—was hooking up with a college guy. And not just any college guy. This was Sven, and he'd looked at her with heat in his eyes.

Sparks igniting at the thought of him wanting her, she deepened the kiss and slid her tongue against his, wringing a full-body shudder from him. His hands tightened at her hip and upper arm, making her aware that they were almost embracing, with her breasts just grazing his chest and their thighs a breath apart. She moved closer, bringing their bodies fully into contact, and the sparks went to flames. Head spinning, she pressed closer, feeling the solid warmth of his muscles and—

"Shit!" He tore his mouth away and in a split second his hands went from holding her close to pushing her away so he could stare at her. This time there was no mistaking his expression. And horror didn't look nearly so good on him as desire had. "Jesus, Cara. No. We can't."

Flushing with a sudden echo of that same horror, she brazened it out, tipping up her chin to say, "Sure we can. So stay, please, at least for tonight." She wasn't sure how much she was offering, only that she needed him to not leave.

"Why? Why is it so important?" His fingers dug in as he searched her face.

But she didn't know how to answer. She was flushed and freaked, and could only stutter, "I-it just is, okay? Can you do it my way, just once, and stay because I asked you to?" She hadn't meant to say it that way, hadn't meant to make him choose. But once it was out there, she couldn't call it back. She could only wait and hope, knowing that if he really cared for her, even a little, he would—

"I can't." The two words sliced through her, as did the regret in his eyes as he let go of her and held his hands out at his sides in surrender, or maybe apology. He might've had those hands all over her only a few moments earlier, but now he seemed a zillion miles away. His expression was closed, his jaw set. "I'm sorry, Cara. I just . . . can't."

Catching the bay's reins, he headed for the door, walking stiffly.

"You're leaving?" She hated that her voice cracked on the last word, hated that she was all churned up, her emotions running right near the surface of her soul and threatening to overflow. "Just like that?"

"It's past noon already," he said without looking back. "I need to get going if I'm going to make the high pastures before dark." But although that was what he said aloud, the subtext was all too clear: Nice try, but it's not enough. I'd rather be out there alone than in here with you.

Which was the story of her life, really. Her father didn't want to spend time with her, so why should Sven? And her mother . . . A sob caught in her throat, then broke free as a harsh, bubbling sound.

Sven stopped. Man and horse were silhouetted in the wide doorway, with the rolling hills behind them topped by a gorgeous blue sky. It should've been a postcard. Then again, if it had been, she would've torn it up. She didn't need this, didn't need him. Shouldn't need anybody. It would be so much better that way.

"Christ, Cara . . . don't cry." He took a step back, but then stopped and just stared at her. With the light behind him she couldn't see his expression, but that was probably for the best. The last thing she wanted was his pity.

"Go." She waved him off. "Just go, damn it."

He hesitated . . . and then turned away, climbed on the rangy bay gelding, and headed for the hills, like always. Only this time he never really came back.

CHAPTER SIX

The memory faded, leaving a wistful ache behind. But despite Sven's apparent belief that their kiss had rocked her world—and not in a good way—it hadn't really changed anything for her. It had—for her, at least—been just another good-bye, another disappointment.

"It was never about the kiss, Sven." Her voice sounded rusty, as if she'd been silent far longer than she thought. Sure, maybe she had used the memory of those sparks as a benchmark for other kisses, other men, but her excitement that day had been more about being seventeen and outdoing her friends than it had been about him.

His fingers tightened on hers. "I made you cry."

"I was seventeen. Lots of things made me cry." Like being scared about her mom and not having anyone to talk to, lean on.

"That time it was my fault," he insisted. "I shouldn't have kissed you back, and I sure as hell shouldn't have taken off like that. You can't pretend things didn't change between us after that."

She pulled her hand away. "That's because *you were*

never around!" She hadn't meant to yell it, but suddenly couldn't dial down the volume. "You missed every birthday, every holiday, every big event. And when Dad wanted to blame someone for you being gone, since he couldn't blame himself, he blamed me. If you want to make that about the kiss, then go ahead. I don't care, because I know the truth, which is that you've always lived in your own world, and it has nothing to do with geography." Making herself stop before she said something she'd regret, she blew out a breath. "You don't get to run away from home and still be part of a family, Sven. It doesn't work that way."

For a moment, there was nothing but silence.

She expected a denial or—worse—pity and an argument. Instead, after a too-long pause while his eyes darkened with sorrow, he sighed and said, "Yeah. Shit. I know. I was just hoping . . ." He shifted, tried to shove his hands in his pockets, didn't have any, and settled for hitching his thumbs in his waistband, which made his sweats slip precariously. "I guess I was hoping that the kiss was the problem between you and me, because that was something I did, which means I could promise to never do it again. As for the other, hell, yes, I'm sorry, Cara. I'm sorry for not being around enough when your mom was sick, and I'm sorry I didn't come back for the funeral. Most of all, I'm sorry that I haven't ever been someone you could count on."

Her throat tightened. "I never asked you to be that guy. In fact, I don't need that guy—I can take care of myself."

"You shouldn't have to, not all the time." His eyes shifted, and for an instant she saw the same heat she'd seen that day in the barn. This time, though, it came from a different kind of frustration. "You deserve someone who'll look out for you the way you always look out for the people around you, someone who'll put you first and foremost, who'll be there for you no matter what."

Zane had said nearly the same thing, but where his words had put her on the defensive, Sven's brought a burn of tears that forced her to blink too quickly and remind herself that he wasn't actually offering. "Sven . . ." she began, but then trailed off, unable to find the words when her emotions were too big, her defenses too low.

"I wish I could've been that guy for you. And I'm sorry I wasn't there when you needed me."

It was the apology she had wanted, needed from him. Or so she had told herself over the years. Yet she found herself whispering, "But?" She heard it in his voice, could see it in his face.

He exhaled. "I can't promise to change. I want to say that I'll be there for you . . . but it would be a lie."

She didn't know when the angry heat had faded. All she knew was that she was suddenly cold, almost numb. "Because of the writs." The Nightkeepers' code spelled out a magc's duty to act first for the gods and mankind, then his king and the other magi and on down, with family near the bottom of the list.

He shook his head. "The writs aren't the problem. I am. I can't . . . I'm just not the kind of guy who sticks around. And as much as I wish I could change that—and by the gods, I do; I swear it—I can't make myself stay put." He spread his hands. "This is who I am."

It was stupid to be surprised or annoyed, yet she was suddenly both. "Bullshit. That's a cop-out. People can change if they really want to."

"You're thinking like a human. Be a *winikin* instead."

He tapped his forearm, where he wore the talent marks that said he was a warrior-translocator, capable of fighting, strategizing, and moving things with his mind. Most prominent, though, was the glyph designating him as a member of the coyote bloodline, with an additional circle and numerical dots representing his bond with Mac. "The bloodline stereotypes are stereotypes for a reason. The jaguars are stubborn, the eagles obsessive, the harvesters nurturing, and the coyotes . . . Well, the coyotes are loners, Cara, and footloose as hell."

"That's . . ." *Bullshit,* she wanted to insist, but couldn't. Because all of a sudden, Sven's behavior—and her father's refusal to blame him for it—crystallized in a way it never had before.

The lean ranginess she had always admired in him, the faint air of wildness that clung to him no matter where he was or what he was wearing, yeah, that was pure coyote. And although the bloodline characteristics had always seemed like a convenient excuse, she'd seen other aspects of the magic at work. Hell, she'd experienced it herself. Given that she'd suffered a string of low-grade illnesses that had vanished the moment she set foot back inside Skywatch, who knew what other tendencies were programmed in at the DNA level?

What if his inability to stay put and deal with real-life problems hadn't been self-centeredness so much as an inborn need to roam? What then?

As if she'd asked the question aloud, he said, "I didn't know I was a coyote when we were younger. All I knew was that I'd rather be out in the backcountry than at home, and then, once I was away from the ranch, it was easier to keep going than it was to turn back . . . at least until I wound up here." He indicated Skywatch and the box canyon surrounding them. "I've done my damnedest to stick it out. Learning to use the magic helped, I think, and swearing fealty to the king . . . But once Mac and I bonded, the restlessness came back. When I'm here, I feel caged in, claustrophobic." He stretched his limbs, as if even that light layer of clothing was too restrictive. "Hell, even on the outside, I can't stay in one place too long."

"You could fight it," she said softly, though the words brought a twinge from her *winikin* self.

Expression hollowing, he said, "I've tried to stay put, Cara. I swear I've tried. But the bloodline wins every time." He paused, his expression flattening. "It's no accident that I'm the only unmated Nightkeeper. Your dad told me once that the coyote magi didn't usually have gods-destined mates. A few had familiars, like I do, but when it came to mates they tended to swing, no harm no foul; have your fun or even your kids and then move on."

She winced, but said, "That's not your style."

"Isn't it? I've never been in a relationship that lasted past the one-month mark."

"You didn't leave any kids behind."

He shrugged. "Different time, different culture."

"You're—" She bit off "not that guy," not because it was untrue—coyote or not, he was a better man than that—but because she suddenly realized she had somehow fallen into *winikin* mode. She was soothing him when she really wanted to grab him by the collar and shake him until his perfect teeth rattled. But that was even worse, because it shouldn't matter to her. He wasn't her charge, wasn't her responsibility, and he sure as hell wasn't someone she should be wanting to make promises to her.

This was a mistake. She should've left the wieners and

Skittles in the hall, then knocked and bolted like it was some sort of apologetic practical joke.

Before she could make an excuse and escape, though, he said, "The main thing I've figured out is that since I can't change who I am, the best I can do is apologize and try my damnedest not to hurt anyone else." He paused, then reached out to her. "I'm sorry for not being there when you needed me, Cara. Please forgive me."

She hesitated, torn by the part of her that still thought he could've gone against his nature if he'd truly wanted to. But in the end it didn't matter, did it? She was getting the apology she'd never expected, the one she'd told herself not to need. So she took his hand. "Apology accepted. And thank you."

She'd meant to shake on it, but before she could make the move, he lifted their joined hands and pressed his lips to her knuckles. And although he'd probably meant it as a more-than-a-handshake gesture, it became far more than that in the moment his lips touched her skin.

Heat seared from the point of contact, racing inward, tightening her chest and stealing her oxygen. Her head spun as all her perceptions suddenly focused on the pressure of his fingers, the soft warmth of his mouth, and the startlement in his eyes as they flew to hers and then darkened, letting her know that she wasn't the only one feeling the unexpected sizzle.

"Don't," she said. Her voice was little more than a whisper, and she wasn't really sure which one of them she was talking to.

"I won't. I'm not. I didn't mean . . . Shit. I'm sorry." But although he lowered their hands, he didn't let go. Instead he tugged her closer, so she was standing in the vee of his legs, near enough that she could feel the heat from his body.

If her defenses had been low before, they were hell and gone now, lost beneath the sudden thunder of blood in her veins. She wanted to pull back but couldn't make herself move; she wanted to look away but his eyes dominated her vision, drawing her in. "Sven?" she said softly, not even sure what she was asking.

"It's the magic," he grated. "I used too much earlier and now I can't . . . Damn it."

"You . . . Oh." Excitement flared at the realization that she wasn't the only one whose defenses were low. Except in his case he was trying to block the powerful, sensual magic of a full-fledged — and unmated — Nightkeeper male, the sex magic that kicked in when his other reserves were drained.

He tightened his grip on her hand. "You should go."

"I know." But she stayed put, rooted by a sudden urgency that came not from the magic, but from her earlier encounter with Zane and the little voice inside her that sometimes whispered that she was remembering it wrong, that she was looking for something that didn't really exist outside her girlhood fantasies.

"Seriously. You need to leave." His free hand came up to touch her cheek and his eyes went dark and intense.

"In a minute. First, I have a confession." She hesitated. "I wasn't being entirely honest earlier when I said the kiss was no big deal. It was, though not the way you were thinking. It's more that I've always compared other guys to what I felt that day. But lately I've been wondering . . . what if that wasn't that great?" Though the way her pulse was throbbing now suggested that the sparks had been real and, more, that the attraction had persisted despite the many times he'd disappointed her.

His eyes darkened, but instead of arguing, he rasped, "Last chance to leave, Cara."

But the pressure of his hands drew her toward him instead, overriding the part of her that said she should stop, pull back, think this through. "I don't want to," she said, though her voice nearly cracked on the words. "I want you to kiss me instead, like before. One kiss, and then you ride off and don't look back." That was what made the experiment okay, the knowledge that he wouldn't be around for long. "I want—"

"Time's up." Eyes flaring with a wildness that set fire to her blood, he moved in on her, curled his fingers around her hips, and kissed her.

Dear gods in the sky, he kissed her. And she had her answer.

As a teenager, she had kissed him and felt sparks. Now, as an adult, there were fireworks, lightning, and more. The sensations seared through her, making her head spin and forcing her to clutch at his arms to keep her balance in a world gone suddenly off-kilter.

She had kissed plenty of guys, slept with a few, and had enjoyed herself just fine, but where before she had wondered why some of her friends put up with bad relationships to get good loving, now she understood. Because as he pulled her into his body so they were touching from hip to brow, curled together as if they truly fit, desire overran her thinking like it never had before.

She reveled in the press of his muscles and the hard ridge of his erection through the soft, yielding fleece of his sweats, and ran her hands over him, kneading as he kissed slowly, deeply, thoroughly. He didn't ask; he took. He didn't seduce; he demanded. And she went weak and pliant against him. Heat thrummed, coalescing in her core, wetting her and making her want. Her breasts were heavy and aching, demanding that she rub against him, and a moan rolled from the back of her throat when he reached to cup one of them and stroke his thumb across a peaked nipple. *Gods.*

She dragged her teeth along his lower lip, nipped his chin, and he growled and reclaimed her mouth in a dark, hot kiss that had her swaying against him, needing him. Their breathing synched, their flavors mingled, and what little coherent thought remained inside her centered on a single word: *more.* She wanted more of the kiss, more of his touch on her body, more of his skin against hers. She reached for the zipper of his sweatshirt, wanting to touch his skin, taste it, and—

Zzziip. The sound was loud and shocking in a room gone silent except for their breathing, and it jolted her back to reality. She jerked away. *Oh, gods.* She had been kissing Sven. Devouring him. Another few minutes—or a quieter zipper—and she might've been naked with him.

Naked. With Sven.

A sharp burst of desire lashed through her, but then turned to a flush of something that wasn't quite horror, but was close. And in his eyes, she saw the same progression, the same endpoint of, *What in the* hell *are we doing?*

They let go of each other, opening their hands in mirrored moves of *not touching you,* and she backed away. Her heart thundered in her ears; her breath rasped in her lungs, quick with excitement and a burgeoning fight-or-flight response that said to run, to get the hell out of there and not look back.

But that would be admitting that she couldn't handle herself—couldn't handle *him*—and she wasn't about to do that. So she exhaled softly and said, "Well. That answers *that* question with a resounding, 'Yes, it really can feel that good.' Now I just need to find that kind of chemistry with a guy who isn't allergic to boundaries."

His eyes darkened. "Cara—"

"Don't." She held up a hand. "Please." She didn't want to know that what they had just felt was more than good chemistry, more than sparks on steroids. "Just leave it, okay? What happened here . . . it didn't mean anything, doesn't change anything. Besides, a hundred bucks says you'll be out of here in a few days." She forced a thin-feeling smile. "Dez isn't going to let you and Mac lounge around here for long."

He didn't return the smile. "What if we stayed put?"

Back in the day, she would've given anything for the offer. Now she couldn't let it matter. "Don't, at least not on my account, not thinking that something could happen between us."

"I'm pretty sure it just did." His low words threatened to send a zing of renewed excitement through her bloodstream. She was highly conscious of the way his unzipped shirt hung open, baring his torso. The play of light and shadow on that warm-toned skin, along with the burn in her blood and the taste of him on her lips, made her want to touch him, lick him, pick up where they had left off and never stop.

Bad idea.

"Maybe, but it's not going to happen again." She backed away a couple more steps, putting herself closer to the door and far enough from him that she couldn't feel the warmth of his body against her skin. "Even if we were any good for each other, the last thing I want to do is give the *winikin* another reason to dislike me. Which means staying away from you for the next three months."

"And after that?"

"If we make it past the zero date, I'm cutting ties and getting out of here. I'm going to give myself a fresh start"—she met his eyes—"maybe even a new identity." She didn't think she could make it any plainer than that. She didn't want to be a *winikin,* didn't want to stay in touch with the Nightkeepers, didn't even want the last two members of her crumpled family to be able to find her. She would be alone, adrift ... and, for the first time in her life, entirely free. And, gods, it sounded glorious.

At the same time, though, sadness struck her as she looked at him, knowing that when they said good-bye after the war, it would be for good. Always before, he'd been the one taking off. Soon it would be her turn, gods willing.

He didn't say anything for a moment. Then, quietly, he said, "You deserve to be happy, Cara. If starting over is what it's going to take, then do it." There was an echo of grief in his voice, banked resignation in his eyes. Those two emotions were so foreign to the guy he used to be that she almost reached out to comfort him.

She didn't, though, because this wasn't about her being a *winikin.* It was about being her own *person,* damn it. So she met his eyes and refused to acknowledge the ache. "I won't be starting over. I'll be learning how to be *me* for the first time in my life."

He didn't say anything for a long moment, and the silence tightened the air between them. For a crazy second that was as much a teenage flashback as anything, she imagined him crossing to her and going to one knee as he begged her to reconsider, to give him a chance. He didn't move, though, except to glance in the direction of the spare room as if he'd heard something. "Go," he said softly. "If you leave now, we can both pretend nothing happened."

"Sven, I—"

"Just go."

She swallowed hard, then nodded and headed for the door, feeling as if she were being carried there by someone else's feet. Pausing on the threshold, she said without looking back, "You guys be careful out there, okay?"

"You too. Take care." It was as much of a dismissal as a good-bye would've been.

Which was for the best, she told herself as she pushed through into the hallway. But as the door closed behind her, she had to swallow past panic and blink away tears. And when she headed for the shortcut leading through the *winikin*'s wing, she felt like she was leaving a part of herself behind.

As the door thunked shut, a low whine sounded from behind Sven.

"It's okay, buddy." He turned as Mac slunk in. He had been aware that the coyote had returned; he'd felt the change in the bond strength, and had caught a mental whiff of concern. Now, though, while Mac had his ears flat in sympathy, his pale green eyes were accusatory, seeming to say, *Well*, that *didn't go the way you planned, did it*?

Okay, that was a stretch—Sven's familiar communicated more in impressions and emotions than actual words—but the question hung in his mind as Mac came up beside him and nudged his hand. The coyote's fur carried the scent of open air and high plateaus, and stirred something hungry and restless inside Sven even beyond the now-draining buzz of sex magic.

Hunkering down, he dug his fingers into Mac's ruff for a good scratching, needing the contact as much as his familiar did right then, because, yeah, that hadn't gone at all the way he had planned. *My fault,* he thought. He had put off talking to Carlos because he was still thinking over Dez's request, and there was no way he could apologize on the one hand and spy on the other. But because he'd been stalling—on both making a decision and facing the difficult conversations—Cara had gotten the drop on him, and he had fumbled. Badly.

And then he'd kissed her.

A low growl rumbled in Mac's chest, though Sven wasn't sure if the coyote was picking up on the vibes or trying to get him to scratch harder.

He dug into the spot as he said, "That shouldn't have happened. Seriously. What kind of a jackass am I? I apologize to her and then go right back and do it again." Granted, he believed her when she said the kiss hadn't scarred her for life—he'd been reaching on that one, had known it pretty much all along. And, yes, she had wanted the kiss, had asked for it, even . . . which was why he'd done it, really. Not because he'd wanted to help her out with her future comparisons, but because it had pissed him off. He didn't want to imagine her with other men, hated the image of her walking away from Skywatch— from *him*—and not looking back.

Mac flinched and flashed his teeth, warning Sven that he was holding on way too hard.

"Sorry." He eased up, scratched the spot on the big coyote's shoulder where he'd dug in, and then stood. He was suddenly restless, feeling caged by the room and the situation—hell, by his own damn clothes. He wanted to pace and growl, wanted to race naked through the afternoon heat, wanted to snap his fingers and be on a beautiful beach with an uncomplicated hookup. That was how he was supposed to do things: no regrets, always looking forward to the next wave, the next port, the next adventure.

And now . . . shit, he didn't know what was next.

Mac whined and shifted, picking up on Sven's urges. Hell, maybe he was even contributing to them—he'd been restless and frustrated lately, constantly on the lookout for a female of his kind. Sven hadn't been able to find others; heck he wasn't even sure where Mac had come from. So, for the moment, at least, the coyote was riding the celibacy train. Which probably explained his fascination with Cara, and why he squirmed like an idiot puppy whenever he saw her.

"She brought you weiners," Sven said, plucking the Skittles off the couch and jiggling the bag in his hand. The candies shifted and clinked like little stones, bringing memories of a wide-eyed girl who had hustled him out of his allowance and into doing her chores. That same girl—now a grown woman—had faced down hellspawn with nothing more than a MAC-10 and a 'tude. And then she had kissed him and walked away. Just like he needed to do.

"Keep an eye on her for me, okay?" he said to Mac, then repeated the order in thought-glyphs. The coyote wouldn't be able to relay a detailed report or anything, but if she got herself in trouble, Mac would sound the alarm and hold off the attack . . . or die trying.

Whuffing as if to say, *Finally!* the coyote wheeled

away and bounded out through the spare room. His mental touch faded with distance until it was just the thin tendril of background awareness, leaving Sven alone with his body still vibrating from Cara's kiss.

He hadn't remembered it being like that before; or maybe he'd locked the memory away with the other half-forgotten goals and dreams that had fallen by the wayside. He had a feeling there wouldn't be any option of locking away these memories, though, not when he could still taste her on his lips and smell her on his skin. And what was he going to do about that?

"Not a damn thing," he said aloud, hearing the words echo in his suite, which was bigger than he needed, yet still felt cramped.

And that was the problem—he needed his space and the freedom to roam . . . but he couldn't have that and Cara too. Did he want her? Heck, yes, he wanted her; that was why he'd sent her away from Skywatch and why he'd made himself scarce when she came back. Only the distance thing hadn't worked this time, because he'd still thought about her. Hell, he'd done more than think about her; he'd used her to beat back the shadows and clear his mind of the things he had seen and done, and to remind himself what he was fighting for. He had never planned on doing anything about it, though. And, damn it, he couldn't do anything about it now, either, because he wasn't any more likely to stick around than ever before . . . and if anyone deserved a man who would make her his absolute priority, it was Cara.

Which meant he needed to keep his hands—and his lips—to himself. Starting now.

CHAPTER SEVEN

Cara plastered a neutral expression on her face as she hurried down the corridor of the mages' wing. *Don't let it show,* she told herself. *Don't give anybody a reason to guess what just happened.*

"Sparks don't change anything," she said under her breath as she powered through an archway and along the polished wood riser that led around the outside of the mansion's sunken great room, beelining for her quarters. It didn't matter whether his inability to stick around was a bloodline trait or a personality flaw; it was a deal breaker. She didn't want to chase him around the globe, and she sure as hell wasn't going to sit around and wait for him to come home. Not that he'd asked her to. He hadn't, and that should've been a relief. The fact that it wasn't coupled with the tears that stung her eyes as she stalked the perimeter of the great room were proof enough that she needed to pull it together. *Please, gods, just let me get back to my quarters without running into anybody. Especially not Zane or—*

"Cara Liu," a peremptory voice said from behind her, bringing her up short with an inner, *Oh, shit.*

Hello, worst-case scenario.

She turned back as her father stepped through the doorway leading to the *winikin*'s wing. He was wearing his funeral clothes and a dark frown, and at the sight of his thunderous expression all she could think was, *Oh, gods. He knows.* Some guilty-child instinct nearly had her blurting that it was just a onetime thing and would never happen again. She bit back the words, though, annoyed with herself because her father's disapproval really should've lost its power by now. *Can I get a cleanup crew in the great room, please? There's been a daddy-issues spill.*

Pressing her lips together to keep from saying something she would regret, she held her ground as he approached. She didn't miss the way his eyes went to her unmarked right wrist. He was the one who had given her the original marks, after all, ambushing her beneath the big Montana sky. He had cut her palm and recited the spell that was one of the very few the *winikin* could use. And then, after it was done, he'd told her that the old family stories were real, the Nightkeepers were real, and they needed her help. At first she had thought he was saying she was one of the magi, a magic-using superhero destined to save the world . . . until he'd told her that she wasn't a superhero at all. She was a member of their support staff. A sidekick at best. And he'd been bone-deep insulted by her disappointment.

That had been the beginning of the end for the shaky relationship they had built in the years after her mom died.

"Did you need me for something?" she asked, telling herself that he shouldn't be able to hurt her anymore and doing her damnedest not to look just-kissed.

"I saw Dez a little while ago, and he mentioned wanting us to do a training run in the next day or so. I thought you'd want to know."

The training runs—mock battles staged at a set of cement-and-rebar ruins the Nightkeepers had built beyond the firing range—had proven invaluable at getting the *winikin* up to speed on the fighting front. Or as up to speed as they were going to get, anyway. Given that the equinox was less than a week away and Dez wanted the entire team ready to go, it stood to reason he would want to make sure they were ready to fight, especially after everything that had happened today.

It took an effort to shift her mental gears into leadership mode, but she managed it, filed the info, and nodded. "Thanks for the heads-up. I'll get with Zane and make sure we're ready." Thinking—hoping—that was all he'd wanted to say, she started to turn away, sketching a "gotta go" wave in his direction.

"About Zane . . ."

She nearly groaned. She was too stirred up and strung out to think about Zane right now, never mind discuss him with Carlos. "What about him?"

"Did you see his mark?"

"I . . ." She frowned, realizing that it hadn't come up. "No. Why?"

Her father tapped his wrist. "He's one of us."

"Of course he's a *winikin*." But then she saw how Carlos's fingers rested on his bloodline glyph, and a low-grade shock ran through her. "He's a *coyote winikin?* But I thought . . . Why didn't you recognize him?"

"The coyote *winikin* were spread thin. When I saw his mark I asked him who his parents were." He named two people she had never heard of, would never meet. "They were both mage-bound," he said, emphasizing the last two words.

"Okay." She shook her head. "So?"

He shifted on his feet, squaring off as if ready to fight. "You should give him a chance, you know. He's a good man from a good family."

Under any other circumstance, she might've laughed at the idea of her father acting as a go-between, might've screamed. As it was, all she could do was sigh in heart-sore exhaustion. "Did he put you up to this?"

"No. My conscience did . . . because as much as I hate to say it, you need to keep yourself entirely separate from the Nightkeepers if you hope to lead the *winikin*." He paused. "Do you understand me, Cara Liu? If we're going to survive the war, you need to be their leader first and foremost. Nothing else can matter."

A chill trickled through her, not because he was wrong, but because he was the last person she wanted to talk to about this. "You saw me coming out of Sven's suite."

He winced, but shook his head. "I saw you with him earlier, out on the ball court. And I remember how it used to be between you two."

"There was nothing between us back then, and there's nothing now."

His look didn't quite call her a liar, but it was close. "If you took up with Zane—"

"You want me to sleep with my second in command to prove my loyalty to the *winikin*?" She wasn't sure which was worse—the suggestion, or the fact that it didn't surprise her that it would come from him.

He hesitated, then said softly, "I want you not to be alone anymore, sweetheart."

"You don't get to call me—" She bit it off as her eyes threatened to fill in earnest. "Damn it. That was a low blow." It was what her mother had called her. Never him, though. Never him. And she was too damn raw to keep it from hurting.

"This isn't a fight," he said, and for a second, she saw the father she had once foolishly idolized in the old man who stood opposite her.

"Isn't it?" Pressure vised her brain, making her want to run and scream. She couldn't do this. Not right now and not with him.

"Think about it, Cara Liu. Your actions don't affect only you anymore."

"Fine, I'll think about it. Now if you'll excuse me?" She didn't wait for his response, just headed straight across the great room for the glass doors that took up most of the far wall. Five minutes earlier, all she'd wanted was to get back to her quarters. Now, though, she wanted the open sky and storm-cleaned air.

She could feel his eyes on her as she pushed through to the deck, where the pool sparkled in the fading sunlight. Bypassing the shimmering water, she headed down the short flight of steps to the main pathway, not letting herself run. Not quite. She took the branch that led past the training hall and cottages and on toward the firing range. She didn't have any real plan—maybe she would shoot; maybe it would be enough to walk off the frustration that churned inside her, making her head feel like a pressure cooker being run too hot. If steam started coming out of her ears, she wouldn't have been surprised. In fact, it might've been a relief. As it was, it helped to be alone.

Really alone. And farther from the mansion than she'd meant to go.

"Damn it." Realizing this might not be the best idea after all, she made herself slow down, breathe, and pay attention to her surroundings. She was near the picnic area, right where the ceiba tree rose a hundred feet and spread its enormous canopy to shade the cacao trees, which stirred in an almost imperceptible breeze. The rain-forest microcosm shouldn't have been able to survive in the desert, but it had grown up from the ashes of the *winikin* and mage children who had died in the massacre. The air was moist and warm, the sound that of moving leaves, the vibe one of peace.

For a second she paused and let the tranquillity remind her that running—or even walking—away wasn't going to fix her problems. She wasn't going to hook up with Zane for her father or the *winikin,* and Sven . . . well, there wasn't a decision to be made there. Sparks alone just weren't enough, and—

Brush crackled, jolting her with brutal suddenness. She pulled her nine-mill and thumbed her wristband to arm the panic button, though she didn't hit it yet. Heart drumming against her ribs, she moved off the path and angled toward where the noise had come from. "Hello?"

There was a jangle of discord in the air, a prickling awareness that said someone—or some*thing*—was out there.

It's just a bird, she told herself. Or it could be Sasha or one of the others harvesting cacao for the upcoming equinox ritual. Maybe just someone going for a walk, like her, or continuing the search for the weak point in the barrier that had allowed the *Banol Kax* to send their creatures through.

Or it could be one of those creatures. Or worse.

Leveling the pistol, she swept the tree line. Not letting

her voice shake, though it badly wanted to, she said, "You've got to the count of three before I call for backup and embarrass us both. One . . . two . . ."

There was a soft *whuff*. Then leaves moved, parted, and a pair of pale green eyes gleamed from the shadows.

"Oh. Christ, Mac." She let her gun sag as adrenaline raced through her, threatening to turn her fight response into a full-on case of the shakes. "You scared the crap out of me."

The big coyote *whuff*ed again, using the low bark that always made her feel like she could almost understand him. Now, though, she didn't need a translation to know what was going on. "He told you to watch out for me, didn't he?"

Mac stepped out of the grove, looking at her with his ears and tail cocked hopefully, as if unsure of his welcome.

She exhaled a long, shuddering breath. Then she patted her thigh in invitation. "Come on, big guy. Let's go kill some targets."

He bounded over to her, barking with joy, and some of that good mood transmitted to her as she headed up the path with the big coyote at her side, anticipating going a few rounds with the simulator Michael had put together to teach the *winikin* how to shoot straight. Violence might not solve everything, but sometimes it was a damn good way to blow off steam. And gods knew she needed to clear her head enough so she could figure out how to deal with Zane, her father, the upcoming mock battle . . . and the part of her that was warning that sparks like the ones she and Sven made together didn't come along every day, and she should grab them when and where she found them. Even if they weren't planning on sticking around.

Coatepec Mountain
Mexico

Anna sat lotus-style in the temple at the top of the mountain, facing the huge *chac-mool* altar with her eyes closed, her dark, copper-burnished hair tied back in a knot at her nape, and her face tipped up to the sun. The sky was a clear, perfect blue, the air a soft seventy-five, and the birds were singing their little hearts out from the trees farther down the peak, near the excavation where she and several of the others were trying to figure out how, exactly, Coatepec Mountain would figure into the end-time war.

Around her at the points of a perfect equilateral triangle stood three ancient stone pillars carved to represent the *balam,* the jaguar that was her bloodline totem. Together, the pillars and altar outlined the place where a vital intersection—the Nightkeepers' connection to the gods themselves—appeared during the solstices and equinoxes. But the equinox was still a week away, and today, save for her, the mountaintop was deserted. Strike and Sasha had 'ported north to Skywatch to huddle with Dez and the others over the latest attack, leaving Anna blessedly alone.

Gods. Finally.

Powerless to help the warriors with anything but teleportation, she had named herself the guardian of the intersection at Coatepec Mountain, and set out to uncover its secrets. So far, though, she hadn't gotten very far. Maybe now, with her mind clear of background chatter, she would be able to sense something in the stones, some clue of how they were to be used, or when.

She picked up the knife she'd brought with her, suppressing a shudder. A brush of her fingertips found the ridged scars on her wrists, old and closed, though they ached with the beat of her heart as she set the knife point to one palm. "Please, gods," she whispered, "let me help."

There was no use asking them to help her—she hadn't felt their presence in a long, long time. She didn't know if they had given up on her because she had turned away from them too often, rejecting their gifts over and over again, or if she was the one blocking them, afraid that if she let one piece of the magic come, the rest of it would follow. It was probably a combination of the two, which might have been a relief if she'd had any ability to control it. But she didn't; it was all in her head. Literally.

It was going to be up to the gods, and maybe—hopefully—a ritual that could convince her subconscious to release whatever hold it was keeping on her magic. She didn't want to be a seer, didn't even want to be a Nightkeeper. But when she weighed those desires against the end-time war, they lost out, big-time.

"Okay," she murmured, not really sure if she was talking to herself or to the voice she sometimes heard inside her head—that of a ghost with unerring logic and a snarly attitude, both of which had transcended death. "Wish me luck."

She didn't hear anything, didn't feel anything, but imagined him making a derisive face and telling her not to be a girl, and go ahead and *cut* already. So she did. Blood welled up and pain slashed through her, but it was familiar and cleansing, and it was terrifyingly easy to switch hands and cut her other palm, gripping the blood-slicked handle tightly.

There was no buzzing hum in the air, no sparkles of red-gold, no sign that the magic even cared that she was bleeding onto the packed earth as she dipped into the pocket of her bush pants and closed her fingers around the small, yellow quartz pendant she carried with her, partly as a talisman, partly as penance.

Anna had been two years away from the start of her training and decades away from receiving the skull from her mother when the king—her father—had declared war on the intersection beneath Chichén Itzá, believing that sealing it would prevent the end-time war. Her mother, foreseeing the massacre and knowing that that was the true vision, had stood by her husband in public, but did three things in private: She tutored Strike and Anna's *winikin*, Jox, on the use of the magical safe room hidden beneath the mansion's library; she faked a still-birth and sent the newborn —Sasha—far away where she might be safe . . . and she gave thirteen-year-old Anna her crystal skull.

Lifting it now, Anna let the silver chain run through her bloodstained fingers until the quartz carving dangled, then began to swing hypnotically. Its empty sockets stared at her, blinking from sunlight to shadow and back again as the carving twisted on its axis.

The skull had power, and she had the innate ability to use that power. There was no other way she could have seen the things she had seen during the massacre otherwise. But the experience had scarred her, changed her, and when the magic came back online for all the others two decades later, it hadn't done so for her. Oh, she had moments here and there, but nothing consistent or controlled, and even those visions had fallen off over time. But the potential was there. She just had to break through the barriers inside her.

Hands shaking, she looped the chain around her neck. The skull settled between her breasts as she focused inward, hearing the beat of her heart and the rush of the blood in her veins, feeling the sting of sacrifice and the heavy weight of the pendant against her breastbone, and seeking the magic that had once come as naturally to her as flirting and laughing. All of which now seemed to belong to another lifetime. And, just as she couldn't summon any interest in flirting or let free the easy laughter she had once loved, she couldn't find the magic now.

Panic flickered at the edges of her mind, but she shoved it aside, because although this felt like every other time she had tried to summon a vision recently, this time she had something new to try: Lucius had given her a piece of notepaper he'd found sandwiched between two leaves of an ancient codex: notes on the vision-quest ceremony of an *itza'at* seer. The paper was modern, the pen blue ballpoint, the writing young and looping, and their best guess was that it had belonged to a girl who, at fifteen or sixteen, had just gotten the talent mark identifying her as an *itza'at,* and was embarking on a seer's rigorous training. Though the spells were supposed to be memorized, never written down, this girl had sneaked notes.

Touching it, Anna pictured a dark-haired teen studying in the archive, sneaking furtive looks at her notes and, upon hearing the tread of adult footsteps, quickly hiding the paper. That was more imagination than vision, though. And with it, she sent a small inner plea: *Please, gods, let it work for me.*

She needed this. They all did.

Closing her eyes, she took a deep breath, braced herself, and whispered, "*Tas teen k'aas wayak.*" It literally meant, "Bring me the nightmare."

And for the first time in her life, the magic came on command.

A yellow glow flared around her—or maybe it was inside her, painting her corneas from within. It was the same color as the crystal skull, glittering and gleaming with patterns of light through a gemstone. She was somehow unsurprised to feel the hard bumps of the amulet clutched in one hand, though she didn't remember reaching for it. Her heart hammered fast and furious, and she was suddenly drenched in a cold sweat that was equal parts flop and fear.

When nothing more happened, leaving her vision clouded with yellow, she sent a plea into the sky. *Show me,* she urged. *Show me what they need to know.* This was about the magi and the war, not about her. Never about her. *Please, gods.* Through lips that felt like they belonged to someone else, she said again, "*Tas teen k'aas wayak.*"

There was another, brighter flash, one that blanked her outer vision entirely, leaving her lost in a world of amber refractions. The world seemed to shift around her for a second, as if the entire space-time continuum had hiccuped. And then, incredibly, a voice emerged from the glowing yellow kaleidoscope—no, many voices, all speaking as one, saying in her mind, *Return the Father to earth. His job there is not yet done.*

Shock raced through her. "What?" This was no vision. It was a message from beyond the barrier!

But as quickly as it had come, the yellow light faded

and then disappeared, leaving her sitting there with both hands—fully healed now, thanks to the magic—wrapped around the crystal skull.

Her mind raced. Whose father? Probably not her own, as that had been an unfamiliar voice, not that of her own ancestral *nahwal*. But what other father . . . *Oh, gods*. Her throat tightened as a possibility occurred, one so huge that it was terrifying.

There was one man who had been known by many as "Father": the sole Nightkeeper mage to survive the first massacre. He had led the dozen or so surviving children out of Egypt along with the loyal servants that had saved the children's lives—captured Sumerian slaves whom he later enspelled to create the *winikin*. When they arrived in their new home—Mesoamerica—he had codified the Nightkeepers' way of life into the writs, and he had written down everything he knew about their history and, more important, the prophecies governing the end-time.

The Nightkeepers had existed for many millennia before his birth . . . but he had made them what they were today.

Anna stared up at the sky, heart lifting with joy. "Thank you," she whispered.

It wasn't a vision or a foretelling, but she had gotten exactly what she asked for: information that would help the magi. Because unless she was way off base, the Nightkeepers had just been charged with the First Father's resurrection.

CHAPTER EIGHT

September 15
Six days to the equinox; three months and
six days to doomsday
Skywatch

"Team one is in position," Cara said, just loud enough that her throat mike could transmit the info to the other three team leaders—Natalie, JT, and Lora—who would sound off when they reached their positions at strategic spots around the Nightkeepers' training ground. The faux ruin was made of cement blocks, rebar, and concrete, but otherwise mimicked a Mayan ruin, complete with a huge central pyramid with interior chambers and booby traps, and smaller pyramids, temples, and dwellings set on causeways that radiated out from the pyramid. Splashes of paint bore witness to earlier training runs, while chunks of blasted cement and char marked the few times the magi had gone at it for real. Today was a mix of the two, part paintball, part real magic. And, gods willing, the *winikin* would pull it off.

Her four teams had scattered from the designated drop point the moment the indicator light went green, indicating the start of the training run. Now, crouched in along the base of a dusty, irregular wall and wearing the urban desert camo of the modern human military, Cara and the seven other members of her team blended—she hoped—with the midafternoon shadows.

"Team three is in position," JT reported. His voice was all business: clipped, efficient, precise, and with none of his off-duty 'tude. Cara didn't know how much of his good behavior came from his days in the military and how much was Natalie's doing, but so far, so good, and she was hoping against hope the other rebels would take his lead. Because there was more than just bragging rights riding on this particular training run.

Way more.

In the four days since Aaron's funeral, there hadn't been any more attacks. The mood inside the compound might've been better if there had been, though, because at least then there would've been an enemy to fight. Instead, the investigation had stalled and a few of the Nightkeepers—including the king himself—had been looking sideways at the *winikin*, as if thinking they knew more than they were telling. Not to mention that several of the *winikin* who had received their bloodline marks had become withdrawn, while others had gotten surly. Then there was Anna's message indicating that the Nightkeepers were supposed to resurrect the First Father, who had been responsible for creating the *winikin* in the first place. Although Lucius and the brain trust hadn't yet figured out how that was supposed to happen, the magi were acting like the Father's return would be the answer to their prayers. And morale among the *winikin* had started seriously circling the bowl.

Fortunately, Dez—to give credit where due—had not only seen the problem, he'd come up with a damn good solution in the form of a Nightkeepers-versus-*winikin* training challenge: If the *winikin*—working in their own teams rather than the usual Nightkeeper-led groups— could infiltrate the Nightkeeper-guarded main pyramid, retrieve a hidden artifact, and get it to a designated rendezvous point for pickup, the king would think about making the *winikin*-only teams permanent.

It wasn't a promise, but it had sure as heck fired up most of the *winikin*. As for the holdouts—Sebastian and several of his cronies—well, Cara and Zane were keeping a sharp eye on them.

Unfortunately, she also felt the need to keep a sharp eye on Zane too. She'd been getting a weird vibe off him over the past few days, and although she hadn't expected things to be normal between them after what happened, this felt like something else. Or else she was projecting, trying to distract herself from the knowledge that Sven was still in the compound and didn't show any signs of taking off. And when he wasn't in her peripheral vision, Mac was.

"Team four is in position," Lora reported. Her appointment as a team leader had gotten some grumbles after the way she froze up under fire the other day, but Zane was convinced that the responsibility would be the kick in the ass she needed to make her step up, and Cara had let him have that one.

"Team two is in the backup position," Natalie's voice said suddenly in her ear. "There are three heat signatures near the primary position, nothing on visual."

"Copy that," Cara said, forcing her brain back on track.

The heat signatures meant either Alexis or Michael was there casting a cloaking shield, or Patience was using her talent of invisibility to hide the ambush. But as part of prepping for the "us versus them" training run, the *winikin* had pooled their observations on the magi, and they had come up with a few workarounds that could—maybe, hopefully—help even the playing field. The heat- and infrared-sensitive goggles they were wearing were just one of many tricks they had up their camo-colored sleeves.

Their sniper was another.

"Zane?" she said into her mike. "How does it look?"

All the way up at the ass end of the regular firing range, the ex-marine sharpshooter was nearly a half mile upwind of the proving grounds, well outside the regular battle zone and higher up than even the main pyramid. From there, his telescopic sights showed him almost all of the grid, and would—according to him, anyway— allow him to hit whatever he was aiming at even that far away, using specially designed paint-containing rounds.

"I've got a good view," he answered. "There are two sentries on the ground level of the pyramid, watching the corners, and at least one, maybe two concealed in the temple at the top. There are two more on the tunnel entrance, and there's a three-man patrol headed west along causeway B."

She glanced at her wrist display to confirm the positions of her teammates, which were marked on a topo map with tiny locator dots. But although the locators and other toys were nice, it was almost time to turn them off, along with the radios and other electronics, in order to simulate the conditions they would be facing during an actual battle, when the barrier flux would often knock out all electronic communications.

Just as she had the thought, an orange flare hissed up into the sky trailing ochre smoke, signaling that they were two minutes to the hard threshold of the pretend equinox and its communications blackout.

Her stomach knotted and sweat suddenly slicked the grip she held on her machine gun. *Don't freak; you've done this before, and for real.* She had been out with five different ops teams. She had killed *xombis,* gunned down *makol,* and seen blood and ichor fly. Always before, though, she had been on a Nightkeeper-led team, safe behind a magical shield and with someone else giving the orders. Now she was in charge. There was nobody looking out for her, nobody making sure she didn't screw this up. And that was a hell of a thing.

All too aware of the seven others crouched behind her—Sebastian, Kels, Foohey, Rinna, DD, Nance, and Tooky, all depending on her to get them through this and kick some Nightkeeper ass—she blew out a breath and concentrated on not letting her nerves show.

"Radios off," she said quietly into her mike. "Stick to the plan if you can; do your best if you can't. And gods be with us." She removed her earpiece, then dropped it in her pocket, conscious of the others doing the same behind her. And although the mike and earbud still pinched awkwardly sometimes, she felt naked without them on. Turning back to her teammates, she made herself wink. "It's almost go time."

Sebastian glowered, but that was no surprise. A couple of the others, though, exhaled softly and nodded.

Then a red flare went up, signaling the start of the battle.

And the fight was on.

The world accelerated to a blur as Cara burst from behind the wall and pounded toward the target with the others right on her heels. The afternoon sun seemed to slam down on her, heating her to broil within seconds and coating her with sweat, but she didn't care. Her strides lengthened; her feet flew as she hit the pyramid and headed up the blocky central staircase, taking the steps two at a time.

She was peripherally aware of the *pop-pop-popp*ing sounds that burst from the other positions as her teams engaged the enemy, drawing their attention away from the back of the ruin. She hoped.

"On your right!" Sebastian snapped, just as a black-clad figure whipped around the step-sided corner, firing as he came. She spun and threw herself to the side while her brain registered Nate Blackhawk's formidable bulk.

Thwack-thwack-thwack-thwack! Blackhawk opened fire and red paint splattered on DD's chest and Tooky's lower body, but then the remaining teammates opened fire. Within seconds, Nate was covered in *winikin* blue, dead by paintball rules. He looked down at himself, shocked. *I'm a mage,* his expression seemed to say. *A* winikin *can't shoot a mage.*

But they could, and had. And the kill had a hot ball of emotion—part elation, part horror—jamming Cara's throat and making it hard to breathe.

The three casualties all sat where they'd been hit. Blackhawk had to wait for ten minutes before he rejoined the fight, mimicking the way most of the Nightkeepers' enemies could regenerate. The *winikin,* on the other hand, were out.

For them, dead was dead.

"Go!" Tooky waved them off. "Kick ass!"

Heart pounding, Cara bolted the rest of the way up the pyramid, leading the charge. Just as she hit the top, she heard a *zzzt-thwack* followed by a curse, and Lucius reeled out of the boxy temple that crowned the pyramid, clutching his blue-splattered heart. After a couple of soap opera–worthy gasps, he subsided to the stone flat and "died" with a last wheeze of "good luck" in Cara's direction.

She sent a quick thumbs-up toward Zane's position, and then slipped quietly into the temple with the others behind her.

At the center of the covered space a dark opening led to stairs leading down into the belly of the pyramid, to the inner tomb where the artifact was being hidden. Instead of bolting straight down, though, she boosted herself up through a hole in the ceiling and onto the roof, which gave her a vantage over the proving grounds.

She scanned the scene, confirming that her teams were all in their places. But her stomach knotted when she saw shadows moving on the far side of the low, blocky building very near where Natalie's and JT's groups would meet up for the next stage of plan A. Worse, four more black-clad Nightkeeper warriors were closing in; they disappeared behind a long, low temple just as Lora and the others reached it from the far side.

Oh, shit. Cara's heart thudded against her ribs as she suddenly realized she was in a hell of a situation. If she gave the signal and the others broke cover on schedule, they were dead. They might be dead either way, if she didn't warn them there was trouble coming. But that warning would draw attention to her team. Worse, she shouldn't go with plan B when there were so many enemy fighters right near the pyramid. The others would scatter to relative safety, but she and her team would have a hell of a time making it back to the rendezvous point with the artifact.

So now what? Her breath thinned as it came down to a brutal, bloodthirsty choice: She could go with plan B and potentially save lives . . . or she could go with plan A and potentially win the game. The girl she had been when she first came to Skywatch never would've considered it an option—she had been raised to nurture, was programmed to reach out and help. But the leader she had become knew that the stakes were high, and the ones they would face over the next few months would be even higher.

And part of being in charge was knowing when to make sacrifices.

Her hands shook as she pulled a high-powered LED flashlight from her pocket, pointed it toward the firing range, and flashed the signal. Then she sent a small prayer skyward. *Please, gods, don't let me screw this up.*

As if in answer, a brilliant yellow flare arced in the sky: It was Zane's signal to the others to let rip with plan A. And once it was fired off, there was no going back. She had made her sacrifice; now it was up to her to make sure it counted.

Pulse drumming, she dropped back down to the temple floor and motioned for the others to follow. "Quietly," she warned in a nearly soundless whisper.

Cool darkness closed around her as she moved down the stairs, and she switched to night vision, which made the outside world seem suddenly very far away. She tried not to imagine the firefight outside, yet at the same time wouldn't let herself blunt the sharp edges by brushing it off as just a game. *This could be real,* she thought as she led the way across a slick landing to a second set of stairs. *It could all be real.*

Zzzt-pop! A miniexplosion flashed, momentarily blinding her. She fell back into Sebastian and caromed off the wall as foxfire booby traps flared to life all around them, further overloading the night vision. She ripped down her goggles, brought up her weapon, and signaled for her teammates to follow her, taking high and low positions.

She went low, came around the corner to find Alexis crouched and waiting, and opened fire just as a spell detonated around her. She lived; Alexis "died," and looked surprised as hell doing it.

Cara didn't stop to gloat, just waved her teammates past. "Move!" she barked. And they moved.

The next few minutes were a blur of gunfire and magical explosions, and a dizzy high-speed weave through labyrinthine tunnels to the inner chamber. "Grenade!" she snapped, and stepped back as Sebastian lobbed his own personal contribution to their armaments—a paint-filled grenade that atomized the spray so finely that it could penetrate a mage's shield spell. There was a sharp crack followed by a vicious curse in Michael's voice.

Another blur of activity followed, fragmented with image memories that burned their way into her retinas: Michael coated from head to toe in blue paint; the surprise—and perhaps reluctant admiration—on his face when she darted in and grabbed the paint-slicked pottery figure that was their goal. Then they were running through the tunnel leading out. She saw blue-splashed bodies, though she didn't know who had cleared the way, didn't hear any more *pop-popp*ing of paintball fire. But as she burst out into the sunlight and the coast was clear ahead, all she could think was that she had the statue—she freaking had it!—and they were going to win. *She* was going to win, and everyone would know it.

Triumph flashed through her, bright, shiny, and unfamiliar. The Nightkeepers would see that she could make decisions under fire, that the *winikin* would obey her and they could fight on their own. She would be a hero. More important, the *winikin* would have a reason to follow her now. Maybe this was what Zane had been talking about that night: the moment when the balance would tip and the last of the holdouts would accept her. And Sven would see that she could handle— Shit, it didn't matter what he saw or didn't see. He was just another mage.

And she wasn't the winner until they reached the rendezvous point.

Yanking her flare gun free, she blasted a trailing track of blue across the sky to signal the retreat, hoping to hell there were other survivors. She and her five remaining teammates raced to the drop point they had started from, darting into the black-painted circle that said they were in place for a teleporter to pick them up from their so-called op. "Come on, come on, come on," she chanted as the seconds ticked by and nobody else showed up.

"Try another flare," Sebastian said.

She fired again, though it was a dangerous move that pinpointed them too closely. Already the enemy would be headed their way, following the flare trail. "We'll give them sixty seconds," she said through gritted teeth as the exhilaration of victory started to wobble.

At T-minus thirty seconds, she headed for the control button that would change the indicator light to amber, indicating that the op was over, that anyone not in the pickup zone had been left behind. Her stomach heaved.

Six survivors—herself and five others. Was that all she would come home with? At the fifteen-second mark, she strained to hear footsteps—something, anything that said more were coming.

Ten. Nine. Eight.

Sebastian grabbed her arm. "Look!" There was a flicker of motion and Dez stepped out from a gap opposite them, weapon raised.

Cara clamped her lips on a scream and hit the button. A siren whooped and the light turned amber. And the game was over.

"We did it!" The cry came from Natalie, who burst from a nearby doorway, eyes shining from a red-streaked face. She flung herself on Cara, spinning them both around in a circle. "We won. We *won!*" Suddenly they were surrounded by *winikin,* all clamoring and high-fiving, and seeming not to care that they were covered with red paint.

"You're dead," Cara said numbly, pulling away from Natalie and staring from one face to the next. "Don't you get it? You're all *dead*. I killed you. I—"

"She was just playing the game." Zane appeared beside her and dropped a heavy arm over her shoulders. "Right, Cara?"

"I . . . What?" Her stomach felt like it was gnawing on itself, yet nobody else seemed to be upset by what she'd done. Even Sebastian was nodding, grinning, and accepting a couple of back slaps from his buddies. They weren't pissed off that she had sacrificed them in exchange for a fake artifact that now weighed heavily in her arms.

"He's right," a new voice said. "You played a good game." She turned to see the king making his way toward her. On the surface, his expression was one of reluctant admiration, as if he'd been surprised by the *winikin* victory, but was willing to roll with it. His eyes, though, were locked on hers, and seemed to be warning her of something. But what? Zane's grip on her shoulders increased as Dez came opposite her and the others fell back, leaving her and Zane facing the king together as the Nightkeepers' leader continued smoothly. "If that was the way you played the *patolli,* I'm not surprised you bilked Sven out of his allowance nine times out of ten."

"He told you that?" It was all she could get past the sudden churn of confusion. She glanced around, but for the first time in days didn't immediately see man or coyote.

"War games are good practice for leadership," Dez said, which wasn't really an answer. It drew her attention back to him, though, and she saw the warning again when he said, "Just like training exercises are good practice for battle, without being the real thing." He held out his hand. "Congratulations."

There were a couple of hoots from the crowd, a few low cheers, and Zane tugged her into a one-armed hug and murmured in her ear, "Go with it. Give them a reason to believe in you, and they'll be yours."

She stiffened as it sank in.

Was this what it was going to take? Was she going to have to pretend she'd been treating the exercise like a game? Her inner self rebelled, saying, *Hell, no. They need to know that was a real decision, and that they shouldn't trust me to lead if I'm going to pull shit like that.* Except that Zane and Dez thought otherwise, as if having a leader who would sacrifice eighty percent of her army to win a single battle was better than letting the *winikin* continue their infighting. And who knew, maybe they were right. She didn't know, but it didn't feel right. *She* didn't feel right.

She looked around again for Sven, then told herself to knock it off. It didn't matter what he thought; it was her decision. Besides, for all she knew, he had disappeared again.

Breathing through the pang brought by that thought, she handed Dez the paint-smeared statuette. Then, meeting the king's eyes, she said, "Thank you, sire. I'm just grateful the gamble paid off." And with that, she bought into the fiction, and hoped to the gods she was doing the right thing.

CHAPTER NINE

Later that afternoon, Sven found Dez in the last place he would've expected: the game room.

When the survivors had first reunited, the big room on the first floor of the mansion had been the go-to spot for their downtime. The magi had sacked out in the comfort of the home theater at one end of the long, narrow space; played endless hours of *Viking Warrior* and *Grand Theft Auto* on the two dedicated gaming consoles at the other; huddled over the pinball machine, billiard table, and foosball set up in the middle; and stocked the built-in shelves with every grown-up toy known to mankind, along with a few that were pure magic. With its wood paneling, neon bar signs, and random collection of laughably bad art, the game room was where they had gotten to know one another, testing strengths and weaknesses and forming the bonds of a team that would—gods willing—see them through the end-time war.

Over time, though, things had changed. Mates had paired off, the threat level had ratcheted up, and there had been less and less time and inclination for playing around. Less need too, as the Nightkeepers knew and trusted one another by that point, and had more important things to do. Sven had been one of the last holdouts, hanging out by himself, sometimes using the games to burn off his restlessness, other times watching too much boob tube in an effort to stop his mind from racing, not realizing until almost too late that the magic had been preparing him for Mac's arrival. Because from the day he and his familiar finally bonded, he hadn't needed video games or TV anymore; he'd needed action.

Since it had been a good ten months since he'd really spent any time in the game room, he shouldn't have been startled to see some changes. One of the pinball machines had been replaced by a full VR setup complete with couch, goggles, gloves, and shit; a Wii station had appeared in place of the Skee-Ball; and the questionable art had undergone a renaissance of sorts, and now trended toward black-and-white photos of the Denver cityscape, though the poker-playing dogs and Led Zeppelin posters remained.

"Wow," he said, letting the door bump his ass on the way shut. "This is different."

Dez had been leaning over the billiard table, shooting a solo game of nine-ball. Now he straightened and turned, shifting the pool cue to hold it like a baseball bat, as if violence were his first reflex. Which it pretty much was.

Relaxing when he saw who it was, the king flashed his teeth. "Couple of upgrades, that's all. Reese and I like to come in and unwind when we're here."

"Don't blame you," Sven acknowledged. But he wasn't tempted like he used to be. He was just there for info. "Got a minute?"

"You have something for me?"

In the end Sven had agreed to spy for the king, but he'd used Mac, a couple of bugs, and some old-fashioned skulking to do it rather than leaning on Carlos and Cara. He'd gotten their forgiveness, though it had taken him a couple of days to talk to Carlos. The *winikin* had made it too easy for him, even claiming it wasn't necessary. It was, though, and he had a feeling they wouldn't be so quick to forgive if they found out he'd been using them to get to the *winikin,* so he'd found other options. Besides, he'd needed to keep his distance from Cara, for sanity's sake ... but that had backfired, because while he'd been staying on the outskirts, it seemed that something must've been going on inside her head. The Cara he knew never would've knowingly sacrificed her people like that, game or not. That hadn't been collateral damage; it'd been a massacre.

He should know. He'd been one of the ones doing the shooting.

In answer to Dez's question, he shrugged. "I've got a few thoughts. But I've gotta ask ... what the hell happened out there today?"

"You first." Dez tossed him a pool cue. "And we'll play while we talk."

Sven caught the stick on the fly and masked his impatience, knowing that the king had his own system, his own agendas. "What're we playing for?"

Turning his back on Sven, Dez started racking up another game of nine-ball. Over his shoulder, he said, "Future claim?"

"Fuck that." There was no way he wanted to owe the Nightkeepers' master manipulator something like that. "Fifty bucks."

"A hundred."

"Deal." It wasn't like the money really mattered, anyway. Even with the dicey economy and some big-ass withdrawals they'd needed for techware and weapons, the Nightkeeper Fund was more than flush. It had been intended for an army of hundreds, even thousands. Not a dozen Nightkeepers and fifty or so *winikin*.

"Shoot for break," Dez ordered. "And start talking."

Sven lined up on the cue ball and shot it straight for the far bumper, trying to land it as close to the dotted line as he could. But it rolled like a damn ball bearing on a foosball table, and went well past the mark. As they swapped out, he began, "For starters, I don't think any of the *winikin* were responsible for letting those things into the compound."

After putting his ball nearly on the mark, Dez set up for the break. "How sure are you?" He shot, scattered the neat diamond, and then muttered a curse when the yellow-striped ball bounced just short of the corner pocket, denying him the insta-win. Nothing else dropped into a pocket, so he stepped back.

"Pretty positive. I've spent the past few days ghosting in and out of their stomping grounds and quartering the compound with Mac, looking for hot spots, and I haven't found jack. There's no evidence—at least that I can see—that any of the *winikin* have the kind of power that would've been needed to punch through the blood-ward and bring those things through the barrier. Hell, I'm not seeing that any of them have any kind of magic, period."

Dez's expression flattened. "Yeah. Shit. I keep hoping for a miracle there." Waving Sven toward the pool table, he added, "How much trouble are the rebels going to be over the next few months, do you think?"

As he lined up his shot, Sven shook his head. "That's a tougher question to answer, especially after what happened today." He paused, looking at Dez with a raised eyebrow.

"Just give me your general impressions."

Frustration kicked, along with the suspicion that there was more going on here than just a debriefing and a game of nine-ball. "Most of them are about where you would expect, given the history. On a personal level they don't trust us Nightkeepers as far as they can throw us, and they hate being under the rule of a mage king . . . but on the save-the-world level they're committed to doing whatever they can. There are a few outliers, of course. Sebastian was talking about taking a band sander to his bloodline mark, and I think he's capable of doing it." At Dez's wince, Sven nodded. "Yeah. Anyway, he's loud and pissed off, but I don't think there are layers to him. You kind of get what you get, ya know? Then there's Threefer, Nance, and Wyeth. They're young, impulsive, and angry. I don't think they would start something, but they'd be the first ones to jump on board." He finally lined up, closed one eye, and shot, banking the one ball and getting it—barely—into the side pocket. Shit, he was rusty. Two years ago, he could've run the table, no problem.

"That it for people who ping on your 'need a closer look' radar?"

"Yeah." Sven missed with the two on a nearly impossible shot, but managed to hide the cue ball in a corner behind the six.

The king curled his lip in an appreciative snarl, but then hopped the white ball right over the six and sank the two. "You sure about that?"

Had he caught something in the tone, or did he have suspicions of his own? Sven wasn't sure, and he didn't know if he really wanted to go there, but after a moment, he nodded. "Okay, no, I'm not sure. There's someone else: Zane."

"Seriously?" The king's expression suggested that either he'd been fishing, or his suspicions had been leaning elsewhere.

Shit, he should've kept his mouth shut, especially when he wasn't sure whether the brush-haired bastard was hitting his radar because of his obvious interest in Cara, or because there was really something going on beneath the military exterior. But it was out there now and he couldn't take it back. "It's just a hunch. A bad vibe, a few looks I haven't liked. Maybe it's just that he's in such a key position that it's hard not to look at him and think that he'd be perfectly placed to make trouble." He shrugged. "Not to mention that I just flat-out don't like the guy."

"Noted." Dez took his shot, and the three ball kissed two bumpers before dropping into a corner. "Question becomes: Is that coming from your warrior's talent or something else?"

Careful. Now he's definitely fishing. And Sven didn't have any intention of giving him a nibble, just in case this conversation wasn't entirely about the *winikin,* after all. "I don't know. The feeling's mutual, so it could just be bad chemistry." That was what he kept telling himself, in fact, trying not to let personal stuff get in the way of his investigation. When Dez just nodded, he pressed, "Come on, spill. What the hell happened out there today? One minute Mac and I were patrolling one of the temples, and the next we're in the middle of a firefight—hell, it

wasn't even a fight, more like a paintball bloodbath."
And it had been too damn easy for him to gun down the
winikin, too much like what he'd spent the past six
months doing.

Dez grimaced. "On one hand, their plan was pretty
impressive. It was a slick move putting Zane outside the
game zone as a sniper and surveillance, the low-velocity
paint grenade was a clever tweak that we're thinking
about using ourselves, and the flares were an effective—
if unsubtle—solution to the radio blackout. . . . But then
Cara took a look, saw the situation, and deliberately sacrificed eighty percent of her manpower in order to get
herself into the pyramid." The king shook his head.
"Sure, she won, but it was at a hell of a cost."

"Deliberately? Are you sure?"

"I was watching on the surveillance feeds. I saw it in
her eyes. She got a look at where our manpower was
headed and she just . . . blanked, I guess. The next thing I
knew, she had signaled the attack, and three of her four
teams were headed straight into enemy ambushes. So,
yeah. It was deliberate." The king paused, grimacing.
"Thank the gods we were able to spin it to the other
winikin as game strategy. A few of them are probably
suspicious, but so far they're not calling for her head."

Sven's gut tightened. "Will they?" He didn't like the
sound of that. Hell, he didn't like the way any of it was
sounding all of a sudden. What had happened out there?
The Cara he knew wouldn't blank under pressure or turn
against her friends like that, no matter what.

"Not if I can help it, and I could use your help." Dez
sank the four, then looked up, his expression deadly serious. "I need to know that the *winikin* are solid, Sven,
more now than ever before." He pocketed the five and

six in quick succession and then said casually, "What do you think of Cara?"

Sven clamped his lips, but the answers were right there, just as she was right there at the edges of his mind. *I think that she's amazing and doesn't realize it. I think she terrifies me because she's so determined to be a good leader that she's losing track of what it means, especially if what happened today is any indication. I think she's strong, tough, independent, brilliant . . . and that she'll kill herself—and maybe everyone around her—trying to prove it.*

Those weren't the thoughts of his logical warrior self, though. So instead he said carefully, "As a leader, you mean?"

Dez cut a sharp look in his direction. "Of course." He missed with the seven, though.

"She's tough, ethical, she works her ass off, and her instincts are generally good."

"I take it that 'generally' doesn't include the stunt she pulled today?"

"I don't know what really happened today, and neither do you until you ask her point-blank." Sven sank the eight with a smooth, deliberate move. "You haven't, which means you don't really want to know. You also said that if they won, you'd think about pulling the Nightkeeper leaders off their teams. So I guess the question is . . . are you going to let the *winikin* lead themselves? And if so, are you going to let Cara be in charge?" Whether the *winikin* liked it or not, the Nightkeepers' king had the final say.

To Sven's surprise, he tightened up waiting for Dez's answer. His warrior self—the Nightkeeper mage who thought in terms of strategy and the war—said it would be a bad idea to change things up this close to the end date, a worse idea to have the Nightkeepers' king be the one to force the change. More, the part of him that cared for Cara didn't like thinking of her making life-or-death decisions for dozens of her friends . . . and, worse, learning how to do it too easily, as he had with the killing. He wanted to protect her, insulate her, like he hadn't done before. He wanted . . .

Yeah. He wanted. And that was the damn problem.

Dez nodded. "Yeah, I'm going to give them the room to do things their way, within reason. The way I see it, that's our best chance of getting their full cooperation. And as far as the leadership goes, yeah, I want Cara in charge. She's still the best choice, for all the reasons Jox picked her." He paused. "But I want to put a Nightkeeper liaison in place, someone who'll be a guiding hand, an advocate, that sort of thing."

A prickle walked its way down the back of Sven's neck. "Nine, corner pocket," he said, indicating the shot with a wiggle of his pool cue. Then, casually, "You got someone in mind?"

"You."

He had seen it coming, could see the logic, even. But he still missed his shot. And, as the nine ball rolled into near perfect alignment with the far corner, giving Dez a winning lie that a blind spider monkey couldn't have missed, Sven's hands went numb from his sudden death grip on the cue. "I don't think that's such a good idea."

"Why?"

Because I've dreamed about her, kissed her, want her. Because no matter how many times I tell myself we don't make sense together, I've never been able to get her all the way out of my head. And because I know that no matter

*what happens between us, in the end I'm just going to let
her down.*

Dez lined up and sank the nine. "That's the game. You
owe me a hundred bucks . . . and an answer."

"You'll get the money," Sven said slowly, trying to for-
mulate a response that wasn't a lie, but wasn't all of the
truth, either. Finally, he said, "As for the other thing . . .
I'm a tracker, not a politician, and I do my best work on
my own. I'm not saying I won't do it—you're my king
and I'll follow orders. I'm just thinking that plenty of the
others would do a better job of liaison than me . . . and
that I could probably be more useful somewhere else."

The king took his time racking his stick before turning
back to Sven with steady, serious eyes. "There's no question I could use you off property. I'm sending a team
down to the First Father's tomb, and you and Mac could
be a huge help there. But I've gotta ask . . . are you sure
this is the direction you want to go?"

He knew, Sven realized with a jolt. Somehow, the king
knew there was something going on between him and
Cara—or at least the potential for it. And what was
more, he wasn't issuing a warning. If anything, he was
offering them the room to let nature—the fates, the gods,
whatever—take its course. Maybe he thought that the
power boost of Sven's pairing up would be worth the
inevitable toll the relationship would take on rebel relations, or that sex magic might trigger in Cara the latent
power he wanted to believe was inside the *winikin*. With
Dez, it was hard to tell what he was thinking sometimes,
and not worth asking. More, Sven thought he was dead
wrong in this case. Even if he managed to win Cara over
for real—and that was a big-ass *if*—there was no way the
winikin would forgive and forget. The rebels would be

pissed that their leader was messing with a mage, the traditionalists would be horrified that they were crossing social lines, and Cara would bear the brunt of their disapproval. More, he and Cara would both know that it was only a matter of time before his DNA kicked in and the restlessness came back. He could fight it for a little while, but in the end it would win—it always did—and he and Mac would take off without looking back.

And he couldn't—wouldn't—do that to her.

"Send me south," he grated. And, yeah, maybe he was running away again, but at least this time it was for a good cause.

CHAPTER TEN

The *winikin* could throw a hell of a party, and their celebration to mark the Nightkeepers' defeat—albeit only in paintball form—was no exception. But as Cara nursed a beer from a corner stool at the end of the bar, she thought the revelry carried an edge of desperation. The training hall was too loud, full of people who seemed determined to have a good time but kept looking sidelong at one another like they were wondering how many of them were still going to be around next week, next month . . . and next year.

She keenly felt each of those looks, because she knew darn well that if they had gone into battle for real today, the answer would've been almost none of them, thanks to her. Worse, she wasn't sure she could promise it wouldn't happen again, because in the heat of battle, it had seemed like the exact right answer, the same way it had felt so very necessary for her to rebuff Zane. Yet those same instincts hadn't so much as peeped a protest when she'd gone into Sven's arms.

What was *wrong* with her? Was she in the middle of

some sort of existential crisis, or had she always had shitty judgment and it just hadn't really mattered until now? Because, by the gods, right now she wasn't sure she should trust herself to pick a movie or order another beer. Especially given that the microbrew she'd chosen kind of tasted like feet.

She rolled the cool, sweaty bottle across her forehead, wishing she could call a time-out on her life.

"Hey!" Natalie appeared beside her, snagged an empty stool, and leaned in to give her a one-armed hug. "Congratulations again! You were awesome out there today!"

Cara didn't shake her head in disbelief, but she sure as heck wanted to. *If that had been real, you and JT both would've been goners.* But that didn't seem to be registering, or if it was, the *winikin* were shrugging it off. It was like today's training exercise had been the catalyst they had needed to finally come around to wanting to believe in her . . . which would've been great, except that now she didn't believe in herself.

Natalie's face went from party-level exuberance to concern. "Cara? What's wrong?"

"I need to get out of here." She set her smelly-feet beer on the counter and slipped off her chair. "I want . . . Shit." Her heart pounded and her eyes prickled with the threat of tears because she couldn't have what she wanted, didn't want what she was being offered, and couldn't handle any of it. "I need to walk."

Nat slid off her chair. "I'll go with you."

"No. Don't." Cara softened the refusal with a quick hug, then turned away before her friend could see that she was on the verge of sniveling. "I'll see you tomorrow."

"Cara—"

"I'll be fine," she said without turning back. "I just need some air."

But once she was outside, she found that it didn't help to lean back against the steel wall and breathe when the atmosphere was thick and heavy with another storm. The horizon was leaden, the stars invisible, and the fine hairs on her arms stirred with a static charge that reached inside her and made her want to move. Giving in, she started walking, not caring that she was running away.

"Cara?" The soft call came from behind her and brought her up short at the edge of the floodlit illumination from the training hall.

"Damn it, not now," she muttered under her breath, but then schooled her expression as she turned back. "Yes?"

She had known it wasn't Natalie from the voice, but was a little surprised to see Lora step out of the shadows. Wearing her fatigue pants, boots, and an army green T shirt, she looked more ready for a training run than a party, and her expression was all business. "Zane sent me to find you. He'd like a word."

Damn it, really not now. It didn't matter whether he wanted to call her out on what'd happened earlier, clear the air between them, or just talk strategy; she didn't want to deal with him right now. But she couldn't blow him off, either. So she nodded. "Where is he, inside?"

"No. Back down at the proving grounds."

"The . . . Really?" Cara twisted around to look in the direction of the big steel-and-cement pyramid, which was just barely visible as an angular silhouette against the stormy night sky. Her hair blew across her face, moved by a gust that smelled of rain. "What's he doing down there?"

"He said he had something important to show you."

"He . . . Right." Thus why he hadn't hit her up on her wrist unit using an open channel, instead snagging a messenger he thought he could trust. He'd done similar things twice before, when his anti-Nightkeeper paranoia had gotten the best of him. Both times, the intel had been good, if not necessarily up to cloak-and-dagger standards. Interest starting to stir despite everything else, she nodded. "Okay. I'll go."

"Alone." Lora's pointed look went to the darkness beyond the floodlights.

"What? Oh." A faint flush touched Cara's cheeks, though she hoped it was hidden by the dimness. Then again, she had also hoped that the others wouldn't have noticed her furry shadow. "Mac won't bother anyone. He's just playing bodyguard." And only because Sven was feeling guilty.

"If you say so." Lora started back toward the training hall. "Do whatever you want. I'm just the messenger." Duty done, she turned and headed up the stairs. Swinging the door open to emit a blast of noise and movement, she stepped through and was immediately swallowed up in the party.

As the door thunked shut, cutting off the clamor, thunder growled low on the horizon, followed by a soft whine from closer by.

Cara glanced over to where a pair of eyes glowed from the shadows. "You heard her." Actually, she wasn't sure how much the coyote actually understood of human speech when Sven wasn't around. Sometimes it seemed like he looked straight into her and understood everything she was thinking or feeling, and then other times the information seemed to go right past him, unacknowledged. Kind of like a human male, really, when she thought about it, only this one had fangs and claws and would offer her a hell of a backup if she ran into trouble, no questions asked.

She had gotten used to having him around over the past few days, she realized with a sudden pang. Having him there made her feel safer ... and it let her know that Sven was still around. And she shouldn't need either of those things. She could take care of herself, damn it. An apology didn't change anything, and neither did a kiss.

The coyote gave a soft *whuff* and advanced a step, so the light picked out the shape of his angular head and thick, furry ruff. His eyes seemed to plead with her not to send him away, but she needed to make the break and stick to it. She couldn't let herself halfway depend on Sven and his familiar; it would hurt too much when they next took off.

So, even though Mac was giving her puppy-dog eyes, she pointed toward the main mansion and said, "Go on, Mac. Go back to him."

His ears went flat; his eyes practically welled up.

Steeling herself, she shook her head. "No, Mac. You can't follow me around anymore. Go on. Git."

Hanging his head, he went a few steps, then paused and turned back. When she just kept pointing, he whined low in his throat, sounding like she was breaking his heart. But he slunk out of the light and down the pathway toward the mansion. Watching him go emptied her out and made her feel like total crap. But at the same time there was also an odd, hollow sense of satisfaction.

She could take care of herself, damn it, and she could handle whatever Zane wanted to throw at her. Maybe she couldn't give him what he wanted on a personal level, but they both wanted the same thing when it came to the war. They would make it work somehow.

The weather was closing in fast, drawing the air tightly around her as she headed for the training grounds. The lights were off, the only illumination the unearthly luminance of the storm, until she dug out a small key-chain flashlight from her pocket and flicked it on. The feeble beam didn't do much more than glint off a shiny bit of sand here and there along the path, making her wish for her night-vision goggles, but she knew the way and could make out the irregular shadows of fake temples and pyramids in the middle distance.

The rising breeze tugged at her hair and clothing as she continued onward, drawing her nine-millimeter in what had become a habit over the past few days. *Don't go anywhere alone without carrying your weapon,* she'd been telling her people. *And I'm not talking about in its holster.* Now, without Mac ghosting at her heels, she took her own advice and kept her eyes moving, her senses sharp, though she wasn't getting any bad vibes as she reached the edges of the training grounds. At least, not like she had right before the funeral. But the thought of the funeral brought a kick of instinct, because it had been stormy then too, and the demon creatures had come from fire and lightning. What if there was a connection? Could a storm weaken the barrier?

A scuff of movement to her right caught her attention, coming from a narrow alley between two low-slung temple-size buildings. Stopping just short of the main pyramid, she swung around. "Zane? Is that you?" The wind picked up suddenly, carrying a splat of raindrops that hit with staccato force, soaking through her shirt in an instant. "Ugh. Can we get inside somewhere?"

There was another scuffling noise, this one coming from the other side. Heart suddenly thudding, she spun toward it. "Damn it—"

A heavy weight slammed into her, drove her sideways, and sent her crashing into the pyramid stairs. She screamed as she hit and skidded down, scrabbling for purchase as she lost her grip on her gun, her flashlight, everything but the sudden fear that slashed through her.

Her attacker—heavy and human-shaped, though she couldn't see in the darkness whether he was a man, a *makol*, or something else—pinned her against the sharp-edged staircase. "No," she cried. "Help me! *Help!*"

She went for her panic button, but he jammed a knee on her forearm and tore her wristband off. Seconds later, something sharp pricked the back of her thigh, followed by the burning rush of an injection. She twisted and surged, but couldn't break free, couldn't get leverage, couldn't do anything but scream, "No!"

The wind whipped to an answering howl and a splash of cold, stinging rain.

Disbelief ripped through her. Panic filled the empty spaces and overflowed, then went swimmy as the world fogged. She didn't know whether it was a drug or a spell, but as she slipped under, she caught a glimpse of a hand and sleeve, the edge of a face, and not only saw the darkness of normal human eyes, but *recognized* them too. It wasn't any demon. It was—

Darkness.

The storm hit hard and fast, going from the moan of wind to a machine-gun fusillade against the windows of Sven's suite just as he finished packing—one knapsack, no bullshit, as usual.

"Shit." He scowled at the moisture-pelted night beyond the glass, but didn't have anybody to blame but himself that he was about to get his ass soaked on his way out to the *winikin*'s hall. He'd been stalling, alternating between the struggle to come up with a good way to tell Cara he was leaving . . . and the suspicion that she wouldn't give a damn. And that, too, wasn't anybody's fault but his own. So he dragged out an old, battered slicker that had migrated to the back of his closet, and headed into the storm.

It was pitch dark beyond the lighted pathway, which went slick and slippery under his boots as he fought his way into the teeth of the wind, feeling like he was reliving one of a hundred sea squalls, though this one on solid ground. When he reached the *winikin*'s hall, lightning flashed for a long three-count, showing him that the cacao grove was lying almost flat beneath the pounding rain, while the branches of the ceiba tree whipped the air above as if trying to protect the precious crop. The rain hammered down onto the steel panels of the training hall with a din that drowned out everything else.

The party was still going—he saw the door open and close, flashing orange-yellow light from within as two figures staggered down the stairs, holding each other up and laughing into the rain. Sven had seen them around but didn't know their names. They quit laughing when he approached and ducked under the overhang that sheltered the doorway.

"This is a Nightkeeper-free zone," one slurred, gesturing with a beer bottle that was down to the watery dregs, yet still managed to slosh onto his buddy. "Piss off."

"Shut it," his slightly more sober friend advised, then

blinked rapidly, trying to focus his reddened eyes on Sven. "C'n I help you?"

"*You* shut it," Beer Bottle said, elbowing Blinker. "We don' have to help 'im."

"I'm juss bein' polite." *Blink, blink.* "Nothin' wrong with that, izzere?"

"Absolutely not," Sven said. "Could you tell Cara I'd like to talk to her out here?" Then, not wanting anybody to get the wrong idea, he tacked on, "I have a message for her." Which he did, sort of.

Beer Bottle sneered. "Whassa matter? You don't want to go inside?"

"Do you blame me?"

The sneer flattened, then got a little confused. "Well . . . no."

"I don't want to make trouble; I just need to talk to Cara. Please."

Blink, blink. "She's not in there."

"She's not—" Sven let out a breath. "Where did she go?"

"Dunno. Saw her leave, though." Blinker did the blinkety-blink thing, then added helpfully, "It was a while ago."

"Did you— You know what? Never mind. Thanks."

Beer Bottle scowled and jabbed an elbow at Blinker. "I tol' you not to help him."

"Nothin' wrong with bein' polite." And they were off again, wobbling around the same conversational circuit as Sven popped his hood and jogged back out into the rain, leaving them to it.

He was just about to head back to the mansion, thinking he'd missed her, when a faint tickle hit the edge of his mind, a pulse of agitation. "Mac?" He stopped in his tracks and opened his mind to their bond.

Instantly, thought-glyphs seared themselves across his mind, seeming ten feet high and glowing red-hot: *Emergency! Come now! Danger! Comenowcome!*

Gut knotting even as his body spun toward the signal, which was coming from the firing range, he sent back: *What? Who?*

Followfollowfollow! was paired with a glimpse of the main pyramid of the proving grounds.

I'm coming! Catching that Mac was poised to bolt after something—or someone—Sven sent an emphatic: *NO. Wait.* Then he put his head down and booked it, adrenaline shrilling through his body as his warrior's talent came online, juicing his magic and getting him ready to fight. A foxfire spell lit the night around him, though he didn't remember calling it. Was it more of those demon creatures? Something worse? He wasn't getting images from Mac anymore, just fury.

When he reached the ruins, he caught sight of Mac's bristling silhouette up ahead and swerved in that direction, skidding in a patch of mud and nearly going down. He kept going, though, racing toward where the big coyote was standing splay-legged with his head down, as if guarding something—or some*one*.

"I'm here," he called over the growl of thunder. "What's wrong?"

There was no answer from the coyote. When Sven reached him, the foxfire spread out to shed bright white light on the scene. The rain had plastered Mac's fur to his body, making the coyote look lean and lethal. His eyes were slitted against the sideways-whipping wind, and a growl grated at the back of his throat.

The big animal was staring down at a churned-up section of ground that was going rapidly smooth under the pelting hammer of rain. But as Sven hunkered down, he shifted slightly and the foxfire glinted off something metallic being shielded by the big coyote's bulk.

"What have you got there?" Sven leaned in, reached for it ... and froze for a second at the sight of a torn, muddy piece of desert-camo cloth snagged on a *winikin's* wristband. It had the initials CL etched inside.

Ice sluiced through his veins. *Cara!*

Mac's eyes met his and a wash of guilt poured through their bond, along with two piteous thought-glyphs: *Gone! Hurt!*

Sven's body kicked into action while his mind screamed inside. He went for his armband, slapping the alarm and the all-transmit in the same move. "Mayday, mayday!" he said, raising his voice above the thunder and rain. "There's been—" He broke off because there was no signal light, no whooping alarm. The storm was screwing with the transmission.

No. Not now. Fuck! He hit the buttons again, then the reset, saw the readout lights flicker but didn't get a damn thing.

He was cut off.

Mac whined urgently, his thought-glyphs becoming a jumble of distress and, *Come on, this way!* as he circled the scene of the attack, his paws turning dark with mud.

Sven hesitated. Protocol and the good of the many said he should go back for his teammates, that it was too big a risk. But Mac's thought-stream filled with the need to hurry, follow, run—along with the smell of fear and blood.

Cara. Her name lashed through him on the next bolt of lightning, driving him to his feet as Mac spun and bolted into the night.

"Godsdamn it, wait!" Sven took two steps after him, then saw in the next flash that the coyote had paused at the edge of the pyramid, eyes wide and wild, lips drawn back in a snarl. There were no glyphs to his thoughts now; there was only instinct and the pounding need to chase, find, protect.

Then Mac whirled and galloped off, disappearing into the night and the storm.

Cursing, Sven plunged after him. And as he ran into the teeth of the wind and rain, he hoped to hell they weren't already too late.

CHAPTER ELEVEN

Cara awoke to a bone-numbing chill that was so intense that she didn't remember ever not being cold, as if the sensation had lived in her marrow forever.

On some level she knew that was crap, that she'd been warm before, that she'd been many, many other things. But as she swam up through the layers of unconsciousness that flowed like water and clung like mud, she knew only the cold. It bit into her, locked onto her, and made her want to sink back down to where she didn't care that she was freezing, didn't care about anything.

Screw that, said some stubborn core within her. *Stop whining and get your ass moving.* Something bad had happened; she knew that much. But what? How? *Wake up and figure it out!*

Huge shivers clamped her muscles tight, and her chattering teeth nipped the tip of her tongue and drew blood. The sharp, bright pain brought her closer to consciousness, letting sounds penetrate from the outside world: She heard the roar of thunder above her, the splash of water all around her.

For a second she was back on the *Discovery,* riding out a squall on the whale-watching boat that had been as much a home for her as she'd ever known. She imagined Captain Jack up in the wheelhouse and the passengers huddled inside over cocoa and barf bags, leaving her alone on the forward deck, leaning into the wind and rain as the deck surged beneath her feet. But then the image fragmented, because the air wasn't salty or ocean clean; instead, her mouth was foul with sandy grit and a chemical aftertaste that brought back newer, far less pleasant memories.

The desert. Skywatch. War games.

Heartache.

As reality returned with sledgehammer blows, she sucked in a breath that was a harsh sound over the other noises. Suddenly, she was sickeningly aware of all sorts of tactile sensations, none of them good: There was a solid surface beneath her, ties binding her in place at her chest, hips, wrists, and ankles. Terror lashed as it came back to her: the pyramid, the storm, a splash of rain. . . . And Zane coming for her with cold, determined eyes.

Zane. Gods. That wasn't him, couldn't have been. It was a trick, a demon, magic. Only how was that possible? Her stomach lurched with the alternative: that he'd betrayed the *winikin,* the Nightkeepers. And her. *Impossible,* she thought, but she knew what she had seen. And now—

"Shit, she's waking up." It was a woman's voice, distorted by distance, echoes, and the noise of rippling water. A woman? Who? Why?

"Good." A man's voice, familiar. Zane.

Panic and fury slashed through Cara, breaking the last hold of whatever drug or spell they'd used. She wrenched open her eyes and blinked into a bright, harsh camp light that was hung on a folding pole very near her. It was a cave; that much she could tell from the echoes, though she couldn't see beyond the lantern. Its glow showed only that she lay atop a flat stone altar that was on a sandy island in the center of a muddy subterranean pool. The rest of her surroundings was lost to the shadows. As her eyes adjusted, she saw down her body, where straps held her clamped to the altar. She couldn't see the details, but she could guess what it looked like: waist-high and carved on the sides, a ritual piece of the Nightkeepers . . . or, worse, the Xibalbans.

A moan bled from her lips, stirring movement from behind her, a low masculine chuckle. Moments later, she heard splashes, and then Zane and Lora came around into her view. They were both wearing black on black, armed to the teeth and wearing ceremonial daggers, like they were magi themselves.

"Lora." Cara whispered the word, though there was little surprise in it. The signs had been there, she supposed. Or maybe her instincts had known all along that something wasn't right. Dismissing the sharp-eyed ex-cop as the follower she'd always been, Cara focused on Zane and felt a sharp, painful twist beneath her heart, not from betrayal, but from self-disgust. She hadn't seen it. How had she not seen it? There was derision in his face now, a mad gleam of triumph in dark blue eyes that she had thought carried the calm of a professional soldier, but instead had been hiding his true thoughts behind a terrifying level of control. "Why?" she asked, the word pulled from deep inside her. "Why are you doing this?"

"Because the gods chose me," he said simply, and

there was a fanatic's belief behind the statement. "I knew they had chosen you too, but I was wrong about your purpose." He glanced beyond the circle of lantern light, to the walls of the domed cave, where she could just barely make out huge four-legged shapes, giant cave paintings that ran around the perimeter, where the rock walls met the rippling water. His lips curved, though she didn't know why. Then she saw that the water was higher than it had been only moments before, her island smaller.

The lake was rising!

A whimper caught in Cara's throat as her mind flooded with horrified understanding. Sacrificial near-drowning was part of the magic—it was how the Night-keepers connected with their gods during the cardinal days, a way for them to access their greatest powers. But there wouldn't be any "near" about it for her—she was no mage, and this wasn't one of the cardinal days. And, as in the paintball game, dead for a *winikin* was just dead.

"It won't be long now," Lora said softly. Her gleaming eyes were locked on Zane, her lips parted in worship, or maybe hunger.

He didn't acknowledge her. Instead, he turned back to Cara. "It was the mark." He tapped his forearm, where he wore the familiar glyph of the coyote bloodline. "Up until then, I thought it meant we were to be mates, that I was supposed to forgive the blood and take you as my queen. I dreamed of the mated mark, you see. But when the gods didn't give it to us, I finally understood. It's not about forgiving at all." His eyes glittered suddenly. "It's revenge."

"What blood?" Cara whispered through lips gone numb. She was trapped, helpless. Terrified. *Keep him talking.* As long as he was there, she wasn't drowning. "What revenge? What did I do to you?"

"Not you. Your father."

Carlos. The name twisted something inside her. "What? Why?" Thunder rumbled outside, vibrating the altar beneath her and letting her know that the storm was still overhead. If it was the same storm as before, she hadn't lost much time, hadn't traveled far. Yet she might as well have been on a different plane. Her voice broke. "He said he didn't know your family."

"Zane," Lora said, shooting a look into the darkness. "We should go. The doorway is almost all the way under-water."

"I lied about who my parents were," he said without taking his eyes off Cara. "Carlos knew them, all right. They would've made it out safe if it wasn't for him. *That's* why this is revenge."

The massacre, she thought. He was talking about the days right before the massacre, when the king cracked down on the rebels, declaring that any mage or *winikin* caught trying to leave would be considered guilty of treason, which was an executable offense. He hadn't ac-tually executed anyone, but he had sent teams of loyal-ists to keep the rebels in check.

Some had gotten away. Most hadn't.

"My father wasn't on one of the teams." She'd asked him directly.

Zane spit into the water, which had covered the small sandy island and was edging up his boots. "He did it per-sonally, talking them back into doing their duty and sav-ing the world for their son." He thumped his chest. "For me. I tried to get them to leave like we had planned, but he'd brainwashed them—the whole fucking *system* had brainwashed them—and they locked me in my room, telling me that everything was going to be okay." He bared his teeth. "I got away, though. They nearly caught me, nearly killed me, but I got away . . . and the gods led me here, so I would know what to do when the time came."

He shifted, and for a second she thought he was going for his dagger, that it was all over. Instead, he turned up the camping lantern full blast, so it reached the farthest reaches of the cave. And even through her terror, she gaped.

Water surrounded them on all sides, brown and rippling, and churning to dirty foam at a narrow spot where an arch of deep darkness and a flicker of lightning said there was a way out.

Cara yearned toward it. *Please, gods*.

The huge cavern roof was decorated with cave paintings of people and animals, hunting scenes that leaped into sharp focus and left her reeling. Directly overhead, there was a throng of painted creatures—birds, mammals, reptiles, they were all there. The brown, rust, and ocher colors were vivid and breathtaking even in her panic. But it wasn't the paintings that had Zane's full attention; it was the lower ring of images that ran the circumference of the cave.

Coyotes. Everywhere, coyotes.

Zane's eyes were lit with terrifying fanaticism. "I was injured, sunstroked, desperate, and the gods brought me here. I lay in the shade, drank the water, and waited for my parents to come for me . . . but they never did. And when I went back to the compound, it had disappeared." His expression flattened. "Your father helped the Nightkeepers lead my parents to their deaths . . . and then the magic took the only home I'd ever known. So . . . I left. I survived. And for years, I thought it was all over, that the massacre had severed the magic forever. But then you came for me—a *coyote* came for me, and I knew the gods still favored our bloodline. I just didn't know how until a few days ago." He was breathing heavily now, still staring at the painted coyotes. "I dreamed of this, of you." The island was gone now, the water up past his knees, though he didn't seem to notice or care.

Tears stung Cara's eyes but didn't fall. "Please," she said softly. "Let me go. You can have whatever you want."

His eyes went back to the paintings. "I want to become what the gods intend. And you're going to help me." He glanced at Lora, jerked his chin toward the exit. "Let's go. This is between her and the cave."

"But I thought . . ." Lora touched her knife with fingers that trembled slightly.

Zane shook his head and started slogging away. Over his shoulder, he said, "No. She drowns. That's the way the magic works."

Cara's heart seized in her chest even as anger lashed through the fear. "There is no magic, damn it!" Her voice cracked with the force of her shout. "You're a *winikin!*"

"I'm a coyote *winikin,*" he called back over the sound of the water. "That makes all the difference in the world."

"It doesn't—" She broke off—there was no point arguing with a madman—and switched her attention to Lora, who stood there with a strange look in her eyes and her hand on the hilt of her blade. "Don't you see he's lost it?" Cara said softly. "Let me go and we'll fix this. We'll fix everything; I promise." She was pleading now, begging. Whatever it took. "Please. Don't do this."

"Lora." Zane snapped his fingers. "Come on."

"Don't—" Cara began, but then broke off because it was no use. Lora heeled up like an obedience-trained retriever, warning that there had been more going on in the *winikin*'s wing than Cara had even begun to guess. Was she that blind? Had she been so wrapped up in her own problems that she'd failed to see that something was so wrong?

A sob rose up and locked her throat as Zane and Lora—her teammates . . . hell, her team *leaders*—slogged through the narrowing gap and out into the night. Then they were gone, leaving her alone with a single lantern and the water more than halfway up the face of the altar.

Cara screamed, "Help! For gods' sake, somebody help me!" Her only answer was a flicker of lightning that made the cave paintings dance as if they were alive. She twisted against the cargo straps, unable to get any real leverage. The bonds bit into her chest and hips, drew blood from her wrists and ankles, and didn't budge at all. Panic bit into her, raced through her, and she filled her lungs as far as she could, straining to scream, "*Help me!*"

The rain rattled like bullets on the scant windshield of the ATV Sven had boosted from the firing range, and slashed into his exposed skin, cutting into him so hard he was surprised he wasn't covered in blood. It was just water, though. And even if it'd been acid burning holes in his body, he would've kept going, following Mac's trail through the rainy, shitty darkness.

This really wasn't good.

They were outside the compound, vulnerable, and nobody knew where they were or what was going on, but he couldn't stop now. He was focused on the lightning-lit glimpses of his familiar up ahead and, like now, when Mac bolted ahead and out of sight behind a rocky outcropping, the mental link that drew him onward with: *Followfollowfollowfoll—*

The sudden break in the litany snapped Sven's head up and put a nasty clutch in his gut. But then he heard a flurry of excited barks and a new glyph burst in on him: *Found! Found! Foundfoundfound!*

"Cara!" he bellowed, though her name was quickly swallowed by the wind. He could still hear the barking, though, along with a new sound, a deeper-throated roar that prickled a whole lot of bad down his spine.

It was the sound of water in the desert. A flash flood.

Gut knotting, he whipped around the corner, hit the brakes, and brought the four-wheeler to a slithering, slewing stop, cursing as the headlights shone on a bad situation rapidly going worse. "Son of a *bitch*."

Mac was running up and down the bank of what had probably been a dry wash or slow-moving trickle an hour ago, but was now a rushing, seething mass of muddy water. Right where the coyote was pacing in fast-forward, the water foamed slimy brown against a wall of rock and then slipped through an opening in the stone, where a cave mouth was just barely visible.

Killing the ATV, Sven bolted toward Mac, past him, splashing to the edge of the water and staggering when the ground gave beneath him like quicksand. "Cara! Are you in there?" *Please, gods. Holy fucking please.* "*Cara!*"

He didn't get anything but Mac's background litany of: *Yes, yes, yes!*

"Shut it," he snapped. "I can't hear anything."

The coyote went to quivering silence, but between the

pissing rain, the churning current, and the grumble that wasn't quite thunder, he couldn't hear dick.

Then, faintly, his name. "Sven?" The word was nearly lost beneath the din, but it was real. By the gods, it was real.

"*Cara?*"

"Hurry! I'm trapped, and—" Thunder drowned out the rest.

"I'm coming. Hang on!" He forged deeper into the water, forcing his feet through the shifting sand and cursing when the icy cold bit through his clothes and the current dragged like a bitch.

Mac howled from the bank, racing up and down. *Followfollowfollow!*

Sven lurched back around just as his familiar gathered to leap into the deadly current. "No!"

The big coyote skidded into the muck at the edge, then floundered back to solid ground, barking, yipping, whining, and sending a steady stream of, *Followfollowfollow!*

"You can't follow. I need you to get help." When that didn't register, Sven sent it in thought-glyphs, pushing them hard through the familiar bond. *Need help. Get friends.* Then he pictured JT, who had unexpectedly clicked with the coyote during the *xombi* exterminations, playing hours of fetch and cracking a series of Lassie jokes that had gotten real old real quick, but had lightened up the horror a little. The *winikin* might not grasp how close they were to "Timmy fell down the well. Lassie, get help!" but he would know there was a problem, and he'd be smart enough to follow the coyote.

Hopefully.

Mac barked. *Friend!*

Sven pictured a crowd of people, everyone he could think of who was at Skywatch, then the Jeeps. *All friends. Jeeps. Then come back. Fast! Fastfastfast!* He didn't dare send more than that, hoped that wasn't too much. But, damn, he needed help and he needed it twenty minutes ago, and both his armband and the comm device on the ATV were dead, killed by a storm that had to be something more than weather.

Mac barked twice in answer, and lightning flashed as he wheeled and bolted away, flying back up the way they had come. Sven felt him heading away, moving fast, purpose fixed in his mind. *Hurry,* he thought, though the mind link was already growing faint with distance. Then he turned back to the cave, bellowing, "Cara?"

There was no answer.

Roaring her name, he forced his legs through the clinging muck and shoved his body through the churning current, slogging, gutting it out, aiming for the cave mouth. The force of the water pounded into him, dragged at him, but he held fast. Ten more steps. Eight. Seven.

Then he stepped onto emptiness as the ground disappeared beneath him. And, bellowing her name, he flung himself into the foamy churn.

The icy water closed around him, blocking out the sound of the storm. For a second the freezing liquid felt entirely alien, like he'd never surfed the big waves or dived the Great Barrier, never even fucking dog-paddled. Then the current grabbed him and yanked him into its flow, and nearly two decades spent above and below the ocean came back between one heartbeat and the next.

He instinctively read the undertow and the counter-current that said he was headed for the rock wall. Instead of fighting it, he wrapped his arms around his head and went limp, and let it happen. He slammed into the rocky surface with bruising, slashing force and smothered an underwater groan. *Fuck, that hurt!* But when his head broke the surface, he struck out, swimming with the current that curved around the base of the wall, knowing that when he reached the cave mouth, the undertow was going to be a bitch.

The roar of water surrounded him, threatened to consume him, but he had to get in there; the seconds were ticking beneath his skin. *Please, gods, let her be okay.*

Then he was at the huge vacu-suck where the floodwaters raced into the cave. Every survival instinct he possessed said to get the fuck out of there, but instead he frog-kicked down and in. The current grabbed him, yanking him down and corkscrewing him in a dizzying spin. Blood pounding in his head, he let the current carry him, pummel him, pull him, spin him around. Then, finally, it softened, eased, let go, and he broke back into blessed air.

"Son of a bitch." He sucked in huge lungfuls while registering that the water noise and eddies around him said he was in a big cave. "Cara?"

"*Sven.*" It was barely a gasp, but he heard it. He heard it!

Calling on his magic, he cast a foxfire that lit a water-filled cavern and illuminated bright, vivid cave paintings. The images moved and swirled, and he wasn't sure if that was a trick of the light or some sort of storm magic. Because there was definitely magic in the cave; it suddenly hummed in his bones and sparkled in the air, making it seem that a zoo's worth of animals spun and dipped. Lower, down near the waterline, coyotes danced in a circle.

For a second, his eyes locked on those coyotes and something stirred inside him. Then he tore his attention free to scan the cave. "Cara!"

There was no sign of her. There was only the water.

Gods!

He'd been going with the current, but now he struck out swimming, casting around, trying to find her. The water coming in through the cave mouth piled up against the far wall in a foamy mass, but not nearly as much as he would expect; it had to be going somewhere. Which meant there was an outlet somewhere in the chamber, submerged. Had she been swept farther downstream?

But her words echoed in his head. *I'm trapped.* Okay, but how? Where? He dived beneath the surface, searching for some clue, but the water was murky brown, the current chaotic, the base of the pool nothing but smooth sand.

"Cara!" He shouted her name each time he surfaced, calling her over and over again. And, finally, he thought he caught a gurgled scream. Kicking to rear himself as high out of the water as he could, he cast another foxfire, a third, lighting the cave day-bright. And he saw a place at the center of the pool where the water swirled and churned rather than flowing. There was something down there!

He floundered toward the spot, sucked in a breath, and submerged, hands outstretched. He found stone and followed it to a cargo strap, felt along the tight strap, and touched a hand. It grabbed on to him instantly, clutching in panic.

The move brought a spurt of relief. And he'd found her just in time too, because although the churning water had given her some extra chances at oxygen, she was fully submerged now, wide-eyed and scared, spitting bubbles as she screamed his name and begged for air.

Rearing up, he gulped a lungful, then ducked down, slanted his lips across hers, and gave her his breath in a kiss that wasn't a kiss, but was full of feeling anyway. Once, twice, and again he did it, until her eyes lost a little bit of their desperation. Then, racing time, he hooked his legs on either side of the stone slab she was bound to, pulled his ceremonial knife, and started hacking at the nylon straps, which were tough and slippery. *Come on, you bastards. Come on!*

Rage caught up with him then. Someone had done this to her. Who? Why? He didn't know, couldn't deal with it now. But fury flowed through him, then coalesced to a cold, icy vow: He was going to get her out of this no matter what it took. He was going to find whoever had done this to her. And he was going to fucking kill them.

He hacked through the chest strap and loosened one wrist, and she reared up, clutching at him as she shuddered and coughed, sucking in huge, ragged breaths. Her hair was plastered to her face, so black against her pasty white skin that she looked entirely colorless until her eyes blinked open and locked on his, twin gleams of honey-eyed brown that were warm, vibrant, and totally at odds with the world around them. "*Cara*." The word was a pained groan that ripped at his chest, coming from the place where he kept all the things he couldn't say.

"Hurry," she whispered between trembling, colorless lips. "Cut the others." The water was up to her throat and climbing.

He fumbled with the rest of her bonds, sawing through the one at her hips and then fucking ripping the last ankle strap free on a convulsive heave that was part fury, part relief. Then he dragged her into his arms and clutched her close. "Jesus gods." He buried his face in the crook of her neck. "I thought you were already gone."

She burrowed in, held on. "I'm f-freezing."

He wasn't much better off, his body cold, his wet clothes plastered to him. But now that he had her, knew she was alive, fury kindled in his chest. "Who did this?"

She hesitated, but then turned her face away and said in a low voice, "Zane planned it, with Lora helping. I don't know if any of the others were involved."

"Son of a—" He broke off, knowing now wasn't the time and anger wasn't what she needed. "Sorry. I'm sorry." Sorrier than she knew, because he'd been fucking watching those two and he hadn't seen it. Rage turned his insides murderously cold, and he felt like part of Mac was inside him, telling him to *find, fight, kill!* Not now, though. She needed him, and for a change he was there. It was a new, humbling sensation, one that put a funny twist in his throat as he gathered her tighter against his chest. "We need to get the hell out of here. Can you swim?"

"Yes, I—"

His stomach sank as a rumbling noise started up, coming from gods only knew where, interrupting him. He scanned a full three-sixty for the cause, but didn't find it.

"Look!" She pointed up, face blanking with new terror.

He followed her gesture and his heart stopped—seriously fucking stopped—at the sight of the cave roof dropping down toward them, running along a seam that hadn't been visible before. Magic, machinery, it didn't matter how it was moving, only that it was, and what it meant. *Holy fucking shit.*

They were in a trick cave, a damned magical hot spot.

The Nightkeepers' original intersection, a circular ceremonial chamber buried beneath the main pyramid of Chichén Itzá, had been able to magically seal itself off and drop into the subterranean river below it, subjecting the magi trapped inside it to a near-death experience by drowning: one of the most sacred sacrifices, bringing the sufferers close to the gods themselves. The room at Chichén Itzá had been designed for the Godkeeper ceremony, and had worked only during the cardinal solstices and equinoxes. But although this was no cardinal day—it was just another freaking Tuesday—when Sven looked up, he saw that the zoo was way closer than it had started. More, only the lower halves of the coyotes were visible. Cara's eyes, wide and terrified, snapped to his. "What *is* this place?"

"Doesn't matter, because we're getting out of here." He threaded her fingers through his weapons belt. "Swim as hard as you can and don't let go of me, no matter what. Okay?"

At her nod, he got an arm around her waist and, with a powerful thrust of his legs, launched them off the altar toward the cave opening.

The current grabbed them, tumbled them, but they fought it inch by inch, swimming hard. She struggled gamely beside him, but he could feel her flagging, her cold-sapped strength no match for his enhanced reserves. "I've got you," he said over the rumble of the ceiling and the rush of water. "Just hang on." He would get her out of there, get her safe, get whoever had done this to her. And then . . . Shit, he didn't know what he was going to do then.

Suddenly, a new sound joined the rumble and the

rush: a stone-on-stone grating noise that had the knots in his gut coiling to the snapping point.

"Look! *Hurry!*" Her voice cracked on the words, and she started swimming harder with a burst of terrified energy, headed for the place where a stone slab was sliding across the little bit of the cave mouth that was still visible.

"*Shit.*" He called his magic and threw a shield spell into the narrowing gap, but it fizzled and died, warning him that, same as the ceremonial chamber beneath Chichén Itzá, his magic wouldn't work in the chamber. The low-level foxfire spell was the best he could do, and even those lights were dimming as the ceiling crowded them down to the waterline while, with a grating noise, the slab slid into place, trapping them.

Cara gave a wordless cry and stopped swimming to stare at the place where their exit had been. She turned back, looked up at him with pleading eyes. "Tell me you brought backup."

"They're on their way." Gods willing, Mac had got the message across. "But without magic . . ." He trailed off. Even if Strike or Anna could detect them within the stone chamber, they wouldn't be able to 'port in. And if they were truly locked inside a ritual chamber—and that was sure as hell what it seemed like—all the fireballs in the world wouldn't be able to get them out until the cavern's spell had run its course.

But what spell? What ritual? And by the gods, how was he going to get her out alive? She wasn't a mage, didn't have the same natural resilience he did. And although her big personality and the huge effect she had on him made him forget how small she was sometimes, he was acutely aware now of the size difference between them. She was light and lithe against him, and so fine boned he thought he could break her if he held on too hard.

Either she had shifted or he had changed his grip; he wasn't sure. But they were holding each other now, wrapped around each other as they treaded muddy water. The magic must have closed off whatever outflow normally let the subterranean lake drain, because the water gradually stilled around them, leaving only the rumble of the ceiling as it dropped nearer and nearer still.

There was less than a foot of headroom left. They were running out of time. His mind raced. He had to do something. But what?

Cast the spell. It came to him on a whisper of thought, an urgency that seemed to come from the moist air around them. One of the foxfires touched the surface and blinked out, even though the spells could usually withstand water. This wasn't normal water, though; it was water inside a ceremonial chamber, a magical hot spot. And maybe that was the answer. He might not know what ritual he was supposed to perform, but he was a coyote, and there were coyotes on the wall. Maybe his magic would be enough to trigger whatever spell needed to be completed before the chamber would drain. *Please, gods, let it be enough.*

Heart thudding suddenly in his chest, he lifted his knife and rasped, "I need to—"

"Do it," she said. "I don't care what it is; just do it. This is your world, not mine. You're the one who's got to get us out of here." She tightened her grip on him for a beat, though he didn't know if she was reassuring him or saying good-bye.

No, damn it. Not good-bye. He was going to get them out of there.

The ceiling bumped his head, forcing him down as he caught her hands in his and gripped them tight, holding on to her. In that moment, he was achingly aware of the way she fit seamlessly, perfectly, even though they were so different in size and temperament. But where those differences had loomed so large in the past, now they mattered far less than the heat that rose between them, making the water seem suddenly warmer than before. He couldn't let that matter as much as he wanted to, though. He never could.

The water hit his chin and crept higher. His heart hammered in his chest, but he forced himself to stay calm and meet her eyes, hold them as he cut his own palms, first one and then the other, so he bled into the water. The air began to hum, singing the high, sweet note of power. *Magic.* The second foxfire died, then the third, but it didn't matter, because the magic was there inside him, racing in his veins and lighting up the water around them with red-gold sparkles. It poured through him, expanding his very soul, until he felt bigger, stronger, more powerful than ever, yet still not enough to fight the earth and stone that held them prisoner. He was going to have to rely on the gods for that.

The gods . . . and Cara. Because somehow he needed to bring her with him into the magic. It was the only way.

Drawing her close, he cut her palms to match his own and then threaded their fingers together so their palms aligned blood to blood. He didn't feel a blood-link, didn't feel anything but her narrow fingers in his, yet that was enough to shift his heart in his chest. *Please, gods*, he whispered deep in his soul as he took a last deep breath and straightened to sink beneath the water. When she did the same, trembling against him, he touched his lips to hers and whispered against her skin, "*Pasaj och*."

The magic of a barrier connection flared inside him, even though it shouldn't have been able to form with them still several days away from the equinox. The power was bottomless, eternal, and it reached out of him to surround her as her eyes went wide in the red-gold sparkles. Then he leaned in and kissed her, and this time he didn't hold back, instead pouring into her all the wishes and longings he'd kept locked inside for so long. She stiffened, clutching at him. He could feel her surprise, her confusion, and the heat that leaped up in answer. Then there was a soundless detonation. The bottom fell out of his soul. And he dropped into the magic, taking her with him.

CHAPTER TWELVE

Somewhere in the magic

The surprise of Sven's kiss—the heat, the intensity, the fireworks—turned instantly to shock as the cold water went hot and Cara's world lurched like a trampoline.

Suddenly she was moving without changing place, her consciousness leaping out of her body and accelerating through a dizzying, zigzagging blur of gray, green, and brown. She still felt like herself, but an insubstantial version. Part of her was cold, wet, and drowning, while another part flew free. He had brought her into his magic. She hung on to his hands, squeezing tightly. *It's working!*

They swerved and slewed, and then plunged down, up, sideways, and into a corkscrew spin that flipped her insubstantial self head over ass—*wham, wham, wham*—like an airplane barrel roll. Her heart leaped into her throat; she couldn't breathe, couldn't scream, couldn't do anything but jam her eyelids shut and hang on for the ride. The spinning got worse, until she didn't know up from down and the motion stopped feeling like movement and became the spinning of her mind, which knew only that she was still clutching his hand like a lifeline.

Then, gradually, the spins slowed. Her vision cleared. And she found them standing together in a beautiful underground grotto, facing each other and holding hands as if waiting to hear, "You may now kiss the bride."

It would've been a ridiculous thought—she wasn't a wedding kind of girl—except that the color scheme carried the vibe too. He was wearing combat black-on-black without the body armor or weapons, while she was somehow wearing a filmy white dress made of a woven fabric so light it felt like she wasn't wearing anything at all. It clung to her, seeming to be a single piece of fabric wound intricately around her body, showing every dip and curve. It ended high on her thigh on one side and trailed down to touch the ground on the other. Her hair hung loose down her back, fully dry; his was slicked back as if he'd just gotten out of the shower. To add to the what-the-fuck factor, they were both barefoot. Soft grains of sand shifted between her toes, and it was as if she could feel each inch of her body individually: the brush of her dress, the blunt pressure of his fingers on hers, squeezing as if to say, *It's okay*.

"Where are we?" she asked softly. "Is this the barrier?"

"No, not the barrier. We're in a vision," he answered, voice equally quiet, though the echoes were picked up by the arching walls of the circular cave.

"It feels so real."

"It is, just on another level of reality."

She stared around her, wide-eyed, heart drumming with a mixture of fear and exhilaration. *This is what all the fuss is about,* she thought, borderlining on awestruck.

This is magic. The air was warm, humid, and redolent of the rain forest she could see through the fallen-through spots high overhead, where green vines draped through and sunlight splashed down at a late-afternoon angle. They stood together on a wide, flat spot beside a deep pool. In places, stalactites dripped down from the ceiling or stalagmites pushed up from the water, thick, blunt, and slick with moisture.

Then, suddenly, the shaft of light nearest them brightened, as if the sun had been cloud shrouded and now burst fully to life. Then it brightened further, went supernova. Sven shifted to put his body in front of hers, and Cara lifted a hand to shield her eyes, scared yet somehow not as scared as she probably should've been. When the light dissipated, a figure stood in front of them, man shaped but genderless, with thick skin that stretched over bone and sinew, and featureless black eyes that stared, unblinking, at her and Sven.

A nahwal!

She gasped, but Sven's fingers tightened on hers, warning her not to back away. So she held her ground, staring at an entity she had never, ever expected to see for herself. Creatures of the barrier, the *nahwal* contained the collective ancestral wisdom of the Nightkeepers. Some held the experiences and personalities of the strongest magi of each bloodline; they passed messages to their descendants and could be both help and hindrance. Others were all-knowing and could answer questions, while some were cruel and vicious. This one's forearm lacked the coyote glyph, which meant it didn't belong to Sven's ancestry, but it wasn't volunteering information and hadn't made any move to attack. So what was it? Why was it here?

"Are you the Father?" Sven asked quietly. "Are you the one we're supposed to resurrect?" A shiver raced across Cara's skin at the thought.

"No. I am his messenger." The voice was a descant of many, as if a church choir were speaking. "The seer is blind and deaf, but the information must be passed, and here you are among us, son of the coyotes. So it comes to you."

A message! Hope flared, tightening Cara's throat. "What information?" she whispered, not sure whether the *nahwal* would even acknowledge her.

It kept its featureless black eyes fixed on Sven, but answered, "In order for the Father to arise, the magi must bring the screaming skull to Che'en Yaaxil on the cardinal day." Then, shifting its attention to her, the *nahwal* said, "That was one question. You have two more."

Cara gaped, first because the creature—the *nahwal!*— had acknowledged her, and then because of what its question meant. "You're a three-question *nahwal!*"

Rabbit had killed the prior version of the oracle, defending himself when the creature went rogue and attacked him. The Nightkeepers had searched long and hard for another, needing the answers it could provide if it chose. The "if it chose" was an important caveat, though, because the answers given by the prior three-question *nahwal* had been riddles at best, useless at worst, and almost always seriously obscure.

"Is that your question?"

"No!" she said quickly. "That was a statement, not a question."

"Careful," Sven said in an undertone. "The last one had a temper."

"No shit," she said, anxiety pushing her tone sharper

than she'd really intended. Blowing out a breath, she whispered, "What should I ask?"

"Request not of others what you must decide for yourself," the *nahwal* said flatly. "These are your questions, not his. Ask for your true heart's desire and the answers will be yours." Its eyes bored into her, reaching inside as the thing said, "What do you want, *winikin*? Ask it of me now . . . but ask wisely."

Cara suddenly had to swallow hard, choking down the bitter thought that she didn't remember the last time someone had asked her what she really wanted. She wasn't even sure she knew anymore, and boy, did that suck. This wasn't the time for selfishness, though, either in questions or dreams.

Her mind raced, bringing a skim of panic. *What should I do next?* she thought frantically, but didn't say it aloud because it would be too broad a question. *How can we get out of the cave?* she thought to try—she might feel solid and real, standing there in the lush cave, still hanging on to Sven like she had the right, but in reality their bodies were far away, drowning. Maybe even near death. But she hoped—prayed—that the *nahwal*'s message meant there was a chance she and Sven would make it back to the magi. *Why didn't I get my mark?* she almost asked, because the *nahwal* was talking to her, not Sven, and that had to mean something. Unless it didn't.

Think! This was a shared vision, a shared message. *Focus on the details.* There wasn't enough to the message for the brain trust to work with, was there? Taking a deep breath, she said, "What does this screaming skull look like?"

"It is the size of a man's fist, made of obsidian, and looks as you would expect it to from the name." There was no tone or inflection, no hint that she'd asked the right or wrong question. Sven, though, tightened his fingers on hers and gave the shallowest of nods.

Taking too much solace from that, she said, "What is the location of"—she stumbled over the ancient words—"Che'en Yaaxil?"

"We are there." The *nahwal* gestured to the subterranean pool and almost ethereally beautiful surroundings. "It is an hour's walk from the tomb of the First Father. That is your third and last question." Sunlight brightened through the opening once more, limning the *nahwal* with a white halo.

"Wait." Sven held out a hand to the ancient being. "What about me?"

The halo brightened and blurred, forcing Cara to squint and then look away. From within the flameless white fire, the *nahwal*'s multitonal voice said, "I will not take your questions, mage, but I will give you your answers: The vision belongs to both of you; it is how you want to be seen. And this is your charge: Do not waste the gifts you are about to receive."

Hope flickered. What gifts?

"What gifts?" Sven asked as if reading her mind. But even as he got the question out, the *nahwal*'s image grew thin and began to fade. "Wait. Come back!"

"Gods go with you both." The multitonal voice was soft, almost wistful.

The pillar of light flared brightly, reaching out to surround them in a warm wash of energy and a thundering, shuddering noise that sounded like an off-balance clothes drier running at top speed: a syncopated *thumpa-thud-thumpa-thud* that sent Cara's heart into her throat.

What was happening? What were they supposed to do next? "Stop," she cried. "Stop this!"

Sven shouted something, but she couldn't hear him over the noise, could only hang tightly on to his hand. *THUMPA-THUD-THUMPA-THUD!*

On the last *thud,* the ground shuddered beneath her feet and her palms burned sharply as the cuts reopened and split wide. She cried out in pain, and then with shock as the blinding light winked out and they were suddenly standing on a featureless gray surface, surrounded by a huge mass of fog that churned around them with a deep-throated, windy roar.

She gaped, paralyzed by helplessness as the mist became tendrils that snaked out, reaching toward her and Sven.

"Get back!" He lunged in front of her and called a shield spell but nothing happened; he cast a fireball and cursed as it failed.

Standing there in warrior black, unarmed and shouting into the fog, he looked at once majestic and vulnerable, and her heart shuddered with a sudden gut-deep certainty that this would be the last time she would see him like this.

"Sven, don't!" She reached for him, but just as her fingertips brushed his sleeve, the tendrils whipped around him and yanked him forward. Her heart stopped and her voice broke on a shattered scream of, "*No!*"

He shouted and fought the mist's inexorable grip, lashing out with magic that fizzled as it was cast. Twisting back, he reached for her with one hand while warding her off with the other. His eyes were tortured, his face stark with horror. "Cara, I—"

The tendrils yanked him into the mist, and he disappeared.

"*No!*" She bolted after him, but stopped after only a few steps because she was suddenly, utterly sure that he wasn't just gone from sight, but from the vision, the plane, wherever the hell they were.

She was alone—she could feel it on her skin and deep down inside. And with no magic, she had no way to get back to her body. She was trapped, locked into—

Movement snaked into her peripheral vision and she spun in a defensive crouch, then screamed when a foggy tentacle latched onto her thigh, burning with cool fire. Another wrapped around her in an instant, dropping on her like python coils; they slid and tightened until she couldn't move, couldn't breathe, couldn't do anything but scream as she was dragged into the mist.

Terror lashed through her. The fog was all around her, and then, gods, *inside* her—a terrible invading presence. It filled her up, pressing inside her chest and her skull as if searching for something and not finding it. The head and heart were the seats of a mage's power, but she was no mage. As if suddenly realizing that, being angered by it, the fog seared through her, burning and tearing. *Agony!* She screamed, fell onto her side, and curled fetal as blackness washed across her vision and her entire world tunneled down to the presence inside her, the burning pressure in her head and heart. Weakness washed through her. Impotence. Then anger, because she didn't want to be weak anymore, didn't want—

Blackness overcame her, shutting down her systems and leaving only a last despairing cry to echo through her fading self: *Help me!*

*   *   *

Sven jerked awake, heart hammering as he blinked into pitch blackness. "Cara?"

She lay in his arms, with her body pressed against his and their legs intertwined, a soft, yielding layer of moist sand beneath them. But she didn't answer, didn't move, barely even breathed. Her cry for help echoed in his soul, but not aloud.

"Mother*fucker*," he grated. The words echoed in the pitch-black, bringing back the sound of stone all around him, water nearby. He didn't need the inputs to know where he was, though: the coyote cave. He was back in his own body, out of the vision and returned to the earth plane without her, spit there by the gray vortex. Its whirling power had been incalculable, searing his veins with a strange magic that had felt like the familiar bond times a million, as if he weren't just bonded to Mac; he had *become* Mac, if only for a moment. Even now, that same feral power expanded his senses, sharpening his instincts and making him feel like he could do anything, fight anyone . . . except his own fucking selfishness. Because he might have held on to her in real life, but in the vision—where she'd been depending on him to get them safely back—he'd left her behind.

He snapped the spell word to light a foxfire, and it blazed instantly, bigger and brighter than his usual, amped by the power that thrummed through the coyote cave. The ceiling had returned to its original position so the animals hung high above the coyotes, and the water had drained away, leaving just a thin river that circled around the central altar. The entrance was still sealed, though, and the magic was thick in the air, heavy and expectant. And Cara lay against him, her breathing far too slow. Her dark hair was a stark contrast against the milk of her skin and the startling white stripe, making him think of Sleeping Beauty, poisoned apples, and evil queens. Only he was no prince, and it was going to take more than a kiss to wake her up.

Pulse thudding, hoping like hell this would work, he went for his knife, cut his palm, and let the blood fall to the sand as he whispered, "*Pasaj och.*"

There was a burning in his blood, a jolt in his soul, and the wild magic snapped and snarled within him. But there was no sense of movement, no mist, no vision. Instead of jacking in this time, he stayed stubbornly inside a body that suddenly seemed not to fit quite right. And instead of calling her back or sending him into the barrier after her, the spell called something else instead. Sparks kindled in his gut and his blood heated, and he was suddenly so very aware of her curves, and the way they fit somehow despite their differences.

Her breath feathered across his throat, bringing a low growl from the gray fog inside him—one that shimmered to life as thought-glyphs: *Want. Take.* It wasn't Mac's inner voice, though; it was his own. And although he'd told himself a thousand times why he couldn't take what he wanted, he couldn't remember any of the reasons right then; he could only wrap her tighter in his arms, pull her closer to his body, and ride the fierce surge of possessiveness that suddenly burned in his veins. His senses heightened and his skin grew sensitive as his cock hardened and the urge to mate took hold. He wanted to have her, hold her, bury himself inside her. He wanted to feel her clawing at his back, wanted to hear the sounds she made when she came. And then he wanted to come himself, lose himself inside her and steep his scent into her pores, marking her as his own.

Don't. It's sex magic. The words seemed strange, as if coming in an unfamiliar language from a part of himself that was so much smaller and less important than the flames that raced through him, a mix of power and desire, and the sharp ache that came with having denied himself for so long.

"No, damn it." He wasn't going there, didn't dare even touch the fringes of the electricity that sparked between them. She was magic, power, glory, and goodness all wrapped up in a tiny yet perfect body, but he knew better than to even take a taste, not knowing whether he would be able to force himself to pull back and not take it too far. She was his weakness, after all.

Sacrifice isn't supposed to be easy. The reminder might have come in the *nahwal*'s many voices, might've come from deep within Sven himself. But it blazed with new certainty, bringing the knowledge that this wasn't just a test; it was a chance for him to be there for her as he'd failed to be so many times before.

Rearing back, he looked down at her for a moment, memorizing the sight of her curled against his chest as if she belonged there. Then, not letting himself hesitate any longer, he clasped her hands in his, aligning their cut palms and feeling the low buzz of the forming blood-link. *Here goes nothing,* he thought, but what he really meant was, *Here goes everything,* because in the next instant he dropped all his shields and opened himself to her, holding nothing back.

Power blazed inside him and flowed through the link into her. Then *he* flowed through the link, as well, and for a disorienting second, he wasn't inside his own head anymore. He was in hers. He felt her strength, her determination, her insecurities, her loneliness, and the lifelong fear that she wouldn't be good enough, that she would let down the people who were counting on her, so much longer a list now than ever before. And each of those things resonated inside him. Oh, holy shit, how they resonated. But although those core emotions were in place, that was all. Her essential self, her full consciousness, wasn't there. All he could sense was the hollow echo of his own soul as it ate itself from within.

She was lost in the darkness. Because he'd left her behind.

Guilt slashed, but he didn't ease back. Instead, he tightened his grip on the blood-link and focused on pouring his power—his magic—into her. *Cara. I'm here. You're here. You need to find your way back.* He thought it like a prayer, sending it into her and hoping to hell it would find her and lead her home.

Silence was agony. Brutal, crushing defeat.

He sagged against her, held her closer, tried to wrap himself around her until he wasn't sure where his flesh ended and hers began. And all the while, he was sending the magic. It rushed from him to her and back again, bringing only lonely echoes and the growing fear that he was too late, that it wasn't enough, that he'd already—

Hello? It was so faint that for a second he thought he'd imagined it. But then he heard it again: *Hello? Anyone?*

Jesus gods. Relief slammed through him, weakening his defenses even more. "Here! Gods, Cara, yes, I'm here!" He said it aloud, heard it reverberate off the cave walls.

Sven?

Yeah. This way. Come toward my voice. He sensed movement in the fog, caught a shimmering outline, a thread of desperate joy as she flung herself at his magic.

For a second, his essence caught hers and they held on and clung as they had done before, in the vision. And then—thank the fucking gods, she was back, once more fully inhabiting her body and soul, and pushing him back into himself. Suddenly he could taste her on his lips, smell her on his skin, and feel her body warming and shifting against his as she turned in his embrace. And that was no dream or vision. It was real.

His eyes flew open as she flung her arms around his neck and clutched him so tight he almost couldn't breathe. "You came back for me." Her words were muffled against his throat, her face hot against his skin. "You did. You came back."

"Of course." Pain stabbed that he'd given her such reason to doubt it. He eased her choke hold and rolled them onto their sides, partly so he could pull away and get a look at her, but mostly so she wouldn't feel the big-ass tent pole he had going in the front of his pants. *Hold it together,* he told himself. *You can do this.* Furiously, he shunted the churning, sexual magic to the foxfires, which glowed so brightly they seemed to drip with light. The move leveled him off enough that he could stop himself from grabbing her, though, and bought him enough breath to grate, "Are you okay?"

"Yes," she said, but her eyes were locked on his, her pupils dilating. "No." Her breathing synched with his, fast and shallow. "I don't know."

Her pulse throbbed at her throat, beating in time with his heart and the heavy thrum of blood lower down, where he was hard and ready. Needy. But that need didn't matter if the desire went only one way. Except that unless he was misreading the vibe that had sprung up between them, the sizzles were going both ways all of a sudden. Magic flared through him, putting red-gold sparks in the air and heightening his senses to an almost painful intensity. And when he shifted to stroke the place where color rode high on her cheeks, his hand shook with the effort it took not to bury his fingers in her hair and dive in for a kiss. But if he took a taste he knew he wouldn't be able to stop there. He would want a nibble, a bite, and then more. Everything.

At the thought, his body tightened and a growl rose up from somewhere deep inside him, sounding greedy and feral, and not at all like the man he wanted to be with her, for her. Worse, he was suddenly looming over her, leaning too close, his mouth only a breath away from hers. "Sorry," he said, easing back. "I didn't mean —"

"Don't be sorry." She followed him up, one hand suddenly wrapped in the collar of his shirt, anchoring them together. Her breasts brushed his chest with her every breath, and the contact flared through his body like a perfect sunrise over the ocean — brilliant and blinding, and making him feel like he could do anything. Against his lips, she said, "We're the only ones who will ever know what happened inside this cave. Which means we can do whatever we want. And right now, I want you."

"Cara, this isn't real. It's —"

"Sex magic," she interrupted softly. "I know. I can feel it. Whatever you did to bring me back, I can feel you inside me, connected to me. I want to feel the rest of you that way too."

"Gods." He was dying to be inside her. Fucking dying. He pressed his hand atop hers, trapping her palm over his heart. He told himself to ask if she was sure, give her another out, or, hell, walk the fuck away. But somehow he knew it'd been too late for walking away the moment he saw her wristband in the mud and everything else had ceased to exist. He had found her, saved her. And maybe right now she could save him a little too. So he leaned back in, pausing only to say, "Last chance."

As she drew breath to say something, he closed the gap and kissed her. Madly, wetly, deeply he kissed her, holding nothing back and asking for everything in return.

Want me, his kiss said. *Need me.* And hers in return said, *I do.* Which was a damn good thing, given that he wanted her like he wanted his next heartbeat, his next breath, his next sunrise. So, beneath an endless ring of coyotes, he kissed her and let the rest of the world fall away. And if somewhere deep inside him warning bells were going off, he ignored the hell out of them, because he was so fucking tired of holding himself back when it came to her.

CHAPTER THIRTEEN

Cara gave herself up to the kiss and the moment, not stopping to care what would happen next. She had been lost in the fog, would have stayed there forever if he hadn't come for her. And there, in that endless gray world, she'd had a moment of sudden clarity: She didn't want to die with regrets.

If that had been the end of it, she would have hated leaving the earth plane without getting back at Zane and Lora and wresting them from the *winikin* before they did any more damage. She would have wished she had done things differently with her father. And she would have deeply regretted giving up her chance at fireworks. Now, though, it seemed that she was being given a second chance. There was magic in the air and a man—*the* man—was holding her, kissing her. And he wasn't pulling back this time. Instead, he slanted kisses across her mouth, along her jaw, and up to the sensitive lobe of her ear. He urged her closer in the soft, shifting sand, and when their bodies pressed together, she felt his arousal, his need.

No regrets, she thought. Free to touch him, finally, she was bold with her lips, and with hands that no longer stung from the cuts on her palms, which had healed to scars already. *Magic,* she thought as the heat raced through her, making every sensation ten times more acute. More, it was sex magic and she, a *winikin,* could feel it, which should have been impossible. Right then, though, she didn't care what it meant; she only gloried in the burn of desire.

He shuddered and pulled away a few inches, so his eyes were very close as they searched hers. Then he surprised her by skimming his fingertips along her jaw and up to her temple, then to touch the place where her hair went from dark to light. Growing up, he had teased her about it so fiercely she had tried to dye it dark, but had succeeded only in staining the bathroom wallpaper and earning a month of double chores. Now, though, he rubbed a few of the white strands—coarse and heavy in comparison—between his fingers in a move that said that he knew who she was—not a vision or a casual hookup, but her.

"Cara," he began on a sigh.

"Shut it." She pressed a silencing finger to his lips. "Don't make this more complicated than it needs to be. We want each other. More, we know this won't work in the long run, but that hasn't stopped us from wondering. Who knows? Maybe this is the gods' gift the *nahwal* mentioned. Maybe they're giving us this one time together to get it out of our systems, so we can move on." That could explain why she felt the magic too, and why the cave hadn't opened back up even though the water had drained away.

His breath feathered across her hand; his eyes bored

into hers. From behind her restraining fingers, he said, "There's only one thing I want more than this, and that's to not hurt you ever again."

A small sliver of pain jabbed below her heart, because while she knew he meant it utterly, she also knew that was impossible. *No regrets,* she reminded herself, and said, "Sorry, I can't promise that." Nerves buzzed through her, but beneath them was a heady stir of courage. She almost never told the full truth, instead editing to keep the peace and bottling up the rest inside. Not this time, though. "It hurts to see you around Skywatch and not be able to touch you or even talk to you. It hurts to know that you and Mac are going to take off at some point, or that if you don't and we make it through the war, I'm going to be the one leaving. But the thing is, none of those things will hurt extra if we do this. If anything, it'll hurt worse if I miss this chance, because then I'll have regrets. That much I really *can* promise." She dropped her hand and replaced her silencing touch with a kiss that started soft but quickly turned hot and needy. When it ended, she pulled away and whispered between heavy breaths, "When it's all over, let's not have regrets. At least not about this."

He stared at her for a heartbeat, his face etched with intensity as he weighed her promise. "Be sure," he rasped. "Be really fucking sure."

"I am."

His eyes changed, kindling with a new and potent fire. She could almost hear his noble intentions shatter, but he said only, "Thank Christ." Then, groaning a dark and delicious curse, he rolled suddenly, pressing his big, hard body fully atop hers as he kissed her, tasted her, touched her, rose over her, and *took*.

And, yes, thank Christ, because this was what she wanted. More, it was what she needed in this moment and this place, with this man. She was finally—oh, gods, yes, *finally*—telling the world to go screw itself, at least for an hour or two. Gods, did that feel good.

Her heart thundered as she grappled to touch him, taste him, then bowed back on a hiss as his fingers brushed the edges of her breasts, the lines of her waist and hips. He cupped her ass and then slid his touch inward to brush the sensitized flesh. Heat gripped her, ground at her, and she sagged against him with a low cry. She was hot, wet, and needy, her clothing a barrier that had to go.

She tugged at his stretchy, formfitting shirt, got it up and off, and purred when she was able to play her fingers along the muscles beneath. The purr turned to a gasp, though, when he slid a hand under her shirt, cupped a breast, and then dragged a thumb across one nipple in a move that sent sparks shooting through her system.

"Oh, gods." She bowed against him, curled around him, her mouth an "O" of pleasure.

"Off," he growled. "All of it."

Their clothing made a nest in the soft, yielding sand at the edge of the pool, and his magic heated the air as they twined together, kissing, licking, sucking—it was all fair game when sex magic burned in the blood.

Murmuring something low and reverent against her lips, he slid a finger along the crease between her legs, easing forward, forward, and then finding her. His low groan echoed her pleasure and she let her breath hiss out as he teased the opening, his touch an erotic shock to her system.

His erection was sandwiched between their bodies, pressing hard and insistent against her mound. As her blood burned higher and hotter, driven by the rhythm he set with his fingers, she slid a hand between their bodies and rubbed her palm across his testicles and up along the heavy, distended vein that lined the bottom of his hard, upthrust cock. He groaned, then shuddered when she closed her fingers around him.

There was no hesitation in her, no second thoughts. She wanted this, wanted *him,* and had for years and years.

His cock was thick and long, with a bullet head that pearled moisture when she ran her thumb across the engorged slit. He groaned and intensified the rhythm.

An early orgasm slapped through her without warning, bright, brittle, and glittering with the pleasure that vised her muscles and left her shaking. She cried out and clutched at him, wordless and needy as her body pulsed around his fingers.

"Fuck, that's hot," he rasped against her lips. Then, his voice going commanding, he said, "Do it again."

"I . . ." she began, but then trailed off when he eased away to scatter kisses down her throat. Then he moved lower, bending and kneeling in front of her.

He stroked his hands down her legs, first the outsides and then the insides, urging them apart and angling her body so her spine pressed against the smooth curve of the cave wall. With a smooth and unexpected move, he hooked one of her legs over his shoulder, opening her, laying her vulnerable.

"Wait." She tried to pull away. "Let me . . ." The protest died on her lips as he turned his head and pressed his lips to her inner thigh.

"No, let me," he said against her skin. "Just let me." And he kissed her again, brushing his lips up her inner thigh and then inward to draw his tongue along the center of her in a long, heated lick that had a moan rolling from her, had her head falling back against the stone and her body going limp in sudden, unfamiliar submission.

Oh, gods, yes, she thought as he bent his head. He kissed her more deeply, more intimately, and slipped his hands around her once more, questing until his fingers found her, entered her again.

There was pressure and pleasure, a fullness that seemed somehow so much more intense than it did when she was alone. Helpless to do otherwise, driven by her body's needs now, she arched into his mouth, rocked against his fingers, and cried out. As he drove her up toward the next peak, she started shaking. Not just because of arousal, though that was part of it, but because she didn't know what was coming next, or what any of it meant. She was lost in the moment, unable to care about anything other than the orgasm that gathered within her and the lover who was bowed down before her.

She held his head against her, worked herself against his mouth, totally taken within the maelstrom of sensations. And as the inner knots tightened around his fingers and tongue, all she could think was, *Thank the gods.*

Then he moved away, leaving her to cry out in frustration, then hiss in approval as he moved back up her body, heavy and solid, letting her feel every inch of him. He rose over her and she gloried in the heavy press of his body into hers, and the glide of his hard cock along her slick folds. Excitement built; she wanted him inside her, wanted to be pounded into, hollowed out. She wanted to sink her teeth into him and mark him as her own. Instead, she turned her face into his throat and whispered, "Now. Please, oh, please, now."

"Hell, yeah, now," he growled in return.

There was no fumbling with protection or questions, no need with a mage. He just poised himself and nudged within, the press of his cock head so intense she bowed against him, her eyes falling shut once more.

A moment of pressure was followed by a twinge as her body stretched to accept his girth. Then he slid deep in one sure thrust that parted her flesh, filling her, and setting off red-gold sparks wherever he touched.

Magic, she thought, and dragged her nails across his shoulders and down along his sides, fingers flexing as he withdrew and thrust again, impossibly deep. She made a low noise at the back of her throat, part purr, part growl, and he groaned in response and thrust again. Her body matched his as they found their tempo, and she was gripped by the sensations, acutely aware of the contrast between his skin and her own, the delicious friction, the heat, and the push-pull of their bodies.

Then he shifted to align their palms and twine their fingers together, and everything got sharper, deeper, more real. She bit her lip to will back the sudden swell of tenderness, and the tears that prickled behind her closed eyelids, not sure whether the move was an automatic one, impelled by the sex magic seeking more of itself, or whether he had formed the link on purpose, seeking that connection with her.

The bond was there, though, stringing her muscles tight and making her arch beneath him and suck in a hot-feeling breath that contained their mingled scents. Her body moved faster beneath his, urging him on, and he growled low in his chest and answered her, setting a tempo that made her feel like they were racing together across the desert.

"Yes. Oh, yes. Gods." She broke the connection, letting it be about the moment and the sex as she gripped his tense forearms where he was braced above her. Her senses turned inward, concentrating on the place where they joined. Her body tightened around his driving hardness, pulsing, not under her control anymore. Pleasure shifted, coiled, and kindled a warm, tingling fire in her belly. "Please!"

He groaned and dropped down to gather her against him, wrapping his arms around her and pressing them together in an embrace that was suddenly far too intimate. He wasn't just inside her anymore; he was holding her, surrounding her, whispering her name in a ragged gasp that brought a surge of tenderness, a sense that yes, this was it. This was what she had been waiting to find.

Panic lit up inside her. Even without the blood-link, it was too much, too huge, too—

"Gods, *Cara!*" He surged against her, shuddering, and the friction of his full-body press brought an ecstasy that swept away her doubts and fears and left her helpless to do anything but join him in the rise and plunge of bodies, the wild abandon of racing together toward the crest.

She tried to keep up with him, but her muscles tensed as her body locked itself in a breathless, tingling moment. She couldn't breathe, couldn't move, couldn't do anything but cry out in a chain of, "Yes, yes, oh, gods, yes!"

And then he slipped a hand between them, touched her where their bodies joined, and her body ignited. Sparks flared and fireworks detonated as he hammered home a few more times. Then he seated himself to the hilt and locked his arms around her in a shuddering, bucking release that set off a series of implosions within her.

The orgasm left her gasping beneath him, her arms and legs wrapped around him, locked there tightly. And then, as it faded, she stayed right there, wanting the moment to last and last. She loved the feeling of him against her—his heavy weight, the heave of his hot breathing, the knowledge that he was just as wiped out as she was.

They had had each other thoroughly, wonderfully. And she wouldn't change a second of it. Not here, not now.

No regrets.

"Gods. That was . . . Hm." He shifted against her, stretching and easing off to one side. "Sorry. Crushing you."

She nuzzled the side of his sweat-slicked neck. "Yeah, but in a good way." But even as she said it, her instincts stirred. That was the kind of thing lovers said to each other, and therein lay danger. This was a onetime thing, a necessary release. Though if that was what it felt like to share sex magic as a mismatched pair, she could see why the magi were all about their destined mates. More, she could see why humans could get hooked on the fireworks and forget about the rest—at least for a while. Not her, though. She had gone into this with her eyes wide-open and full knowledge of what she was doing, and who with, and now it was time to pull back . . . even if part of her was humming an awestruck note.

Yes, she'd had sex with Sven, fulfilling more than a few of her pent-up, overwrought fantasies from long ago. And yes, it had been amazing, more so than even those fantasies—or anything else she'd experienced since then—had led her to hope. Fireworks, hell. That had been nuclear. But it didn't change anything.

And if she told herself that enough times, she might even start believing it.

Easing away from him and playing it as cool as she could manage, she tipped her head toward the sealed-shut cave entrance. "Guess that wasn't what the gods were waiting for, after all."

A flicker of recognition said he'd made the connection too, knowing that the other sacred chamber had required not just a near-death experience but also the sexual consummation that completed the Godkeeper spell. But he shook his head. "That wasn't what this was about, Cara. At all."

Something shifted in her chest, but she didn't let herself acknowledge the part of her that wanted to say, *Then what was it about?* She knew the answer, after all. It was just that silly, eternally seventeen-year-old part of herself that wanted it to be something more. "I know," she said softly, "and believe me, I'm not trying to make a joke out of this. But we don't need to dissect it either. It was ... I can't ... Hell." She blew out a frustrated breath. "Let's just get dressed and find a way out of here." Not meeting his eyes anymore, she reached for her shirt. "We've got bigger problems than—"

She froze at the sight of a stark black glyph on her inner right forearm.

And. Her. Heart. Stopped.

Oh, gods. Oh, no. Oh, gods, no. The litany beat in her blood as horror hammered through her, chased by pain. She must've made some noise, because Sven whipped around and got big, as if ready to defend her from a dozen hellhounds. But there was nothing to fight except the reality of a coyote's-head glyph enclosed in a round-edged square, with the double dot representing "2" above it, to indicate that the wearer was a coyote with a familiar. Or, in this case, the servant to one.

"*Fuck*." He lifted shocked eyes to hers. "I didn't mean . . ." He trailed off, no doubt because there wasn't anything to say.

"It wasn't you. It was the *nahwal*." Because although it was certainly possible that the blood-link or the sex could have reawakened the servant-master bond between them, her gut said it was the *nahwal*'s doing. Sven hadn't wanted her—or anyone—as his servant. His ancestors, though, would want things lined up according to tradition. *Bastards,* she thought, her arm starting to ache.

"You broke it before," he said after a moment. "Maybe you can do it again."

"It took months, and I was sick as a dog." Her voice threatened to crack but she wouldn't let it. If anything, the mark was a necessary reminder that they were still the same people they'd been before. The vision hadn't changed anything, and neither had the sex. Or, rather, something had changed, and not for the better. *Aj winikin,* she thought bitterly. *Son of a bitch*. If that was the *nahwal*'s gift, the creature could damn well have it back. "Screw it," she said, forcing her chin up and her spine straight. "It's just a mark. It can't make me do anything I don't want to do." That was her story, and she was sticking to it. But where she might've been halfway to convincing herself that the sex hadn't changed anything, there was no way she could say the same about this.

"Cara—"

"Don't," she said quickly. She didn't want to talk about it right now. She wanted to be out and moving, wanted to fill her lungs with the fresh night air. The cave walls pressed suddenly in on her, though this time they weren't moving; the claustrophobia came straight from her soul. "Please . . . can we just get out of here?"

He looked at her for a long moment, then nodded and turned away.

They dressed in silence and headed for the stone slab that covered the cave entrance, their boots squishing in the shallow, muddy river that was all that was left of the flash flood. Even though she knew it was the nature of the magic and the chamber, the difference between before and after made it feel like days had passed, rather than just a few hours.

They paused side by side at the entrance, where the stone suddenly seemed very solid, very heavy. Pressing her palm to it and finding it cool and faintly slimy, she glanced over at him. "You can open it, right?"

He copied her move so their hands were side by side, his bigger and more tanned, hers narrow and fine boned, with one thumbnail bitten down. "Yeah," he said. "I can open it."

She didn't ask how he could be sure, or why his magic would work now when it hadn't before. Instead, new nerves kindled as her mind skipped ahead to what they might find on the other side. What had Zane and Lora done after leaving the cave? She didn't think they would have hurt any of the *winikin*—not when they meant to lead them instead—and she didn't think they *could* hurt the magi. But that was about the only thing she thought Zane incapable of at this point.

Letting out a slow, steadying breath, she nodded. "Okay, then. Let's do this. Open sesame."

He hesitated, though, and the pause drew out long enough that she glanced over. His face was drawn, his eyes fixed on the stone slab like he was X-raying his way through it and not liking what he saw.

Tension coiled within her. "Is there a problem out there?"

"There's a problem, but it's not out there. It's in here. . . . With us." He brought his other hand up, so he was pressing both palms on the stone slab, as if to shove it out of the way. Instead, he let his head rest for a moment between his outstretched arms.

Us . . . The word tugged at her, as did the strain in his big, lean body, which let her know that as an honorable man—and he was that, in his own way—he was having trouble with the idea of her as a one-cave stand. "Don't do this," she said softly. "There's no 'us.' I'm taking the mark out with me, but the rest of it stays here. It has to."

He raised his head and pinned her with stormy eyes that held a yearning heat that set off warning bells even as part of her leaped with excitement. "What if I don't want it to stay here?" he asked softly.

Her heart stutter-stepped and the breath went thin in her lungs. She told herself to shut him down, walk away, do something—anything—to keep him from making this more complicated than it already was. Instead, knowing she was teetering on the verge of a huge mistake, she said, "What *do* you want?"

There was a pause, and the moment hung in the balance. *He won't say it,* she told herself. *He means it another way.* Because there was no way in hell he was going to say—

"You, Cara." His expression was stark, his hands braced against the stone as if it were the only thing holding him in place. "I want you. I want to know that what we just had wasn't just a onetime thing. I want to be with you for real . . . and I have for a very long time."

She tried to find a rational, logical response. All she could come up with was: "Bullshit."

One corner of his mouth twitched. "It started that last summer, even before we kissed. It wasn't so bad when I stayed on the move, but when we wound up stuck here together at Skywatch, I couldn't outrun it anymore. I had to send you away. And then when you came back . . . Shit. It hit me like a godsdamned sledgehammer seeing you get out of that Hummer, all slick and dangerous, like a badass version of the girl I used to know. But at the same time you're still you—you're tough, brave, re- sourceful, and you've got the biggest heart of anyone I've ever met. I want that. I want you, Cara." He kept his hands jammed against the stone slab as if afraid that if he moved he would reach for her, and he wasn't sure what her reaction would be.

She wasn't sure either. What was she supposed to think? To say? She couldn't breathe, couldn't string two words together, couldn't do anything but stare at him. "Then why . . ." she began, then faltered. But although the question went unfinished, it vibrated in the air be- tween them, just as sex magic had an hour before. *Why didn't you say something? Why weren't you ever around?*

"Your father warned me off."

"My . . ." She couldn't keep going. The oxygen had suddenly been sucked from her lungs, and not because she didn't believe him, but because she did. She could practically see it, could all but write the script.

Carlos never would've allowed anything to happen between her and Sven—a *winikin* and a mage. And not just because of tradition, but because she'd never measured up.

Sven lowered his arms and turned to lean against the stone. He let his head fall back against the solid slab and looked up, though she didn't know if he was seeing the animals or memories. "That was why I was all hell-bent on riding out without talking to you or your mom that day. He said he'd seen the direction I was looking, and told me to stay the hell away, that you were just a teenager and it was up to me to be the grown-up."

And that too had the ring of truth, though she suspected there had been more to it than that. The breath whistled in her lungs as she tried to wrap her brain around this new information, tried to slot it into what she knew, or thought she'd known. Not about her father—she'd long ago stopped trying to fix things there—but about Sven. She'd spent big chunks of the past few years telling herself not to dwell on ancient history, but now it was there in her head, replaying that summer in such detail that she knew she hadn't forgotten the past, after all. Now, though, the memories shifted and shivered, trying to realign themselves.

"That's why you didn't come back to visit after that summer?" she asked in a voice that didn't sound much like her own.

He hesitated. "I wish I could say that was the only reason."

Disappointment kicked, warning her that a small, stupid spark of hope had kindled inside her. *Don't go there,* she chided, even though it was already too late. But at the same time it was ridiculous to think even for a second that she'd been the reason for his wandering. She might have been a catalyst, but ranging free was bred into him, bone and soul.

"I haven't been a teenager for a long time." It came out sounding far more choked up than she wanted to admit to being. "Why didn't you tell me?"

"Carlos is still your father. Even before I knew that he'd saved my life the night of the massacre, I knew I owed him for keeping me and raising me like he did. He'd never really asked me for anything before that day, so I did my damnedest to give it to him all those years, not realizing that it wasn't just about you being his daughter; it was about me being a mage."

"And me a *winikin*." But it was more a question than a statement, because that had never seemed to bother Sven. If anything, he'd been the first one to ignore the traditions when it came to class and status at Skywatch.

He shook his head. "No, never. When we first got here, I kept things to myself because I was trying to cope with the what-the-fuck shock of becoming a Nightkeeper and dealing with the magic and everything that comes with it." He paused. "And let's face it . . . you hated it here."

"I . . . Yeah." Even now, her chest tightened when she thought back to those months. She had bitterly resented being indentured without permission, and to the one person who could pull strong emotions out of her without even trying—or seeming to notice. Except he *had* noticed . . . and he'd sent her away.

"Then, when you came back, there was no way in hell I could say anything. Jox was right when he chose you to lead the *winikin,* and I knew I couldn't fuck with that." He shifted, looked at her with eyes that reached inside her and kindled sparks of desire amid the confusion. His voice roughened as he said, "I wanted to, though. Seeing you, being around you . . . Gods. So I took off. But I couldn't get you out of my head. And when I got back here and saw you again . . . everything was suddenly right in the world, because I could talk to you, tell you some of what I had figured out. I couldn't tell you how I really felt, though, because things were still so unsettled with the *winikin*."

"But—" She had to break off and swallow past the huge lump in her throat. "None of that has changed. If anything, it's going to get worse."

The corners of his mouth turned up in rueful acknowledgment, though his eyes stayed very serious. "You're not kidding."

"Then why . . ." In the end, she could only get out, "Why now?" She was floundering in emotional waters that were way over her head.

His expression softened, going almost sad. "It's because of what you said about regrets . . . and what you did about it."

"What, you mean jumping your bones?" The words came out fast and brittle.

"Don't." He reached toward her but stopped short of making contact. "The humor-as-defense thing doesn't work on me. I've had way more practice at it. Besides, I'm not just talking about the sex, though that was fantastic. I'm talking about not letting moments get away from us." He paused, looking over at the cave paintings. "You're right, you know. We may not have all that many moments left, and we owe it to the gods to use the ones we're given to the fullest, and live without regrets."

"That's not exactly what I said." Her voice didn't quite tremble, but it sure as hell wanted to, because suddenly this all felt very real and important.

A corner of his mouth kicked up, then flattened again. "Okay, so I'm interpreting a little. But here's the thing. I don't want to go into the last three months of the countdown without you knowing that I have feelings for you that go way beyond what happened here today. And maybe us having a chance to see what could happen between us for real." He paused, his expression caught somewhere between wary and expectant.

If he had kissed her then, she thought she would've gone up in flames, thrown herself at him, and agreed to damn near anything. He didn't so much as lean toward her, though, leaving it her decision. She nearly cursed him for it.

"I . . ." She swallowed and tried again. "I don't think . . . *Damn it.*" She rubbed both hands across her face, trying to get herself centered enough to have a conversation, or even a logical thought process. But that wasn't easy when one part of her was busy singing a happy chorus of hormones, while another part was sending up warning buzzers. As she lowered her hands, though, her eyes were caught by the new mark on her forearm.

Gods. How was she supposed to deal with all that had happened in such a short time? Zane, Lora, Sven, the cave, the mark . . . it was all suddenly too much. Panic had her heart racing and sweat chilling her forehead; claustrophobia had her stomach knotting so tightly it hurt. "I can't do this right now." Her voice broke on the words. "I need some time, some space." The last was nearly a whimper.

"Are you okay?" His face instantly falling into concerned lines, he reached for her.

She edged back, out of reach. "Yes. No. I need to get out of here."

"You . . . Oh, right." His disappointment was evident, but so was his understanding. He of all people would get what it meant to feel trapped and unable to deal, needing to run free.

Without another word, he nodded, palmed his knife, and called his magic with a few murmured words.

She didn't feel anything this time, but there was a low rumbling sound and the stone slab began to move. Relief slashed through her, followed by a sharp twist of grief. She didn't let herself dwell on either, though, as the doorway cracked open.

From outside, Mac gave a joyous bark. A burst of radio static erupted from Sven's armband, followed by Dez's voice, a low growl of, "Tell me that's you, Sven, and that you've got Cara and you're both okay."

"It's us," she called. "We're fine. I'm coming out." Without waiting for Sven, she surged through the widening crack and back out into open air and into a whole new reality, with no idea of how she was going to deal with the changes . . . or what tomorrow was going to look like.

CHAPTER FOURTEEN

Skywatch

"Hang back here for a minute," Sven said in an under-tone, waving Cara into the shadows of the cacao grove beyond the *winikin*'s hall, where the celebration was still going strong even though it was nearly two in the morning. "I'll check things out and give you the all-clear."

In the starlight he could just see her spine stiffen and her head come up, but he couldn't see her expression, and vice versa. Which was probably for the best.

After the briefest hesitation, she nodded. "Roger."

The two syllables were about all she'd said directly to him since they left the cave and reunited with Mac and a dozen very worried teammates. And for the thousandth time since then, Sven wished he'd kept his damn mouth shut.

In the middle of the cave, the magic, and the aftermath of the kind of sex that was guaranteed to make a guy say too much, too soon—telling her had seemed like the right thing to do. Hell, it'd seemed like the only thing he could do, because deep down inside, he'd known that if he didn't tell her then, he might not ever do it.

That probably would've been better, though. It'd been bad enough when he had been the only one running from his feelings. He was an old pro at it, after all. For him to add that onto her plate now . . . Shit, bad timing.

So much for the whole "no regrets" thing. He didn't regret the sex—that would be like saying, "No, thanks," to breathing, especially when it had been just the one time, no harm, no foul—but he badly regretted bringing the other stuff into it. Because what was he offering her, really? He was the same guy he'd always been, and that guy wasn't good for anything more than a short-term fling. Dozens of women could attest to that, and Cara knew him better than all of them put together.

Go? Stay? The thought-glyphs appeared in his mind at the same time a warm, furry body pressed against his leg, almost hard enough to knock him off balance, in the canine version of, *Get your shit together and let's do this*.

"Stay," he told Mac. "Protect." Actually, he would've liked to have the coyote with him for the recon, but he had a feeling it'd take some doing to peel his familiar away from Cara. He wasn't sure how much Mac understood about what had happened, but the coyote had been practically glued to her since they got out of the cave, bristling when anyone so much as got too close to her.

Then again, so was Sven.

He had managed to hold his frustration in check through their debriefing on the *winikin*'s treason, the coyote cave, his and Cara's shared vision, and the *nahwal*'s message. He hadn't let on to the others that anything sexual had happened between them, hadn't even let himself look too long at her, trying to figure out what she was thinking. Instead, he'd done his damnedest to focus on helping come up with a plan to deal with the traitors.

In the end, it had circled back around to the two of them anyway: Cara needed to be in on their arrest for the obvious reasons; Dez had wanted only one mage involved, so the *winikin* wouldn't feel like they'd been ganged up on; and Sven had volunteered with enough of a back-off glare to keep the others from chiming in.

Yeah, they could both probably use some distance, but he'd be damned if he took it at her expense this time. Besides, he wanted to get his hands on Zane.

Moving quietly, he crossed the packed-dirt open space between the grove and the training hall, then eased up the stairs for the second time that night, which brought a flash of disbelief at how much had changed in . . . what, six hours? Less? Christ, that was a mind-fuck.

The porch was deserted, the noise level muted compared to what it had been before, and when Sven eased to a window and took a look inside, he was unsurprised to find that there were only twenty or so *winikin* left. Those twenty were the hard cores, though: hard-core drinkers, hard-core rebels. And they were sitting at a central table, riveted to whatever Zane was saying.

The bastard's body language was animated, but his eyes were cool and hard, like part of him was standing back and watching his own performance, weighing it. Was he trashing Cara's leadership style and making a full-on argument for his own, or was he manipulating things more subtly, pointing out flaws in a seemingly positive way and trusting the others to reach the conclusion he wanted? Or, hell, maybe he was singing her praises, planning to play the bereaved suitor and friend when her body was discovered, and only then letting the others convince him to take command.

Lora was there too, sitting on the other side of the table, looking as rapt as the rest of them. Cara said she'd acted like she'd been brainwashed, as if Zane had found a way to give her the certainty and security she craved, albeit his own twisted version of them. As far as Sven was concerned, though, a weak character was no excuse for attempted murder.

Fuckers. Anger burned his veins at seeing them there, acting like it was nothing to have left Cara tied up in a flooding cave. If he hadn't gone looking for her, or Mac hadn't been able to track her . . . *Shit.* Forget Dez's plan to question them; he should just fireball their asses where they sat.

Instead, he waved for Cara and Mac to break cover, and did his damnedest to harness some of the rage that snarled and snapped inside him. Because the plan wasn't just to bring the traitors to justice; it was to keep Nightkeeper-*winikin* relations intact while doing it.

When Cara got up close beside him at the door, he said in an undertone, "They're all at a central table. I'll go in first; you stay behind me in case he panics and starts shooting."

In the yellow illumination coming from the porch light, there was no mistaking the stubborn *I'm in charge here* set to her jaw. "That'll make it look like I'm hiding. Nope, I'm going in first. You'll just have to move fast if he threatens me." She pinned him with a look, then lifted the sawed-off double-barreled shotgun she held across her body. "And remember, I've got this and you've got cuffs. Only use magic as a last resort."

"Yeah, I got that part." He didn't like it, but he got it. A few days ago, the idea of a Nightkeeper blasting away at a bunch of *winikin* would've seemed ludicrous. Now it was far too easy to imagine, along with the political shit-storm it would create. "I'll do my best." He wasn't promising any more than that. But he also wasn't going to argue with her about going first, because she had a point. He needed to look like backup, not heavy artillery. So he eased open the door, which led to an entryway that would let them stay concealed for the first ten or fifteen feet. "After you." His voice softened. "And, Cara?"

Her eyes went wary, then slid away from his. "Let's just focus on the job, okay?"

"I was just going to say that I'll be right behind you."

"Oh." Faint color touched her cheeks. "Thanks." Then, without another word, she slipped through the door.

And as Sven followed with Mac at his heels, he put the other stuff out of his mind—or tried to—and brought up his magic to a background buzz, ready to defend or attack at a moment's notice. Because right now, it didn't matter what had happened between them or where they were going to go from here. All that mattered was not letting Zane and Lora hurt her again . . . and paying them back for their betrayal.

Cara's heartbeat thudded unevenly as she crossed the short antechamber leading to the main hall. The adrenaline pumping through her body didn't come entirely from anticipation of the coming showdown, but she couldn't dwell on what was happening between her and Sven.

She had to focus on the here-and-now, and do her best to get through this confrontation—hell, call it what it was: an arrest—while keeping the rest of the *winikin* as intact as she could. Dez, the Nightkeepers, and, hell, the war effort and therefore the whole freaking earthly plane were counting on her to not let her people decompress.

The knowledge had her pausing just shy of the doorway and taking a deep breath that whistled in her lungs.

She heard Zane's voice coming from the room beyond, though she couldn't make out what he was saying over the belligerent staccato of U2's *Rattle and Hum*. It sounded like he was joking, but his tone carried an edge that raised the hair on the back of her neck and made her feel suddenly trapped, drowning. Claustrophobia pressed in on her without warning, but she dug her fingernails into her palms and shoved it away, pissed that she'd given him that much power over her, even for a few seconds.

The anger cleared her head and unlocked her feet, though, and before she was aware of even having made the decision, she was through the door and beelining for her betrayer.

Zane's back was toward her, like he'd been trying to prove that he didn't need to watch the door, and Lora was staring so raptly at him that she didn't notice Cara's entrance. The others, though, caught sight of her immediately. She knew their names, knew their stories, but in that moment she didn't see them as individuals; she saw a potential stampede. And as a rancher's daughter, she knew she needed to deal with that or risk getting flattened.

Their party-reddened eyes went from her to Sven, and their expressions fired at his invasion of their turf. Some shouted; others surged to their feet and sent chairs flying.

Cara bellowed, "Freeze!" and fired the sawed-off from her hip, making her own ears ring and aiming way over their heads, going for shock value rather than bloodshed.

It worked. They froze. All except for Zane, who whipped around. For a second, there wasn't even a spark of recognition in his face, as if he'd already wiped her from his memory banks. Then he got it, and blankness turned to astonishment and dawning horror.

"That's right." Cara leveled the sawed-off at the center of his chest. "I got out of the cave. Guess you should've killed me yourself after all, huh?" She was watching the faces of the others, and was relieved to see the anger and disgust that had been aimed at Sven and Mac now shift to confusion.

Zane sagged back against the table hard enough to make it grate a few inches across the floor. "That's impossible. The gods led me there. They told me they would take you in exchange —"

"They didn't tell you shit," she said flatly. "You came up with all of it on your own so you'd have an excuse to take over the *winikin*. You and Lora both."

As if that had been her cue, the woman in question gave a low, broken moan, then turned dead white as Mac came around and stood right by her with his teeth bared and his ruff bristling. A few of the others shifted uncertainly, but their glares were aimed at Zane and Lora, not the coyote or his master.

Cara, though, was very aware of Sven standing right behind and to the right of her, letting her handle things even though he probably wanted to tear Zane apart. She didn't let herself think that it was very like what her younger, more idealistic self had imagined, with Sven as her destined mate and protector, and the two of them fighting to save mankind.

The reality was at once very close to that, and yet so very far away.

Zane's eyes darted around the room, to her, to Sven, and then back to her. "Lies." He hissed the word, then glanced back at the others. "What did I tell you? She wants to get me out of the way and bring her master on board as the leader of the *winikin*. It'll be just like before the massacre—we'll be no better than a drafted army. Cannon fucking fodder commanded by leaders who hide behind invisible shields."

And even though only seconds earlier he'd all but admitted to attempted murder, a couple of the *winikin* looked at each other, then at her. She felt Sven square himself, and knew she had to defuse this, and fast.

Exhaling softly, she addressed the others, members of a herd that was suddenly thinking of stampeding again. "Zane lured me to the training grounds, knocked me out, and carried me to a cave miles outside the compound— one that he's never told any of us about, even though it could be a valuable asset. There, he and Lora bound me to an altar and left me to die in the floodwaters." She paused, not letting the memories come. They crowded close, though, choking her slightly as she said, "I would have died if Sven and Mac hadn't come after me. They saved my life." She paused for a beat. "But that doesn't make him my master. My allegiance is to the *winikin*."

"Then what's with the ink?" Zane nodded to her wrist. "That's not just the coyote's mark. It's *his* mark . . . and you weren't wearing it when you went into the cave."

She didn't give him the satisfaction of seeing her look down to where her sleeve had ridden up. "I didn't go in there voluntarily . . . And you said it yourself—the cave has coyote magic."

He sneered. "So does the coyote mage." To the others, he said, "You'll see. She'll bring him in on decisions, bit by bit, until one day we'll wake up and he's in charge. Meanwhile, she'll be spreading her legs and giving up whatever he wants—"

There was a blur of movement, a crack of fist on bone, and Zane flew back onto the table with his arms outstretched.

Cara gaped as Sven bent over him, fist drawn back for another blow. "Keep talking," he warned in a low growl that Mac echoed from the other side of the table. "I dare you."

Zane grinned to reveal teeth that were rimmed red with blood. "Go lick your own balls."

"Insult me all you want," Sven grated. "But not her, not like that." His eyes raked the others. "And it doesn't have a godsdamned thing to do with politics."

The *winikin* didn't react to that, but they also didn't come to Zane's defense. They just watched, stony eyed and rapidly sobering, as Sven dragged the other man up off the table and fished the cuffs from his pocket. As he started securing Zane's wrists, he said down low, "If it was up to me, you'd be headed straight to Xibalba, do not pass go or collect dick. But the king wants Rabbit to ask you both a few questions, so—"

"No!" Lora exploded from her chair and lunged toward them. Mac yelped and grabbed for her with a flash of sharp teeth, but he missed as she came over the table and flung herself on Sven. He reeled back as she raked at him while screaming curses in a thin, high voice.

Jerked off balance when Sven dragged at the half-attached cuffs, Zane stumbled and went down to his knees, but when he came up, he had a cuff dangling off one wrist and was holding the .22 he kept in an ankle holster. He aimed at the back of Sven's head and thumbed the safety.

"Gun!" Reacting instinctively, Cara swung the sawed-off as hard as she could. She hit Zane's hand and the small pistol went flying, but her grip slipped on the follow-through and the shotgun went off with a roar.

And all hell broke loose.

CHAPTER FIFTEEN

As the shotgun blast echoed against the background music, one of the *winikin* shouted and went down, writhing. There was a frozen moment of shock—Cara's, theirs—and then the others broke and, shouting in drunken fury, hurled themselves into the fight.

She screamed and stumbled back under the onrush, but tripped on something furry and went down. Mac yelped and skittered out from underneath her, then reoriented on her attackers and lunged with a deep-throated snarl. The coyote slammed into the closest—Sebastian, who was reaching for her with blazing eyes. The *winikin* staggered and shouted in pain as Mac locked onto his forearm with grim intent. Cara scrambled to her feet and fumbled with the shotgun, hands shaking as she tried to get two more slugs loaded. She dropped one, got the other one in, and brought up the weapon to—

"Freeze!" This time it was Sven's voice shouting the command, and there was a punch of magic behind it.

The sleep spell took hold instantly, dropping all of the *winikin* except Cara. Their bodies went limp and they fell, some hitting the floor directly, others bouncing off tables or one another on the way down, so the music—it was the Battlefield Band now—gained a bass line of meaty thuds and scraping furniture, along with Mac's surprised snarl as he tore free from Sebastian and darted out of range of the tree-trunk fall of his body, which was the last to land with a heavy *thunk*.

And abracadabra, the fight was over.

Or rather, Cara saw with dawning horror, this particular fight was over and a new one was just about to get started. Because this was a *winikin* catastrophe of epic proportions.

"Oh . . . shit." Blood speckled the floor and cloyed the air, and the fallen bodies were strewn like the losers of a battle. But she was the real loser here.

She had shot Breece in the leg. Mac had mauled Sebastian's arm.

And Sven had magicked the whole bunch of them.

There hadn't been a case of magic being used against a true *winikin* since Scarred Jaguar press-ganged the prior generation into the Solstice Massacre. This wasn't on that scale, granted, but the timing sucked.

Back on his feet now, standing among the fallen with Mac at his side, Sven glared down at Zane. His fists were clenched, his body tight, and when the music swelled in the background, he flicked a hand and killed the stereo from across the room.

The silence echoed louder than if he'd shouted something over the music. More, it made her viscerally aware of his power and shifted something inside her, setting aside her dread for a precious moment and forging a tight pressure in her chest. One that felt like . . . awe.

He could drop twenty men with a single word and

silence music with a gesture. He could throw fire, cast an invisible force field, telepathically communicate with a hybrid coyote, and move things with his mind.... How had all that gotten commonplace in her head?

It was impossible. Amazing. Incredible.

She had grown up dreaming of being part of the Nightkeepers, and while she might not be a mage herself, she was allied to one, connected to one. And, for an hour earlier that day, she had been his lover.

Letting out a soft breath, she tried not to shiver as the sudden heat rushing through her clashed with the cooler air and raised goose bumps on her arms.

He glanced over, eyes dark. "Damn it, Cara, I—"

His armband pinged and Dez's voice grated, "We heard shots. You've got ten seconds before we come in."

Sven tapped the transmit button. "We've got everything under control now, but a couple of *winikin* are going to need to see Sasha." With a magical talent for healing and manipulating life energy, she was the Nightkeepers' answer to first aid.

"Ah, fuck me. How bad are the injuries?"

"Superficial, but they're going to be pissed when they wake up. I, uh, had to knock out the whole lot of them."

"Damn it."

"It couldn't be avoided. There was a situation."

"There always is," Dez said, sounding suddenly very tired. "Okay, we're coming in."

The next few minutes were organized chaos as the Nightkeepers poured into the training hall, looking remarkably unfazed by the scattered bodies.

Then again, they probably were unfazed, Cara thought, mind whirling on the strange, shivery currents that were suddenly racing through her body.

Dez muttered a curse, but it didn't seem to be directed at anyone in particular, and he looked more resigned than angry as he said, "Give me the four-one-one." Voice flat and careful, Sven made his report. When he was finished, Dez just shook his head. "Yeah. That didn't go down the way I had hoped." His eyes flicked to Cara. "You okay?"

She swallowed, then said, "I'm not hurt. As for repercussions . . . well, the fallout is going to start the moment these guys wake up."

"Which we're going to leave until morning," Dez decided. "If we're lucky, they'll think they blacked out." His eyes went to the two injured *winikin,* who were being field-patched for the ride back to the mansion. "Okay. Maybe not."

Turning on his heel, he rapped out a string of orders to the assembled team: Zane and Lora were consigned to two of the mansion's basement storerooms, which doubled as cells, the wounded were turfed to Sasha, and the others were dispersed to their beds to sleep it off. Things shifted into high gear for a few minutes, and then, with a pop of displaced air as Strike 'ported them back to the main house, the last of the group disappeared, leaving Cara and Sven standing alone in the training hall, amid what looked like the aftermath of a decent bar fight: one tipped-over table, a little blood, and a lot of knocked-over chairs.

She stared at the place where Zane had been lying, and the only thing she could think through the spinning in her head was that there should've been more actual damage. Some rearranged furniture wasn't nearly enough. "Tell me that didn't just happen," she said hollowly. "Tell me I'm still dreaming."

She knew she wasn't, though. She hadn't dreamed the cave, the crazy-hot sex, or his confession, and she hadn't dreamed this.

He moved to her side and gripped her shoulder. "Hey. It's going to be okay. We'll deal with it."

"We," she echoed, finding that the word jarred.

"Sure." He squeezed and let go, moving a few feet away to flick a few chairs back upright—one with his foot, several more with his magic.

As before, the show of power stirred her juices. This time, though, there was also a jangling discord, a sizzle of warning. And as he put the table back into place with a gesture, the heat drained away, leaving behind a gruesome realization.

He wasn't hers to desire, and they weren't part of a "we." She wasn't a member of the Nightkeepers' team, not really. She was supposed to be the *winikin*'s advocate . . . Yet she had fallen entirely under Sven's spell, and hadn't even noticed the change. Worse, when the time had come for her to get her justice against Zane and Lora she had hung back while Dez and Sven made their plan. Just like a good little servant.

Nausea pressed, forcing her to swallow hard.

How had it happened so fast? How had she not noticed? And how in the hell was she going to break the spell?

Pushing back her sleeve with a shaking hand, she stared at the coyote's mark. "Is this what you want?" she asked, aiming the question at the gods, but a little bit at him too.

"What—" Sven began, but she cut him off.

"This shouldn't have happened." In hindsight there was almost no way the plan could've worked the way Dez had painted it. Even if they had managed to get Zane and Lora subdued without resorting to magic, there was no way a group of drunken, revved-up rebels would've let them walk out of there unchallenged. "We should've waited until they were back in their rooms and done it quietly."

But what was twenty-twenty clear to her now hadn't been before.

When Dez had proposed the plan, she'd nodded along, imagining the look on Zane's face when she swaggered through the door with Sven right behind her. She didn't know whether the urge had come from those long-ago superhero fantasies of hers, from some inherent ability of the bloodline mark to make her accede to the Nightkeepers' king, from a deep-down urge to stay near Sven and try to figure out whether he really meant what he'd said back in the cave, or all of the above, and then some. All she knew was that she hadn't been thinking about what was best for the *winikin*. Far from it.

"What happened here was stupid grandstanding," she said bitterly, furious with herself for not seeing it at the time. "Dez wanted to show that the Nightkeepers are so powerful that a single unmated mage can control a whole room of *winikin*. He wants us to be able to rule ourselves . . . but only as long as we remember that he's allowing us to." It wasn't the first time she'd had the thought, but this was the clearest evidence to date. She shook her head. "I should have refused to be a part of this plan. More, I should've stopped it."

"Why didn't you?" Sven's voice came from nearer than she'd thought him, and she glanced up to find him standing close enough to touch her, though he didn't. Instead, he held her eyes with an intensity that urged her to confide in him, to trust him.

She could do that, she knew. But only to a point.

"I think I got caught up in the idea of the two of us working together as a team, just like in the stories." She hesitated, heart suddenly thudding, even though she knew what the outcome had to be. "I used to pretend we were gods-destined mates."

And there it was. The impossible.

His hands moved as if to reach for her, but he restrained himself. "Then you have feelings too."

"Had," she corrected, then sighed. "Maybe 'have' too. Who knows? It's all so screwed up." Strangely, the knots in her stomach smoothed out when she admitted it. If anyone had told her that morning that she'd be talking to Sven this way, she would've laughed them out of her suite and then taken her own temperature to make sure she wasn't delirious. "It doesn't matter, though. Not really."

"It could," he said carefully. And the fact that his eyes slid away from hers let her know that it did matter, very much, to him. "We might be able to find a way."

Her stupid heart picked up a beat, but she shook her head. "I can't risk it. Zane was right when he said that I can't be connected to you—not as your servant and sure as hell not as your lover—and still be a hundred percent committed to the *winikin*." She cut him a sharp look. "How can you even ask me to try? Doesn't that go against your oath?"

"The gods outrank the king."

A shiver tried to crawl down her spine. "Why is that relevant?" She lifted her arm, turning her mark to face him. "Because of this?"

"Because of that. Because of the way the vision played out . . . and because maybe Zane wasn't wrong about what the gods were telling him to do, just about what it meant." He paused. "What if everything's happened the way it was meant to? Or, failing that, what if the gods have fixed things so we're back where we were supposed to be all along?"

"The gods don't acknowledge the *winikin*," she said through lips gone suddenly numb. "They only talk to the Nightkeepers."

"Says who? It's not in the writs, same as the part about the *winikin* not being able to do magic." He leaned in. "Think about it. Scarred-Jaguar proved that he would do anything, say anything to keep control of the *winikin*. What if he—or another king like him—started those rumors?"

"That's . . ." *Impossible,* she wanted to say, but the word got stuck in her throat, because it suddenly didn't seem so far-fetched after all.

"The *nahwal* talked to you, not me," he pressed. "And its message was about the First Father's resurrection. The First Father made the *winikin,* Cara. Who better to remake them, bigger and better and able to fight the war?"

A shudder took hold, making her nerves jangle. "How long have you been thinking about this?"

"About wanting you? Years. About the gods being involved in it? It's just now lining up for me." He tapped his forearm, right atop the warrior's mark.

That particular magical talent allowed the warrior-magi to subsume their emotions during battle and gave them increased reflexes and strategic thought. It was that strategy-making at work now, apparently, but to what end? Was he truly trying to make sense of things, or was he finding the path of least resistance? Gods knew that had been his style growing up. "You're looking for reasons to do what you want. Newsflash for you: 'The gods made me do it' hasn't worked as an excuse since the massacre." But even to her own ears, she didn't sound sure.

"I rarely need an excuse to do what I want." And with that scant warning, he closed the distance between them, caught her against his body, and came in for a kiss.

She could have backed away or held him off, probably should have. Instead she stayed put as he cupped a hand beneath her chin, tipped her face up, and fused his mouth to hers.

Sparks caught, turned to flames. And just that quickly, the heat was back inside her, surrounding her, sweeping her up, and bringing an inner whisper of, *Thank the gods.* She didn't want to have to think right now, didn't want to try to interpret the signs or the gods' intentions—if the magi hadn't managed it in nearly four years of trying, why would she have any better luck?

No, she wanted to sink into the kiss and dig her fingertips into the lean muscles of his upper arms as their tongues touched. And as his arms went around her and he lifted to his full height, so her feet left the floor and their bodies were plastered together every inch of the way, she wanted to wrap her legs around his waist and purr into his mouth, wanted to strip him naked, lick him until she discovered which spots made him squirm, which ones made him groan.

But she had to think, had to figure out for herself what came next. Because if she screwed up now, the ripples could affect both the *winikin* and the magi, and from there the war. The knowledge weighed on her, overcoming even the tingle of energy that had gathered beneath her coyote mark and the burn of red-gold sparkles that teased at her senses, hinting at the magic she had experienced back in the cave.

She burned for him, ached to have him pounding inside her with no thought of today or tomorrow, only the now that they made together. Instead, she eased from the kiss and pulled away, levering her forearms against the flat planes of his chest until he lowered her to her feet once more.

He didn't let go of her, though. "Tell me you feel it." His eyes were dark, his voice an aroused rasp.

She told herself to lie, but nodded anyway, mouth drying to dust by thc hcat that seemed to spin from her body to his and then back again.

"This kind of chemistry isn't something you find every day," he said. "It doesn't just happen. It means something."

Which, if true, meant that her search for future fireworks might be a long one. Trying not to let that possibility—and the twinge of dismay that came from thoughts of moving on—bog her down, she said, "Maybe, maybe not. But guess what? The gods aren't my masters any more than you are." Somehow, that didn't twinge nearly so hard, which couldn't be a good sign.

"Christ, Cara." He glanced at the sky as if expecting a bolt of lightning, which might have been funny if it hadn't made her chest ache.

"Wrong religion." She took a deep breath and pressed a hand to her stomach, where a sudden churning suggested she wasn't as comfortable with heresy as she'd first thought.

The *winikin* might not get messages from the gods, but they prayed to them all the same. And it wasn't like these were mythical figures; they were real. Three months ago, when several smaller members of the *Banol Kax* had broken through the barrier and attacked the Nightkeepers' summer solstice ritual, she had watched in awe as Strike, Leah, Alexis, and Sasha had summoned the gods they were bound to. The plumed serpent Kulkulkan, the firebird Kinich Ahau, and the rainbow goddess Ixchel had combined forces to drive the demons back to Xibalba. Then, as the solstice waned, they had returned to the sky in trailing comets of light and color.

It had been beautiful. Moving. And scary as shit, because it had driven home to Cara just how far off she was from the reality she'd grown up with, and just how dangerous this new reality was going to get over the next bunch of months.

The gods were real, they were part of the war, and the Nightkeepers were their servants on earth. That was powerful stuff. But at the same time, it just wasn't in her to follow blindly.

"Maybe you're right," she said after a moment. "Maybe we're part of some big cosmic plan, and maybe the gods are trying to team us up. But if the Nightkeepers have proved anything over the past four years, it's that we've all got free will even in the face of a full-on prophecy . . . And this isn't anywhere close to being a full-on anything."

Her skin cooled where it had been heated by the warm press of his body, but inwardly the heat remained. If anything it ramped up when sparks kindled in his eyes and he leaned closer to say, "It is for me."

"Stop it." She slapped a palm on his chest and shoved. It was like trying to push over a building, but he obliged by backing up a step. "Just . . . stop playing me, Sven. I need to think this through."

His expression tightened. "This isn't a game."

"Isn't it?" Suddenly she saw part of what had made the warning bells go off inside her from the very beginning of his confession, though she'd been too wrapped up in other things to see it clearly until now. "What do you want to have happen here?"

He took another step back, this time without the shove. "What do you mean?"

"Spell it out for me. And be specific." Part of her quailed at the idea that she was talking to a mage—to Sven—like this. But another part ached at the hint of *what the hell?* in his expression. Because with him, "What the hell?" was almost always followed by, "I'm outta here."

But his lips firmed and he moved back into her space. Took her hand. And said softly, "I want you, Cara. I want us to be lovers, teammates." He didn't quite say "mates," but it was more or less implied.

More or less. "How?" she asked, and the single word echoed in the silence.

"What do you mean?" It was the second time he'd said it, making her wonder whether that was his fallback, his way of making the other person do most of the work when the conversational going got tough.

"When I was ten, I wanted a pet dolphin, but I couldn't make the logistics work. The way I see it, finding a way for the two of us to be together without totally screwing up the balance of power here wouldn't be any easier than keeping a bottlenose on a Montana cattle ranch. So what's the plan? Should we go to Dez and get his take on it? Just stand up in the middle of dinner and announce that we're a couple and everyone else has to deal? Sneak around and hope that nobody figures it out? What?"

His eyes slid away from hers. "The gods—"

"I'm not asking the gods. I'm asking you."

Mac whined low in his throat, looking between the two of them with an anxious doggy expression. Cara knew exactly how he felt, but she couldn't back down now. Maybe she would have a few years back, but not anymore. Not when she was responsible for a broken army that badly needed to be mended.

"What do you want from me?" The question was low, sounded almost dragged out of him. Yet he was still trying to turn it back on her. She didn't think he knew he was doing it, really. It was just the way he was wired.

Like a coyote, she thought with an edge of bitterness that hurt to feel. "I don't think there's any way we could keep an affair casual, not under the circumstances. So I want to know exactly how much I would be risking, what I'd be giving up if I decided to be with you the way you want. And I want to know what you'd be giving up in return."

His head came up; his eyes narrowed. "What do you mean?"

And there it was: not just the third repetition of his favorite question, but the shock and *oh, hell, no* expression of a golden boy who had gotten what he wanted all along, too often without any cost. Well, not this time.

"If you want to be with me, then you're with me, no holds barred."

He nodded cautiously. "I don't want anyone else. I haven't in a long time."

Part of her took those words deep inside, held them close. "That matters, Sven. It does. Truly. But it's not what I'm talking about." She paused and took a deep breath, knowing they were on the tipping point. "I need to know that if we start this and I take the hit with the *winikin,* that you're not going to take off and leave me to clean up the mess."

He exhaled like she'd gut-punched him. "You want me to promise to stay."

"In blood. With witnesses."

White edged the rims of his eyes, though his face had otherwise gone to the neutral, reserved expression he wore in battle. Another fallback. "I don't . . . I think . . . Shit. Can't we just keep things casual?"

Her heart cracked and bled a little, though she had known what his answer would be. He might be unreliable in some ways, but she trusted many other things about him, including his honesty. Granted, he'd been known to lie to himself, but that wasn't the problem here. He knew what she was asking . . . and he wasn't going to promise it to her.

She sighed and rubbed the heel of her hand across her sternum, over the achy spot. "If it were just the two of us on a beach somewhere, then hell, yes, we'd keep it casual." She tried for a smile. "I'd probably just be using you for the great sex anyway."

His grin was equally weak. "Too bad we're not on a beach."

The ache intensified. "Yeah. Too bad."

He hesitated, then closed the small distance between them and kissed her forehead, murmuring, "If I could promise to stick around for anyone, it would be you, Cara. Only you."

Tears prickled, but she closed her eyes and willed them back. "Shit. Don't say that." Part of her, though, had needed to hear it. "Just go, okay? I need some time alone."

After a long, drawn-out moment, he said, "You're armed?"

"Yeah. Got my wristband too. I'll be fine." She tensed, expecting him to say something more and both needing and dreading it.

But all he said was, "Mac. Protect." And then, with a scuff and the sound of boot steps, he walked out.

It was a long moment before she opened her eyes, another before she swiped away the moisture that clung to her lashes. She looked at Mac, then away, because she couldn't stand the sorrow and sympathy in his pale green eyes. Which left her looking at the now deserted training hall, empty and dispirited with the leftovers of a party that felt like it had spanned two lifetimes, maybe three.

"Guess that means the next step is picking up the pieces and doing some damage control," she said to the coyote.

Problem was, she didn't know which pieces of the damage she was supposed to be controlling, which ones she was supposed to be letting loose . . . and, damn it, there wasn't anybody left that she trusted enough to ask for advice.

Or was there?

"Shit," she said on a sigh, staring down at her forearm mark while her chest went hollow and funny-feeling. Because whether she liked it or not—and she really, really didn't—she needed to talk to her father.

CHAPTER SIXTEEN

September 16
Five days until the equinox; three months and
five days until the zero date

Sven awoke to the smell of bacon and an inner sense of discontent, and couldn't immediately place either of them.

For a second he flashed back to lying in the Mexican highlands, sprawled restlessly half-off a folding cot, staring up through gauzy bug netting at the ceiling of a pop-up tent pitched in one of a hundred temporary campsites. There, the smell would've been the stink of charred bodies, the discontent the residue of his work. Now, as he blinked up at the white-painted ceiling and slowly turning overhead fan, he got that he was in his room at Skywatch, and the smell was definitely bacon. It took him another groggy, magically hungover moment to place the discontent.

Cara. Oh, shit.

His heart gave a painful squeeze and part of him

wished he were back down south breathing *xombi* dust. Because he'd really fucked things up this time.

So much for being a better man. A better man wouldn't have said anything unless he knew for real what he wanted and that he could get it without screwing things up even more than they were already screwed. Which, as she had pointed out, was impossible.

At the time—in the cave, in the aftermath—it had seemed utterly imperative that he tell her he had feelings for her. Now, though, in the light of day he knew that even though he couldn't remember a time he hadn't wanted her, he could've made it another three months without saying anything. And he damn well should have, because he couldn't promise to stay.

Everyone she had ever cared about had left her: him by running away, her mother by dying, Carlos by being more *winikin* than father. She deserved someone who would stick by her and put her first and foremost, always. And that sure as shit wasn't him.

He tossed an arm over his eyes. "Cocksucking hell."

"Good. You're awake," Carlos's voice said from the doorway.

Shit. The bacon. Dragging his arm off his face and his body upright, Sven faced his *winikin,* who was a familiar sight standing in his bedroom door with a tray of food and a half scowl. What wasn't at all familiar, though, was the twinge of unease brought by the sight.

He'd never before broken a promise to Carlos; and while Cara's age wasn't the factor it had once been, he knew damn well that Carlos would still be pissed at them for crossing what he considered a sacred line. Not to mention, Sven realized with a kink of fatalistic amusement, he'd never before faced off against the father of a girl he'd hooked up with, and sure as hell not the morning after, naked.

Carlos was all business, though. "The king sent me to get you moving. He wants to see you in his quarters as soon as you're up and functional. He's talking to Cara now."

Oh, hell. "How long have they been at it?"

"Half hour, maybe." Carlos gestured with the breakfast tray, which smelled of grease and salt, and for a human would've been a heart attack special. "You want this in here?"

"I'll get dressed and come out." And eat fast. He didn't like the idea of Dez and Cara closeted away together, not because he was afraid of what she would say about the two of them, but because he was afraid of what she would say about everything else. She was too brave for her own good, and so determined to prove that the *winikin* deserved to be independent that she lost track that they were vulnerable in ways the Nightkeepers simply weren't. And that scared the crap out of him.

He was out of bed in an instant, and three minutes later shrugged on a faded green T-shirt to go with his jeans and boots as he walked into the kitchen, where Carlos had laid out the goods on the breakfast bar. Sven couldn't quite place the *winikin*'s expression; he wasn't sure if there was a new disturbance in the force there, or if it was a continuation of the same distance they had been dealing with for years.

As he started shoveling calories on board, he asked around a mouthful, "How much do you know about what happened last night?"

Turning on the hot water to suds up in the sink for washing—which for him was a kind of therapy—the *winikin* leaned back against the counter, eyes sharpening. "Nothing, really. I was out back at the library helping Jade and Lucius with deciphering Anna's latest prophecy and tracking down some lead on a cave in the middle of nowhere, Guatemala. I spent the night, caught a nap here and there, and worked straight through. I'd barely put a foot back in the mansion when Dez sent me to get you moving. Why? What happened?"

Shit, Sven thought. Carlos didn't know Cara had been in trouble, or that the two of them had been the source of the lead, never mind that Zane and Lora were under arrest, and the rebels undoubtedly pissed, maybe worse.

But it also meant that Dez had somehow squelched the rumor pipeline . . . and probably had a plan for how he wanted things let out in public. "Hm. You should probably hear it from Dez or Cara."

Sharp gray eyes got way sharper. "I'd rather hear it from you, right now."

But Sven's fealty oath said to keep his mouth shut, so he said only, "There was an incident. She's fine, but there's going to be some fallout. Let me take this meeting with Dez and find out where we stand."

The *winikin* didn't ask, not even about his daughter. He just nodded. "The king will tell us what we need to know, when we need to know it."

It wasn't the first time Sven had done the stop-and-blink thing over Carlos's acceptance of—and, hell, *defense* of—the hierarchy. Now, though, there was a spark of frustration. Okay, more than a spark. "Don't you want to know what happened to Cara?"

"You said she was fine. And she's made her choices."

"Some of them, maybe." But she hadn't chosen to take her marks in the first place, and yesterday she hadn't chosen to once more wear the coyote glyph. They just kept getting handed to her. And even though Carlos wasn't doing anything out of his norm, it suddenly pissed Sven off far more than usual. "It really gets you that she's trying to find a middle ground with the rebels, doesn't it?"

The *winikin*'s lips turned down. "There shouldn't need to be any compromise, no need to rewrite traditions that have served us for centuries. Especially not now."

"And you're sure all of the traditions are right?"

"I don't think she should be the one deciding which ones to set aside."

"Who, then?" Sven pressed.

"Jox wouldn't have—" Carlos shook his head, scowling. "It doesn't matter, does it? He put himself ahead of the *winikin,* ahead of the war." He didn't quite say the words "selfish bastard" aloud. "And he chose Cara as his successor . . . why? Four years ago she refused to do her duty and took off. Why would he figure she'd be any more reliable now?"

Leave it alone, Sven told himself. *She doesn't want anyone fighting her battles for her.* Or was it more that nobody had ever offered before? Either way, he couldn't just let it go. Not when he'd spent the past few days— and, hell, the past twenty-four hours—seeing her strength and resourcefulness, and her dedication to the *winikin.* So he said, voice low, "She's your daughter, Carlos. Yours and Essie's."

A dull red flush said he'd scored, but the *winikin*'s eyes narrowed. "Don't go there. You have no right."

"Maybe not, but nobody else is going to call you on it, are they?" Breakfast forgotten, Sven glared at the man who had raised him. "She's your daughter, Carlos, your flesh and blood. If you don't think you owe her some love—or at least some damn respect—because of that, then how about a little guilt for not giving her a choice, or, hell, some basic training, before you grabbed her, blooded her, and went, '*Poof,* there you go. Congratulations, I've made you into a servant!'"

"I made her into *your* servant, you fucking ingrate," Carlos said through gritted teeth.

"I never asked you to. I didn't want any of this, but I sure as hell didn't want her waiting on me. For chrissake, that's why I sent her away."

"Bullshit. You sent her away because you were afraid you couldn't keep your hands off her, but you knew damn well there was no place for that sort of a relationship here at Skywatch with war on the horizon. You still know it."

"Then why the hell did you make her my *winikin?*" The question came out in an unintended roar. "Why did you warn me off her and then throw us together like that? Was it a test? Some sort of punishment? What? Jesus, Carlos."

"Language," the *winikin* reprimanded, and for a second Sven was ten years old again and headed for the naughty corner.

Only for a second, though. "Fuck my language and answer the question. Why did you do it?"

"Screw this." Carlos grabbed the tray of uneaten food and headed for the door, sloshing coffee on the floor as he went. "I don't answer to you."

Sven didn't point out the obvious contradiction. "Damn it, Carlos. If you didn't want me around her, then why bind her to me?"

The *winikin* stopped, slammed the tray down on the

side table next to the door, and spun back. "Because it was the only way to get you back here, godsdamn it. When Jox called us all back to Skywatch, I had to be sure you would come. I knew if I asked you would tell me you were on your way, and keep doing whatever you were doing in the first place. Sure, I could have had them send someone out after you, but that would've meant . . . Shit, I couldn't do that."

He hadn't wanted to look bad, Sven realized. So he had sacrificed his daughter instead. He leaned back against the kitchen counter and felt the hard edge press into his kidneys while disgust coated his mouth. "You used her."

"Desperate times."

"You didn't trust me to man up once I understood what was going on."

"Do you blame me?" The *winikin*'s raised eyebrow reminded Sven of his big apology and all those good intentions. Granted, he hadn't repeated his old mistakes by doing a vanishing act when things started getting complicated, but maybe that would've been the lesser sin.

"Yeah, damn it, I *do* blame you. I . . . *Shit*." He paused, trying to rein in his bubbling temper, because he owed Carlos his life. But he didn't owe him unquestioning acceptance, especially when it came to Cara. Not anymore. "You could've talked to me, told me the truth about the Nightkeepers and the situation. I would've come back with you." He wanted to think he would have, at any rate. "You could've tried that first, at least, before using Cara."

Carlos's eyes flared. "Do you think it was easy for me? Do you think I *wanted* to do it that way? For fuck's sake, we were finally starting to get along. With Essie gone, we were eating together sometimes, riding out together. It wasn't perfect, but it was a start. And then Jox called, and I didn't have a fucking choice."

"There's always a choice."

"Fine." The older man lifted his chin to glare. "Then I made the choice. I ruined things with Cara, maybe even ruined things *for* her, in order to guarantee that the Nightkeepers got their coyote mage. Live with it. I know I do."

"You . . . Jesus, Carlos. Who does shit like that?"

"A blood-bound *winikin,* that's who. From day one, I was taught that the war is coming and the magi are the only ones who can save us, and that it's up to the *winikin* to do whatever it takes—anything and everything, even if it means sacrificing our lives and families—to help them."

And he had sacrificed his family, Sven realized. Maybe not directly, but still. "Was it worth it?" The sudden twist in his gut said the answer mattered.

"As long as you don't let infatuation taint your powers, then yes. It was worth it." And the damn thing was, there wasn't an ounce of apology in the *winikin*'s eyes.

Anger flared, roughening Sven's voice. "How can you say that about your own daughter?"

"The truth isn't always easy. If the First Father had meant for the Nightkeepers and *winikin* to mix, he wouldn't have forbidden them from mating."

"Did he? Seems to me that particular rule is a later addition."

"You'd like to think that, wouldn't you? It's easier than admitting that you're risking your magic, sniffing around her like you're doing." Some of Sven's flinch must've shown, because Carlos's eyes narrowed. "Yeah,

I noticed. Everyone has. So how about you do the right thing and stay the hell away from her?"

The words echoed back across the years and left Sven staring. "That day. That summer . . . It wasn't about her being too young. It was that you couldn't stand the idea of a mage and a *winikin* together."

"It's against the writs!"

Sven didn't bother arguing that one. "Jesus," he said, shaking his head, "it wasn't ever about her, was it? All along, I was the one you were trying to control. You couldn't stand the fact that I cared about her. Still do," he corrected. "And that's driving you up a fucking wall."

"There isn't room for sentiment when you're fighting a war," the *winikin* said darkly. "That *is* in the writs. Your responsibility is to the gods and ancestors, mankind, and then your king and the rest of the Nightkeepers. Lovers don't make the list. They're replaceable."

It seemed impossible that he could say that about his own daughter without blinking. "Are you really that heartless?"

"No. I'm that scared."

"You're . . . Wait. What?"

"I'm scared of what's coming. Fucking terrified. You were too young to remember anything about the massacre, and I used to thank the gods for that. But these days I'm not so sure, because I can't help thinking you'd be taking things more seriously if you remembered what it was like. . . ." His expression turned inward; his voice lowered to nearly a whisper. "Gods help us, it was awful. All the blood and the bodies, the screams, the children crying, running, being trampled. I . . . I stepped on them, ran over them carrying you, skidding in their blood and thinking that if I could just get away, we'd be safe."

Sven crossed the room to stand opposite the man who had rescued him that night, and who had raised him the best he knew how. That, of all of it, had never been in doubt. "I'll never forget that you saved my life."

Carlos's eyes came up, and his hand shot out and clamped on Sven's wrist. His fingers dug in and held. "Good. Because now it's your turn. I need you to save my life. I need you to save all of our lives, including hers. And you can't do that if you're letting yourself be distracted. You need to focus on what really matters."

And damned if he didn't have a point, one that resonated deep inside Sven, tugging at his warrior's magic. But at the same time, he couldn't ignore the string of seeming coincidences that had put him and Cara together in the coyote cave, with the scene set for sex. More, he couldn't ignore—didn't *want* to ignore—the heat that flared through him at the thought of her. "What if she's part of what really matters?"

"She's not."

"I think she is." It was all he could say without coming up against his fealty oath, which was already buzzing at the back of his brain, warning him that he needed to get moving; the king was waiting. But that wasn't the only thing banging around inside his head, not by a long shot. Duty was one thing, destiny another, and both were sacred to the gods.

"Do you?" Carlos's expression was hard, uncompromising. "Or are you looking for a sign that tells you it's okay to do exactly what you want with no thought of the consequences?"

Cara had asked him nearly the same thing. Hell, he had asked it of himself. "Not this time."

The *winikin* hesitated, then said slowly, "You made

me a promise once. I'm going to ask you for another one."

"I won't promise to stay away from her. I can't." It wasn't until the words were out there that he realized just how true they were.

"Promise me that you won't do anything about it unless you're absolutely certain of the gods' plan . . . or if you're not certain, that you'll wait until after the end date." Carlos's lips turned up in an utterly humorless smile. "If nothing else, that'll give you something to fight for."

"I won't . . ." Sven began, but then trailed off, because fuck if that didn't sound reasonable. But he wouldn't—couldn't—make a vow he wasn't sure he could keep, or even if he should try, because the magi rarely understood the gods' plans except in hindsight. "I promise I'll do my damnedest not to compromise the Nightkeepers or *winikin* by my actions. That's the best I can do." He held up a palm. "You want it in blood?"

"No, damn it, I want you to do the right thing."

Sven hated this. He was pissed at Carlos, but that didn't change the fact that he owed the older *winikin* for his life, and for shaping him into the man he'd become. There was love there, if not always affection. "I'm trying to do the right thing," he grated. "We just disagree on what that means right now. And the king's waiting for me."

Carlos scowled. "Then go already."

"Do you want me to swing by later and fill you in?"

The peace offering got an irritable shrug. "Dez will make sure we know what he wants us to."

"But Cara—"

"You said she was fine. I'll take your word on it."

Anger kicked anew. "Don't you care about her at all?"

Carlos looked away, throat working, and his voice was rough when he said, "Of course I do, damn you. She's all I have left of Essie." He picked up the tray and headed for the door, shooting over his shoulder, "But if you don't save the world, it won't matter what I care about."

The door closed behind him with a definitive-sounding *thunk,* making that a hell of an exit line. Or it would've been if he hadn't been talking about Cara.

She deserved a father who would've gone for his throat at the first hint of their fooling around, and not because of bigotry; a lover who would've taken her old man down for being a cold bastard when it came to her; family members who would've banded together rather than scattering to sulk in their own corners when things got bad. She deserved . . . *Oh, shit.*

He stood there a moment, staring at the door as he got it. He freaking got it.

She needed someone on her side, someone with an official *don't fuck with me* title and the weight of the king behind him. And he could be that guy, though not in the way he most wanted. No, he wasn't going to be her lover. . . . He was going to take Dez up on his job offer. It would piss her off, granted, but it would put him in a position to protect her not only from her enemies, but from herself. And right now that had to be his first and foremost priority. . . . Because despite all the signs pointing to the value of a quick and painless exit, and all the complications that were bound to come from his sticking way too close to her, he wasn't going to walk away from her this time.

CHAPTER SEVENTEEN

When the door behind Cara opened and boots sounded on the tiled foyer of the royal suite, she gritted her teeth. First, because she had been on the cusp of getting Dez to agree to her strategy and now the moment was lost. And second, because she knew who it was right away, not just because she, Dez, and Reese had been waiting for him, but because the air changed, sending heated currents coursing over her skin and raising the fine hairs on the back of her neck.

She hesitated a moment, then turned, playing it casual and hoping to hell that the king and his mate didn't see her flush like an idiot teen.

Sven was wearing jeans, boots, and a battered T-shirt, and should've looked like the beach bum he'd been when she first tracked him down to bring him back with her to Skywatch. But the clothes were where the resemblance ended. His body was bigger, his swagger tougher, and his eyes homed in on hers immediately, locking there for a moment and gaining a silent question, as if he wanted to ask whether she was okay, or maybe how much she had told the king.

She sent him a small nod, not even sure what she was really trying to convey other than acknowledgment. She was okay on some levels, far from it on others, and her and Dez's conversation wasn't really his business. She had her own relationship with the Nightkeepers' leader, her own agenda, and neither of those things had anything to do with her and Sven.

"Sorry it took me so long to get here," he said to Dez and Reese as he crossed the room. "I needed a few minutes with Carlos."

Cara stiffened. She had tried to find her father last night and again this morning, but he hadn't been in his quarters, the greenhouse, or any of his usual haunts. Had he been avoiding her? Ire gathered, even though by the time she had awakened from five hours of restless dozing, she had all but talked herself out of asking his advice. She knew what he would say, after all: *Don't overreach; be proud of your heritage; don't try to be something you're not.*

Well, screw that. She would decide what she was and wasn't going to do, and right now, she was doing her damnedest to keep the *winikin* on her side in the aftermath of last night's blowout. And Sven was interrupting.

Deep breath, she told herself as he took a wide wingback chair opposite hers, putting the ornately carved coffee table between them. *Wait it out.* Dez hadn't exactly agreed to her requests ... but he hadn't outright denied them, either. He'd seemed on board with still letting the *winikin* lead their own fighting teams. As for the other ... well, he hadn't turned her down yet. Once Sven's debriefing was over and they could get back to—

"We were just discussing what should be done with

Zane and Lora," the king said, startling her. "Your thoughts?"

Sitting up straight, she shot a look at Sven, who didn't seem nearly as surprised as he ought to have been. Instead, he just scowled like he'd bitten into something rotten. "Why is it even under discussion?"

Of course he would see it that way—treason was one of the few things punishable by death under Nightkeeper law, and he'd always hated Zane. Even though she knew some of that stemmed from Sven's wanting to protect her, irritation sparked and grew, and she snapped, "Because not all of us are so comfortable with—" She bit off the word "death," knowing that was a too-low blow. "Sorry. Shit."

He ignored her apology as if it didn't matter either way, though she had seen him flinch. "What's your answer, then? Imprisonment? Why should we waste manpower keeping tabs on those two, not to mention running the risk of looking like we're tossing out the writs left and right, and pretty much doing whatever we damn well please?"

That should've seemed ironic, coming from him. Instead it was an indication of just how serious things had gotten all of a sudden. She could feel time slipping away from them, could feel the balance among the *winikin* threatening to skew too far away from center. Leaning in, she said urgently, "This isn't about you, or even about the writs. It's about needing the *winikin* to come together as a valid fighting force, and fast. Sasha managed to heal up the two who got hurt last night, but there's already some serious rumbling going on, and lots of people pissed off, both because of what Zane and Lora did, and how their capture went down." She didn't blame him

for that, though; there had been plenty of people involved in the plan, including her, so the failure was
shared. If anything, the *winikin* would blame her for not
seeing the Nightkeepers' grandstanding for what it was.
Gods knew she blamed herself for it. Now she needed to
regain their trust as best she could. "The way I see it, my
best chance for getting them to rally behind me is if I get
some concessions from the king, ones that they care
about, and that make them feel like they've got some say
in their own destinies."

She expected Sven to argue that this wasn't a democ-
racy and they all had to follow the damn leader. Instead,
he simmered down and nodded, if slowly. "Okay, I get
that. But I don't see how Zane and Lora play into it.
Don't tell me you want to do some sort of a trial with the
winikin version of a kangaroo court?"

His tacit acceptance probably shouldn't have surprised her, and it definitely shouldn't have warmed her.
Because it did both, there was an edge to her tone when
she said, "A trial would waste time that we don't have,
and I think it would stir up more questions than answers." She shook her head. "No, I want to have Rabbit
reprogram them and then send them home."

There was a beat of silence and a flash of disbelief
before he said, "You're fucking kidding me." He stared
blankly at her for a long moment, then turned to Dez
and Reese. "You're not seriously considering this, are
you?"

The king and queen, who sat together on the couch in
jeans and sweatshirts with their heads tilted together,
had been quietly observing the exchange. So quietly, in
fact, that Cara got a sudden chill of premonition that
there was something else going on here, that they hadn't

been waiting just to get Sven's full version of what had happened during the bar fight. They seemed to be waiting to be convinced. But of what?

Heart thumping, she put in, "Obviously, we would only do it if Rabbit thought it was safe. He's going to be the one questioning them. He'll know if he can block their memories strongly enough to make it work."

Sven shook his head, dividing his attention between her and the royal couple. "Use Rabbit to question them? Absolutely. But don't let them go. What if the blocks fail? What if somebody recognizes their marks and tracks them back here? Hell, what if the *Banol Kax* find them and get inside their heads? They'll know everything there is to know about us."

"You think I don't know that?" All those possibilities and more had kept her awake long into the night, talking it through with herself because there wasn't anybody else she could use as a sounding board. "But think about it. If Dez orders their execution, he'll be no better than Scarred-Jaguar, at least in the eyes of the *winikin*."

"I don't think . . ." But Sven trailed off. "Shit."

"Exactly. He'll be worse, even, because Scarred-Jaguar never actually used the death penalty. And you said it yourself—imprisoning them would be a waste of manpower. Worse, it could give them a chance to win over other rebels and stir things up, and we don't have the time for that."

"Some sort of stasis spell could work."

"After you dropped a dozen *winikin* last night?" she said pointedly, then shook her head. "Even without that reminder of how easy it would be for you guys to overpower any one of us—or, hell, all of us—a stasis spell would come across as an abuse of power."

"And Rabbit mind-bending them wouldn't?"

"It'd be different," she asserted, as she had done fifteen minutes earlier to Dez and Reese. "He'd be stripping them of their memories and implanting a cover story that explains where they've been for the past year. The trads will see it as punishment for them to lose their *winikin* heritage like that; the rebs will think the punishment is them not knowing to defend themselves—or how—when the end comes."

He shook his head. "I still don't like it."

"I don't see a better answer." She shook her head as frustrated weariness started to encroach on the bravado she'd been channeling since she got to the royal suite. "If you do, bring it on."

"Stasis. It's neater, cleaner, and the *winikin* will get over it eventually." He turned to Dez. "I'm taking the job. Which means I get a vote here."

Fatigue took a backseat fast. "Wait. What job?"

Dez, though, got an ominous spark in his eyes as he zeroed in on Sven. "You're sure? You're really in?"

"One hundred percent." He turned to Cara, and there was an implacable sort of wariness in his eyes as he said, "I hope you won't hate me for this, and that we can figure out a way to make it work so things will be easier for you, not harder. I respect the hell out of you, both as a woman and as a leader . . . but everything inside me says that this is the right thing to do."

"Okay, now you're scaring me." And not just a little. Her pulse thudded thickly in her ears and her stomach churned. "What are you talking about?" She turned to Dez, her voice threatening to wobble. "What's going on here?"

"Things within the *winikin* are worse than any of us

thought," the king answered. "You've got factions within factions and your own people are trying to kill you. Now you're asking me to give them weapons and autonomy, and let a couple of traitors go free because it'll make you look like a leader." He shook his head. "That's a tough one to swallow, Cara. A fucking tough one."

"If you were going to say no you would've done it already." She hoped. He wasn't just playing with her, was he, trying to make some other point she hadn't gotten yet?

"I'll give you what you want, on the condition that you accept a Nightkeeper liaison, a mage who will be right beside you every step of the way, helping rather than overseeing, but with veto power over your decisions."

Cara's heart stopped. Literally stopped. "A . . . what?"

"A Nightkeeper liaison." Dez shook his head in sympathy, but said, "Sorry, that's the deal. I need to know the *winikin* are under control, Cara. I can't have this blowing up in my face. Not now. Trust me; you're going to want to take the deal."

This wasn't happening, couldn't be happening. *Oh, gods.* Her heart had started up again, but it was bumping off rhythm, fluttering against her ribs like it was trapped and trying to break free as the second shoe dropped. Sven had brought up the subject. He had said he would take the job. Which meant he had known about this. Worse, it meant he was the guy. Her liaison.

Oh, hell, no.

She was on her feet without having realized she had stood, though somehow Dez and Sven still seemed to tower over her, their presences expanding well beyond their physical bodies, part of the magic of the magi.

Refusing to feel puny, she balled her hands into fists and glared at the king. "What's my other option?"

"I'd rather not go there. I hope you'll take the offer instead."

"But the politics—"

"Have to be secondary to the success of the war."

"They . . ." *Damn it.* "You'll be undermining me, crippling me as a leader. Worse, you'll be running the risk of losing the rebels. We need them, damn it. They're the younger generation, the fighters."

"So you'll find a way to spin it so they stay," Reese put in. "Make this into a positive, not a negative, maybe even a concession you've squeezed out of the king." That got a grunt out of Dez, making the queen's lips twitch. She stayed focused on Cara, though, with eyes that weren't unkind, but said simply, *Deal with it.*

"Not him." She turned on Sven, teeth bared. "Not you."

He spread his hands in a gesture of helplessness belied by the smooth shift of his bulky muscles and the aura of leashed wildness that surrounded him. "Think it through. Now that you're wearing my mark, the *winikin* are going to put us together in their heads no matter what you say. Rather than trying to ignore it, let's use it instead."

It didn't help that he had a point. "How long have you known this was a possibility?" *Tell me you found out this morning, that it was a surprise to you too.* Except that she'd been closeted with the king for an hour and Sven had just gotten out of bed. Maybe Carlos told him. Maybe . . .

"Since right after I came back."

Fury pounded through her. "Five days ago. He talked

to you about being the liaison *five days ago,* and you didn't say anything?" Not even after they hooked up, after he'd told her he cared about her. Which made her wonder how, exactly, he defined caring. Was it when he was horny? When things were convenient? What?

"Originally, Dez asked me to take a good, hard look at the *winikin* right after Aaron's funeral went so wrong. He was afraid it was an inside job." When she did a double take, attention caught, he shook his head. "I didn't see anything that made me think it was ... but then again, I didn't catch wind of what Zane and Lora were up to, either, partly because I didn't like him to begin with, and partly because I refused to use you or Carlos for information."

"Is that supposed to make me feel better?"

"For what it's worth, I'm sorry. But Dez asked me to keep things under wraps."

Which had to trump her feelings, damn it. But that didn't make it okay that he'd gone behind her back, or that he and Dez had been making decisions about her *winikin* without her knowing there was even a discussion going on. And Sven? Gods, she couldn't work with him on a day-to-day basis. It would be ... impossible.

"It's a good offer," Dez put in. "What's more, it's the only one you're going to get, so I suggest you take it."

In other words, she was getting a liaison whether she liked it or not; it was up to her whether it happened smoothly and with a prayer of spinning it to the *winikin* as a positive, or happened with her kicking and screaming, and making things even worse on the solidarity front.

"We can make it work," Sven said quietly. "We know how to get along ... we just haven't had much practice over the past bunch of years." And the damn thing was, he didn't seem at all uncomfortable with the idea. He was acting like their teaming up was the most logical solution, like it should be on some late-night top-ten list of great ideas, despite their having all but agreed last night that they should steer clear of each other.

"For how long?" she asked, hating that the answer mattered too much. "A week? A month?"

"As long as you need me." Which wasn't really an answer, because undoubtedly he'd be the one to decide when that ended.

"I *don't* need you. That's the point." *Go away,* she thought almost desperately. *The longer you stay, the harder this is going to be.* She didn't want to get used to having him around, because it would only hurt worse when he left. She didn't want to have him filling the shadow Zane's absence would leave, didn't want him beside her at meetings and strategy sessions, didn't want him going over all her plans, arguing with her, throwing his weight around and making her defend decisions that should've been hers alone. . . . And if a small part of her wanted exactly those things and so much more, she stuffed it deep down inside where all her other stupid fantasies lived. Shaking her head, she turned to Dez. "This isn't going to work. We're going to spend so much time butting heads and contradicting each other that we'll never get a damn thing accomplished."

"Who else did you have in mind as second in command?" Sven asked unexpectedly.

"I . . . Shit. Natalie, I guess. She's got ties to the rebs through JT, but she's also got a huge appreciation for the traditions. And the others understand why she's working with Lucius, so there wouldn't be a problem there."

"And she doesn't have an iota of combat experience," he countered. "Not to mention that it doesn't make any sense to take one of our few trained Mayan scholars out of the library. I'm not assigned anywhere right now, though, and the *winikin* might not like me all that much, but they like me better than most of the magi." He rose from the chair so they were standing facing each other, with the carved coffee table between them. "I don't need to be in charge, and I'm not going to challenge you or make you look bad. I just want to help you." His eyes softened slightly. "Call it payback, call it guilt, call it whatever the hell you want, but let me do this, okay? I won't let you down this time."

He was right, she realized; she didn't have an obvious choice for Zane's replacement, and she'd proven all too well the day before that she didn't do her best thinking when she was under pressure and didn't have someone else backing her up with a reality check. Maybe the answer would have been obvious . . . if it hadn't been for what had happened in the coyote cave.

It wasn't just the sex—she thought they could have chalked that up to the magic and the moment, and walked away from it. But all the things he'd said after, and then their argument last night . . . that had been them, not the magic. At least, it had been for her, and that'd had her reacting from emotion rather than logic. As for him . . . well, she didn't actually know where he was coming from. It didn't make any sense to her that he would be spouting words of almost-love one night, and then the next morning be ready to work side by side with her like it was no big deal. There wasn't any trepidation in his eyes, no silent plea that she go with it and he'd explain later. Had he pushed his emotions behind the wall of his warrior's talent? Or had he set them aside that quickly? If he had—

"How about you give it a chance?" The suggestion came from Reese. "Just the two of you on a trial run outside of the compound, a two-person op you can work without feeling like your every move is being scrutinized." She shot a meaningful look at Dez. "Sometimes things get simpler when you take some time away."

"I don't want . . ." Cara began, but then trailed off, because this wasn't about what she wanted, hadn't been in a long time. If she agreed to this, she'd be buying Zane's and Lora's lives, not because she sympathized with them, but because they had become political currency. She didn't think Dez understood just how much they mattered, or how much resentment would be stirred up if they were executed, spell-frozen, or even simply imprisoned. With the wounds of the massacre still too fresh in many of the *winikin*'s minds, they needed to know that there was a way out of Skywatch somehow. So finally she said, "I take it you've got an op in mind?"

It was Dez who nodded and said, "You know the screaming skull the *nahwal* mentioned? Well, Lucius tracked it to the Playa Maya Museum in Monterey. We want you to steal it."

CHAPTER EIGHTEEN

Zane's brain was a seriously weird place, and Rabbit felt right at home. The twists and turns made sense, like he was driving in a strange town but somehow knew exactly where to find the gas stations and fast food, as if he'd been there before in a previous life. Or, more accurately, as if he'd recently spent time in a very similar town. Zane might've been misguided and far too ready to buy into his own self-serving interpretations, but he'd honed some of the same skills Rabbit had found himself needing more and more lately, as he tried with increasing frustration to reconnect with his mother's spirit, while hiding those efforts from everyone, including Myrinne. Especially Myrinne.

Secrecy. Suspicion. Righteousness. Contempt. Rabbit sent his consciousness through Zane's mind, passing memories and signpost-bright emotions, picking through the labyrinth until he found what he was looking for.

When he did, he brought his perceptions closer to the surface, to the point where he could feel his own body sitting hunched over beside Zane, and could sense Dez,

Sven, and Cara sitting nearby, waiting tensely for the intel that could make or break the *winikin*'s life. Lora was already free and clear; she hadn't known anything, and had been painfully easy to reprogram. She was the kind of person who would always look for a pack leader to tell her what to do, how to feel. As far as she now knew, she had spent the past ten months or so as part of a whack-job cult, which she'd been lured into by a guy she met online. She was ashamed of the guy and the cult, and didn't want to talk about either of them. She just wanted to get back to her life, and shouldn't present any further problems for the Nightkeepers.

Zane, on the other hand . . . well, they would have to see.

"He thinks he's part Nightkeeper," Rabbit said, channeling the info he was getting from the *winikin*. "It was a family legend that his twice-great-grandmother had a child with either her own Nightkeeper charge or another member of his family, putting mage blood into the mix. That's why Zane was trying to sacrifice Cara—he was looking to activate his supposedly latent Nightkeeper powers. It looks like when he first got here, he had a couple of dreams that reminded him of the coyote cave and gave him delusions of grandeur mixed up with some sort of divine plan. He fixated on Cara, first as his mate, then as his sacrifice."

"Did he talk about it to anybody other than Lora?" Cara asked at almost the same time Sven said, "Did he have anything to do with those creatures showing up at the funeral?"

"Give me a minute." It took Rabbit longer than that to find the information on Lora, whom Zane had barely registered as more than a spare set of hands. The attack was easier to dial into. "I don't think you've got any other traitors to worry about; it was just him most of the time, with Lora helping out at the end, once she really started cracking under the pressure. As for the attack, he didn't know anything about it beforehand, but decided it was a sign telling him to act now."

After a few more questions and answers that didn't really add anything to the mix, Dez sighed and said, "I think he's tapped out. Rabbit, what do you think about reprogramming him?"

"Same as with Lora, I can change his memories of the past ten months so he thinks he fell in with a doomsday cult that was pretending to be the Nightkeepers, and scramble it around enough so he won't come looking for us."

"I hear a 'but' in there," Dez commented.

"Not intentionally."

"But . . ."

"Shit." It felt way hypocritical to rat out a guy whose brain felt more than a little familiar, but Rabbit told himself it was the differences that mattered. "Using Lora was easy for him, and so was leaving Cara in that cave to die. He's not a full-on sociopath like Iago, and not crazy like Iago was at the end, either. But he's not hooked into an ethical code, either human or Nightkeeper. I can change his memories, but I can't promise he won't do something else if we let him go. He's . . . predatory. Hungry. I don't think that's going to go away."

"So what do you think? Should we let him go?"

"I . . . I'm not sure." It felt seriously weird that he was being asked to comment on Zane's moral character, when he himself was a half-blood screwup who had burned down several million dollars' worth of other people's property and fallen prey to Iago's mind games over and over again, jeopardizing the Nightkeepers in the process. He was the Master of Disaster, the guy who gave Murphy's Law a bad name. . . . There was no way he was qualified to make this call.

A little help here, gods? Rabbit thought, automatically using his magic to shape the words into a prayer, even though it had been a long time since his prayers had done anything but rattle around inside him. Instead of rattling, though, the prayer *whooshed* out of him, disappearing and taking some of his magic with it, and leaving stunned silence behind.

Holy shit. What just happened? Heart kicking up a dozen notches, Rabbit sought the prayer, tried to follow it, but came up against the blank walls that bounded his consciousness instead. What the hell? Where did it go? Part of his problem was not knowing whether he was supposed to be praying to the sky or the underworld, not knowing what to think or believe. Were the sky gods the saviors the Nightkeepers thought them, or were they lying schemers, like Zane here?

Hello? he called, hearing it rattle. *Anyone?*

In the outside world, the others were discussing Zane's fate. Sven said, "We can't just let him go. Not with that inside him. What if we—"

Out of nowhere, a power surge hit Rabbit, making his blood sing. It poured through the walls of his mind, up from the floor, down from the ceiling. The rattles got louder and louder, sounding like a crazed mariachi band trying to do "Radar Love" on fast-forward; they swirled around him, tightened in on him, blotted out everything except the noise and the magic.

He must've fogged out for a minute, because when things cleared, he heard the others still talking about what to do with Zane. They hadn't felt the surge. How was that possible?

Because this power is yours alone, Rabbie.

Mama!? The word burst from him with such a rush of hope and joy that it almost made it all the way back to his body, to be shouted aloud.

Careful. Some secrets are better kept until you know more. Finish quickly here and then come to me.

The power snapped out of being, though its echo remained. Rabbit's heart thudded happily in his ears; the flop sweats were gone, along with his hesitation over what to do with Zane. He was powered up, jazzed, ready to get on with things as he tuned back in to the conversation.

Cara was saying, "I don't like it. What's more, the others are going to be pissed if they find out your idea of 'releasing' Zane was to stick him in a mental institution and fake the paperwork to keep him there through the end date. You're getting dangerously close to imprisoning *winikin* to avoid a mutiny."

"Trust me," Dez said. "I'm aware of the parallels. But not everything Scarred-Jaguar did was one hundred percent wrong. And, besides, the rumors are your problem."

"We'll tell 'em he was mind-bent and released," Sven said promptly. "They don't need to know the rest. And, Cara, seriously? Admit it. You don't want him released all the way, either. You know what he's capable of."

She made a noise of disgust, but subsided.

"So I should get started?" Rabbit asked, trying not to let his real body jitter with suppressed excitement the same way his mental projection was doing inside Zane's skull.

"Yeah," Dez said. "Do it. We'll deal with the logistics."

Working fast, riding high on the power that was apparently his alone—the others sure didn't seem to notice it—Rabbit slapped heavy blocks around Zane's key memories of Skywatch and the people inside it, repressing them and installing new surface memories that turned the training compound into an encampment hidden in the Blue Mountains, the Nightkeepers into a doomsday militia that was raided and scattered.

All the while, he was acutely aware of the power flowing through him. It wasn't dark magic but wasn't fully light, either. It was his mother's magic, now his own.

Gods, he had almost started to believe she'd been a dream.

"Rabbit? You okay?" The question came in Dez's voice. "You need a break?"

"Nope, I'm almost finished." Hurrying now, he soldered the last few blocks into place and added a couple of fail-safes, along with giving Zane a newfound craving for garlic pickles, because he liked Cara, damn it, and the bastard had messed with her. He might have done more—*how's a little erectile dysfunction sound, there, Zane, old boy?*—but the magic was tugging him back toward his cottage, to the place where he'd hidden the two eccentrics.

He could feel the small carvings vibrating, yearning to be together for the first time since he'd discovered the second one. He didn't know how or why, but the channel for communication was wide-open, waiting for him to tap into it.

"He's all set," he said as he started backing out of Zane's consciousness layer by layer. Where he usually had to brace himself to pull out when he'd been so deeply enmeshed, now there was just a faint tug of conscience, a protest from the part of himself that remembered what it felt like to have his own brain fucked with, and regretted having to do it to someone else, even a traitor.

Then he was out of Zane's mind and back in his own, blinking to clear his vision while the others talked over his head. The room spun. The magic heated, calling him, begging him.

"Gotta go," he mumbled, shoving abruptly to his feet and heading for the door of the small storage room–slash–prison cell. "Need to . . ." He pantomimed barfing. "He's fine. He's good. Send him wherever he's gonna go."

Cara took a couple of steps toward him. "Do you need something? Food? Help back to your cottage?" As much as she tried not to be a *winikin,* she was a nurturer at heart. Not that she would thank him for saying it, even if he could get a coherent sentence through the pounding beat of magic that filled his head.

"No. I'm fine," he managed, though he didn't think any of them were buying it. "Just need a bathroom."

He made it upstairs to the one on the mansion's main floor, locked the door, and turned on the water in the sink to cover any telltale noises. Then he yanked his knife, blooded his palms, and sank to the tiled floor opposite the john, his body going heavy and lax as he focused inward, knowing what he had to do and sensing that he was running out of time, the channel of communication threatening to fade if he didn't get it right.

Concentrating so hard that sweat popped down his spine and chilled against the cool marble of the bathroom wall, he thought of the eccentrics, stuck in separate socks at the bottom of a drawer. Telekinesis was his weakest talent, but with all the magic rocketing through him right then, he could've moved a frigging mountain.

Instead, he eased the eccentrics out of their socks and slid them together, all of it happening inside his underwear drawer. He felt the pieces move, felt them click into place and fuse. The universe seemed to take a breath and hold it. Then there was a soundless detonation inside him, a *boom* of pressure. For a second his perceptions lurched and grayed out.... And when they cleared, he found himself standing in the middle of a blasted desert that wasn't like anything he'd ever experienced before.

What ... the ... fuck?

He turned a full circle, seeing only gray and more gray: an ashen landscape of dunes and black, twisted trees with a horizon of a black, featureless sky.

It looked like the in-between, the wasteland that separated the plane of the living from that of the dead, and where souls could walk forever and never get anywhere, looping endlessly until they were ready to begin their journey through Xibalba, where they would be tested and earn their way—maybe, hopefully—to reincarnation. But the in-between didn't have a fitful breeze that brought him the sharp, acrid smell of ashes, and it was the reddish brown of sky and soil, not corpse gray. More, this didn't feel like any of the other planes he'd ever been to. If anything, it felt like home, like the earthly plane.

Only it sure as shit didn't look like it.

A shiver worked its way through him. "Mother?" Although he'd called her "mama" before, that was for kids. And he didn't know her, not really.

I am here.

He spun and found her behind him, though she hadn't been there an instant earlier. As before, she wore flowing white and had pale, gleaming eyes. This time, though, she wasn't translucent. Her body was solid and her bare feet left marks in the ashes. She was really there.

Hello, Rabbie. Her words still sounded in his head, not aloud, but they were stronger now, in a voice that stirred long-buried memories, as did the name.

Rabbie. It had been circling inside his head for days now, alternately warming him and depressing the shit out of him, until he'd felt like a fucking seesaw or a dippy bird or something, zigzagging between extremes of emotion underlaid with the deep, dark fear that it had been a onetime thing, that he'd never see her again.

And now here they were.

He reached for her, needing to touch, but his hand passed right through her image. His gut hollowed out on the realization that wherever they were, he was the ghost. That brought a big-ass chill crawling down his spine, as did the realization that he couldn't feel the magic anymore, as if he'd used it up . . . or he was in a place where magic didn't work.

"Where are we?" he asked. "Is this the dark barrier?" The shiver dug in and got claws, but beneath it there was a thread of excitement. Iago might have blocked him from using the dark magic, but the connection—and the fascination—remained.

It's not where that matters, but when. This is your home at the dawn of the coming new year.

"My . . ." Sharp horror flooded him as the twisted black stumps around him stopped looking like random trees and started looking way too familiar. One huge, charred stump rose up above a cluster of smaller tree-skeletons. Beyond that, what he'd initially thought was a series of dunes started looking like the folded-in remains of a steel building buried beneath a layer of ash.

He didn't need to look behind himself to know that the other dunes were more buildings set in an achingly familiar pattern. And even though he'd never fit in quite right at Skywatch, never been able to fall into lockstep with the others, his heart shuddered.

Gone. All of it . . . gone.

He could barely breathe as he flashed back to how it used to be, before things got serious and the fun stuff fell by the wayside. He saw bodies crowding and elbows bumping at the tables, the *winikin*-manned Weber grills set up off to one side, a bruising ball game working its way up and down the open area where the old Great Hall had been, and dappled shadows of sunlight coming down through the lush green leaves of the ceiba tree that marked the center of Skywatch, the heart of their tiny village.

He saw Patience and Brandt, who had taken him in after his old man died, making him feel as welcome as he ever had; he saw their twin sons, Harry and Braden, who had worshiped their Unc' Rabbit and whom he still missed, even knowing they were safer in hiding. He saw Myrinne in the middle of the game, laughing as she fought Strike for possession of the tough rubber ball. He saw Leah, Anna, Sasha, Cara. . . .

Gone.

"We lost the war," he said, his voice rough with emotion. "Or we're going to lose it. Is that what you're telling me?"

No. This is one possible future. It is what will be unless you wish it otherwise. Her eyes kindled to a silver gleam that had his heart thudding once more in his chest. *You are mankind's best hope, Rabbie. The old shaman was right: You must become the crossover and persuade the Nightkeepers to turn away from the sky gods and support the* Banol Kax *in their fight. . . . Or else mankind's champions will lose the war, and the world will become what you see around you.*

The crossover. *Gods.* He sucked in a breath, pulse bumping as the part of him that had been sliding to despair did an about-face and beelined for wary hope. But that hope had a problem of its own. "They won't listen to me," he said, hating the shame of the truth. If he'd been a different person, lived a different life, maybe the Nightkeepers would've paid more attention. As it was, he'd blown up so much shit over the years they wouldn't—couldn't—take him seriously when it came to something that went against everything they'd been raised to believe.

You must make them.

"How?" He had tried. Gods knew he'd tried.

You'll find a way. She smiled, eyes softening through the silver gleam. *You're my Rabbie. You found me . . . which means you can do anything.*

His chest went so tight he couldn't breathe as his heart whispered that same silly lullaby he'd heard earlier, the one he almost remembered. *Rabbie and Tristan, sitting in a tree . . .* The song lightened the gloom within and without, making it seem as if the sun might break through the thick, choking clouds.

Swallowing hard, he said, "I want to see Tristan." He hadn't acknowledged the need even to himself, hadn't realized how important it was to him until his question was met with a telling silence and a dimming of her eyes, and his heart fucking fell to his toes. "Why not?"

It's complicated, my sweet Rabbie.

"I need . . ."

You must be brave, baby. More important, you must work alone. Tristan can't help you, and my powers are limited. And be warned: When you go up against the system, everyone you know will turn against you.

He shook his head. "Not Myrinne." If anything, this would bring them closer together, because he would finally be doing what she'd been on him to try for months now. Longer.

Even her. Especially her. The answer was immediate. Absolute.

No. Impossible. Rabbit's brain seized and then radiated pain, like he'd just chewed his way through a half gallon of Rocky Road that'd been hanging out in liquid nitrogen. "Bullshit. That's just bullshit."

She is an agent of the enemy, and she's using you.

His stomach hollowed out instantly. "You're lying."

She reached out to him, but was unable to touch. *I'm sorry, Rabbie. I'm so sorry to take this away from you.*

"You're not. You can't." Hands balling into fists, he started to take a step toward her, then spun and stalked away a few paces and stood, staring out over the wreckage that had been the main mansion of Skywatch.

His mind flashed on the plaque that hung—had hung?—beside the front door, the one that showed the ceiba tree as the ancients had seen it, with its roots sunk deep in the underworld, its branches touching the sky, and its trunk supporting the earth plane and forming the heart of the village. Beneath it was—had been?—

engraved the motto of the modern Nightkeepers: *To protect, fight, and forgive.*

He had done all that, damn it. He had protected his teammates and by extension all of mankind; he had fought enemies on this plane, the in-between, and even in Xibalba itself. And he'd done his damnedest to forgive his old man for being a prick and a lousy father, and himself for making some pukingly bad decisions over the years. He'd protected, fought, forgiven. He'd done his best to be a good soldier, a good mage.

Yet still he got fucked?

Hot frustration raced through him. Why wasn't it enough? Where was his balance, his good to even out the bad?

There is more bad to get through before you reach the good, Rabbie. Please believe me. Please trust me in this, if you trust me in nothing else. Your good times will come.

"When?" His voice broke on the word. He looked around at the familiar canyon, torn to shreds and filled with ash, and the grayness that stretched in all directions to meet the lifeless sky, and his righteous fury curdled at the knowledge that it would be like this in three months if he made the wrong decisions now.

Which meant he had to abso-fucking-lutely get it right. But Myrinne . . . *Gods.* "If it weren't for her, I'd probably be dead already." Before she came into his life, he'd been on the fast train to self-destructing. She'd made him grow up and be a man.

She saved you because she needed you. A parade of images raced suddenly through his mind in rapid succession: Myrinne as he'd first seen her, peering cannily through racks of pseudovoodoo garbage in her foster mother's tea shop in the French Quarter; her talking —

seducing—him into trying a Wiccan scrying ritual that had gone horribly wrong; and then the two of them together more recently, with her sharp, him frustrated.

"Fine, yeah, she pushes me. But only because she not only loves me, she believes in me. She thinks the same thing you do—that the old shaman was right about my being the key to the war. That's why she nags."

She pushes you where she wants you to go. She wants the power for herself, as did her mother before her.

Feeling like he was clawing to keep his head above the surface of the things he refused to believe, he grated, "That witch wasn't her mother." Mistress Truth hadn't even really been a witch, either. Just a shyster who'd happened to luck into a ceremonial knife that'd carried some major power. She had gotten herself killed for it too, trying to cut a deal with Iago. She was no mother to Myrinne, and hadn't had any power in her own right.

Are you so sure of that? his own mother asked softly. Then, before Rabbit could answer—if he'd even had an answer—she filled his mind with the thing he feared and dreaded more almost than the end-time itself . . . the dream.

He stood in a pool of blood, blank faced and holding a dripping knife, like something out of an episode of CSI. He imagined someone ordering, "Cut to a flashback of the murder in three . . . two . . . one . . . mark." Then the camera pulled back, widening the frame to show a woman's sprawled body, a flare of dark hair, a clever, witchy face with eyes fixed and staring. Then even farther back, to show a mansion in flames.

Myrinne was dead, Skywatch burning. And Rabbit was

just fucking standing there holding his father's ceremonial dagger like he was ready to do it all over again.

He batted at the images, though he knew they were entirely inside his mind, inside *him*. "No, godsdamn it, I wouldn't do that to her! I couldn't. I love her!"

He'd first seen the vision during the scrying spell, when he'd foolishly asked how he and Myrinne could earn their *jun tan* mated marks. First, he'd heard his old man's voice telling him to get rid of the hellmark that had connected him to Iago. Then he'd seen the knife. The blood. Her eyes.

Oh, gods. Her eyes. He pressed his fists against his own closed lids, trying to force away the image, which was a memory yet not, because it hadn't happened yet even though he'd seen it over and over again in his nightmares.

"Please don't make me," he whispered, not sure whether he was talking to his mother or the dream, which was too vivid and unchanging to be anything but prescience. For so long he had thought it was a warning from an ancestor or the gods themselves, a chance to change his course and not make a terrible mistake. But what if the gods weren't warning him off at all? What if they were telling him what he was supposed to do? *Fuck.* Agony rolled over him, centering in the place where his heart had been only moments before. "I need her. I can't do this alone."

The crossover is one alone, not half of a pair.

He scrubbed his face and then leaned back, squeezing his eyes shut, too broken to give a shit that the move let loose a tear. "Don't say that. Please . . . no. Don't." There was no anger in him now, though, no denial.

I'm sorry.

He realized he'd wrapped his arms around himself like a fucking girl, which just drove home how much he'd gotten used to having someone holding on to him, telling him he was going to be okay. Not someone. Myrinne. She was his first, his one and only. His—

Betrayer.

"Never." But he was losing steam. "There's got to be something else going on. I'll talk to her," he decided. "I'll see—"

You cannot let on that you know. Better to watch her closely and discover her plan, her allies.

"I can . . ." But he couldn't mind-bend her. At her request he'd installed a mental block that prevented him from getting inside her. He couldn't remove it without her knowing what he'd done.

Why do you think she insisted? She couldn't let you see inside, couldn't let you know her true agenda. She was the one who called the creatures; she was the one who sent whispers into the winikin *soldier's mind, telling him he could become a mage if he killed one of his own. She wants to disrupt the Nightkeepers while she convinces you to seek the dark magic on her terms—those of the sky gods who control her—because then the magic will destroy you and the dark barrier together. And humanity will be left with this.* Her gesture encompassed the remains of Skywatch, which was the earth's only real hope of surviving the end of days, even though mankind didn't have a freaking clue.

"Stop. Jesus, please stop." Desperation closed around him, making it seem as if the dim, ash-darkened skyline were drawing inward and making him want to claw his way out, screaming.

I will stop. I must. My time is up. Her mental tone was suddenly thready and fading, as if she had moved past him and he was getting the tail end of the Doppler shift. *But remember this, sweet Rabbie. Your brother and I are watching over you even when you can't see or feel us. Which means you're not really alone.* The last was a soft whisper, almost inaudible.

Then she was gone, leaving him in the desolation.

And despite what she had said, he sure as shit felt alone.

The solitude echoed through him, around him, as he realized he could be the only person for miles, maybe even the only living creature. Was this, then, the way it was all going to end? *One possible future,* she had called it, and him the crossover. Mankind's best hope.

Ever since the shaman had suggested the destiny, Rabbit had been wrestling with the utter fucktarded insecurity of being named the savior of mankind. But he didn't know if he could do it without Myrinne. She was his cornerstone, supporting him, lifting him up, and making him believe that he could do so many more things than he had thought.

How could that be wrong?

"Rabbit." His name—nickname?—was a thread of sound in the gray-on-gray world, coming in her voice as if he'd conjured her with his thoughts. When it came again, though, it was accompanied by a lurch of the world around him, like it—or he—had just been shaken. "Come on, Pyro. Time to wake up."

Pyro. That was a nickname he dug, one that reminded him not only of his first and best talent, but also their too-short time together at college, when he'd actually been popular, not just because he had a hot girlfriend, but because he'd actually found things he was good at, and people who thought he was cool. He'd played the part of a normal guy there, and it hadn't fit all that badly. More, it had given the two of them a secret to share, a little wink-wink-nudge-nudge when she called him "Pyro" and warned him not to burn anything down.

The game had been fun. It had been very *them,* and had given him a secret warmth to carry with him when they were apart.

That same warmth pulled him out of the vision now, drawing him back into his body so he could feel the heavy lassitude of his limbs, the quiet, drugging fatigue of having pulled lots of magic without carb loading. There was a mattress beneath him, blankets piled on top of him. And, when he opened his eyes, a dark angel looking down at him.

"You're awake! When we found you in the john, we thought . . . *Gods.* I'm glad you're back." Relief flooded her eyes, and a wave of emotion slammed into him so hard and fast that it took his damn breath away before he'd even had a chance to catch it in the first place. With her dark hair pulled back in a ponytail and her face bare of makeup save for a touch of something dark at the corners of her eyes, and wearing one of his sweatshirts—so big that it fell off her shoulder at one side—she looked like the hottest coed ever, like the girl who had winked at him across the dining hall and called him Pyro.

In that moment, as the worry in her face dissolved to relief and a mist of tears, he realized that he knew three things without question: He loved her. He trusted her. And, somehow, his mother had to be wrong. He wasn't sure how, or what he could do to prove it, but she was wrong. Myrinne was . . . Myrinne. She wasn't working for anyone else, wasn't plotting behind his back. He loved her, believed in her.

More, she was his. And anybody who wanted to mess with her was going to have to go through him to do it . . . including his mother's ghost.

CHAPTER NINETEEN

September 17
Four days to the equinox; three months and
four days until the zero date
Monterey, California

"I'm sorry, sir," the little blue-haired docent said, "but that particular piece has been relocated. It was a last-minute substitution into the display we sent out for tonight's gala."

"For—" Sven stopped himself. "Right. The gala." He didn't need to take another look around the wood-paneled, elegantly appointed Playa Maya Museum or at the rock on the docent's ring finger to have his mental cash register give a *cha-ching*. Of course they needed funding, and a chichi party would be par for the area. "Are there any tickets left? We had planned on attending, but things came up—you know how it is—and I never got around to RSVPing."

Her lashes fluttered down over eyes gone suddenly

bright and interested. "As a matter of fact, yes, there's one stateroom left."

Cara turned from the display of three-legged pots she had been pretending to study. "Stateroom? The gala's on a cruise ship?" She frowned prettily, somehow managing to look a little ditzy, which he would've thought impossible. It was the third or fourth time she had slipped into a conversation with the museum staff with a perfectly timed question, bouncing off his conversational openers until they had the information they needed without the other person ever suspecting they were being pumped.

She was wearing sleek, upscale black, with her hair in a twist that showed the white in a repeating pattern that made him want to touch. Then again, pretty much everything about her had his hormones on red alert, and had since Anna zapped them to the drop site and disappeared, leaving them alone together, far from Skywatch. What was it Reese had said about it being good to get some distance? Shit, as far as he could tell, that was a matter of perspective. For her and Dez it might be a good break. For him and Cara . . . dangerous. He was far too aware that they were away from witnesses, away from judgment. And now it was looking like their quick in-and-out was going to turn into an all-night affair, unless they could figure out how to get at the screaming skull before the gala.

"It's just an overnight trip," the docent said brightly. "You'll be back bright and early in the morning. Shall I ring you up for that last stateroom, then?"

Overnight. Brilliant. "Sure, thanks"—he belatedly glanced at her name tag—"Doris." He touched Cara's arm and together they followed her to the gift shop, where he handed over the magic plastic—aka one of the limitless AmExes that were linked to the Nightkeeper Fund—and didn't let himself look at the number when he signed the slip.

Meanwhile, Cara chirped away, pleasantly wringing Doris dry of information about when, where, and how the screaming skull was being moved and displayed. The answers pretty much added up to there being no way in hell for them to get at it before the party. Seeming entirely unfazed by the prospect of spending the night, Cara burbled, "Is there anything we need to know about the gala? Dress code, silent auction, that sort of thing?"

"The dress is black and white." Doris leaned over the counter toward Sven, giving him a whiff of something lavendery and old-ladyish. "And between you and me, the food isn't very good—it's supposed to be Mayan, but one of the board members is some sort of health nut and pitched a fit, so dinner is going to be faux-veggie Mayan. The staff did their best, I'm sure, but it's all very ... healthy." She lowered her voice conspiratorially. "I'm smuggling in a couple of Big Macs and some homemade brownies to hold me over."

Despite his inner turmoil, Sven grinned. Old Doris might've just hustled him for a few thou—okay, he peeked—for what had to be the most expensive room on the ship, but a fellow junk-fooder couldn't be all that bad. "I'll keep that in mind," he assured her, and sent her an eyebrow wiggle on his way out the door, making her laugh and shoo him away.

Outside the museum, he and Cara found a small, secluded spot among the lush landscaping, and hunkered together to call Anna and update her on the situation. After a quick confab with Dez, she came back on the line, her voice slightly distorted as she said, "If you get in trouble, call me and I'll come for an emergency evac. Otherwise, I'll meet you on the dock in the morning. I'd rather not have to target a 'port onto a crowded boat in the middle of the Pacific."

"In other words," Cara said dryly after they signed off, "Dez said to leave us alone together for the day to duke it out." She didn't meet his eyes when she said it, though, and a faint flush stained her cheeks.

"It's not the worst idea." He leaned back and looked up at the sky, which was almost painfully blue through a feathering of brilliant green leaves. The day was bright and sharp, the air subtly scented with flowers, the niche a perfect little spot for a kiss . . . and three months from now, it could all be gone if the Nightkeepers and *winikin* didn't get their shit together. Which meant that he and Cara needed to get to work. But when he looked back and found her sitting there with her eyes closed and her face turned up to the sun, something shifted in his chest. She looked peaceful, almost happy. It wasn't until he saw the difference in her that he realized just how tense she was at Skywatch, like she was always braced for the next disaster. And he didn't want to put that look back on her face. "Fuck it. Let's play hooky."

Her eyes flew open, then narrowed. "That's so not happening."

"Why not? They're not expecting us back until morning, and we can't do anything with the skull until the gala. We've got all day." He shifted to face her but didn't let himself reach out. This wasn't about sex; it was about . . . Shit, he didn't know. He just knew that they needed this. "Come play with me, Cara," he said softly. "I think we could both use a day off."

Come play. He used to be the guy who surfed instead

of studying but aced his tests anyway, the guy who was always the first one into the pool and the last one to leave the party. When had he forgotten how to play? When had he gotten so freaking serious? The answer was right in his heart, though: He had stopped being that guy when he bonded with Mac. It was the first time in his life that he had made a real and lasting commitment to something, putting him on a different track with the magi. He was their hunter now, just as much a killer as Michael with his death magic. And, damn it, he wanted to play again.

"I don't think that's such a good idea." The shadows in her eyes tugged at him, moved him, and suddenly there was nothing he wanted to do more than take them away—for a few hours, at least.

And he thought he knew how. "Come sailing with me." The ocean was the one thing they had in common as actual people.

Her gaze sharpened. "That's not fair."

"So sue me. . . . But do me a favor and wait until after we've run away to sea for a few hours." His voice dropped. "Think of it—the wind in our faces, the sound of the waves, the feeling of the boat moving under us . . ." And in thinking of it, he yearned for the days when that had been his whole world, back before the Nightkeepers, the magic, and Mac. Maybe he'd been young, cocky, and irresponsible, but he'd been, at his core, happy.

He didn't know whether she was humoring him or if she too missed her days on the water, but she hesitated only a few seconds before she nodded. "Okay. I . . . Okay, let's do it."

Feeling like the bell had just rung on the last day of classes, he surged to his feet. "Come on. Let's go find ourselves a marina."

She joined him, eyes lighting with a glint of the excitement that was suddenly racing through him—not the toxic restlessness that dogged him when he stayed in one place too long, but the anticipation of the rush and the roar of the ocean.

"You find the marina and charm someone into renting you a boat you'll be happy with. Text me when you've got something and I'll meet you there."

"Where are you going to be?"

"Shopping." Her lips twisted in a rueful smile. "We both need bathing suits . . . and unless I miss my guess, we're short on some black and white."

"I'll do it." The words were out before he knew what he was saying.

Her startled eyes flew to his. "Wait. What?"

"I'll do the shopping. You find us a boat." And if that wasn't a vote of trust, he didn't know what was. But with her wearing his mark on her wrist, the last thing he wanted was for her to do his chores.

Faint color stained her cheeks. "Are you sure?"

Yeah, if it made her look like that . . . then yeah, he was sure. "Positive. Let's go."

The next hour was, mercifully, a blur that mainly consisted of walking into the first high-end place he saw that had a tux in the window on one side and a sparkly dress on the other and throwing himself on the clerk's mercy.

The bathing suits were easy enough—after getting a baleful look for his semiobscene charade of, "She's about this big," he texted Cara for the info the saleslady wanted, and then went off to the other side of the store for a pair of trunks and the joy of having his inseam politely groped. The tux was a no-brainer—he just nodded and let the sales guy go to town with the caveat of, "Anything, as long as I can walk out with it"—and when the ladies' attendant came back with three gowns she thought would work, he "eenie, meenie, miney, mo'd" it . . . and then picked the one he liked because it sparkled like the sea in bright sunlight, washing everything to white and glitter. And when he reached the register and a gleam of black and white caught his eye, he added it to the pile and got a gush of thanks in return.

This time he went ahead and looked at the total, and he chuckled when he signed off. Granted, it wasn't as fun as back when Jox was handling the purse strings—it'd been entertaining to watch the poor guy twitch when Alexis had killed a rented BMW and left it on the AmEx—but it still felt just illicit enough for him to get a kick out of it.

It took him fifty-two minutes from in to out, and when he hit the street lugging a bunch of bags, he was feeling pretty damn proud of himself. And, as he headed for the marina, he caught himself whistling and realized that, for that precious moment, he was at peace, headed out to sea with Cara. It might've been one of the fantasies he'd had down south of the life he would've liked to live if he could've done anything he wanted. But for today, it was real.

Ditching his purchases for the gala in a couple of guest lockers, he headed for the water with the bathing suits, still whistling.

"Hey!" She waved from a slip halfway down the dock, where she sat perched on the gunwale of a jaunty motorboat with sleek lines and a big-ass engine. When he came level with her, she said, "I went with horsepower over wind power so we'd be certain to make it back in time for the gala." A grin lit her face. "And because I feel like going really, really fast."

"Then let's get going. Fast."

They set about casting off, working smoothly as a team, just as they had back at the museum. And as they did, he made only a token effort to hold back a surge of pure male appreciation for a gorgeous woman dressing up a powerful machine. With her hair slicked back into a tight braid and the gleam off her narrow black sunglasses mimicking the startling white streak in her hair, wearing a new polo shirt emblazoned with the marina's logo over her own black pants, she could have passed for anything from an employee to a rich owner, and would've gotten second and third looks no matter what. More, she moved about the boat with the easy grace of someone who hadn't just spent a few months aboard a whale-watching boat, but was a natural, to boot.

She turned around, caught him looking, and went still. He fully expected her expression to flatten out, maybe go annoyed. But then her lips curved and her eyes warmed, and she called, "Less staring and more doing, mister!"

His heart kicked a funny beat and he snapped a salute. "Aye, Captain."

That set the tone for the afternoon, as they roared out to sea and then up the coast with the throttle wide-open and the wind in their faces. They didn't talk much, didn't touch each other aside from a friendly shoulder or hip bump in passing as they traded off on driving, or maneuvered around the narrow space belowdecks where she had stored food from the marina's snack bar, which was predictably overpriced but not half-bad.

Beyond the galley was a low-ceilinged room with a wide sleeping platform, but they kept the door shut by unspoken consent and stayed mostly on deck, breathing the salty air and leaning into the whip of the wind. And although they both kept a sharp eye on their surroundings and had weapons hidden beneath their clothes or, once they were in their bathing suits, close at hand, the threats all seemed mercifully far away.

At noon, as they throttled down to *putt-putt* past a sea lion rookery and did bad impressions of the hugely raucous creatures, Sven was as relaxed as he'd been in the past . . . gods, he didn't even know how long, eased by the roll of the waves beneath the boat and the way they could just *be* together, without chattering or trying to impress each other.

At two, as they turned back with a shared look of reluctance, he was in a pleasant haze brought on by the warm sun, moist sea air, and her company. And it wasn't that she was so unobtrusive that he could pretend she wasn't there, that he was alone as he often preferred. Exactly the opposite, in fact, as he found himself turning toward her to point out the things he saw—here a small pod of dolphins, there a rocky outcropping that should be a postcard and probably was, and beyond it a cormorant just coming up from a dive and hopping up onto a rock to cock his long black wings and hang himself out to dry.

Gods above, he thought as she laughed up at him, her expression open and animated, and so damn beautiful it made his heart hurt. *Why can't it always be like this?*

Why couldn't they just be two normal people who'd met in a normal way—at a bar, on the beach, somewhere that didn't come with the rules and ungodly pressure of Skywatch? If this was the kind of thing she was picturing when she talked about the life she wanted to lead after the war, he could see now how it could be a powerful motivator. He'd never really thought that way, never really looked beyond the war. Now, though . . . it twisted him up inside to know that if they were seeing her future now, he wouldn't be in it. Not only because he believed her when she said she was going to walk away and not look back, but because his instincts said so. He was no prescient, but somehow he was certain that whoever the guy was in her future happy day on a boat, it wasn't him.

He must have stared at her too long, because she tipped down her sunglasses to look at him. "What's wrong?"

"Nothing." When she didn't look convinced, he crossed to her and took her hand. Her eyes widened, but she didn't pull it away, not even when he brushed his lips across her knuckles. "Right now, in this moment, it's nothing."

She shook her head and reclaimed her hand, but squeezed his fingers in parting. And for the next couple of hours they were mostly silent, lost in their separate thoughts.

Still, at five, as they motored back into the marina and did the seesaw routine required to slide the boat back into its original position, crowded one among many, he didn't want to let go of the day.

In the past, by now he would have been chafing for some time by himself. Instead, when she would have hopped out of the boat he talked her into one more soda, a few more minutes of them quietly chatting about nothing in particular—the view, the birds, the strangeness of being on the water after spending so long inland, and how quickly it felt like home. He didn't want to leave, didn't want the day to be over.

"It's not over, not really," she pointed out when he

said it aloud. "But it *is* time to shift gears, get suited up, and head for the gala." Her fingers worked at the beads of condensation on her can of Diet Coke, suggesting that she was tensing up and getting excited for the op, just as she had been that morning.

He couldn't blame her—the cloak-and-dagger stuff *was* pretty cool, and he was usually just as excited to get rolling. He wasn't, though. . . . If anything, he wanted to full-throttle it back out of the bay and not look back.

I've got a bad feeling about this, he thought but didn't say. The equinox was only a few days away and they needed the screaming skull. So instead, silently vowing to make damn sure she made it out in one piece no matter what, he said only, "Promise me you'll be careful?"

Her eyes sparked, but she must have seen something in his face, because after a brief hesitation, she nodded. "Okay, I'll promise . . . if you do the same."

How long had it been since anyone had told him that before he headed off into action? Shit, he didn't know, just like he didn't know why it hit him so hard now, punching a tight fist beneath his heart. Or, rather, he knew, but it was better if he pretended he didn't. Not because Carlos was worried about his magic and focus, or even because of the other *winikin,* but because she had been right to call him on his bullshit. He didn't get to have her unless he was ready and willing to be there for her a hundred percent . . . and that was the one thing he knew he couldn't give her.

Damn it all.

He could give her this, though. "Yeah. I promise."

Her expression firmed, going more serious than it had been only moments before, as if she had caught some of his mood. "Okay, then. Let's do this."

They headed for the marina's clubhouse, where she had gotten day passes as part of the rental, and they separated to their respective locker rooms to get gala'd up.

He emerged sometime later and settled down to wait in the pretty cobbled courtyard that the marina maintained for its guests. Pulling out his phone, he cleared a few texts and skimmed through the e-mails, finding nothing critical. He was just starting to type a reply to the forward an old wreck-diving buddy had sent him—bad joke, even worse picture—when movement from the ladies' locker room caught his attention.

He looked up and saw Cara. He froze.

And he stared.

The snow-white gown shimmered with the movement of beads and unidentifiable glittery things that picked up the light and dipped and clung to her curves. One of her shoulders was covered, the other bare, and the subtle contrast between the gleaming white and the cream of her skin made him want to touch and taste, as did the severe perfection of her twisted-up hair with its zigzag stripe, and how it was softened by a couple of curled sections that fell free to cover the earpiece she wore to match the one he had on. The skirt had seemed longer when the saleslady had held it up, but he wasn't complaining about the way it hit Cara midthigh, showing off legs that seemed far longer than her diminutive size would suggest; nor was he complaining about the narrow silver shoes with their crisscrossed chains and funky zippered fastening, which punked things up and took the look from "wow" to "wow, it's Cara."

No, he wasn't complaining at all. In fact, he wasn't saying anything, because he didn't have the words.

She glided over, heels tapping unerringly on the cobblestones without a wobble, as if some feminine magic were at work. She carried the gleaming white shoulder bag he'd insisted on despite the saleslady's objections that it was too big for evening wear. When she got up close to him, he caught her light, flowery scent and saw that she'd put on makeup, had somehow been carrying it with her even though they'd had no hint of the gala. Magic again. As she drew near, her eyes warmed and a smile grew. "Thank you."

The drool, it seemed, was a sufficient compliment.

He wanted to give her more, though. Going for the inner pocket of his tux, he pulled out the long, narrow box that held the necklace that had caught his eye ... and suddenly felt awkward as hell standing there, holding it while her eyes got big.

Too late, he heard the mental warning sirens and recognized the inner *what the hell are you doing?* He was supposed to be proving to her that they could work together without the personal stuff getting in the way. Not dressing them up in clothes out of their shared vision and handing over bling. He concentrated on breathing, trying to get his tongue unstuck from his epiglottis. This didn't have to be a big deal. *It was just funny money,* he told himself, and it wasn't like he could put the box away and pretend it hadn't happened. So he would give it to her and try not to make this into more than it needed to be.

He wasn't quite sure how he was going to pull that off, though.

"I don't know what this is or what it's supposed to mean," he said, holding out the box. "I just know I needed to get it. How about we call it a peace offering, or a symbol of our new working relationship, or some such shit.

Anyway . . ." Taking a deep breath, he flipped open the lid. "It reminded me of you."

The single strand of sparkling black gems drew the eye down to the central stone, which was a clear, pure white that shimmered and glowed when the light hit it. It was sleek, sophisticated, and dramatic as hell.

"Oh," she breathed, reaching for it and then pulling her hand back as if afraid to touch, instead putting her hand over her mouth.

Some of the nerves smoothed out inside him. Okay, good. This was good. He could do this precisely because it *was* Cara, and because she deserved to have someone do something for her now and then, rather than the other way around. More, he had a feeling from the way she inhaled and squared her shoulders that she was being careful not to read too much into the gesture.

"Let me," he said, not realizing until after the words were out there that he had said the same thing when he'd gone down on her in the cave. But he'd meant it then and he meant it now. She gave and gave to everyone else, and deserved to have someone give back to her for a change. And if he was playing with fire, he could handle himself. Had been for a long time now.

Her eyes were steady on his for a moment; then she turned away and presented him with her back, which was bare down to nearly her waist. Her spine was straight and proud, the curve of her neck elegant, the soft skin behind her ear terrifyingly vulnerable. He wanted badly to touch her, thought from the rhythm of her breathing that she wanted it too.

"I'm not wearing my gun," she said, but although she had probably been going for a conversational tone, it came out breathy and suggestive. Or maybe that was because his brain immediately supplied the detail that she also wasn't wearing a bra.

He cleared his throat. "Stay close to me. We're better off shielding up and getting the hell out if there's any trouble."

"Okay." The word was soft, as if she were agreeing to more than just the plan. Or maybe that was wishful thinking.

He fumbled a little with the box and the way it held the necklace in place, then lifted the glittering strand free and draped it around her front, absurdly conscious of the way his own breathing hitched as she bent her head forward so her coiled hair would stay free of the clasp. The moment suddenly seemed very intimate, as if this were something he should be doing in a bedroom, not a cobbled courtyard, with a couple of people pretending not to watch from one of the café tables nearby.

Her skin was soft and warm, her bone structure impossibly delicate. It took him far too long to slide the clasp's little tongue into its little receiver, in an act that he told himself not to read too much into—not that he wasn't already stiff and uncomfortable inside the tux trousers, and sorely tempted to reach down there and readjust.

By the time the mechanism clicked into place, he was breathing hard and sweating. He backed away fast, holding out his hands in a gesture of *nope, didn't touch anything,* more to reassure himself than her. "Okay, you're good."

She took a deep breath and turned back to him, eyes bright with emotion. "Thank you," she said simply. Easing up on her tiptoes, she got a gentle grip on one of his lapels and tugged him down so she could kiss his cheek.

The gesture was as simple as her words—a pure thank-you that didn't ask anything more of him, didn't seek or give promises. And for the first time in his life, he wished there were questions and promises, wished there were something more. But there was only gratitude in her eyes when she settled back and took a moment to smooth his lapel back down, stroking the place over his heart, and there was nothing more than polite inquiry when she chirped, "Ready?"

No. "Yep." What was she thinking right now? When they were younger, he'd almost always been able to read her thoughts from her face, except when they were wagering. That was one of the things that had made her so damn tough to beat at the *patolli*: her ability to bluff. Was she bluffing now, or had she really managed to set aside her feelings and frustrations and put him back in the friend zone?

Never mind that—what was *he* thinking? He couldn't give her what she needed, yet he wanted her to want him. "Selfish" didn't even begin to cover it.

Unaware of his inner morass, she said brightly, "Well, then, the gala awaits us." She took his arm as if it were the most natural thing in the world.

Was she already playing the role of his ditzy arm candy, or did she really not feel the heat crackling in the air around them? His skin was tight, his magic revving a sharp spark in his blood and a deep ache in his wrist, beneath his marks. Frustration snapped at his heels, thinning the control he'd kept on himself all day as he'd watched her bask in the simple one-piece bathing suit the saleslady had chosen for her, or sat beside her as she drove the boat with reckless enthusiasm, winding up the motor past redline now and then, and laughing at the slap of the wind in their faces, the feeling of freedom. He'd wanted her then and told himself to keep his hands to himself. He wanted her now even more . . . and the sight of her wearing the sparkling black collar he'd chosen for her sliced right through that self-control and had him reaching for her before he was even aware of having made the decision. He caught the back of her neck and felt the necklace brush the side of his hand as he drew her close.

And then he took her mouth in a kiss that had his pulse going from zero to a buck twenty in no time flat.

Their first two kisses had been her idea, and things in the cave had happened partly because of the magic . . . but this kiss was his. He slanted his lips across hers and took, levered her mouth open and claimed. And when her surprised gasp trailed off on a moan of surrender, he didn't back off and give her a moment to catch up; he moved in and took more.

Then she murmured and crowded closer, blossoming open into the kiss, and he stopped being aware of anything beyond the woman in his arms and the heat they made together. Some warrior part of him was still monitoring the world, ever vigilant, but the rest of him was lost in the kiss. They twined together, seeking and tasting. The texture of her dress reminded him not to rip and tear, not even to wrinkle, as they had a job yet to do. But that constraint only added to the sharp excitement as he ran his hands gently down her body and then back up again, grazing the sides of her hips, ribs, and breasts and wringing a moan from her.

The sound startled him. He tore his lips free and pressed his brow to hers. He was breathing hard, laboring to suck in enough oxygen to keep him on his feet, but that battle was nothing compared to the one inside his skull. "You should slap me for that," he said, his voice raspy. "Hell, punch me. Shoot me, even. I frigging deserve it."

She pulled away but didn't go far. Instead, still in his arms, she blinked up at him, then pressed her lips together as if tasting him. "Why? Because you kissed me?"

"Because I kissed you, because I talked you into a hooky day we both knew would only make it harder to pretend we're just working together . . . Hell, because I went behind your back to spy on the *winikin* and didn't tell you about the liaison thing." He paused, exhaling. "Most of all because I should be guilty as fuck-all over the way I'm handling this. I know things can't go anywhere between us, and we're screwed if even this much gets around back home. . . . But I can't keep my damn hands off you." He skimmed a fingertip along the edge of the necklace, which was warm from her skin. "You're going to have to be the one to stop this . . . because I'll be damned if I know how."

A flush deepened at her throat and on her cheeks, and her eyes took on a dangerous gleam that had him bracing himself for a slap, a punch, maybe even a shot.

Instead, she eased in and brushed her lips across his in a gentle, fleeting touch that poured lightning into his veins. And when she eased away, she was smiling with wry humor. "Let's let it go for tonight, okay? We're here; the others aren't . . . and this is the first time in my life a guy has cared enough to beat himself up over me. If you don't mind, I think I'll enjoy it while I can. Besides, we're running out of time if we're going to get this job done."

"Cara . . ." But what was he supposed to say to that? He'd known her all his life, and she could still startle the hell out of him. Then again, he probably shouldn't be surprised—she'd shown over and over again that she was tough, resourceful, and resilient, and able to deal with whatever was thrown at her. Only . . . he didn't want to be something she had to deal with. He didn't know what he wanted, except to keep that light in her eyes. So instead of pushing her like he wanted to do, getting her to tell him what she was really thinking, he crooked his elbow and held it out. "Ready to become a thief?"

"Absolutely." She took his arm and they set off along the courtyard, heading for the piers where the cruise ships docked. And if there had been a flash of relief in her eyes, a hint of vulnerability at odds with her tough-girl demeanor, he let it go. For now, anyway. They could figure out the other stuff later. Right now, they had to get their hands on the screaming skull artifact and keep each other out of trouble . . . and his instincts said that was going to be easier said than done.

CHAPTER TWENTY

The *Monterey Princess* was huge and slick, the crowd was glittery and ornate, and Cara was a wreck. Oh, she camouflaged it well—she'd had plenty of practice burying her emotions, after all. But she was seriously shaky inside as she and Sven boarded the small, luxurious cruise ship, handed over their scant luggage to an attendant with bushy eyebrows and bulging pockets, and joined the flow of expensively decked-out humanity headed for the main ballroom.

She was only peripherally aware of the touches of polished wood and sparkling crystal that went into making up the aura of understated elegance surrounding them, or the more overblown glitter of the crowd. Instead, she was wholly aware of the man beside her: the heat of his body; the leashed strength beneath her fingertips, where she had her hand loosely at the crook of his arm, not letting herself cling. . . . And the deceptive lightness of the necklace he'd bought her, which skimmed across her skin when she moved, reminding her of his touch.

Focus. She'd poked at him about needing to keep his mind on the job, but she was the one who needed the reminder. She might have convinced him that she was cool with the way things were between them, but exactly the opposite was true. She was heated and churned up, and all too ready to make a mistake. The boat ride and the kiss, combined with clothes that were far too close to the black-and-white of the *nahwal*'s vision . . . it was all too much. She was restless, twitchy, and anxious. Fine currents of heat ran through her body, coiling in her belly and warming her inner wrist, right where she wore his mark.

In the main ballroom, the crowd had formed an amorphous line that wound through the main salon, where the artifacts were being displayed in gleaming cases that looked deceptively flimsy, but weren't. Brightly colored signs adorned each case.

Making herself dial into their surroundings—and not her escort—Cara scanned the scene, noting three exits and four guards: solo guys in their twenties and thirties, wearing tuxes and earbuds, with weapons under their jackets. The bulk of the partygoers were elegantly put together in tuxes and nice dresses, with a few outfits leaning toward tacky. One in particular had her doing a double take, checking that the body stocking and artistically placed white feathers covered all the relevant parts of its fiftyish female wearer. They did, but the dress, combined with bright orange sandals that laced up to her knees, evoked a Henny Penny mascot far more than it did anything else.

"Wonder if she thought that was Mayan?" Sven said in an undertone, with a head tilt in Henny's direction. But although he went for the joke, his expression was serious as he searched Cara's face, no doubt wondering whether she was going to be able to handle the op.

"If it is, you can count me out of that ritual," she tossed back, shooting him a hard-edged look out of the corner of her eye, hoping it came off as purposeful rather than brittle and a little desperate.

It must have worked, because he nodded toward the display that held the screaming skull. "Shall we wander in that direction?"

"Lead the way."

They should have blended in as they rambled from display to display, pretending to be more into each other than the artifacts, but even in the well-heeled crowd they drew looks, no doubt because of the glossy gleam of perfection that came with Sven's Nightkeeper genetics. The tux was off-the-rack and a bit tight in the shoulders, his hair disheveled from the ocean breeze, but he drew the eye and held it, and made a girl think about stripping off that tux and running her fingers through that hair.

When a sleek blond twenty-something model-type on the arm of a much older man turned her head to arch an eyebrow at Sven, Cara nearly bared her teeth. *Back off; he's mine.* Only he wasn't, wouldn't ever be. So she ignored the trophy blonde and forced herself to focus as their calculatedly wandering path brought her and Sven into range of their target.

The sturdy base of the elegant wood-grained stand was bolted to the floor, and a see-through dome shaped like a step-sided pyramid covered the top and was locked into place. Within that fairly formidable vault—well, formidable to anybody but a translocator—a velvet-covered stand shaped like a human hand held a gleaming black stone as if preparing to hurl it, sinkerlike. Only this was no game ball; it was carved into the shape of a human skull, with its mouth agape in a terrible scream. The screaming skull, which represented the Nightkeepers and their duty to save mankind from the end-time war, had been found in only a very few Mayan sites and on only a handful of artifacts. Of the artifacts, most—including this one—had been dismissed as modern-made fakes, when, really, they had been made using magic, not machines.

Cara's skin prickled to goose bumps and she had to fight a shiver, though the ballroom had been too warm only seconds earlier.

"Cold?" he asked with a sidelong look.

"No, it's just . . . Never mind," she decided. There was no point in letting him know she was more nervous than she'd expected to be. Even though they would be magically swapping the statue for a good fake and making an anonymous donation that would more than cover the theft, it was still stealing. The knowledge had her on edge, as did the heat that pulsed beneath her skin, a whole-body awareness that she couldn't afford to feel. She shook her head, trying to clear the wayward thoughts. "Let's do this."

She started to move off toward the farthest guard, but Sven reached out and snagged her hand. When she turned back, startled, he tugged her closer, then leaned in to say with quiet firmness: "You don't have anything to worry about, Cara. I've got your back. I swear."

Another shiver worked its way across her skin, because she didn't think he'd ever promised her anything before. That he was doing so now meant something. She didn't ask what or why, though. She just squeezed his hand. "Same goes. I've got your back—promise."

She would have tugged free and turned to go, but a

strange warmth suddenly rose up inside her, stealing her will to move. Her feet grew roots, her fingers curled around his, and for a second it was like they were *connected,* not just physically, but mentally as well. She could feel the pulse of his heartbeat alongside her own and could faintly sense the humming magic within him, throbbing just beyond the threshold of her understanding. Heat kindled in her core, a potent mix of awe and excitement that urged her to go to him, be with him, bind herself to him, and give him—

No! Wrenching herself out of that litany, she tugged away, breaking the palm-to-palm contact with a sharp jerk that drew too many eyes.

Aware that they couldn't cause a scene, she made herself smile, made herself reach up and cup his cheek, which was smooth beneath her overheated palm.

His eyes were hard and hot, churning with the magic she had felt within him. "What just happened?" he grated, voice low. But his expression said that he knew. They both knew.

She said it anyway. "I think it was the First Father's magic acknowledging a *winikin* swearing to protect her Nightkeeper charge." *Damn it all.* She glanced at her wrist and exhaled a small, relieved breath to find that she still lacked the *aj winikin* mark.

"That promise goes both ways," he said quietly.

Maybe so, but the magical bond put on the *winikin* was a one-way street, and it wasn't one she wanted to travel.

Making herself move by force of will, she took a big step back, smiling brightly and pitching her voice to carry. "No, you go ahead and look around, and I'll get the drinks. I'll be back in just a second."

The last few people who had been paying attention to them—mostly bored spouses looking to liven up the evening with a good fight—went back to their own business.

Sven gave her an intense look of *we'll talk about this later,* but nodded and stuck to their roughed-out plan. "No ice in mine."

She rolled her eyes like she'd heard that a thousand times, and with that little exchange, they fell entirely off the radar screens of the humans surrounding them.

Cara headed for the bar area, slipping easily through the crowd. She didn't draw nearly the amount of attention he did, though a few male heads turned as she approached, then pivoted back when she was gone. One of the guards gave her a once-over and a small smirk that she didn't want to think about, while two of the others looked through her as she passed where they were stationed near the premier pieces of the showing.

A set of low, wide stairs fanned out from the two exits nearby; from there, she had a clear view of the ballroom and was close enough to three of the four guards to keep a close eye on them. Sven would have to watch out for the fourth himself. Not that the Nightkeepers couldn't get them out of trouble if things went wrong, but it was better to keep things as quiet as possible.

Right now, things were looking nice and quiet. The crowd was starting to thin as couples headed for the dining room, the guards were vigilant but relaxed, and Sven was alone by the display case that held the screaming skull. From there, he could use low-level magic to make the switch, and then they would find a private spot on deck for the higher-level magic he needed to send the thing back to Skywatch.

As if sensing her eyes on him, he glanced up, found her, and sent her a *where is my drink?* gesture. They were on plan, on point, and good to go.

So why was her pulse pounding? More, why did it feel like she was still down there on the floor, surrounded by people while she stood in front of a display case?

You're talking yourself into this. There's nothing to be worried about. Just breathe. Everything will be fine.

"How's it look?" his voice murmured in her earpiece, creating an odd disconnect from the scene because she couldn't see his lips moving.

Far less adept with the communication device, she pretended to look out the door while she answered, "Seems clear."

"Seems clear or is clear?"

She took a deep breath. "You're good to go." *Please, gods.*

Turning back, she kept an eye on the guards, the crowd, and Sven himself as he lingered a moment longer in front of the screaming skull, leaning over the step-sided display case as if studying the piece in detail. Sudden heat flared through her body, wringing a gasp that caught the nearest guard's attention at the very moment that her oversize evening bag suddenly bulged and grew heavy. Then the heat was everywhere—inside her, all around her, not burning her but instead making her head spin. Her vision blurred and she wobbled.

"Ma'am?" The nearest guard took a step in her direction. "Are you okay?"

No! She couldn't screw this up, not now. Fighting through the haze, she clutched the bag to her chest when it threatened to slip from her fingers. "Seasick!" she blurted. Then she hunched over, channeled all of the *oh, crap, I'm going to puke* faces she'd seen on the whale-watch boat, and bolted out the door.

She hurried along the railing and then up the first set of stairs she came to, then another, heading higher and higher until she reached an open observation deck that was mercifully deserted. Sinking back against the nearest wall, she concentrated on breathing.

Holy shit. What just happened there?

Pull it together. Breathe. Focus.

Footsteps rang on the stairs coming up, but her instincts—or rather, the bond created by the coyote glyph she wore on her wrist—told her it was Sven. This time the burn was one of unease.

"Sorry," she said when he joined her in the small niche, crowding her back against the door with a broad-shouldered body that all but blocked the light. His protective stance settled her, smoothing out the edges. But at the same time it made her more aware of her screwup. "I didn't mean to draw attention like that."

"Don't worry about it. It was a nice distraction, and if it comes to questions, people are going to remember that you were by the far exit, nowhere near the skull. Hey." He caught her chin in his hand and tipped her face up into the light. "What happened?"

"Nothing. I . . ." She trailed off as a long shudder racked her body. "Shit. Sorry. I think . . . Damn it." She didn't want to say it out loud, but didn't see an alternative. "I think that because I don't have the *aj winikin* mark to balance off the coyote glyph, the bond is acting funny. I caught the backlash of the magic when you sent me the skull, and it just about knocked me on my ass."

"I didn't feel anything."

"That's because it only goes one way." She tipped a thumb from her chest to his.

"Not from where I'm standing."

"Tell that to the magic," she said, her voice threatening to crack.

"Cara—"

"Not now. We need to stay focused." She held out the bag. "Let's get this bad boy headed home, okay?"

He hesitated, then went for the knife he'd hidden in an ankle sheath. "Hand it over."

The carving was heavier to hold than it had felt in the bag, and oddly warm to the touch, the stone slick and smooth. Her heart thudded in her chest as Sven blooded his palms and said the spell words that jacked him into the barrier's power. Then he took the artifact from her, held it in both hands, and closed his eyes in concentration.

The skull vanished with a huge thunderclap and lightning flared overhead in a jagged slash that broke the sky. Which shouldn't have happened.

Cara choked off a startled scream and spun, then gaped at the sight of dark, angry storm clouds where there had been a clear sky and stars only moments before. Oh, gods. Had the *Banol Kax* tracked his magic? Were they somehow using the weather to attack?

Sven shouldered in front of her, using his body to shield her from a sudden whip of wind. "What the *fuck?* Where did that— *Get down!*" He pushed her back into the lee of the wall, crowding her into a small, sheltered space. Heat raced through her in a magical backlash, and suddenly the air around them sparkled faintly red-gold. She didn't have time to marvel at being able to see his shield spell, though, because the sky suddenly flared with another huge bolt of lightning.

It ripped straight for them and slammed into the ship, making the huge vessel lurch and wreathing the observation deck with an eerie blue-white glow. There were shouts and screams from below, where the main decks had gone dark, with emergency lights springing to life here and there. A lone siren began to blare.

Sven cursed and went for his armband, which he'd folded into the shape of a phone and stashed in the pocket of his tux. "Fuck. Nothing!"

Suddenly, horribly, the glow started to draw in on itself, rising up from the deck, taking on shape and details, becoming . . . "Oh, shit," Cara breathed. "Do you see . . ."

The blob was stretching and elongating, growing ears and a long tail even as it darkened to shadows and two burning eyes that glowed gleaming red. It was the hellhound that had attacked her at Aaron's funeral!

"Get ready to run when I say the word."

"I can't."

"Cara—"

"No!" She wouldn't risk leading it down to the others. "We need to stop it here!" She scrabbled in her bag for the gun, though jade-tips had barely made a dent the last time.

As if spurred by the sight, the beast roared and charged.

"Leave her alone!" The air turned suddenly scorching as Sven lunged upright, summoned a huge orange-red fireball, and unleashed it with a yell.

The magic slammed into the creature, encircling it with fire and driving it back and down. The thing gave a hideous mewl of pain and collapsed as the flames flared higher, growing so bright that Cara had to squint and then turn away.

Sven stood planted in front of her with his hands balled to fists as if he would've fought the thing with his bare hands rather than letting it get to her. But before she could think about the spreading warmth that ran through her at the sight, new horror kindled. "It's regenerating!"

Lightning lashed the sea around them, bringing thunder and wind, and letting them see that the creature wasn't just regenerating. It was getting *bigger*.

"Motherfucker," Sven said. And braced for the fight.

We're dead. That was all Sven's brain could cough up at the realization that they were out in the middle of the fucking ocean without backup or additional weapons. His shield was good for now, and he would try again with the fireball spell, but already he could feel the drain on his magic. He had burned too much of it sending the skull back to Skywatch.

The hellhound snarled as lightning flickered behind it, painting the scene with St. Elmo's fire.

Gods help us.

Cara came up beside him with her puny little pistol, eyes hard and determined. Her dress glittered in the blue-white lambency of the storm, her hair trailed from its twist in tendrils of white and black, and his magic haloed her with sparks of red-gold. In that moment, she looked like a goddess, and so damn beautiful it made his chest ache.

He wanted to hold her, have her, protect her. But he couldn't—

Join. You are more powerful together than apart. This is as it was meant to be. The *nahwal's* voice echoed in his head, followed by her soft gasp. She turned to him, eyes wide and scared, even as his pulse thudded with mingled shock and excitement.

"You heard that?" he grated.

She snapped her mouth closed and nodded. Then she held out her hand, palm up, to offer her scar. "Do it."

There wasn't time to weigh the options; hell, there weren't any options. He needed the kind of boost that came only from another mage . . . or a lover.

He took her hand as the beast struggled to its feet with a gurgling roar that called thunder and a howl of wind. He scored her palm and drew blood as the creature started stumbling forward, its eyes locked on his faltering shield. Then he took her hand in his, aligning them blood-to-blood, and hoping to hell this wasn't a huge mistake.

He felt the jolt of a low-level blood-link, but needed more than that. Way more. Calling his magic, he reached for the barrier and whispered, "*Pasaj och.*" But nothing changed. It was just the two of them and his nearly tapped-out magic.

"Hurry!" She gripped his hand, urging him on. "Kill it!"

He called a fireball, but it wasn't much, wasn't enough.

"It's not working!" she cried, voice cracking.

He shook his head. "I don't know—"

You to her and her to you. The bond must form or all is lost! And for a nanosecond—the briefest of instances, there and gone so quickly he almost missed it—pounding restlessness flared through him and he flashed back on a hot, baking desert floor burning his feet as he raced along, searching for the one who would complete him. Those were the dreams he'd had last year, the ones that he hadn't realized were coming from Mac. But how . . .

"That's it!"

His magic wasn't searching for a mate; it wanted a familiar. He was a coyote, after all.

Heart banging against his ribs, he tightened his grip on her and concentrated, not on his magic or the barrier connection, but on his bloodline mark. He focused on it, poured his magic into it, and opened himself to the soul bond he shared with Mac, even though the coyote was too far away for it to function. The magic pooled, searching for a target, then zeroing in on her.

His magic found her, recognized her, wanted her. It arrowed from him to her and back again, and his body convulsed as something tore inside him. Then blazing heat fired in his veins, burning down to his soul and then outward again, shooting down his arm to his bloodline mark.

"No!" he shouted, afraid the magic would burn her, hurt her, but he couldn't call it back, couldn't shut it down. Then the power raged through him, coalesced into a huge fireball that hung in the air, bleeding flames. And for a brief instant he saw double, perceived double—hell, he *was* double, sensing things not just with his own faculties, but with Cara's as well.

Connection. It burned through him, forging new pathways in his soul. He could feel her terror, but also the determination that was overriding it to put her at his side, facing the creature with nothing more than a Glock nine. Through her senses, he could feel the heat and sizzle of his Nightkeeper magic, which she shouldn't have been able to sense. And through both of their eyes, he saw the hellhound gathering for a leap.

"Now!" she shouted, or maybe he did. It didn't matter as he launched the fireball with a tremendous heave, straight at the onrushing creature.

Boom! Magic detonated on impact, wreathing the beast in flames. The hellhound screeched and reared up, snapping. But this time the fire raged higher and hotter as Sven poured more magic into the fireball, keeping the attack going. "Die, damn you!"

The magic kept coming and coming—from him, from her, from the greater power they somehow made together. He didn't question it; he used it, searing the beast, charring it. On one level there was dull horror and the too-familiar stench of burning flesh. On another, he knew only that he had to protect Cara and the humans below. Nothing else mattered . . . and if deep down inside he put her ahead of the masses, and went against the writs in doing so, he was fucking fine with that.

The creature struggled horribly, resisting death with keening cries until it finally collapsed with a shudder. Still, he kept it burning, holding on to the magic while lightning lit the night sky, and the wind whipped around them, pitching the huge ship from side to side. He burned the beast to cinders, but before he could call it done, the noise of the storm changed, rising to the scream of an unrushing funnel cloud.

"Hang on!" He grabbed Cara and shielded them both, but the twister didn't head for them. It went for the creature's ashes instead, sucking them off the deck and back up into the storm. The wind howled and lightning flickered, but even as the answering rumble of thunder trailed off, the storm was breaking up, dissipating.

Between one eye blink and the next, it vanished, leaving no sign of disturbance save for a slow roll beneath their feet and a rising clamor coming up from the decks below.

"Gods." Cara let out a shuddering breath. "The creature got stronger."

"Yeah, but so did we." And it was only just beginning to hit him how much stronger they had gotten together . . . and what it meant.

She looked at him then, and her eyes held a gleam that stirred his already stirred-up blood even more. But before she said anything more, shouts sounded from the staircase just as his armband pinged, doubly interrupting.

"I'll stall," she said. "You answer."

Without waiting for his nod, she stashed her gun in her bag and ran to the stairwell with a cry of, "Did you see that? What's happening?" Her tone notched up with each question, ending on a wail of, "Are we sinking?" That stalled the human tide that had rushed up thinking there was something going on up on the observation deck. Her near-sobs of "There's a *fire?* Where?" and "Oh, God, are there enough lifeboats? Sven, for the love of all that's holy, stop trying to upload that to YouTube and come on!" completed the turnaround.

Most of the looky-loos headed back down, while a few stalwart souls—all male, big surprise—stuck around to calm her down and shoot him dirty looks.

"You there?" Dez said the moment Sven answered the phone. "What the hell is going on? The skull arrived hotter than hell, and with a blast of magic like I've never felt before. And then your dog went nuts."

"He's not— Shit, never mind. Here's the deal." Sven rattled off a quick rundown of the attack, ending with, "I don't know what's going on here, but there's got to be some connection between the storms, the creature, and Cara."

"And between the two of you."

"Yeah." He didn't want to make a big deal about that yet, though. Not until he and Cara had a chance to talk about it. It might not make any difference, really.

Or it might change everything.

"You want us to try a midocean pickup?"

"No, don't risk it." When Cara called his name, Sven looked over and saw her and a couple of cruise employees waiting by the stairs. "I've got to go. They're sending us all to our cabins while they turn the boat around and head in. If we disappear now, there'll be questions."

"We can handle it. The credit card won't lead them anywhere if they try to trace you."

"Still. I'd rather stick it out." Cara could use a few hours to process what had just happened. Hell, he needed the time too.

"You think it's safe?"

"We can take care of ourselves," Sven said, and clicked off. It wasn't until he had tucked the communication device back in his pocket and was headed over to rejoin her that he realized he'd meant it—not just that he would take care of her, but that they would take care of each other.

Holy shit. He missed a step at realizing that he was suddenly part of a "we." How had that happened? His gut fisted. He might not have liked it when she said the *winikin* magic went only one way, but that was because it wasn't fair to her that the gods and circumstances had conspired to take the choice away from her, not because he'd wanted a two-way magical bond with her—mated, familiar, or otherwise. Yet now the choice had been taken away from him too.

Or had it? He had promised to watch her back, after

all. And their new connection had given him the power to do it. That couldn't be a bad thing.

Right?

"Hey." She caught his hand as he reached the small crowd at the stairwell. "Did you get through to your parents and let them know that we were hit by a storm, but we're fine?"

"Yeah, I talked to them." He slid an arm around her waist. To the two crewmen who had stayed behind, waiting to herd them to their stateroom, he said, "Did the boat take any damage? Are there more of those squalls coming?"

"Everything's fine, sir, but you really need to get under cover."

They joined the flow of humanity down below and headed for their stateroom in a silence that seemed out of place amid the babble that surrounded them, a mix of, "Did you see that lightning?" and, "It looked like something was on fire there for a few minutes!" and, "Are you sure we're not sinking?"

When they reached their room—an exterior cabin with an ornate door and a key-card slot designed to look like old ship's brass—he swiped his card and held the door for her, and then stepped through and closed and bolted the door. Shutting out the din was a huge relief, but the pressure inside him skyrocketed again as he took a look around what proved to be the sitting area of the two-room stateroom.

The place was decorated like a damn French bordello.

There was gilt and red velvet practically everywhere he looked, and in the nearby bathroom, brass and marble picked up the theme and promised hot tub action and all the slippery bath salts and massage oils he could ask for. *Come on in, get comfortable, and get busy,* the decor practically screamed. *Get naked. Get it on.* Or maybe that was just him, he thought. But then Cara turned back from taking her own long look around, and he saw an answering heat in her eyes, along with a disquieting click of connection. It felt almost like he'd jacked into the barrier, but it was faint and far away, just a buzz of magic in his blood, a stir of echoes in his soul.

Their bond—whatever it was, however it worked—didn't just come when he called his magic, then. The realization brought a skim of disquiet, as did the way she linked her fingers together and stared down at them as if bracing herself.

He crossed to her, didn't let himself touch. He wanted to soothe, to fix things, but wasn't sure if they were fixable, or if he should even try. "I'm sorry. I know this wasn't what you wanted."

"No, it wasn't." She let out a slow breath, then looked up at him, and he was surprised by her calm. "Part of me is glad it happened, though. It makes things easier." She paused. "After all, I did ask for a sign, didn't I?"

A buzz of fresh heat entered his bloodstream as he remembered. "Yeah, you did." Along with the heat came a sense of inevitability. *Join,* the *nahwal* had said, *or all is lost.* She had wanted proof that their being together was part of the gods' plan before she risked the *winikin* by becoming his lover for real. But . . . "I'm still the same guy, Cara. I can't change who I am."

"There's a newsflash." Brief humor lightened her expression; then it softened to something he didn't remember seeing from her before: peace. "I'm okay with that. More than okay, really. I didn't ask for a sign that we were destined mates or meant to be together forever.

That's not what I want. I just needed to know that we weren't talking ourselves into something that's not real."

As much as he was dying to touch her, he held himself back. "The magic is real," he said, the words coming from deep inside him. "The connection we made upstairs ... that's real, and it means something. But at the same time, the magic shouldn't force you to do anything you don't want."

"It's not forcing me; it's giving me permission." Her lips curved, her eyes lit, and she held out her hand, palm up, to show a thin scar where a scab should have been. "Will you be my lover until the end of the age? Will you stand with me, fight with me, and help me lead my people beside yours?"

Said that way, it somehow took on the weight of a spell. He hesitated, though not because of the magic. "What happens after?"

"We say good-bye." Her smile didn't waver. "I'm not trying to trap you into anything, Sven, and I'm not letting the magic trap me. We'll do our duties and, gods willing, save the world. And after that, we'll go out there and live our lives knowing that each day after the twenty-first of December is a blessing. What could be better than that?"

They were the right words but they somehow struck him wrong, making him want to argue the inarguable. Instead, he took her hand and cradled it for a moment in his, surprised anew that hers was so small in comparison, yet held such strength. "You're sure? This is what you want?"

She nodded, then looked up at him. "Yeah. You?"

He let his body answer for him, leaning in and sliding his hand up her arm and down to her waist, skimming over the textures of the dress and the woman beneath.

Her eyes darkened and her breath caught, and a primal response surged up from deep inside him. Suddenly he wanted to nip at her neck, herd her into the bedroom, cover her with his body, and thrust into her warmth, pounding hard and heavy. He could see it in that instant, not just through his eyes, but through her senses, as well. He could smell their mingled scents, hear her cries, feel the furious pleasure of taking her as his own.

Do it, his overheated system chanted. *Do it!*

Instead, he eased in and skimmed his lips over her cheek to the corner of her mouth, lingering there while her hand crept up his arm and her fingers curled around his shoulder. He waited until she softened against him, until her lashes fluttered shut and she murmured his name, and then he claimed her mouth in a deep and drugging kiss, one that said, *I want you,* and, *I need you,* and, *We're going to take our time and make this last.* And if on some level he knew that by holding back those mating urges he was trying to prove to her that there was more to them than just magic and circumstances, more than the gods' intentions, he tried to let that go for now.

After all, he had known from the moment he kissed her in the coyote cave that neither of them was going to walk away from this unscathed.

CHAPTER TWENTY-ONE

They went through the door into the bedroom together, kissing and dragging at clothing with reckless abandon.

Sven slapped the switch near the door and the room came to life, with light fracturing from a central chandelier and a series of wall sconces. Cara got a glimpse of gilt, and a huge, crimson-covered bed overwhelming the small shipboard space. Then he slammed the door and spun her back against it, lifting her and then pinning her there. And instead of, *Am I really doing this*? all she could think was, *Oh, gods, yes*.

She didn't need to think any further than that—she'd gotten her sign in the *nahwal*'s message, and even without it, she knew that this was right for her, here and now. She would lead the *winikin* but she wouldn't live her life in fear of them. If the future was only a few short months, she wanted to live those months with all the pleasure and magic she could find. And if "after" went beyond that, she would have fully experienced passion for the first time in her life, giving her a benchmark for her next lover to meet and exceed.

Not that she wanted to think about that next lover now.

Instead, she found Sven's mouth with hers and poured herself into the kiss, taking it dark and wicked with her palms and tongue. He groaned in answer and ran his hands up her legs to push the dress high, and she stretched to wrap her legs around him, arch into him, and ride the hard ridge of his erection. The move wrung a growl from deep within his chest, and he lifted her higher to feast on her throat while she wrapped her arms around his neck, needing to hold him, touch him, be close to him. Closer still.

His kisses were ardent, his breathing fast and furious, his body a solid, immovable wall that brought nerves and the breathless weight of panic flashing through her as one part of her knew it was trapped, but another said, *Yes, please, more.*

She gave herself up to it, gloried in the way he held her off the ground without effort, pinning her with his lower body so his hands were free to touch and take. The dress was bunched at her waist now, his mouth at her breasts as she remained trapped between the flat press of the door and the yielding hardness of her lover.

Her lover. Yes. Sven was about to become her lover for real. *Gods.*

She buried her fingers in his hair and tugged back his head. His eyes were wild and glazed, his focus entirely on her, and when she drove her lips onto his, he met her stroke for stroke, with a rattling groan that echoed from him to her and back again, seeming caught in the heat and the magic that thrummed just beyond her senses.

"Not here. Not this time." He spun them away from

the door, cupping her ass so she rode him, as he carried her to the bed, kissing her, needing her. His hands raced over her, nearly violent in their speed, yet gentle when they connected. She leaned away, unfastened her dress, and skimmed it up over her head to fling it wonderfully free, so she was wearing only stockings, panties, and heels, and was wanton with it.

He lowered her to the bed but kept his weight off her as he kissed her and then drew away to stand over her, strip off his jacket, and reach for the buttons of his shirt. Then he went suddenly still, his eyes darkening as he looked down at her.

She lay deliciously sprawled, letting him look his fill while the blood pumped through her, making every inch of her tingle.

"Gods," he said, his voice raspy, the word seeming to come from deep down inside him. "Cara."

"Yes," she said. Yes to all of it: to having him, taking him and being taken. This mattered; the rest of the world didn't, not now. She rose to her knees and reached for the studs of his shirt, nudging his hands away. "Let me." She opened his shirt and trailed kisses along his center line as it was revealed, undid his cuffs and slid the material back to kiss his marks, because they were a part of him. Then she unfastened his belt and the placket of his pants, and tugged them down in a slippery slide of expensive material to bare the flesh beneath. The sight of him straining against the fabric of his boxers quickened her breath, gripping her with frantic desire.

His boxers were a quick yank and gone, his shaft hard and pulsing with the beat of his heart, his testicles a warm, yielding weight that she could trail kisses across while she stroked his thighs, his buttocks, the cleft between. He shuddered and slapped for a bedpost, clutching it as his legs and body went rigid. He caught her shoulder, tried to urge her up his body, but didn't try very hard.

"Let me," she whispered against his inner thighs, thrilling to the way he swayed against her, hissing out a breath as she moved higher to lick along his stomach, then kiss a sweet path up the underside of his thick, pulsing shaft. And where before she had been in awe of his power, now she was the one who felt powerful.

His breathing went ragged, his muscles corded where he gripped the bedpost, his hands viciously gentle as he touched the back of her head, her nape, fingers dragging along her skin as if he was reassuring himself that she was really there, that this wasn't one of the figments he had used to keep himself sane down in the war zone.

He had thought of her, fought for her. Knowing it, and that he cared for her deeply in his own way, unlocked something inside her. Murmuring his name, she opened her mouth and took him deep. He jolted against her and groaned a short, earthy curse, then went still as she slid her lips around him, encompassing him, taking as much of him as she could.

His breathing hitched and fine tremors raced along his muscles. He wasn't a mage right now, wasn't a spy or a warrior; he was a man desperate for what she could give him. Not sparks now, but flames. Pleasure. Acceptance. Affection. And a hell of a blow job.

She worked him, laved him, gloried in the surge of his body and the slick heat his excitement generated in hers as she brought him up to the pinnacle and—

He grated her name as he pulled away and bore her back onto the bed, stripping away her nylons and panties as he came down atop her. One shoe clunked to the floor; the other he took off and winged at the light switch by the door, plunging the room into a warm darkness lit by a glow from the bathroom and the blaze of security lights outside.

The night wrapped them in an intimacy she didn't trust, but then he covered her with his body and nothing mattered but the press of his weight, his hot breath on her skin, and his kisses. Oh, his kisses. Their lips caught and held; their tongues slid; their breathing shuddered and hitched. And through it all, she burned for him, throbbed for him, reveled in knowing he needed her as much as she needed him.

He got a hand between their bodies and touched her core, murmuring dark praise at her wetness. He worked her, caressed her until she felt slick and swollen. Pleasure shivered through her at each slide of his hand, and then again as he shifted against her, intertwining them in a full-body embrace that had his hard, swollen cock sliding between her thighs. She rode the pleasure, rocking her hips against him, finding the perfect combination of pressure and friction almost immediately, and rocketing herself to the quick, bright slap of an orgasm.

She cried out as it gripped her, consumed her, raced through her, and then passed on, leaving her body vibrating at a higher level of sensation, driving her onward rather than leaving her wrung out.

Sven reared up over her and his face caught the light. His eyes were fierce, his hair a wild corona, his face set in concentration. The sight of him sent new shivers racing through her like lightning. His bloodline wildness was there in the elegant arc of his body, the lethal grace of muscle and sinew. She wanted this, wanted him, but not in any civilized way.

Heart pounding, she levered herself up to kiss him, seeking his taste, his strength, the quickening of his breath, and the groan that rumbled deep in his chest. Then she turned beneath him, pressed her bottom up against his pelvis, and offered herself, not just to Sven the man, but to the mage as well, the Nightkeeper who embodied his bloodline more than any other.

His breath shuddered out of him on a harsh groan of, "Christ, Cara," and he caught her waist hard, holding her there, pressed up against him as he throbbed. And then, with no more than a shift of his body, his hard shaft found the entrance to hers. "Holy Christ," he hissed, and then he drove into her from behind.

Her lungs filled with a moan as he parted her, forged deep and deeper still. Her senses coalesced to the point of entry as her inner muscles clenched around him while he withdrew and surged into her again. His body was slick and strong as it arched over her. He surrounded her, filled her, kissed the back of her neck as he thrust into her again and again in a primal, atavistic rhythm that started fast and then went faster still.

The resting heat of the orgasm she'd just had snapped tight in an instant as her body said, *Yes, this and more.* She wanted to give more, take more, take all of him.

Widening her stance, so the outsides of her thighs slicked against the insides of his, she wrapped her arms around his braced forearms and arched her neck back to press her cheek to his jaw, feeling the heat of the two of them together.

"Cara," he whispered, and it sounded like a prayer. Then he shifted his weight to one arm and freed the other to touch her breasts, her thighs, and the place where they were joined.

At the first brush of his fingers to her sensitized flesh she jumped against him. At the second, she leaned in and purred, arching up against him as he moved. Pleasure coiled anew, raw and unfettered, and she swayed and might have collapsed entirely had it not been for his strong arms holding her, caging her. She convulsed in the throes of a second orgasm, this one coming so much stronger than the first, overwhelming her.

"Ah, *gods!*" Sven gripped her and quickened his tempo, driving surer and deeper for three strokes, four, and then surging into her, and growling long and deep as he shuddered and cut loose.

He held himself rigid while a groan drained from him, ending in her name. They stayed like that for an endless-seeming moment. Then, breathing like he'd just run the entire proving grounds with a demon at his heels, he collapsed against her, bringing them both to the bed on their sides, still joined by the flesh that stayed hard within her, pulsing.

Wow, she thought. *Oh, holy . . . wow.* Or maybe she said it aloud; she wasn't entirely sure, though he pressed his lips against the back of her neck as if in answer. But he too seemed to have lost the words.

They lay there, locked together and unspeaking, for a long time. Long enough for their breathing to level off and for them to separate. Long enough for the air to feel cold and him to tug up the comforter over them. And long enough for her to know, as she slipped into a light doze and then deeper, that things between them would never be the same.

Skywatch

Rabbit crouched over Myrinne's body, holding a stained knife that dripped blood onto her lifeless face and open, staring eyes, knowing he was in a dream.

It wasn't the same dream, though. It was day instead of night, and they were inside Sven's coyote cave. But she was still dead; he was still standing over her, breathing heavily, his blood racing with a mix of grief and rage.

"How could you?" He heard the words echo like he was in someone else's mind, only he wasn't. He was himself, inside his own skull. "Why did you do it? For chrissake, why would you—"

He lurched awake with a strangled cry, slashing at the air with his empty knife hand, trying to ward off the images, the nightmares. Then the fog cleared and he found himself sitting up in bed, surrounded by the familiar walls of his old man's cottage—*his* cottage—cast with the bloodred light that oozed from the scarlet-eyed skull night-light Myrinne had gotten him as a joke last year.

"Sorry," he said blearily. "Didn't mean to wake—" He broke off, because she wasn't there. Her side of the bed was cool to the touch, and the cottage had that echoing feeling of emptiness, silent save for the hum of the fridge, that said he was alone.

"Myr?" he called anyway. "You there?"

He didn't expect an answer, didn't get one.

He sighed and scrubbed both hands over his face, trying to erase the dream, though he knew that was futile. Even if he managed not to think about it for a few hours or days, it would always come back. Him. The knife. Myrinne.

He couldn't pretend it wasn't prophetic anymore; if it had just been the same flash over and over again, maybe . . . but ever since his mother's spirit had visited him that second time, the nightmare had been changing. First he'd dreamed the scene with Skywatch whole and untarnished in the background, not burning. Then the time had changed from night to day. And now the location had shifted.

The body and the knife were always the same, though.

One possible future, his mother had called the devastated landscape, which meant that unlike the *itza'at* seers, her spirit could see varying outcomes, not just a single incontrovertible one. So the changes in the dream had to mean that his actions were affecting the most likely outcome of that night, which was good. But so far, all he'd changed was the setting, not the act. "I don't care where it happens," he said. "I want it to *not* fucking happen."

In the lonely stillness of the night, though, his words lacked any real punch. Because the hell of it was, he was having doubts.

Where did she go when she slipped out of bed at night? She left her wristband behind, which meant she didn't want him to be able to track her down. Before, he had told himself there was no crime in her wanting to be alone sometimes. Now he couldn't stop wondering what the hell she was doing.

He'd been watching her during the day, keeping tabs on where she was, who she was talking to, and he had noticed her getting chummy with some of the *winikin*. Was it true? Had she somehow orchestrated Zane's breakdown, as his mother had said?

No, impossible, he'd told himself over and over again, trying not to read too much into each conversation, each witnessed head tilt and overheard laugh. And later, when they were together, the guilt would come crashing down and he would get stiff and awkward with her, or cling too hard and then, when she asked what was wrong, make up some shit about the screaming skull and the First Father.

She knew he was lying; he could see it in her eyes. But she didn't call him on it. Instead, she would rub his back, make love to him, fall asleep next to him . . . and sneak out several hours later, headed gods only knew where, leaving him too much time to think. With Zane and Lora cleared of any involvement in the funeral attack, there was still the question of how the creatures had gotten through the ward. Which could—maybe, possibly—leave Myrinne as a suspect.

Gods, please, no, he thought, digging his fingertips into his eye sockets and trying to work away the pain that had become a constant companion over the past few days, along with blurry vision and a shitty appetite. It was depression, he knew, confusion. Giving it a name didn't make it feel any better, though, so he reached for the Pepto he'd installed in his nightstand and knocked back a third of the bottle, using it to wash down a few Tylenols for good measure.

After all the times Myrinne had stood up for him, stood beside him, behind him, wherever she freaking could stand that would help him make the most of himself . . . after all that, he hated that he was having doubts. But even if his mother was wrong about some or all of it, that didn't explain two years of nightmares.

As the Pepto smoothed the sandpaper in his gut and the Tylenol took the edge off the knives being driven into his brain, he dragged himself out of bed and into the second bedroom. Part "toss it in there and we'll get to it later" and part workspace, the spare room mostly held Myrinne's Wiccan woo-woo stuff and their school crap. A few months ago, he had cleared out a corner and set up a private altar.

Rather than the Nightkeepers' standard *chac-mool,* he had filched a carved stone turtle from the library. Roughly two feet across and resembling an oval coffee table with a domed top and turtle head, it had the calendar glyphs carved around the rim of its shell and a circular depression in the center of the dome. Affiliated with neither light nor dark magic, the turtle symbolized the earth and its waters. Which he figured made it an okay choice, because he wasn't breaking his "no dark magic" promise to Dez, but he wasn't praying to the sky either. He was more opening himself up to the possibilities.

Now, though, as he pricked his finger with a stingray spine and smeared the blood onto a small piece of parchment, he was feeling more churned up than opened up. He wanted answers, not more questions; he needed to prove that his mother's beliefs were flawed in some logically explained way and Myrinne wasn't using him. He needed both of them to be right.

Then again, the universe hadn't exactly given a shit about what he wanted in the past. What were the odds it was going to start now?

He lit the parchment and set it in the central pit atop the turtle's shell, and as it burned he brushed the smoke toward his face and breathed deeply, trying to find some scrap of inner calm through the headache and nausea. Normally he had a tough time praying—he often spent more time watching the patterns the smoke made than he did actually communing—but tonight the words came straight from his soul. "Please help. I need to know, is the dream something I need to stop from happening . . . or are you showing me what I'm supposed to do?"

CHAPTER TWENTY-TWO

September 18
Three days to the equinox; three months and
three days to the end date
Skywatch

"Bullshit!" Carlos stormed across his sitting room and into the kitchen. "That's just bullshit."

Apparently this was where she and Sven had learned to use the word so forcefully, Cara thought with grim humor. "You're not the first to say that." Though Dez's tone had been more wondering than disbelieving, and he'd gotten on board pretty damn quick with the idea of her having a connection to the magic and the gods. "But just because it sounds crazy on the surface, that doesn't mean it's not true."

He glanced at her out of the corner of his eye. "I know you're not a liar, Cara Liu. But you're reaching."

Glasses clinked as he rearranged the dirty dishes in the sink, then turned on the water to let it warm in an old habit that had started as a gesture of housekeeping after her mom died—it had been his way of saying, "I help out around here too"—but over time had become a tic, a defense mechanism. If he saw a hard conversation coming, on would go the water. Tears? Bring on the dish soap.

Seeing it now put a lump in her throat and made her miss her mom more than she had in years. By the time the cancer finally took her it had been a blessing, and they'd all had their chances to say good-bye—sometimes it had felt like too many chances. Now, though, as she stared at her father and saw a stranger, she wished she had someone to talk to, someone who understood him.

She was on her own, though. Sven had offered to come with her, but she'd turned him down. Things between them were still too new. She hadn't expected to come back to Skywatch as his lover, hadn't expected it to have changed her outlook as much as it had.

Besides, this was between her and Carlos.

Forcing her voice steady, she said, "I don't think it's a reach. Look at the evidence—the *nahwal,* the visions, the mark, the skull statue, the way the hellhound seems focused on me . . . all of it points to the *winikin* being part of the gods' plan, with me leading them."

"Zane thought the same thing."

It would have stung if she hadn't already thought it. "Zane was a solo act. Sven and I have shared the visions."

A plate banged. "I'm guessing that's not all you've shared." His voice was cold, his shoulders set.

She fought not to let him see that he'd made a direct hit. "I know you didn't want us together."

"Still don't." He slapped off the water and spun to

glower at her. "You don't get to say that you're doing what the gods want, but do it by defying the writs."

"There's nothing in the writs forbidding a relationship between a *winikin* and a mage. And you know as well as I do that the First Father wasn't a god. He was just the guy who got the Nightkeepers out of Egypt ahead of the death squads, and led them to this continent for a do-over."

"Yet you think his resurrection will win the war, and that you and Sven are meant to bring him back."

Another direct hit. But rather than argue, she blew out a breath and said, "I'm just doing my best here. I'd like to think we all are ... but we're running out of time."

He turned back to the sink. "What do you want from me? You must want something, or you wouldn't be here."

"I ..." She trailed off as angry tears threatened, not just at him, but at herself for not realizing how bad things had gotten between them. She had thought they were peacefully coexisting. *Wrong.* If she'd had a plate in her hand she would have banged it louder than he was doing as he attacked a stubborn speck. "What is your problem? What have I done that's so awful, really? Is it because I refuse to behave like a proper little servant? Because I left? Or is it because Jox put me in charge rather than you?"

"I've had about enough of this."

"Bullshit. I'm the one who's had enough. I should have called you on this when I first got back and you made it clear that you didn't want me here if I wasn't going to do things your way."

"Stop it," he said, louder this time, but he wouldn't

look at her, just kept scrubbing away like he wanted to take the design off the plate.

But she couldn't stop. The words were tumbling out now, propelled by years of frustration and the inner voice that whispered, *No regrets*. "Or maybe you just don't want me around at all. If I hadn't been at the ranch, Sven wouldn't have needed to stay away for all those years, would he? Or maybe I should go all the way back, to when Mom got pregnant with a half-blood. Is that why you spent all your time with Sven and left me to her? Because I'm half human, not even a real *winikin*? Is that why you never cared as much about me ... because you didn't want me in the first place?"

Her eyes were dry, her chest hollow, because none of it was news. She'd thought it all before, though never said it aloud. And for a moment it seemed like she still hadn't, because she got zero response.

Her father kept working, methodically washing and rinsing the last glass and then setting it in the drainer. He turned off the water and wiped his hands on the towel he'd tucked at his waist. And then—and only then—he turned to face her.

She wasn't sure what she had been hoping to see in his expression—grief, perhaps, or guilt. Maybe the hint of a tear ... some acknowledgment that he'd been a shitty dad. What she got was ... nothing. There was no guilt, no anger, no nothing but the face of a man who thought himself blameless in this mess. "I did my duty by both you and Sven."

"Your duty according to the writs, you mean."

"Of course." For a second she thought she saw something in his eyes, as if maybe he wasn't as sure as he seemed, but needed to cling to that certainty rather than admit there might have been other ways to go. But when she looked again, it was gone.

Anger bubbled up from some inner store she hadn't even been aware of keeping deep inside. "Was it your duty to force the marks on me without any explanation, never mind training?"

Impatience flashed. "I did what needed to be done."

"You needed Sven and used me to get him."

"The Nightkeepers are the keys to this war. Not us."

He was so sure of it, so immovable. Pressure vised her chest, making it hard to breathe. "You could have told me what was going on. You could have asked. That would have taken what? Five minutes? Ten?"

"Would you have agreed to try it?"

She had asked herself that more than once. "Yeah. I would have." But she would have known what was going on, what to expect . . . and how little of that expectation to put on him.

"Well, then."

"That's not the point. The point is . . . Shit." It didn't matter, really, did it? He wasn't going to apologize or change and she didn't need him to do either. She was doing fine without him. "Thank the gods you married Mom. You got that one right, at least."

There it was again—that nanosecond flash of emotion. But then he squared his shoulders. "Is that what you came to tell me?"

"No, I . . . no." She exhaled, trying to push past the pressure in her throat that said she'd been hoping for more without even realizing it. Which was dumb, because she damn well knew better.

She and Carlos might have gotten closer in the years

after her mom died, when they'd had only each other left, but all that had changed when the barrier reactivated and Jox called the Nightkeepers home, and any sense of family loyalty her father had picked up in the outside world had disappeared. Whatever warmth might have remained between them after that had been dealt a death blow when she left Skywatch, and then slaughtered utterly when she returned, took over the *winikin,* and refused to force the rebels into the traditional mold. He hadn't been able to deal with that, hadn't even tried.

Doesn't matter, she told herself. What mattered was that she needed to stop wishing things were different and just work with what she had. Neither of them would change, and both of them thought they were right. In that sense, they were both doing the best jobs they knew how under the circumstances.

It sucked, but she needed to find a way to work with it. And she didn't have much time.

Taking a deep breath, she said, "Fine. Here's the deal. I'm calling a meeting to announce that Zane and Lora are gone—and why—and that Sven is stepping in as my coleader."

"You'll lose the *winikin.*" He said it flatly, as if it were a foregone conclusion.

"Not if I have the support of some key people."

"And I'm one of them."

"I have JT and Natalie on board. They'll help sway the more moderate rebels. If you stand up for me, the older generation will follow." She hoped.

"They'll think it's only because I'm your father."

She smiled with zero humor. "Bullshit."

He scowled, but relented slightly with, "You'll want to tell them what happened with Zane, and about the cave and your mark, and everything that happened yesterday too. There are rumors flying like a bitch, and they'll get you in more trouble than the truth."

"I know. I'm going to lay it all out there. If they know what's going on, they'll make the right choice, especially if I've got the support of people they trust." *Fingers crossed.* "So . . . can I count on you to back me up on this one?"

He hesitated, then pushed away from the counter, brushed past her, and headed for the second bedroom of his suite, which had been her room when they first came to Skywatch, but was now an office, with zero evidence that she'd ever been there. A desk drawer rasped open and then slid shut, and she heard the sound of a pencil scratching on paper, an archaic noise that made her think of childhood and essay tests.

She was being tested, all right, but she waited him out, and eventually the pencil scratches stopped and he emerged from the office, holding out an index card. "For you."

"What is it?" She met him halfway, took the card, and skimmed the lines of text. Her blood chilled and a shimmy took root in her stomach at the sight of unfamiliar words that somehow struck a chord. "Some sort of spell? What—" She broke off, realizing what it was, what it had to be—one of the few spells granted to the *winikin,* and the only one she knew for certain Carlos had used: the binding spell that gave a winikin the *aj winikin* glyph, officially marking them as a servant to their bound bloodline. She would have dropped it, but couldn't make her fingers move. "You want me to fully bind myself to Sven?"

"I want you to swear that you'll be his *winikin*, but not his lover."

"You . . ." The air leaked from her on a vicious hiss. She wanted to lash out at him, but knew that wouldn't make a dent. Logic might, though, and she still needed to get his support somehow. Not this way, though. There had to be another. "You'd risk going against the *nahwal*'s message?"

"It said you needed to join, but didn't specify how. The *aj winikin* bond is the obvious answer." He plucked the index card from her fingers, folded it once, and tucked it into her jacket pocket.

She swatted at his hand, but the damn thing was, he had a point. The magic had come through the bloodline mark . . . or had it? "Zane said there was mage blood in the coyote *winikin*. What if the magic is coming through that connection instead. What if . . ." She trailed off and pressed her lips together, not wanting to say it aloud. Words like "mates" and "destiny" didn't have any place in her and Sven's relationship . . . but that didn't mean she was going to give up that relationship to buy her father's vote, especially when every instinct she possessed said not to.

Her father looked disgusted. "You're reaching, saying anything you can to keep him as your lover."

"And you'd do anything to stop us, wouldn't you?" She breathed past the tightness in her throat, her chest. "Why is that, really? Is it because you see it as your failure as a *winikin*, or is there some real reason you don't want us to be together?" As a woman and a daughter she was trying not to care. But as the leader of the *winikin*, she had to ask.

His face hardened. "You risk him, risk tainting his magic."

"Bull. His magic is stronger when we're together. Ask him yourself."

"He needs to focus. Sex is a distraction."

She couldn't argue that one, because she was coming to learn that it certainly was—especially the way Sven did it. But she shook her head and drummed up a weak smile, trying to defuse things a little. "By your logic, nobody here should be getting any until the zero date. Good luck selling that idea."

His expression shifted, but not to one of amusement. Instead, he looked almost wistful. "Can't you trust me to know what's right?"

And for a moment, she saw him as he used to be, back when the four of them had sat around the card table as a family, betting chores and pretzels. Back then, she might have gone along with anything he said, thrilled to be included. But that was a long time ago. "Your version of 'right' is outdated."

"Perhaps. But everything I know, everything I've experienced in twice as many years, says that you're talking yourself into this, and that's going to get you in trouble." He paused, and for a second she thought she might be getting somewhere. But then he said, "If you two are meant to be together, truly meant, then your feelings will still be the same three months from now. If you take the mark, stay out of his bed, and fight the war, you'll have the *winikin* behind you."

Her stomach knotted into a tight ball, and she didn't want to look too closely at the reasons why. "But—"

"I'll support you as Sven's *winikin* . . . but not his lover. That's the deal. Take it or leave it."

If she hadn't been convinced that her and Sven's relationship was connected in some way with the gods and the war, she might have taken the deal . . . at least she wanted to think she would have. But it wasn't; it couldn't be. So she shook her head. "No deal." She was going to have to win over the *winikin* without her father's support. She headed for the door, saying over her shoulder, "Meeting's in the training hall in an hour."

He didn't call her back.

CHAPTER TWENTY-THREE

From the shelter of the cacao grove, Sven watched the *winikin* file into the training hall. Mac sat on his haunches nearby, with a confused whine ghosting in the back of his throat, not getting why they were hiding from the good guys.

"It's complicated," Sven said, because he didn't think there were enough thought-glyphs in the world to cover what was going on in his head.

He didn't want to go in there alone and cause a scene, but he hadn't been able to make himself wait up at the mansion for Cara. And that was a problem—while part of the twitchiness had come from knowing that she was talking to Carlos, the rest came courtesy of a familiar itch that said, *Get out, get moving, get some distance.* And although for a long time he had embraced that itch, now he wished he could take a damn pill and get rid of it. Or maybe a spray or something. A bug bomb. Whatever.

He didn't want the restlessness. More, it worried him that he'd awakened that morning from a bright, vivid dream of running through a closely growing rain forest, searching, always searching, though he didn't know what he sought. Part of the time in the dream he'd been himself, but the rest of the time he'd had four legs and tough-padded feet that flew across the soft earth.

He'd had the same sort of visions in the weeks leading up to Mac's finding him and the two of them becoming linked through the familiar bond. But he already had a familiar, and that was an exclusive partnership, so these dreams and vision flashes had to be something else. And the only thing he could think was that some part of his coyote magic was coming to the fore, telling him he needed to move on, that a true coyote mage didn't stay in one place—or with one mate—for long.

But he didn't want to leave Skywatch, damn it, and he didn't want to leave Cara. She needed to know he was capable of sticking around.

And he *was* sticking, damn it, would continue to stick, no matter what it took.

He must have muttered something under his breath, because as the last few stragglers jogged up the stairs to the hall and the door banged shut a final time, Mac cocked his head and rolled an eye back in inquiry.

"We'll go down there in a minute. I'm just waiting for . . . There she is," he said as he spotted Cara coming down the path, stalking stiff legged with her hands jammed in the pockets of her studded jacket. "Uh-oh. I'm guessing things didn't go so well with Carlos. Come on."

They slipped out of the cacao grove and angled to intercept her near the picnic area. Up close, Sven caught the snap of anger in her eyes as she glanced at him, then watched her try to shove it behind a calm facade. "Hey, wait up," he said, catching her wrist and drawing her into the lee of the huge ceiba tree. "Give yourself a minute. You don't want to go in there looking like that."

She glared up at him. "Looking like what, exactly? And are we really hiding behind a tree? Seriously?"

"You look like you're about to rip a chunk out of the first person who crosses you, and I'm pretty sure the goal was to keep this meeting as calm and controlled as possible. As for the tree thing, yeah, but only because it means I can do this." He drew her into his arms, but when she shot him a *don't even think about kissing me right now* glare, he tucked her head beneath his chin, wrapped his arms around her and held on tight. "Give yourself a minute, okay? Just breathe and remember that he's not going to change."

She stayed tense for a moment, then exhaled a shuddering breath and relaxed against him. "Damn it, don't be nice to me. I need to go into this meeting a little pissed off."

"How about calm, focused, and ready to kick some ass?"

Laughing a little, she sneaked an arm around his waist and squeezed. "Yeah. That'll work." She eased away, then looked up at him. "Thanks. You're not a bad guy to have around."

"That's what I've been trying to tell you," he said lightly, though the comment brought the same sort of clutch he used to get when one of his casual hookups had dropped a not-so-casual remark about him sticking around. Only this time he was the one trying to hem himself in. Stifling the urge to hold on to her too hard, he let her go instead. "Ready to go blow up the hierarchy?"

She groaned. "Don't say it like that."

"Sorry." But as they headed for the training hall,

walking side by side but not touching, he took heart from the fact that she looked more resolute than grim, and her eyes held a gleam of *step off; I'm in charge.* And, damn, that was sexy.

He let her take the lead going up the steps and through the doors, and then on into the main room. It was packed with *winikin,* some sitting at the round tables, others lounging at the closed-down bar. Pretty much every one of them took one look at her and then another, longer look at him and the big coyote that slunk at his heels.

Some of those looks were friendly enough, but most weren't. Especially the ones coming from the two guys who'd gotten hurt in the dustup two days earlier. Sasha had patched them up, but they still had some healing to do.

There were mutters of, "Now what?" and, "What's he doing here?" and, "I heard he's schtupping her."

Sven zeroed in on the last commenter, a twenty-something guy who met his glare for about five seconds before looking away. A couple of the guy's buddies shifted as if looking for a fight, but Sven just raised an eyebrow and kept going through the throng.

His restraint got an approving look from Cara as she reached the place opposite the bar where a couple of risers formed an impromptu stage for meetings and ka-raoke. There was no sound system, so she stepped up on the stage and gave the room a minute to settle.

Moving around behind her, so he was off the risers and thus not looming, and Mac was more or less out of sight, Sven took up his *I've got her back* position and tried not to picture Kevin Costner in *The Bodyguard,* because gods knew he'd never admit to having watched it.

Like a good bodyguard, he scanned the crowd, trying
to figure out where the biggest threat was going to come
from. And he found Carlos staring daggers at him from
the back of the room.

A pang went through him at the look in the *winikin*'s
eyes, but he locked gazes for a long moment, then sent
the other man a nod. Carlos grimaced and looked away,
but Sven figured the message was clear enough. He had
followed through with his promise to Carlos, and waited
to get his sign. Cara's father didn't need to know that
the sign hadn't really mattered, though, because despite
everything else, he just bloody well felt *right* when he was
with Cara.

Even now, as she held up a hand and waited for the
mutters and shuffles to subside, and he stood there knowing that they had a hell of a fight ahead of them, he was
exactly where he wanted to be.

It was when they were apart that the doubts—and the
visions of being somewhere else—crept in.

"Okay, I'd like to get started," Cara said, pitching her
voice to carry to the far corners of the room, where the
radicals had gravitated—Carlos and a few of the old
guard on one side, Sebastian and a dozen or so rebels on
the other. Sven kept his eyes moving as she continued. "I
know there have been some major rumors flying over
the past couple of days. Some are true, some aren't, and
most are a mix of the two. I had thought about apologiz-
ing that I'm just now calling this meeting, but the thing
is, I'm not sorry for the delay. We needed the time to
figure out the facts, what we think they mean, and what
we're going to do about them."

Sebastian called, "And by 'we,' do you mean you and
the Nightkeepers' king, or you and lover boy there?"

One of his buddies thumped him to shut up, but a couple of the others nodded.

Cara shot him a cool look. "Do you want to tell this, or should I?"

He snorted. "Spin away, boss. Go ahead and tell us how you sent Zane and Lora to live on a nice farm some-where, like you'd tell a six-year-old when her dog bites someone and gets put down, or how you're not fucking us over by hooking up with that one." His chin jerk went in Sven's direction. "And how it makes total sense for him to be in charge, even though the king said we could damn well lead ourselves, because you think that you might be able to use his magic, and that's why the hell-hound came back after you. Like that makes everything hunky-fucking-dory."

Sven raised an eyebrow at the extent of the rumors. It seemed that there wouldn't be much in the way of sur-prises, then. Just some clarification and—hopefully redirection.

Nodding to Sebastian, her face set in falsely pleasant lines, Cara said, "If you're finished?" When he grumbled and subsided, she swept the room with a look before clasping her hands at the small of her back in almost a parade rest. Sven could see that her fingers linked and held and turned white from the pressure. Her voice, though, stayed steady as she said, "Okay, then. Taking it from the top . . ."

Clearly and concisely, she led her people through the events of the past week, giving them the facts and inter-pretations, the caveats. She told them more than Sven would have, maybe even more than Dez had intended for her to reveal, but at this point it was probably the only way to go. Given the depths of the rumor mill, whatever she left out would come back to bite her in the ass somehow.

Which meant Sven got far more play than he would've liked, and he had to fight not to squirm at times. She glossed over the sex and his push-pull of affection and alluded to their history only in passing, but any idiot could have filled in the gaps, and while a number of the *winikin* were pains in his ass, none of them were stupid.

He tried not to react as she built her case. Instead, he watched the crowd. And damned if he didn't see faces smoothing out, then a nod here and there. It started in the middle of the room, where Natalie and JT sat at the intersection between the two cliques, and then edged outward in an almost imperceptible ripple, one that might've been invisible to anybody in the thick of things. Sven, though, was on the outside looking in, and he saw it.

Pride trickled through him. She had them. She fucking had them. Or most of them, anyway. As for the holdouts ringing the room . . . well, they were going to be the wild cards, weren't they? He just hoped to hell the others would be enough to trump.

Finishing the recitation with a quick rundown of the evidence suggesting that the ancestors—and presumably the gods—had paired her and Sven against the odds and perhaps even the writs, she went on to say, "I won't claim to be infallible—far from it. I should have handled things differently during the war games, I should have figured out what Zane was up to, and I should have insisted on handling his and Lora's arrests differently. But I'm determined to learn from my mistakes and put us in the absolute best position to survive. To do that, I need to be partnered up with Sven, and I need your support."

This time when she paused, there was some shuffling and sidelong looks, but nobody—not even Sebastian—spoke out.

She waited a beat, then said, "Jox put me in charge of you without a vote, and there's no vote mandated by writ or tradition, but I think we need one, because these are your lives we're talking about. These are all of our lives. But first . . . questions?"

For a three-count, the loudest sound in the room was Mac's breathing. Sven had his eye on Sebastian and his cronies, so it was a surprise when the first question came from the other side of the room. "The *nahwal* didn't specifically say that you and the mage should be lovers, and a similar bond could be achieved by your taking back the *aj winikin* mark. Wouldn't that be a better way to show your loyalty?"

It was Carlos.

Sven stiffened and Mac gave a low growl, responding to his sudden flash of ire. Cara, though, showed no outward response. She just said, "Over the past four years, the magi have had to rely on their instincts when the prophecies and magic have failed. I may not have magic of my own, but I have good instincts, and they're telling me that this is right and good. I don't need to take the *aj winikin* to prove anything to anyone, except maybe you." Her voice cooled. "You forced the servant's mark on me once before. You're not going to do it again."

That got a bunch of nods from the rebel side of the room, but Sven got an *uh-oh* feeling when he saw a few of the other, older *winikin* shifting in their seats.

"There's no evidence that you're supposed to be sleeping with him, is there?" Carlos persisted.

She lifted her chin and met his eyes, but she was talk-

ing to all of them when she said, "I'm not sleeping with
Sven because of the *nahwal* or the gods. I'm sleeping
with him because I've wanted to be with him for a long
time now, but only recently became convinced that our
being together will in no way be a detriment to the
winikin or the war. And I'm sleeping with him because
when I was strapped to that altar with the water over my
head, he was the person I thought about, the one I
wanted to see."

Sven's throat lumped as, for the first time since the
meeting began, she turned to look at him. And for a moment her eyes were those of the woman he'd woken up
with, the one he'd made morning love to. He wanted to
tell her what it meant to hear her say that, wanted to give
her something in return, but couldn't.

Her eyes warmed, though, as if he had, and she turned
back to the crowd and said simply, "Then there he was.
He was there for me when nobody else was." Her eyes
went to Carlos. "If you want to condemn me for putting
myself first in this, then that's certainly your right. But I
think you're wrong. The other magi have shown that
there's room for love and family in their society. I think
the same should be true for ours."

She paused a beat, and then swept the crowd. "Next?"

There was a quiet moment—Sven thought a few people in the middle of the room were teetering on the
brink of applause but didn't dare try it—and then JT
said, "Okay, I'll go."

"Fire away."

He asked about the First Father's resurrection—Sven
had a feeling Cara had planted the question, and gave
her points for anticipating the need—and that turned
things away from their relationship. She fielded two

more questions along those lines, ignored a third that tried to circle back around to the bedroom, and went into more detail about the hellhound's second appearance and what it might—or might not—mean.

And, watching her cool competence and grace under fire, Sven's brain chewed on an old refrain: *I don't deserve her*. But this time it wasn't because of his restlessness or the knowledge that he couldn't give her what she needed. Instead, it was because she flat-out awed the shit out of him. She was tough, edgy, and sexy as hell, but with an inner vulnerability that she didn't mind showing. Yet at other times, she could be an elemental force, immovable and yet flexible, facing down her father on one side and kindling hope on the other. And she did it all without magic, without having been raised into the belief that she was somehow special, better than everyone around her. She did it simply by being her.

Nope, Sven thought with sudden clarity, he didn't deserve her . . . but he was damn well going to try to live up to her for the next three—

Dizziness slapped through him with the suddenness of a squall, nearly dragging him to his knees. He stayed on his feet by force of will, not wanting to embarrass either of them by passing the hell out in the middle of her speech, but his vision blurred and brightened, and suddenly he wasn't in the hall anymore; he was in a rain forest, racing along a narrow game trail with his nose to the ground. *Searching, searching. Hot sun. Cool shade. Thirsty but can't stop now. So close, but where?* He glimpsed a cave mouth, heard the sound of water inside, caught the whisper of a hated scent, and felt a low growl rumble in his chest. *Enemy!*

Adrenaline chased away the vision. The rain forest

fragmented, disappeared, and then he was back in the hall. He was still on his feet, thank the gods, and the only one staring at him was Mac. His familiar's ears were plastered forward, his eyes intent, but he stayed silent.

Sven didn't know what to make of that. Hell, he didn't know what to make of any of it. If this was his subconscious telling him to move on, it was going to have to work harder than that, because he was staying put, damn it.

Gritting his teeth, he refocused on Cara.

She seemed to be wrapping things up. "We can't pretend the Nightkeepers don't exist, or that we can do this without them. That's just dumb. We need to work with them, and yes, we need to support them while they do the things we can't. But we have what they lack, what they need, and that's the strength of numbers. So I'll ask you now to work with me and Sven, and with the Nightkeepers, while we all do our absolute damnedest to pull this plane through the end-time and into a new cosmic cycle."

Pausing, she looked around, then pointed to the chair JT was sitting in. "From there to the window is the center line. If you agree to follow Sven and me, stand on that side." She indicated the traditionalists' side of the room. "If you refuse, take the other side." She waved to where the rebels sat. "I'll give you a ten-count. When I hit ten, that's the vote."

She started with "one" and there was a generalized shuffle. By "three" the pattern was clear: The middle of the room was drifting to the "yes" side, the outskirts to the "no." On "five" it looked like a fifty-fifty split, and Sven's gut knotted with a rising tide of frustrated anger.

"Six," Cara said, her face starting to go grim. "Sev—"

"Hold it," Sven snapped. "Just hold it right there." She stopped the count and turned to him with a warning head shake, but he wasn't having it, wasn't having any of it. "Wait a minute," he said. "I've got something to say."

He halfway expected the *winikin* to shout him down or tell him he was out of line. It was a tribute to Cara's impassioned speech, he supposed, that they didn't. Or maybe they were waiting to see what she did. A test of allegiance.

She gave him a long look, as if trying to decide whether he was going to help or hurt her case, but then nodded. "You're out of order, but I'll allow it. You're just as much a part of this as I am." And with that he thought she might have lost some ground, which meant he damn well better make it up, and then some.

Taking a deep breath, he stepped onto the risers with Mac right behind him, conscious of the way all eyes had to zoom up to keep him in range, seeming to halo him with a big old neon sign that said, *He's not one of us*.

No, he wasn't. But he thought he could help them if they would just give him a chance. *Man up,* he told himself. *Get this right. She deserves better than your usual best*. Starting now.

Problem was, he saw only one way to tip the scales. And it was going to be a hell of a risk.

Clearing his throat, he said, "I know some of you are pretty pissed at me right now, at least a couple of you with good reason." He sent a nod toward the two guys who'd been hurt in the fight; one looked startled, the other thoughtful. "And what I'm about to say probably isn't going to win me any points from the rest of you . . . but are you out of your fucking minds?"

That got him a stirring of the crowd, a few scowls, and Cara's low warning of, "Bad idea."

Maybe it was. But it was the only one he had. "Look, I know you're probably saying, 'Who the hell does he think he is, talking to us like that?' But that's the thing—I don't see *winikin* or magi; I never did. I see people. And as one person to a bunch of others, I'm asking whether you're out of your fucking minds. We have a chance to do something good here, something special. Fuck, we've got the opportunity—hell, the mandate—to save the gods-damned world here, and you're dicking around over semantics?"

"Semantics to you," Sebastian called from the "no" side of the room, "freedom to us."

"Newsflash: The *winikin* don't have a monopoly on that one. Do you think I volunteered to be one of the last dozen or so survivors of a dying race, or to get slapped with a big old, 'Hey, howdy, the world is going to end if you guys don't pull off the impossible'?" He shook his head. "You want to think I had it easier than you, go ahead; at least some of you are probably right. But keep in mind that I'm just as bound by the magic as you are, probably more. And if you think about it, any one of you probably has a better chance of living past the end date than I do, because sure as shit the demons are going to come gunning for me first."

An ache started in his chest as the adrenaline drained, and he notched the volume down to say, "Look, here's the deal: The brain trust has found a resurrection spell they think will work, but it's going to be big magic and a serious power drain. Which means two things: One, the second they start the spell, the *Banol Kax* are pretty much guaranteed to be coming after the spellcasters; and two, they're not going to be able to spare more than a couple of magi for defense . . . the rest is going to be up to us." He jabbed a thumb at his own chest, then to Cara, and then waved a hand to indicate the whole damn room.

There was a restless shift in the crowd, and somebody muttered, "Cannon fodder."

"Not the way you mean," he said. "It won't be like it was during the massacre. First off, you're not being forced to fight—this will be strictly voluntary. And second, you'll have weapons of your own. Jade and Lucius hit on a spell they think they can tailor for you guys to use. It's part shield, part weapon, and way cool. And you'll get one if you vote to fight."

"It's not about fighting," Sebastian countered. "We're willing to fight, just not for a Nightkeeper and his girl-friend."

Mac's growl echoed the spike of Sven's temper. "This is *entirely* about fighting, dumb ass. In three days, we need to be in Guatemala defending the hell out of Che'en Yaaxil, and as far as I'm concerned, it doesn't matter whether there's a *winikin*, a Nightkeeper, a human, or, hell, a wombat in charge, as long as I have reason to believe they're competent. Defending the barrier is what matters. That's my duty. It's your duty." He pointed at Sebastian, then started pointing at the other *winikin*. "And yours, yours, and yours." He ended with Carlos, said softly, "It's your duty to fight. You can defend your charge, your family, your future . . . whatever it takes. We're all in this together."

He fell silent, glaring at them in challenge.

Cara stepped up beside him and took his hand. Said softly, "Seven."

Nobody moved.

"Eight."

Still nothing. Sven's chest had a rock on it, making it hard to breathe.

"Nine."

Carlos looked up to the ceiling, to the sky, and said softly, "Is this what you want? Truly?" Then, as if he'd gotten an answer from the slow thump of the overhead fan, he headed from "no" to "yes."

And damned if the others didn't follow him, trad and rebel alike. Cara's fingers tightened on Sven's hand, and he could feel her shaking as she whispered, "Ten."

The "no" side was empty. Even Sebastian had gone over, and looked resigned to have done it. They had won the vote, and to a *winikin* a vote was tantamount to sacred. There was no turning back from here.

"Thank you," Cara said, her voice cracking. She started to say something else, but then pressed her lips together and shook her head. "I don't have the words, except to say that I've never in my life been prouder to be a *winikin*."

Sven gave that a moment to settle in, then said, "I know it's going to take some time for all this to sink in, but I'm afraid time is exactly what we don't have. Lucius is going to meet us out at the ball court in twenty minutes with one of the new weapons, and we'll start from there."

With that, he drew Cara down off the riser and out the back door, not just because he was suddenly itching for open air but because he had a feeling she could use it too. She was pale and drawn, and rather than triumphant at her victory, she looked like she'd just been given a terminal diagnosis.

He had a feeling he'd looked something like that when he found out that the whole Nightkeeper thing was more than a bedtime story. It hit you like that when you suddenly had the weight of the world riding on your shoulders.

Once they were outside and away from the training hall, he angled them back around toward the cacao grove, where the leafy greens provided some privacy, albeit with the smell of the southlands, and the memories that provoked. He wasn't worried about memories right now, though. He was worried about Cara.

"Come here." He drew her into his arms, and his concern notched up when she latched on and clung, shuddering. "Hey," he said into her hair. "You're okay. It's okay. I'm here. I'll be right here every step of the way." His stomach jittered as he said it, but he ignored the discomfort, knowing there would be worse to come. "We can do this. You're not alone, okay? I've got your back."

"I know." She exhaled a shaky breath. "I know. It's just . . ." Pulling away, she looked up at him. "What if I'm fooling myself? What if all this is just as much a lie as Zane's reality?"

"It's not," he said firmly, because she needed him to be firm right then.

"But what if it is?"

"Don't make me repeat myself."

His mock-stern growl got a ghost of a smile and another deep breath. Then she nodded. "Okay, you're right. I know you're right. It's too late to turn back now." She hesitated. "Will you do me a favor?"

"Name it."

"Hang on to this for me." She pulled a folded card out of her jacket pocket and handed it over.

He unfolded it, read it, and whistled. "The *aj winikin* spell? You sure you don't want to burn it?"

"Thanks, but no thanks. Keep it close, just in case Carlos is right and I'm wrong." She shook her head and went back into his arms, this time burrowing softly against him and letting her breathing slow to match his.

He curled his arms around her and rocked them both, needing the contact as much as she did, maybe more.

CHAPTER TWENTY-FOUR

September 21
Equinox

In the dark blue of early predawn, Cara could just make out Sven's silhouette at the window. She didn't know what had awakened her—maybe him getting out of bed, maybe her sleeping self feeling the empty spot beside her—but she knew the tense line of his body as he stood alone, and how the sight brought a clutch inside her.

"Sorry." His voice came out of the darkness as he turned toward her. "Didn't mean to wake you."

"I don't know how you do that." And it wasn't just that he knew when she was awake, either. Over the past few days, as they had worked nearly around the clock to get the *winikin* ready to defend Che'en Yaaxil—teaching them to use the shield stones and fire-tipped projectiles that together gave them almost warrior-class armaments—he had seemed wholly attuned to her moods and fears too. He knew instinctively when to soothe, growl, or give her room. She couldn't say the same, though; there were times with him when he got quiet and faraway, and she didn't know what to do to help, or even whether she should try.

Like now.

Logic said he was a grown man and would ask for help if he needed it. More, for a man who had spent most of his life alone, she imagined it was a shock to suddenly find himself in charge of a small army, with all the demands that went with it. So she was trying to give him room. But at the same time, something—maybe her instincts, maybe the bond between them—kept telling her that he needed her when he got like this, quiet and withdrawn.

"It's magic," he said, and she could hear the smile in his voice. But there was strain there too, and as he stepped toward her and his face came clear in the faint illumination from the bathroom night-light, she saw a silent plea for her to believe the smile and ignore the other.

It was on the tip of her tongue to ask what was wrong, but she didn't. She wasn't sure she wanted the answer, not today of all days, when their partnership needed to be its strongest.

Instead, she smiled back and, when he got into bed beside her, she let the dip and pull of the mattress draw her into him, so bare skin slid and heated. "No," she murmured, "this is the magic."

"Ah, Cara," he whispered into her hair, but said nothing more.

Instead of asking, she tipped her face up to his for a kiss, and drew her hand down his body in a long, slow caress that made him tense and groan. This was what he needed right now. It was what they both needed.

Seeming to agree, he wrapped himself around her and took her under with a kiss that wiped everything else from her mind. Gone were her doubts and fears—about him, the *winikin,* the coming battle—leaving only sensation behind.

Her perceptions coalesced to the press of his lips on hers and to the good, solid strength of his body. She caught her breath when he skimmed his lips down along her throat and across the upswell of one breast to capture her nipple in his mouth and suck, hot and wet and mimicking the act of love.

Moaning, she clasped him tightly, urged him on. They kissed and clung, touched and teased, until the blood sang in her veins and her heartbeat trip-hammered with a rhythm of: *more-more, more-more, more-more.*

She might have said it aloud, must have, because he rasped her name, along with hot praise and dark promises as he rolled atop her, poised to enter her. She dug her fingers into his hips and arched against him, waiting, waiting, wait— *Ah!* She cried out as he thrust home, filling and stretching her, and making her see starbursts behind her closed lids.

Then he was moving, setting a hard, urgent rhythm that slapped her body from zero to sixty in no time flat, and from there to overdrive. She held on to him, bowed beneath him, and buried her face in his sweat-slicked neck, where she whispered his name, a moan, a litany of, *Yes-yes-there-more-oh-there,* as her body tightened around him.

Her breath stilled as her senses rushed inward and then pushed her up, up toward a huge-seeming goal, and then *over.* The orgasm flared through her, locking her muscles and leaving her helpless to do more than cling and cry Sven's name as he thrust into her again and again, prolonging her pleasure and wringing out his own until, with a rattling groan, he plunged into her and held tight, body jerking as he came.

Then he held tight a few minutes longer, as they both shuddered in the aftermath and breathed each other in.

"Sweet Cara." He kissed her cheeks, her lips, her forehead, then rolled to his side, parting from her body but taking her with him, so they were curled together. "Sweet, sweet Cara." His words were drowsy, his breathing soft.

"Sleep," she said, kissing him. "Turn it off for a while."

He said something more, but it was lost in a sigh as, with a final nuzzle, he complied and let himself go lax. Within moments his breathing deepened and he was out. But although she badly wished she had the same option, her mind wouldn't let her sleep. She kept coming back to his silhouette at the window, as he stared out toward the open mesas and the world beyond.

Don't think about it, she told herself. *Not today.* She would talk to him about things after the equinox . . . or maybe not. He was giving her everything he had promised her, after all—he was protecting her, helping her, being there for her. How fair was it, really, to push him for more than that when he'd been honest from the start? She knew what she was getting into. And maybe— probably—she needed to find a way to let this be enough.

Somehow.

You must not let her destroy the gateway!

Rabbit lunged awake with his heart pounding, his ears ringing with his mother's voice, and the power of the equinox coursing through him.

He was disoriented for a few seconds, but then the spins turned into panic, because not only was Myrinne's side of the bed empty and cool, but there was another void, this one inside him.

Understanding stabbed like the sharpest knife. *The eccentrics!*

In an instant, he flashed back on last night, when Myrinne had met him at the door wearing nothing but a strand of obsidian beads. She had kissed him and led him to the bedroom, and they'd made love like they hadn't done in months. In the aftermath, all loose limbed, stupid, and so damned tired of being inside his own head, he'd asked her where she went at night, and had somehow wound up telling her everything—about the eccentrics, his mother, and even her suspicions. It had all come gushing out, a vomit of emotions and self-pity that had damn near wrung him dry. And through it all, Myrinne had kissed him, held him, told him that she loved him and it was all going to be okay, and he'd believed her, believed *in* her.

Only now she and the stones were gone.

"No!" He threw on clothes, left his armband on the table, and raced out the door, sticking his old man's knife in his belt as he hauled ass. He could just barely sense the stones, but it would be enough to track them. And her.

Traitor. Seducer. Betrayer. He wasn't sure if the whisper was his own or not, but it fit all too well with the evidence. His chest hurt and his head was spinning.

There were Jeeps by the training hall, keys tucked neatly into the visors. He launched himself into one, fired it up, and sped across the compound in a spray of dirt and gravel. He said the quick spell to drop the blood-ward, used telekinesis to open the wrought-iron gates, and then restored both once he was through. His magic was running high, his temper and sense of betrayal higher as he figured out where she had taken the stones.

"Son of a bitch." Nausea surged. He hadn't been able to escape the dream after all. She was in the coyote cave, where he'd last envisioned her death. "Is this what you want?" he asked the gods that didn't seem to be in the sky or the underworld anymore, but rather inside him. He tasted salt and for a second thought he was bleeding, but then realized it was tears.

Jesus Christ. Was this really happening?

The trip passed in a blur of kicked-up dirt and spinning tires. He didn't bother with stealth, couldn't think beyond the rage and grief that pounded through him along with the pain in his head and the soul-deep whisper of, *You have to get them back, become the crossover, and save all mankind.*

He didn't question how he could hear his mother's voice without the eccentrics; he knew only that he could.

The cave mouth gaped wide and the once muddy ground surrounding it was cracked and crazed. The flash-flood river was gone, the earth parched, and his boots rang on the hard surface as he called a shield spell and strode through. His brain buzzed, filled with whispered echoes in his mother's voice and the pull of the stones. And though there was a part of him that raged against both, saying that this was Myrinne—he loved her, trusted her—those thoughts were drowned out by the others that said she had betrayed him.

Inside the cave was cool, damp, and shadowed, and felt crowded with the animals that danced on the walls and ceiling.

Myrinne was at the altar, slim and lithe in jeans and a cropped tee that flirted with her tattoo. Her head came up at his entrance; her mouth went round with surprise and horror. And he felt nothing but murderous rage.

The scents of vanilla, patchouli, and lavender filled the air, and the eccentrics lay in a round dish beneath a layer of fragrant oil that flamed blue, then red as his magic filled the space. He had dismissed her Wiccan stuff as useless, thinking it was her way to feel like part of the team. He'd been wrong, though. There was power here. Betrayal.

"*Rabbit*." She held up both hands. "Wait. I'm just—"

"Don't!" he thundered. "No more lies!" There was a wrenching, tearing pain in his chest, and he broke, shattering from the guy he had been with her into a new man, one who could see what she had done to him, all the ways she had manipulated him.

"I'm not lying. I—" She screamed as the eccentrics erupted from the oil in twin burning sprays and flew to land in his outstretched palm, where they seared into his skin without pain.

Stuffing them into the pocket of his jeans, ignoring the way his black Windbreaker gaped open across his bare chest, he advanced on her. "Were you going to destroy them right away, or were you going to summon her first? What were you going to do to her? Damn it, tell me!"

Tears streaked her face. "I wasn't going to hurt anybody. I was just trying to help. After what you said about the stones, I got this idea—"

"*Don't*." The word cracked like a whip. "Don't pretend this was for me. It's always been for you, hasn't it?"

"No." Her lips shaped the word but almost no sound came out. Her eyes were wounds, her mouth a slash.

"You've fooled me, manipulated me all these years,

but now I'm seeing things clearly." He was at the edge of the island, where baked mud went to shifting sand. A *drip-drip* made him look down. His hands were bleeding from twin slashes across his palms, though he didn't remember making the sacrifice. He was filled with equinox power, though, overflowing with it. More, beneath the red-gold sparkle there was a faint rattlesnake hiss. A clatter. Exhilaration pounded through him. It was the first time he'd heard the dark magic's song since Iago took away his connection to that half of himself.

His lips pulled back in a feral snarl. "This was what you wanted, right? You wanted me to use the dark magic again. But why? Who are you working for?" He leaned over her and got in her face to yell, "Damn it, *what are you trying to do to me?*"

"I'm not doing anything! Snap out of it, Rabbit, *please!* This isn't you." Tears ran down her cheeks in fat, glistening drops. She was shaking, gripping the edge of the altar as if to hold herself up.

The fog was thick now at the edges of his mind, his vision tunneled to her face above the burning oil. He slapped the pan aside, splashing scented oil, and smiled as she screamed and backpedaled. Deep down inside him, a weak, puny kid heaved, puked, and beat at the walls of his mind, screaming, *What the fuck are you doing?* But that kid was a pussy who'd never done anything right, and was easy to ignore when another voice, so much louder, said, *Yes, Rabbie. My Rabbie. You are the crossover. Do what needs to be done.*

The dark magic rattled again, filling his veins with flames and terrible power.

Sobbing now, Myrinne cried, "Call for help, Rabbit. You need to call the others. Please. I'm begging you."

"They can't know until it's over," he said, hearing another voice beneath his own.

Her eyes went wide, stricken, terrified, as she understood. "No." Again, it was more the shape of the word than the word itself, and then, louder: "No!"

She spun and bolted. He didn't even move, just flicked a finger and sent flames searing around her in a bright, crackling cage of fire. She screamed and stumbled to a halt. "Rabbit, *no*." She collapsed to the ground sobbing, shouting through her hands, "I was only trying to help. Please!"

He barely heard her over the dark magic, which thrummed through him, and coiled at the black quatre-foil mark on his arm. Nearby above the altar, the fog swirled, gathered, and began to glow in the shape of a doorway. He stared up at the spot and a smile split his face.

We're waiting. Make the sacrifice and call us through.

She said "we"! His blood leaped at the promise of seeing his twin, his other half.

"Yes, Mama." He whispered the words, afraid that if he said them too loudly the dream would disappear. This wasn't a nightmare, after all. It was the promise of a new future.

At his command, the fiery cage moved toward the gathering gray cloud, forcing Myrinne to move with it. She staggered, went down, and cried out when the lattice burned her. Her hair was soaked with sweat, her eyes blank.

The pussy inside him wept and railed, but his mage self—his better, stronger self—extinguished the flames and then reached for her with his blood-streaked hands. He got her by the hair and forced her onto her knees.

Her eyes focused, went wet with grief. "Rabbit, please."

He set the knife to her jugular. "My name is Rabbie."

"No," she whispered, "you're Rabbit. My love. My one and only." She reached for the knife, grabbed the blade, and yanked her palm along it, and then clutched his free hand, matching them blood-to-blood.

The connection clicked into place instantly, traveling along neuronal pathways that had been burned into place by two years together and the love—or the illusion of it—they had shared. He fought to yank free, to shake her off. "Get the fuck—"

Then she dropped her mental shields. And for the first time, she let him all the way into her mind.

Vertigo spun around him as he plunged into the whirlwind without preparation. Then he was seeing what she saw, feeling what she felt, and knowing what she knew.

Terror, grief, horror, betrayal. The emotions slammed through him as he looked up at his own face, nearly unrecognizable in its fury. But beneath the fear there was Myrinne, opening herself to him. He caught memory flashes of the things that had made her the person she was: the abuse she'd endured at her foster mother's hands, so much grimmer than he had ever suspected, kindling the drive to be more than herself—better and stronger, so nobody could hurt her ever again. He saw himself—as rescuer, lover, antagonist, friend, and, finally, betrayer and murderer, or close to it—and he felt the emotions of each.

But what he didn't sense was duplicity.

She was pushy and ambitious, but she wasn't a spy, a traitor, or a saboteur. She was, quite simply, Myrinne. The rest of it was lies.

"No." He tried to yank away from her, tried to deny what he was sensing, what he had done. He succeeded in getting his hand free and breaking the bond, but he couldn't get the truth out of his head.

Oh, gods. She hadn't betrayed him.

But he had just betrayed the hell out of her.

"NO!" His shout echoed in a blast of power that was pure and gleaming, neither dark nor light, but a combination of the two. At his cry, the gray fog went utterly black and the hiss of dark magic rose up to a steampipe roar.

"Don't let it through!" Myrinne cried. "Rabbit, for gods' sake, *shut it down!*"

He stayed frozen, locked in place with horror as a presence boiled within the fog and then reached for him, whispering, *Rabbie!*

"No!" Myrinne lunged up and flung herself between him and the morphing cloud, then jolted and screamed when it lashed out at her, hit her. She was thrown back, struck the altar, convulsed, and went still.

Rabbit's heart stopped.

The fog lifted from his eyes.

And he saw what he had done, what he had become.

"Myrinne!" He surged toward her, only to be brought up short by a blast of sound and power that came from behind him, nearly flattening him. He spun and saw the cloud fully for the first time—black and ugly, coiling from a split in what had to be the dark barrier. Revulsion lashed through him. Rage. "No!"

Flames shot from his fingertips, blasting into the cloud, which recoiled with a high keening noise. In his mind he heard, *Rabbie, no!* but he didn't let that stop him. He didn't know what that voice was—his mother, a demon, a member of the *Banol Kax*—but he didn't care anymore. *It* was what had betrayed him, not Myrinne. And he had been so fucking hungry for a mother that he'd believed it. He hadn't done the right things, asked the right questions. He'd been so caught up in wanting to know where he had come from, why he was the way he was, that he'd bought into the fantasy . . . and he'd become a monster. The dark barrier wasn't the answer; the demons weren't the good guys.

Shouting, he poured fire into the darkness again and again, moving forward as the cloud retreated back into the tear, then vanished. Even after it was gone, he kept hammering the rip in the barrier with his magic, building up layer after layer until there wasn't a tear anymore, but rather a hard, scarlike strip.

Then he let the magic die and went down beside her on his knees. "Myrinne?"

There was no response. She was utterly still, her body twisted oddly, her muscles lax.

He caught her bloodied hand and matched their cuts. His reserves were drained but he didn't care. She could have everything if that was what it took. He funneled his magic through the blood-link, giving her his power, his strength . . . and his love, though he didn't have any right to offer it to her anymore.

She wasn't responding. Dear gods, she wasn't responding.

"Myrinne!" He dived through the link and into her mind, not looking for answers this time, but rather looking for *her*. But the place where she should have been echoed with emptiness. "Nooooo!" He howled the word within and without, roaring the denial of what he had done. His heart shuddered and threatened to stop entirely, and part of him thought that would be a relief. He couldn't go on without her, couldn't live knowing that he had killed her, that she had died with his accusations ringing in her ears.

Wait, said the pussy inside him, the smarter self that had believed in her all along. *Wait. Don't you see? There's no such thing as coincidence.*

"It's all just the will of the gods," he said, finishing the quote from the writs. "But what—"

Then he saw it. He fucking saw it.

And he knew what he had to do.

Sven was running through the forest, first on two legs and then on four, searching, always searching. Sharp frustration burned in his marrow. He wasn't where he was supposed to be, but couldn't find the way there. Where? He didn't know, knew only that he was running out of time.

Up ahead, a break in the trees, a gleam of sunlight and stone, a burst of adrenaline. There! He charged along the path, burst into the clearing, saw the cave mouth, and—

Bright white flared across his senses and he staggered, banged into a carved stone wall, and leaned against it for support, chest heaving as his surroundings came clear. He was in the ball court at Skywatch, helping pack the last of the shield stones and fire-tipped rounds for the teleport to Guatemala.

And he'd blanked out for a minute there.

"You okay, man?"

Sven squinted, trying to place the *winikin.* "Yeah. I'm fine, Rog—Ritchie." He stumbled over the name, though they'd been out humping equipment together for a couple of hours already. Meeting too many new people in three short days had his head feeling stuffed full. "Maybe dehydrated a little."

"Here." Ritchie tossed him a water bottle. "Don't want you conking out on us in the middle of things."

Sven caught it on the fly. Although he wasn't exactly Mr. Popularity, some of the *winikin*—most of them, actually—seemed to be accepting his involvement. "Thanks."

He drained the bottle and set it aside while he tried successfully to keep from puking, and unsuccessfully to keep from thinking about the vision, the dreams. He couldn't *not* think about them, because the clock was ticking and his gut said that when they got to Che'en Yaaxil, he was going to recognize it, not just from the inside.

"Maybe you should chill until it's time to leave," Ritchie suggested. Which wouldn't be long now. Unlike many of the Nightkeepers' rituals, which happened either in the dark of night or at the exact moment of the equinox or solstice, the resurrection spell called for broad daylight. The *winikin* shouldered the last of the packs and started to head for the mansion, but then hesitated and turned back. "Do you want me—"

"I'll be fine." Sven waved him off. "You go ahead." He was dealing, would keep dealing. "If you see Mac, point back this way and say, 'Go to Sven,' will you?" The coyote was out of range, and he was too light-headed to call him back.

"He's right behind you."

Sven froze. Then, trying not to let the other guy see him getting rattled, he glanced back over his shoulder to find Mac on his haunches nearby, with his head cocked in a *Hello? Sitting right here, dude.*

Which would've been fine . . . except the familiar

bond was silent. There was none of the live-wire effect that told him Mac was nearby, and when Sven opened himself all the way up, he couldn't hear the background chatter—typically a litany of warm sun, interesting smells, and itchy balls—that he usually tuned out.

He sent a thought-glyph: *Speak?*

Mac chuffed, still looking at him like he was an idiot. *What did we have for breakfast?*

If the coyote could have furrowed his eyebrows, Mac would've been doing that and more. But there was no response . . . at least not one that Sven could hear.

The messages were getting out, but they weren't coming in.

Oh, hell. This wasn't good. Not good at all.

Ritchie took another step back toward him. "You're not okay. I'm going to call Cara, and—"

"No, don't. I'll find her myself."

The *winikin's* eyes narrowed. "I think I should go with you."

Sven dredged up a reassuring smile that felt more like a grimace. "It'll be fine. Don't stress." *And don't start any rumors about how the boss's boyfriend is off his game. That's the last thing we need.*

Actually, the rumor was the next-to-last thing they needed. Having him actually off his game was the last.

"If you're sure . . ."

"Positive. Go on. Drop that off in the hall and then you're off the clock until 'port time."

Finally appeased—Sven hoped—Ritchie headed toward the mansion, casting a last look over his shoulder. When he was out of sight, Sven closed his eyes, summoned magic that felt far too sluggish for an equinox, and cast a shield around him and Mac.

It failed.

"Fuck me." A big-ass pit opened up in his gut. He had known he was risking a backfire by staying put longer than his magic wanted him to, but he had counted on his warrior's talent to keep things working until after the battle. And now . . . *Shit.* He didn't know what the right answer was going to be. All he knew was that he couldn't help lead the *winikin* into battle without his damn magic.

Tapping his armband for a private channel, he hit up Cara's identifier. When she answered, he said, "Hey, where are you? I need a minute."

"I'm in my suite. Everything okay?"

"Nothing we can't deal with." He hoped. He honestly didn't know what he was going to say or what he hoped to get out of talking with her, only that he needed to see her, touch her. "I'll be there in—"

A strident *beep-beep-beep* cut him off, coming from his armband, with deeper echoes sounding elsewhere throughout the compound, and then the emergency channel went live, and JT's voice snapped, "We need serious help in the main mansion. Rabbit's barricaded himself into the altar room with Myrinne's body and the screaming skull. He says he's going to use it to resurrect her!"

CHAPTER TWENTY-FIVE

"Just do your thing; that's all I'm asking," Rabbit said to the screaming skull's hollow-eyed, skeletal face. Desperation hammered at him, making his hands shake as he clasped the skull between his and Myrinne's cut palms and whispered, "*Pasaj och.*"

He felt the burn of the barrier connection and saw the red-gold of Nightkeeper power, but other than that ... nothing.

Sunlight poured through the glass-and-steel roof of the circular chamber at the center of the mansion, creating patches of light and dark on the carved stone walls. The ashes from countless Nightkeeper funerals had been used in the mortar and set beneath the *chac-mool* altar, skewing the magic heavily toward the light. Which was why he'd brought her here—he needed all the good-guy vibes he could get.

"Come on, come on!" he chanted. There had to be a way to invoke the resurrection spell without being down at the First Father's cave, *had* to be. But how? He had shields on all the doors, but soon he would be surrounded, outnumbered. When that happened . . . Shit, he needed to think, *think!*

He had placed her on the altar, curled on her side with her hands beneath her cheek as if sleeping. Only she wasn't. He couldn't find a pulse, couldn't sense her inside her own skull anymore. If she wasn't already gone, she was so very close.

His heart pounded a sick rhythm in his chest. Sweating, shivering, he leaned over her. "Come on, sweetheart; stay with me. I'm sorry. I'm so fucking sorry. I'll make it up to you somehow; I promise. Just stay with me." He tried the spell again. "Come on, come *on!*"

Beneath the desperation, grief and anger blossomed. Huge, horrifying, *crippling* guilt. Of all the things he'd fucked up in his life—and there had been many—this was the worst. She had trusted him, loved him without reservation—he knew that now for certain. She had only been trying to help him. As always. And he had killed her for it.

"Think, dumb ass." There had to be some way to connect the skull's power to Myrinne's soul as it slipped away. Some kind of magic, or artifact, or . . .

What about the eccentrics?

He froze, feeling them weigh suddenly heavy in his pocket. They were powerful, they could forge a conduit to the dead, and the room was skewed so heavily toward light magic, his gut said there was no way the demon that had called itself his mother could break through.

Fumbling, he pulled out the stones. The blood from his cut palms streaked along their slicked surfaces, muddying the black and ocher as he placed them together and put them on her chest, above her heart. "Please, gods," he whispered, thinking it was fitting that he was on his knees already. "Please bring her back."

He clasped the skull between their palms once more, and whispered, "*Pasaj och.*" And—holy shit and thank you, gods—brilliant red light flared from the eccentrics and whizzed around Myrinne, wrapping her in a cocoon of magic. "Yes, that's it. That's it. *Pasaj och!*"

The skull heated.

Pulse racing now, he dug down and called all the magic he could will up from deep within him. Then he leaned in and pressed his lips to hers in a kiss, shuddering at the coolness of her lips, their unresisting softness. She was worth ten of him, a hundred, because what use was all his power if he kept losing sight of right and wrong? "Please, baby. Please come back," he whispered against her mouth. "*Pasaj—*"

Glass crashed suddenly overhead and shards rained down. Cursing, he flung himself over Myrinne, protecting her face and upper body as he cast a shield of pure fire energy around the two of them.

Black ropes slapped the stone around him and figures descended through the unshielded skylights, and then dozens of *winikin,* lighter and faster than the magi, hit the ground running to fan out around him, weapons hot. One among them, though, was bigger and hit harder. Sven.

"No!" Rabbit shouted, and gripped the skull, frantically casting a second shield around it so— *Too late.* Power surged, and the artifact dissolved from his hand and reappeared in Sven's grip. "Noo!"

"It's over," Dez said, stepping through the main doorway, which was open now that Rabbit's shield was concentrated around him and Myrinne. "You need to let us have her."

Wild eyed and beyond himself, Rabbit grabbed the eccentrics, which burned to the touch, feeling strange and fleshy. "It's not over. I won't let it be over. I love her; don't you get it? I love her; I've always loved her, ever since that very first day. Nobody but her." He lurched to his feet, kicking his old man's knife aside as he brandished the joined eccentrics like a weapon, and only then realizing that together they formed a sharply pointed sacrificial blade. How had he not seen that before? Had they changed, or had he? Reversing the blade, he realized the truth. He had changed the nightmare after all—it wasn't his knife dripping blood anymore; it was the joined eccentrics . . . and he was the one who needed to be sacrificed. "Balance," he rasped, finally understanding what he had to do. "A life for a life."

The fog rose up inside him again, reaching for him, calling to him.

"Rabbit, no!" someone cried through the mist. "Don't. Let us—"

He drove the blade into his gut, angling up for his heart. It was like being punched in the stomach by a fist made of fire—a solid thud and then burning, radiating pain.

Then something went *pop* inside him, and he knew he'd found his target.

Sadness—sweet and profound—welled up with the tears that suddenly flooded his eyes. He collapsed across Myrinne. "Take me instead," he grated to the gods. The knife was buried in his heart, and he was giving of his own free will. "Send her back," he said, his voice bubbling with blood. "Take me inst . . ."

His shield spell faltered and— *Crack*! A brilliant burst of power that originated from the eccentrics momentarily painted everything in the room with the oily brown sheen of dark magic. From inside it emerged the demon who had claimed to be his mother. She wasn't a ghost anymore, wasn't even human—her eyes glowed red and her teeth were pointed to fangs. Power surrounded her like an unholy halo, shielding her when the Nightkeepers attacked with fireballs, the *winikin* with guns. Seeming not to notice them, she grabbed Rabbit and dragged him off Myrinne.

He tried to struggle, to reach out for her, but couldn't move; he was too far gone. He hung limp in the demon's grip as she summoned the magic of the eccentrics and began a transport spell.

"No!" Dez shouted, and lunged, only to come up against the demoness's shield.

Rabbit saw the king's face etched with rage and horror, saw the others trying to get to him, saw their despair. But what mattered in the last instant before the 'port spell took effect was seeing the faintest flutter of Myrinne's lashes. Then the spell took hold and *crack!* Skywatch was gone.

Over the next hour, even though her heart was heavy with Rabbit's disappearance and the inability of the magi to track him, Cara did her damnedest to hold herself—and her *winikin*—together as the minutes ticked down to their planned departure for Che'en Yaaxil.

Myrinne was barely alive, and nobody had a clue what had happened, or what sort of apparition had taken Rabbit. It hadn't been a god or *nahwal,* hadn't been anything the magi had seen before. So what, exactly, was it?

How had it gotten inside Skywatch? What did it mean for the coming battle? They still had the screaming skull and it appeared undamaged, but would it work to bring back the First Father? Gods, she hoped so.

Regardless, the *winikin* had their marching orders: *Defend the magi, and no matter what happens, don't let the enemy interrupt the resurrection spell.*

"Fifteen minutes to teleport," Strike called from the hallway, his voice ragged. He'd been hit particularly hard; Rabbit was his younger brother in every way that mattered.

Cara and several other volunteers were cleaning up the sacred chamber, which had originally looked like something out of a TV crime scene. It was still pretty bad, though, so when a broad-shouldered figure filled the doorway, she held up a hand, thinking it was Strike. "Stop there. Don't . . ." She faltered at the sight of Sven. "Oh. Hey."

He tipped his head toward the hallway. "Can I have a few minutes?"

She hadn't forgotten that he'd called her right before the alarms went off, or how serious he'd sounded. And, as she took in his grim expression, she knew that was a big part of why she had found some busywork to do with her last half hour before the teleport. She tried to tell herself it was a good sign that he'd come looking for her now, that he wouldn't do anything to damage their rapport right before the battle . . . but her heart lumped in her throat as she stripped off her gloves and moved to join him, and her stomach shimmied as he guided her through a little-used door off the east side of the mansion.

It opened to a small tree-filled courtyard that was

tucked behind the garage and faced away from the main compound, so all that could be seen beyond the mansion was sand and sky, and a lone bird riding an airstream high above them. The sight stirred something inside Cara, making her want to run fast and far, and never look back. But that was his MO, not hers, so she faced him squarely and said, "Tell me. Whatever it is, I can handle it."

"I know you can." He brushed a few strands of hair back from her cheek, tucking them behind her ear. "I think you can handle anything you set your mind to. I just wish you didn't have to. I wish . . . Shit. I'm not doing this right." He took both of her hands in his own, so they were facing each other, fingers intertwined.

The scene was suddenly very like that first vision, making her instantly aware of their clothing. He was wearing combat black and she was in a white T-shirt, albeit with camo pants and combat boots. Black and white, hands joined beneath a bower. Her heart went *thudda-thudda* and her throat dried to dust at the sudden crazy thought. *No, impossible. There's no way. He's not—*

"I need you to release me from the promises I've made to you."

"You . . . Wait. What?" That was so far from where her head had gone that she stuttered for a second while her stomach went freefalling. "Which one?"

"All of them."

"Bullshit." But his expression held grim apology rather than any hint of an ill-timed joke.

He squeezed her hands like he never wanted to let go. But he said, "I'm sorry, Cara. I need you to set me free."

Nausea surged as she flashed on the sight of him standing at the window last night, staring out at the world. But that didn't do a damn thing to take the edge off the shock that raced through her, didn't come close to filling the yawning pit that opened up inside her. Yes, she'd seen his restlessness, felt him pulling away, but she'd thought they had more time. She had thought he would settle down, get into the rhythm of being back at Skywatch . . . and being with her. But he hadn't even given it a chance.

Anger flaring, she burst out, "Seriously? You're doing this *now?*"

"I have to." His face was stark, his voice flat, and something in his expression made her think that this wasn't just about him getting squirrelly.

She took a deep breath. "Talk to me, Sven. Help me understand what's going on in your head, because by the gods, right now it feels just like old times. Only it's worse. Much, much worse, because I care about you so much more now." She swallowed. "Please tell me you're not bailing already."

"I've been having dreams, Cara. Dreams and waking visions of being in the rain forest near Che'en Yaaxil, searching for something. They're like the flashes I started getting right before Mac and I bonded, only they're more . . . I don't know. Frantic, I guess. Like something really bad is coming."

She exhaled softly. "You're afraid you won't be able to react the way you need to if you're caught up in managing the *winikin* and trying to watch my back." She squeezed his hands, tried for a smile. "We can work with that."

"That's part of it, yeah. There's something else, though. . . ." He returned her squeeze, but didn't smile. "I'm blocked, Cara."

"You're . . ."

"Blocked. My magic isn't working right. Mac can hear me but I can't hear him, can't tap into his senses. Worse, I nearly used myself up zapping the skull away from Rabbit, and that was a short-range translocation. Power-wise, I'm back down to where I was before Mac and I bonded, maybe less."

She glanced down at their joined hands, and stretched her senses toward the small trickle of warmth that was so new yet already a part of her. "I can still feel you."

His eyes went sad. "I can feel you, but I can't tap into that connection for power. I can't tap into *anything,* and that's a huge problem."

Panic sparked. They were ... what, ten minutes to teleport? Less? "Maybe it has to do with the cave, or the skull. Maybe—"

"I don't think the blockage is related to the visions, at least not directly." He glanced away from her, toward the horizon. "I think that it's coming from inside me."

Ah, she thought, and then ... *Oh.* Disappointment surged through her—disappointment in him for being who he was, in herself for forgetting. "Because you're fighting your nature."

His eyes flicked to hers. "You knew?"

"I ... Yeah. I didn't want to see it, though."

"I didn't want to feel it. These past few days have been like a dream, a fantasy. A few times I've woken up in the middle of the night or early in the morning, and just watched you sleep for a minute, thinking to myself, 'There she is. After all these years, there she is.' And I was as happy as I can ever remember being." He met her eyes fully, and she saw everything she had been hoping for in him as he said, "I wanted—I *want* to stay here with you, be with you. I swear it, Cara."

"Then stay. Be with me." Emotions raced through her, jamming in a huge lump in her throat.

"I can't. I tried to ignore it, but . . . this is who I am." He raised their joined hands and pressed his lips to her knuckles in a move that shouldn't have put distance between them, yet somehow did. "We don't have much more time. I'm sorry as hell to do this to you, but I need you to release me from my vows to protect you and help you with the *winikin*."

The blood rushed in her ears. "Then what?"

He didn't pretend to misunderstand. Pressing his forehead to hers, he said, "Then I'm going to block our bond and open myself back up to the urges of my bloodline. I'll stay and fight with you for as long as I can . . . but I can't promise anything more than that."

She told herself not to ask, to let it go until after the resurrection spell had been cast. But she asked anyway. "What about us? Is this it?"

"I hope not. I don't want it to be." He eased back, searching her eyes. "Cara, I'm crazy about you. I want to be right next to you every moment that I can. I want to help you, protect you, show off for you. . . . Hell, I've never felt like this about anybody, ever, and I need you to believe that."

Her eyes filled, damn it. "So what are you suggesting?"

"We could take it day by day, see what happens." He brushed a thumb across her lashes. "You could take me as I am. A coyote . . . but one who cares for you very much. Can we make that be enough for now?"

Part of her wanted to say, *Yes, absolutely. We can make it work.* Anything to not give in to the heartache that was beginning to claw at the thought that this was the end of the fireworks. Gods, in a few short days he had become part of her world. He had been everywhere with her, done everything.

Can we make that be enough for now? It echoed in her head, in her heart. And the thing was, it should have been enough. It was just supposed to be fireworks and good times, a way to live the next three months to their fullest in case they were her last. So it shouldn't matter if he was there some nights and not others. She was fine on her own, after all.

But it *did* matter. She had learned many things over the past couple of weeks—about herself, about him, about the two of them together—and although there was plenty she didn't know yet, plenty she didn't understand, she knew one thing for certain: Day by day wasn't going to work for her. Not when it came to Sven.

Maybe a different woman would have been able give him the "I'll see you when I see you" that he was looking for. She couldn't, though. After a lifetime of being low-priority for everyone except her mom, she wanted more, damn it. She wanted what she'd had for the past few days. And she wanted to know he was there for good, and that he was staying because of her, not because of the gods, or the *nahwal*'s message, or the coming battle. For her. If she gave in now, she'd be giving up what she wanted, what she needed, so he could regain his power. But in doing so, she would lose her own power, and that was just as important.

And that wasn't just the woman talking now; it was the *winikin*'s leader.

Her heart tore as she stood on her tiptoes to kiss him,

then ached when she saw a flicker of hope in his eyes. "I release you from your vows," she said. "You are a free man, not bound to me in any way."

"That's not true. You have my heart."

She yanked away from him to stand on her own with her hands balled into fists. "Don't! You don't get to say things like that if you're not going to back them up."

"I can't—"

"You won't. There's a difference." Aware that she was shouting, she took a breath, tried to level off. "You say you want to be with me? Then be with me. You say you want to stay? Then stay."

"But the magic won't—"

"Bullshit. The way I've heard it, the magic gets blocked when a mage shuts himself off from his emotions. Which means the problems you're having aren't because of your bloodline or your visions . . . it's about making a commitment."

And damned if he didn't wince. "Cara. Babe. You don't know for sure that's what's going on."

"You don't know it isn't, and don't call me 'babe.' Save that for your endless string of beach bunnies." An inner churning warned her that they were out of time, but she knew that they needed to settle this now, that they both needed to go into battle as strong and whole as possible, whether together or apart. Swallowing, knowing this was her last-ditch, she continued. "You say you've wanted me for years, but you stayed away because of my father. Now you've got me—you can keep me—but you're turning away because of the magic. Well, I'm calling a final 'bullshit' on that. More, I'll bet you ten bucks—a million, name your ante—that if you open yourself up fully to our bond, your magic will come back online, maybe even stronger than before."

It didn't escape her that neither of them had much practice with love and healthy relationships. If they had all the time in the world, they could have let this one develop more slowly ... but time was something they didn't have. Her throat was raw, her heart a wound in her chest, her pulse a fast, syncopated *thudda-thud* that seemed to be urging, *Say yes, say yes, say yes.*

But he shook his head. "Cara ... I can't. I've got to go with my gut on this one, and it says I need to be true to my bloodline."

She tried not to hear the echo of her father's voice in that, tried not to think he'd finally come between them for good. Because this was it. She'd given Sven his last chance to prove that he could stick it out and be the kind of man she knew he could be, and he was blowing it.

"Don't do this," she whispered. "Please."

His eyes glistened. "It's already done."

As if on cue, the compound's alarm system gave a two-note *bleep-bleep* of warning. It was time to go.

She instinctively clutched at her wrist, as if covering her mark could prevent him from blocking her out. For a second, she thought he was mistaken; the glimmer of connection was still alive. But pain pierced her as she realized that it wasn't the same. It was muted now, sluggish and still. A one-way street now rather than two.

Her wristband buzzed, followed by JT's voice. "Cara? You copy?"

Eyes still locked on Sven's, she raised her wrist to answer him. "I copy. We're on our way." Lowering her arm, she said stiffly, "We should go."

"First, tell me that you're okay."

"No. I'm really not. But I will be." She turned her back on him and headed for the rendezvous, hoping to hell they hadn't just fucked things up for everyone else . . . and wishing that the day was already over, so she could go back to her room, pull the covers over her head, and weep.

CHAPTER TWENTY-SIX

Candelaria Caverns
Guatemala

According to Lucius's report, the Candelaria cave system had probably been the cradle of the ancient Mayan religion, because it was the one place that had all the elements symbolized by the pyramids: a mountain climb leading to a cave mouth, with a river inside it that descended down into the earth to a hidden tomb. And since the river was supposed to lead the dead to the afterlife, that made Che'en Yaaxil—a hollowed-out cavern buried deep in the forest and well off the radar screens of Candelaria's tourists and researchers alike—a damn good place for a resurrection.

In theory, anyway. In reality, there was a big question mark all of a sudden, because where the Nightkeepers' early scouts had reported that the place practically vibrated with power, it had suddenly become a dead zone, and not just of the radio variety. Yes, the communications were down because of the equinox's power fluxes . . . but there also wasn't a scrap of magic to be felt.

"You're sure this is the right cave?" Dez asked, keeping his voice down so the others nearby—mostly *winikin* setting up the stone-shield perimeter—wouldn't hear.

"It's the one we saw in the vision," Cara confirmed, not letting herself glance across the cavern to where Sven was helping with the setup. She was holding it together, but just barely, caught in a tug-of-war between grief and guilt, with a heaping side of anger—at him for not wanting her enough to fight for it, at herself for falling so hard that it had suddenly become all or nothing.

She was pretty sure the timing of the blowout had come from the magic, though. Maybe Carlos had been right that she had been reaching all along, that the signs hadn't meant what she'd wanted them to.

"You're positive this is the place," the king pressed.

She nodded. The circular cavern, the irregular domed roof with the fallen-in spot that let sunlight filter through, the waterway and sandy beach were all the same. "This is where the *nahwal* told us we needed to be."

"Okay. Then let's do this, and let's hope to hell the spell can bring the power level back up and that Rabbit didn't damage the skull. Without his magic amplifying the uplink . . ." Dez shook his head. "I've got a bad feeling."

Me too, Cara thought as Dez strode to the spit of dry sand, where the skull had been placed on a tripod altar made from carved bones.

"You okay?" Natalie asked, coming up beside her and sending a look in Sven's direction.

"Is it that obvious?"

"Only to me, and only because I've seen that look

before in the mirror when JT's being particularly irascible. I recommend chocolate, alcohol, a chick flick, and some target practice, not necessarily in that order."

A laugh bubbled up in Cara's throat, where it choked to a sob. "I think I'll have to take a rain check. And I don't . . . Damn it." Sudden tears burned her eyes, and she turned away from the others. "I can't do this now."

"Are you sure? What if—"

"Don't," Cara said sharply, having already done the what-ifs herself. What if he didn't make it through the op? What if she didn't? What if they'd met as normal people doing normal things, and discovered fireworks? What if, what if, what if. "We're at an impasse, and talking about it any more now would only distract us from our priorities."

"That sounds like something your father would say."

"Maybe. But that doesn't make it wrong."

"Places, everyone!" Dez called, waving for the magic wielders to form an inner circle and the *winikin* to form the perimeter, along with the two magi who would be acting as their backup.

Cara's eyes skimmed over Brandt and went to Sven, who was checking weapons and ammo. As if sensing her gaze on him, he looked up, and their eyes locked. She caught a flash of pain in his face, felt it in her soul, and, without thinking, took a step toward him.

"Go on," Natalie urged. "It doesn't have to be all or nothing, not right now."

But then, from outside the cavern, Mac let out a shivering howl, followed by a flurry of furious barks. Sven's head whipped around. And Cara's heart sank as he hesitated a split second and looked back at her with heartache and apology written on his face. Then he turned and bolted for the short tunnel that led out of the cave, chasing after the sound.

And he was gone.

It was only a few seconds from the first howl to the moment he disappeared into the tunnel's darkness. But Cara stood staring at the empty tunnel entrance for nearly half a minute. One part of her couldn't comprehend that it had happened so quickly; another said it had been inevitable.

Oh, gods. It had really happened.

Dez waved for Patience to join Brandt in the *winikin* line, and she did so without missing a beat, which told Cara that the king had known about Sven's visions, probably before she did. That should have hurt far more than it did, but it seemed that the parts of her that handled grief and pain had overloaded. She felt dead inside. Dull. And so very cold, partly from shock and partly because there wasn't any warmth coming through the connection anymore, not even a trickle.

"Cara, sweetie . . ." Natalie reached out and clasped her arm.

"I'm okay," Cara said, though that was a lie. "He warned me this would happen." She hadn't believed him, though. Somewhere deep down inside, she must have told herself that it wouldn't come to this, or that if it did, he would stay with her.

Apparently parts of her were still seventeen and stupidly optimistic. Or they had been. She could feel them now, dying inside her as she turned away from the tunnel mouth and focused on her team. Hers now, because she no longer had a coleader, no check to her balance. It was going to be up to her to lead the *winikin,* up to them to protect the magi.

And Sven ... *Gods, please keep him safe.* But that was the only thing she would ask for when it came to him, because she had a job to do and a team to lead.... And he had just bailed on her for the last time.

Sven ran along a narrow game trail in the rain forest, searching, searching. There! Up ahead, a flash of movement, a stir of leaves, and then gone. Lungs burning. Close now, but where?

The vision blurred to reality and then back again, making him feel desperate and schizo. He ran on two legs, on four, and then back again, following the whip of Mac's tail, glimpsed briefly and then gone. Leaves and branches lashed at him, and a troop of monkeys screeched overhead, sending parrots darting from the trees.

Mac didn't slacken, didn't look back.

"Damn it, get back here!" Sven's voice sounded strange and alien in his own ears. "What's going on here?" The strange double vision felt like it did when he was deeply linked with his familiar, but their bond was silent. He couldn't call the coyote back, couldn't ask what he was chasing, didn't know why they were running away from the cave and their teammates—away from *Cara*, damn it.

What more do you want from me? he asked the gods, anyone who might have an answer. He was following the vision, but he didn't have his magic back, couldn't hear Mac, hadn't gained anything except a broken fucking heart.

He had known it would hurt like hell to end things, but he hadn't even begun to guess how much it would suck to see her walk away and not look back.

The trail widened and he saw Mac fully for the first time since the chase had begun. The big coyote was flattened out with his nose to the ground and his tail flagging, tracking, searching, all the things Sven kept envisioning. Only he wasn't inside Mac's head in the visions. He was . . . Shit, he didn't know where he was, or why.

He stopped dead on the trail. The skewed double vision cleared abruptly, as if he'd shut off some other channel without being aware of its existence. He was alone in his head once more, brain no longer fogged by something else's dreams. And he didn't like what he saw.

What. The fuck. Was he doing?

He was running away. That was what.

Brush crashed up ahead, then faded as Mac kept going without slackening speed. But Sven let him go as his head did some crashing of its own. Part of him wanted to keep going, keep running . . . but the rest of him said to turn his ass around and go back to where he belonged. Not just with his teammates or the *winikin* army, but with his woman. *Cara*. He had come back to Skywatch determined to make amends for having let her down time and again, and what did he do instead? He hurt her a thousand times worse and told himself it was the right thing to do.

She was the one who'd been right, though. He was running from her, from his growing feelings, though he'd talked himself into believing that the urgent, out-of-control sensations were coming from his bloodline magic. And in doing so, he'd blocked that magic, just like she'd said. At least, he hoped that was what had happened, because that should mean it was fixable.

He couldn't explain the visions or Mac's odd behavior, but it was time to make a choice. He could keep following the vision, or he could go back to the fight, the team, and his woman.

"I'm going back." He said it aloud, daring the *nahwal,* the gods, or the universe to tell him different. Then, not waiting for an answer or caring what it might be—this was his life, his choice—he spun and bolted back the way he had come.

No lightning struck him dead; no demon appeared to drag him to Xibalba as he raced through the rain forest on his own two feet. He didn't feel the slashing branches, didn't stress about his magic, Mac, or anything else he couldn't control right now. The one thing he could control—the thing he should've been in better control of all along—was himself. Starting now.

As he ran, he prayed that Cara would give him one more chance to apologize, one more chance to prove that he wanted her, that he was willing to make whatever amends she wanted, whatever sacrifice would prove that he was committed to her the way she wanted, the way she deserved.

He didn't know yet how he was going to do that. But he would do it. That was a promise.

The way back seemed shorter than the trip out; he was there within minutes, chest heaving and legs burning from the sprint. He'd made it!

But as he neared the edge of the clearing at the mouth of the tunnel, a terrible rattle split the silence and the air shimmered in a smudged gray curtain across the cave mouth. The surface bulged and rippled obscenely, warning that the barrier was almost breached at that point, which wasn't something they had planned for. If the demons came down that tunnel and caught the Nightkeepers unprepared . . . "No!" Sven surged toward the breach. "Cara!"

A blur came hurtling at him from the side, too fast for him to defend. It slammed into him and he went down beneath a huge projectile of fur, muscle, and sinew.

He hit hard and rolled, shouting, "Mac, godsdamn it, stop!"

But the coyote that faced him in an aggressive crouch wasn't Mac, he saw with sudden shock. It was a sable-coated female with dark, frantic eyes. She lowered her head and snarled, then jerked up with an utterly canine look of surprise as Mac burst from the undergrowth with a roar.

The bigger male hurtled over Sven and thudded to the ground in front of the female with his teeth bared and a low growl revving in his chest. The female's snarl ratcheted up and the two tensed to spring, to fight, to—

"Hold it!" Sven surged to his feet. "Mac, hold! Look!" He pointed to the cave entrance, where the dark curtain was folding in on itself and curling around to enter the tunnel, moving fast. "She was protecting me!" As the bigger coyote subsided, Sven repeated in an *oh, holy shit* tone, "She was protecting me."

Moving around Mac, he put himself right in front of the female, who was still crouched, but had stopped snarling. She watched him with wary eyes and her whole body shook, but she held her ground as he hunkered down.

"Dear gods. You're real, aren't you? Where did you come from, sweetheart? What are you doing all the way down here?" Mac had appeared unexpectedly, but at least they could theorize that a pack of the coyote blood-line's carefully selected hybrids had escaped after the massacre and gone feral. Down here . . . he didn't have a clue.

But she was real, all right. And she was powerful enough that her visions had reached him all the way up in New Mexico.

Heart thudding with sudden excitement, he tried to think of how it felt when the visions came, how he'd run after Mac seeing double, once as himself and once as another coyote. And, seeking those feelings, he sent a pulse of magic, along with a thought-glyph. *Friend.*

The female barked, high and excited. *Friend! Talk! Where? Man where? Searchsearchsearch, where?*

The "man" concept was one he knew from when Mac had been trying to track him down, their mental link somehow activated before Sven really understood what was happening to him. It was gender neutral, and meant the one particular human being that the coyote was meant to bond with. The female was a familiar in search of her person.

And there was only one other person on the planet who wore the double-dotted coyote glyph.

Excitement flashed in his veins like wildfire. "In there!" He pointed to the cave, where the dark, roiling shimmer had entirely plugged the tunnel. "She's in there! Is there another way to get inside?"

His mind filled with scattershot images coming in a suddenly very familiar mental tone. *Running. Searching, searching. A cave. Enemy! The enemy is in the cave. A back way. Another tunnel. Run. Hurry. Fast-fast.*

He didn't know how she had learned thought-glyphs or come to be in the Guatemalan rain forest, or how she'd managed to contact him, but right now none of that mattered. All that mattered was getting into that cave.

"Go!" Heart hammering, he waved her off. "We'll be right behind you."

Following her thought stream like a beacon, he and Mac chased the sable female through the trees and up a nearly vertical cliff face, to where a crack led to a narrow, twisting tunnel. And, gods willing, all the way inward to the cavern of Che'en Yaaxil.

"What the hell is that?" Natalie cried. But she knew. They all did. The chatter of dark magic coming from the tunnel was just as the magi had described it: like the noise made by an Amtrak-size rattler.

"They're coming," Brandt confirmed. He and Patience were helping the *winikin* with the shield stones that Lucius and Jade had magicked up for the *winikin* to use for protection. They worked either singly or as an overlapping domed defense, which was what they had in place now.

"Stand your ground," Cara called to her teammates, amazed that her voice stayed steady. The rattling noise shifted and slithered and made her want to claw at her own skin. She held it together, though, just as she'd held it together up to this point in the op, by focusing on the immediate situation and dealing with whatever small piece of the whole needed to be dealt with.

The big picture was too damn scary right now: The Nightkeepers were having zero luck activating the screaming skull, there were nasty things coming up that tunnel, and it was her job to make sure they didn't get to the Nightkeepers.

So she concentrated on the pieces that needed to work. "Breece," she directed, "go help Sebastian." The shield stones had their own power sources, but they used a blood-link as the catalyst. The more a *winikin* hated magic and the magi, the harder they found it to link up, even if they were honestly trying, as if something deep inside them still rejected the connection.

Trying very hard not to think of the parallel to Sven, she made a couple of other moves, shoring up faltering spots in the shield-stone dome, which was visible as a pale blue glow all around them. Through it, she could see a dark mist gathering at the tunnel mouth, then thickening to an opaque fog that began to roil and spin.

The rattlesnake hiss amped, but she held her ground, all too aware of the magi in the center of the dome. They were blood-linked and deep in the magic, nearly insensate as they focused all their energies on the skull and the resurrection spell. They were trusting her people with their lives, and she wasn't going to let them down.

She had their backs, even if nobody had hers.

"Weapons ready," Brandt called out, his voice ringing over the din. "Wait to fire until we see —"

A vicious rending noise tore through the cave, and the fog split in half, gaping to either side as terrible creatures poured through into the cave. At first she saw only a roil of dark body parts, glimpses of clawed hands and feet, and wickedly barbed tails, but then the creatures fanned out and she saw the demons for real.

They were human shaped, eight or nine feet tall, with wingspans of twice that, made of dark skin stretched across fingerlike bones. Their faces looked like they'd been caught in the middle of a shape-shift between human and pug, with squashed-in noses and beady eyes that kindled and glowed red as they solidified. And if that wasn't enough to warn her that these were the bat demons JT and Natalie had once faced, barely escaping with their lives, then the ID was sealed by their whiplike tails and grotesquely oversize penises, which had flat, leaflike scales at their tips.

"*Camazotz!*" JT shouted, confirming her guess and sparking new fear, because the powerful demons could be killed only up close and personal—cutting off their penises puffed them to smoke—and because where he and Natalie had fought a nest of newborns, these *camazotz* were fully mature.

As they came through the tear in the dark barrier, their burning red eyes locked onto the *winikin* and their mouths split in terrible screeches that started in the audible range but then ran up from there to a supersonic whine that made Cara's bones ache.

Someone screamed, snapping the terrified silence of the *winikin* line and unleashing a chain of cries and shouts that warned of a stampede.

"Hold your shields!" she shouted. "Stay open to the magic! For the love of the gods and tomorrow, don't lose those shields! And get ready to shoot!" She checked her weapon—an M-16 modified to handle the new exploding-tip jade bullets—with hands that shook so badly it took two tries to get the clip back in.

The *camazotz* poured through the rip. There were twenty of them, then thirty. And then, as if they had reached some critical mass or were answering some command given outside human hearing, they raced to surround the shielded circle.

"Steady," Patience called. She and Brandt were blood-linked, adding their magic to that of the shield stones, and they each had a pulsing, glowing fireball conjured and ready to hurl through the one-way shield, which would let things out, but not in.

The *camazotz* moved closer, eyeing the shield as if trying to figure out whether it would burn them. But the shield stones gave off only a passive force field, and one that hadn't yet been truly tested.

Please, gods, Cara whispered inwardly, but then didn't know what she dared ask for, or even if the gods were listening. For a few brief days, she'd felt like part of the prophecies, part of the war. Now, though, it seemed like she'd been talking herself into the impossible-seeming logic. What were they doing here? Was this even the right place, the right spell? On some level, she had expected the *Banol Kax* to send the shadow creatures to attack: the hellhound, the eagles, all the other beasts that had erupted during Aaron's funeral. Those were her enemies, hers and the *winikin*'s, and would have meant something.

The *camazotz,* though, were pure killing machines, an army sent to wipe out the resistance. Which meant ... what? That her signs that the *winikin* were crucial to the equinox hadn't been signs at all, just wishful thinking? Or, worse, had she and Sven gotten it wrong, after all? Because something wasn't right; that was for sure. The Nightkeepers didn't seem to be making any progress; they were uplinked in a circle, heads bowed, with Dez leading a chant. He had the skull artifact in front of him; faint smoke rose from it where they had burned their blood offerings. But aside from that, nothing was happening. All the magic was dark, the newcomers demonic. And they were closing in.

Focus. It was way too late to turn back now. All she could do was concentrate on the task at hand. Hold the shield. Protect the Nightkeepers.

"Ready," Brandt said in the same calm tone as his

wife, the two of them working together with a seamlessness that put a lump in Cara's throat.

A huge, burly bat demon grabbed a smaller one standing nearby and shoved it into the shield. The nearest *winikin* shouted and stumbled back, but the shield held. It held!

But it also didn't fight back. Unlike some of the Nightkeepers' shields, it couldn't deliver an electric shock or slash of fire. It was a forcefield, not a weapon.

The *camazotz* roared in triumph, and attacked.

"Now!" Patience shouted, and let rip with her fireball. It slammed into the surging churn of demons, grazed one, and hit another squarely, engulfing it in flames. A nanosecond later, Brandt's fireball hit a huge male nearby.

"Fire!" Cara ordered, and let rip with a burst from her machine pistol. The rest of the *winikin* started shooting a nanosecond later, and for a moment the only thing she could hear was the chattering hail of automatic weapons followed closely by the *crack-boom*s of the explosive-tipped rounds detonating to drive shards of sacred jade deep into the demons' flesh.

The world outside the shield erupted with bestial screams and oily sprays of black ichor. The creatures reeled as their blackish flesh peeled away under the searing, magic-wrought fire or was shredded by the jade shrapnel. Within seconds, nearly a third of the *camazotz* were on the ground, writhing, but a dozen or so had reached the shield. They scaled the sides like spiders, wings outstretched so they blocked the light and made it hard to see what they were doing. They were moving like they had a plan, though, which wasn't good.

"Get them!" Cara ordered, gesturing. "We don't want them to—"

Suddenly JT shouted, clutched at his chest, and dropped to his knees. Natalie cried out and raced to him, only to fall partway there with her hands over her heart. Above them, a pair of *camazotz* clung to their sections of the shield and were regurgitating a dark ooze onto the surface of the magic. It burned where it hit, eating through the shield-stone spell and somehow knocking down the stones' wielders.

"No!" Cara unloaded her clip into the first of the bat demons, which fell back with its face gone to pulp, leaving a gaping opening in the shield. Sebastian and Breece took aim at the second breach.

"I'll patch the gaps!" Patience said to her. "Help them!"

Cara raced to Natalie as several others converged on JT, who was normally their medic. His kit lay beside him, but in the terrifying moment when she leaned over Natalie and couldn't find a pulse, breath, or hint of life . . . Cara couldn't remember who was next on call for medical emergencies. Suddenly everything was jumbled up inside her head, competing for space. Panic lashed through her. *Don't lose it. Don't you dare lose it.*

She automatically turned and said, "Who—"

There wasn't anybody there to ask.

"It's the blood-link," called the man who was bent over JT's unmoving body. "You've got to break the blood-link!" It was a sandy-haired *winikin* with steady blue eyes. Cara couldn't remember his name or anything about him.

"Wait!" Brandt snapped. "Let me take over their

shields first. The punctures aren't affecting me or Patience, and we can hold the spells. . . . Okay, go!"

The guy stripped off JT's wristband, breaking his link to the shield stone. The second the band was off his flesh, JT arched up off the ground and sucked in a harsh, rattling breath. "It's working!" the guy barked. "Get Natalie's band off!"

Fumbling, Cara yanked off the device, which burned her fingers with cool fire. Natalie convulsed and then rolled over, gagging wretchedly. But she was alive. Blessedly alive.

Thank you, gods! "Ritchie," Cara called, remembering his name as her brain unlocked, then went into overdrive. "Over here. I want you to—"

"Here they come again!" Brandt warned. "They're regenerating faster than we can blast them back."

"You've got to get out there and cut their dicks off." The pained rasp came from JT. "It's the only way to banish the fuckers. At least it was a year ago." Which was an ominous caveat, as the magic was stronger now.

"Fire at will!" Patience cried, and let rip, driving back the front line once more.

But Cara heard additional screams, shouts, instructions, and knew that other sections of the shield had been breached, other *winikin* taken down. Any minute now, the *camazotz* would break all the way through, and they'd be fighting for their lives, and for those of the Nightkeepers.

The huge, burly bat demon that had started the charge rose up from behind the line, screeching at the edge of her hearing, driving the others on as they got blown back, regenerated, and rushed forward again and again.

"Transfer all the shields over to me and Brandt," Patience shouted. "Then get over here and give us your blood-links. We should be able to hold it that way."

Cara didn't move, though. She stayed staring at the huge *camazotz* leader. As if feeling her glare, it pivoted and glared back with burning red eyes, then jerked its chin as if to say, *You and what army, bitch?*

But that was the thing. This was her army. These were her people, and it was her responsibility to get them out alive. That might not have been her priority the day of the mock battle back at Skywatch, but it sure as hell was now. She couldn't hang back or hide out, not when there was something she could do to help.

Her hands shook as she scooped Natalie's wristband off the ground and added it to her own, then activated the shield-stone spell links of both, not as part of the larger shield, but to create a tough shell of magic surrounding her. Protecting her. Heart drumming a quick rhythm that was half terror, half determination, she slung her machine pistol on its harness and pulled her combat knife in its place. Then she headed for the shield.

Brandt caught sight of her. "Cara! What are you—"

His words went muffled as she plunged through, striking sparks where shield met shield.

The noise on the outside was worse than she had expected, even through two layers of shield-spell. Her pulse hammered in her ears, and she wanted to double over and puke with terror, but she didn't let herself give in to the fear, didn't let her determination waver. Instead, trusting the others to cover her with whatever firepower they had left, she bolted for the bat demons' leader.

Before, she had used her people as a distraction to save her own ass and get the win. This time she would do the reverse. *Please, gods.*

A dark shape closed on her from the left, another from the right. *No!* She dodged, tripped, and nearly went down, and then a roar of magic exploded behind her with a shock wave that nearly flattened her. She didn't look back, just kept racing across the sandy surface until she was within range of the huge *camazotz,* which was standing there with its hands out to its sides in the apparently universal gesture of, *Bring it on, bitch.*

But although she was five-foot-nothing and weighed a hundred or so pounds soaking wet, she hadn't grown up on a cattle ranch for nothing. And the fight training at Skywatch had been brutal but effective. She went in low, dodged the bat demon's first swipe, ducked under the return, and felt the whiff of a wing slash right above her. The thing's second blow caught her squarely on the shield and sent her flying back to crash into the cavern wall.

She hit hard and found that the shield didn't do a damn thing to buffer the impact, leaving her dazed. She thought she heard someone shout her name with frantic worry, but she couldn't stop now. The *camazotz* approached her, loomed over her—

And she yanked her machine pistol off its harness, fired screaming, and blew its head to mush.

Reality shifted around her as the creature's body wavered for a moment, still upright, and then toppled in slow motion, crumpling forward onto her. She tried to roll clear, but shock and the power drain of the bloodlink slowed her reflexes and the body hit her, slid sideways, and pinned her lower legs to the ground.

"No!" She shoved at the huge creature. "Gods, no!" It didn't move. But already she could see the wounds beginning to knit as the thing regenerated.

The battle raged around the dome in a cacophony of gunfire, explosions, and screams, but the leader's silence hadn't gone unnoticed. A pair of *camazotz* detached from the dome and headed for her, eyes blazing.

Panic slashed through her and adrenaline flooded her bloodstream; she struggled, shoving at the big creature, trying to move the immovable— *Shit! Don't be an idiot.* Going for her knife again, she risked turning off the shield to grab the bat demon's limp penis. It was as thick as her wrist, slick with sweat and ichor.

Gagging, she set her knife to the base and started hacking. Ichor spurted, but she kept going, sawing through the surprisingly tough flesh until, with a last rasping knife slice, the thing's penis parted from its body.

And all of it—bat demon, dick, ichor, and all— disappeared in a puff of oily smoke.

"Cara!" Her head whipped around at the sound of Sven's voice, and her heart clogged her throat at the sight of him charging down from a narrow ledge with Mac right behind him.

"Sven!"

"*Behind you!*"

Magic boomed suddenly at her back, driving her to her knees. A wing whipped where her head had been, and a clawed hand slashed through the nearly empty air, just grazing her shoulder. But even that small slice burned like unholy hell, more painful than anything she could remember experiencing before.

She screamed, fell, and rolled, trying to get away from the *camazotz* that rose over her, its eyes burning with feral hatred.

"No." She grabbed for her pistol, but the harness was empty and her hands were rapidly going numb. Dimly she remembered Natalie talking about how one small scratch from a *camazotz* could knock out a full-grown man for twenty-four hours or more. "Noo!"

It furled its wings and leaned in, reaching for her with wicked claws as its mouth gaped wide to reveal viciously sharp reddish brown teeth. But then a dark blur raced up behind the demon and launched itself into the air with a feral roar, and a lean, dark-furred coyote slammed into the bat demon, driving it off her with a ravenous snarl.

"Mac?" Cara slurred, confused, yet beginning to hope against hope that this was real and she wasn't already dreaming. Yet her vision blurred and it suddenly seemed that there were two coyotes attacking the *camazotz*. Which had to be a dream.

Then, as her consciousness wavered, she saw Sven coming toward her, saw all the world's anguish in his stormy eyes, saw his mouth moving, shaping her name, and—

Nothing.

CHAPTER TWENTY-SEVEN

"No! Cara!" The words tore themselves from Sven's throat as he raced toward her, aware that JT was closing from the other direction, shielded and carrying his medic's kit.

The *winikin* didn't waste words; he dumped the kit, drew his knife, and killed his shield as he strode toward where Mac and the sable coyote were standing over the body of the demon they had taken out. When the female snarled at him, Mac barked a warning, or maybe an explanation.

And Sven didn't catch a word of it. The new coyote hadn't spoken to him since that first blast of communication, and he was deaf to Mac. More, his magic was dead. Finished. He'd used it up fireballing Cara's attacker ... and he'd been too damn slow to do it.

"I'm here, babe," he said, dropping to his knees beside her and gathering her in his arms. His voice broke at the limp, unresisting feel of her normally strung-tight body and the pale gray-green cast to her skin, the fierce reddish black of the claw scratch on her shoulder. JT joined him, his face going grim, and Sven's voice broke as he kept talking to her. "Sorry. You don't like 'babe,' do you? I'll have to come up with something else."

He was babbling but he didn't want to stop, because if he did, JT would tell him what he already knew: that the equinox and the closeness of the end date had strengthened the venom of the *camazotz* from a soporific to a poison.

"Let's get her inside the shield," JT said, his voice equally ragged. "Natalie fought it off in a quarter the time it should have taken her to wake up, I think because she was connected to the magic. You can boost her, help her."

Sven nodded and gathered Cara up, hating how light she was in his arms, as if the life had already drained out of her.

"Hurry!" Brandt called from the center of the chamber, where the defenders had knocked back nearly all of the *camazotz,* buying a brief window of safety while they all regenerated. Some of the *winikin* were out hacking away and puffing the bat demons to dust, but the creatures were regenerating faster than they were being banished. "Run!"

Sven ran, with JT leading the way and the coyotes on his heels. They made it inside the shield-stone perimeter just as the first demon lunged to its feet once more, screeching and pissed off, only to get a faceful of explosive-tipped jade bullets and go down again.

"Everyone back inside the line!" Patience commanded as six other *camazotz* regained their feet, then four more. "Retreat, *now!*"

Most of the *winikin* responded instantly. Breece, though, kept hacking away, calling, "Just one more—"

She broke off with a strangled cry when the demon yanked itself from her grip, grabbed her by the neck, and bit down.

The crunch was horrific; the sight of her body going limp and then getting tossed aside was even worse.

Closing his eyes on a moment of silent prayer—for her, for all of them—Sven carried Cara to the little spit of sand where they had stood in their first shared vision, the one that had started them down the path to this place, this horror.

He cast a look around at the chaos of a battle going badly wrong. The Nightkeepers had managed to raise a glimmer of red-gold magic around the screaming skull and were bearing down, repeating the chant over and over again, trying to pierce the barrier between this life and the next and not getting far. The *winikin* were battered and exhausted; their blood-links were faltering even with Brandt and Patience acting as buffers, and the shield was flickering in and out.

Most of the *camazotz* had fallen back, but not because they had lost their leader. No, they were keeping up just enough of an attack to wear out their enemy. Then, once the shield was down all the way, they would move in. And feast.

Sven's blood chilled, but he found a prayer. Or maybe more a question. A challenge. *Is this what you wanted, gods? Is it? Or did I fuck everything up by turning my back on the woman I love?*

His brain hiccuped a little at the "l" word, but his heart didn't miss a beat.

Cradling her to his chest, he breathed her in and found himself thinking simply, *Please, gods.* It was what she always said when she wasn't sure whether she had the right to ask for their help. And for the first time, he knew how that felt.

He didn't deserve her, hadn't fought hard enough for her when the time was right, and now he might be too late. But he loved her, damn it. He fucking loved her.

"Give me one more chance," he said softly—to her, to the gods. "I promise I won't let you down ever again."

And, wonder of wonders, he felt a quiver of magic run through him at the vow.

Heart jumping from zero to sixty in no time flat, he opened himself to the power, sought it, latched onto it, and threw his soul into its warmth. He tore open the *winikin* connection he had blocked so self-righteously that morning, and welcomed the pain. Then he channeled all of his energy and that tiny quiver of magic straight into the *winikin* bond, whispering in his soul: *Please, gods.*

For a second nothing happened. And then, just barely, he felt the thinnest thread of a connection, a faint trickle of warmth.

Come on, come on! He held nothing back, but still it was more a stream than a torrent. Why was he so weak? He had come back to make amends. He knew what the visions were now. Yet still his magic didn't return. Had he damaged things with Cara so irreparably that even his power had turned away?

"Give her your magic," JT urged. He was crouched down on the other side of Cara now, though Sven hadn't sensed his presence. The *winikin*'s expression was urgent. "It's the only way to burn off the poison." And although he didn't say it, they both knew the *winikin* were down to the dregs of their energy, and probably the Nightkeepers as well. They needed a boost and they needed it now.

A few days ago—hell, even a few hours ago—he and Cara together could have put some serious power into the mix. Add in Mac and the sable coyote, who was crouched near Cara's head, watching her with worried eyes, and they might even have been able to turn things around.

Now, though, he shook his head. "I'm trying. It's not enough."

Worse, she was fading, getting weaker, letting go. He could feel it, but couldn't stop it. And for the first time in his life he felt truly helpless, truly at the mercy of the universe.

A ragged sob tore at his throat. "Don't you dare give up on me. Not now. Not—" He broke off at a tap on his shoulder, jerked his head up with a growl. And saw Sebastian standing there, offering his bleeding palm.

Twenty more *winikin* stood behind him, a mix of the factions. Beyond them, a skeleton crew was doing their best to hold the shield around the magi, who were bleeding from their hands and tongues as they called on the First Father to return. Worse, the *camazotz* were massing once more, their blazing eyes fixed on the shield with hungry intensity.

"Take it," Sebastian said, turning up his bloody palm to the light. "She's ours too." There was a quiver of magic in that, as well, as if the *winikin* had already made a new promise to their leader.

Nodding, Sven clasped Sebastian's hand in his.

The punch of power that rocketed through him nearly blew his damn head off his shoulders.

"Holy shit," he managed to gasp as the united might of the *winikin* roared inside him, immense and powerful and seeming to be searching for something. *Searching, searching* . . . "Holy, holy shit."

"Can you do it?" Sebastian grated, his voice seeming to come from very far away.

Sven nodded. "We'll get her back. I promise." The vow made a bigger ripple, augmented this time by the power of the *winikin* and everything that was inside his heart as the blood-link wove together, gaining strength and becoming something real and whole. And, riding the wave, Sven opened himself to the *winikin,* to the magic . . . and to Cara.

The response wasn't anything he expected.

A sudden wind whipped up inside the cavern and lightning lashed down and hit the domed shield, scattering along it like a science museum exhibit gone badly wrong. The *camazotz* screeched and charged, hammering into the shield and making it groan beneath the force of their attack. But suddenly it didn't look like they were trying to break the shield so much as get inside it. Their eyes were wild, their wing beats frantic.

"Shit!" Sven tried to pull the power back in, rein it tight, but it was out of control, whiplashing through him and up into the storm.

Overhead, near where the fallen-through spot let in the light, a huge cloud gathered, overlapping the rocky ceiling of the cavern, somehow existing both on this plane and another. Lightning struck the dome again, frying a bat demon with a huge and meaty bug-zapper noise. It shrieked, fell to the ground, and lay smoking.

Thunder rolled in the air, making the ground tremble.

"Sven, no!" Dez shouted, lunging up and breaking the blood-link to wave him down. "Stop! You're calling the hellhound!"

"I can't stop it!" Whatever chain reaction was happening had reached critical mass. Magic flowed from the *winikin* into him, from him to Cara, and then back up again in a feedback loop that filled him up, made him invincible, and terrified him all at once.

Searching, searching... He didn't know what the magic was looking for, only that it was very near. It had two legs, four, wings, fins, a crocodilian tail.... *Searching*... The sable coyote's head whipped up and she gave a joyous bark. *Found!*

The magic snapped out of him, cut dead, and if he hadn't already been on his knees, he would have fallen. He sagged.

Cara shuddered in his arms and her eyes flew open and locked on his.

Relief hammered through him, though there was fear too. Fear that she wouldn't be willing to give him one final chance. "I'm sorry." He caught her against him, held her tight. "Jesus, gods, I'm sorry."

She avoided his eyes. "What's happening?"

Stomach sinking, he answered, "I don't know anymore. I thought I did, but—"

Thunder barked and lightning speared from the storm cloud, arrowing through a ragged hole in the sagging shield-stone spell and whipping toward them.

"Move!" Sven called a quick shield that flared to life strong and sure, shocking him even as he hooked an arm around Cara's waist and dragged her aside. Mac lunged after them, leaving the sable coyote behind. She froze there, splay legged and wide-eyed.

And the lightning hit her squarely, as if she had been the target all along.

"No!" he shouted, heart shuddering at the horrible howl and the smell of burning hair. But when the flash cleared, she stood there unscathed, eyes bright and alert, and locked on Cara. The female didn't even look like she'd been singed; she seemed totally unharmed.

"What is she?" Cara asked, voice hushed.

"I thought . . . Oh, shit!" The female's body blurred and stretched without warning, expanding, enlarging, growing until the sable coyote—or demon?—was the size of a horse, stiff ruffed and vicious-looking, with coal red eyes that fixed immediately on Cara, suddenly all too familiar.

The hellhound had arrived in the flesh. And this time it wasn't letting her get away.

CHAPTER TWENTY-EIGHT

"Come on," Sven yelled, dragging at Cara's arm. "Fall back. I can shield us!"

Heart pounding, she turned to run. "Go!"

No! The *nahwal*'s voice cut through her panic and confusion. *Join now or all is lost!*

And she stopped dead. "Oh, gods."

Sven spun back. "Here? Now?"

But Cara got it. She freaking got it.

They had been right about some things, wrong about others. And they'd been very wrong about the two of them. "It's not talking about us joining," she said softly. "The signs have been pointing toward this guy all along." She indicated the hellhound, which was crouched with its head low, its hackles raised, and its huge teeth bared. "He's not the enemy. He's tried to reach me whenever I've been deeply linked to the magic through you."

Sven shook his head, but there was a look of dawning wonder on his face. "He's a she, and she's the one who's been sending me the visions. She's been looking for you." His voice quieted. "I thought she was your familiar."

Cara caught her breath. *My familiar. Gods*. And in that instant, she yearned . . . and then she let it go, because the creature facing her was nobody's familiar. "No. I think she's the key to the resurrection spell. Her and the *winikin* together."

That was what the signs had meant. Not that she and Sven were destined.

He took a step toward her. "Cara—"

Shouts interrupted, coming from the shield. The Nightkeepers were breaking the spell and rallying with the *winikin* as more *camazotz* poured from the tunnel. They were going to need help, though.

Cara held out her hand to Sven. "I need to borrow your magic. It's working now, isn't it?"

He avoided her eyes. "Yeah. Good as new."

That shouldn't have pinched, but did. She accepted the pain, though, just as she accepted the terror that took root and grew as they approached the hellhound. Mac stalked at her side, bristling, though she didn't know whether that was coming from his instincts or Sven's thoughts. Maybe both, because the creature was monstrous up close, fierce and fanged, and smelled faintly of burned hair and ozone.

The storm had gone quiet, but the clouds remained. Now, as the hellhound's growl notched up, thunder grumbled beneath their boots.

"Don't be rude," Cara said in a reproving voice. "You came looking for me, remember?"

Lightning flickered and the air grew heavy and storm-charged.

Out of the corner of her eye, she saw Dez say something to Strike, who shook his head. When Anna did the same, her stomach clenched. The Nightkeepers were exhausted, the shield failing, the teleporters possibly too spent to evacuate.

So when the beast shifted, looking ready to charge, she pulled her combat knife, opened the slashes on both her palms, and held out a hand to Sven. "Okay. Let's do this."

He hesitated. "Cara, I—"

"Not now," she interrupted. Because if he gave her one more empty apology right now, she was afraid she would be the one to block him, not the other way around. "Tell me after."

He said nothing more, but nodded and took her hand, and when the blood-link formed, it carried with it a huge upwelling of warmth and support. She nearly staggered from the impact of it, the aching sweetness of feeling magic coming through the bond once more when she had thought it lost forever, and from how much she wanted to send the same back to him. But the difference was that while she would mean it wholeheartedly, his would last only as long as it was convenient.

So, saying nothing, she accepted the warmth along with the magic, and crossed the last few feet that brought her into the hellhound's range. Coal red eyes watched her approach, but the huge beast didn't move.

Lightning flickered, though, followed by a growl of thunder.

"You came looking for me," she reminded the beast. "Well . . . I'm here. I don't know what you want from me. But whatever it is, you can have it."

"Cara . . ."

She ignored Sven's warning growl and, with his magic inside her and his blood-link making her feel like she could do anything, be anything, she held out her hand and opened her fingers to let the blood trickle free.

The beast moved like a striking snake, snapping its jaws to trap her hand in its massive teeth. She screamed in shock, but when Sven and Mac both surged forward, she said, "No! It's okay. It's . . ." She trailed off as the huge animal's tongue swiped her palm and new heat seared through her, new magic.

"Holy shit," Sven said, and looped an arm around her waist to support her when she sagged. "What is this? What the fuck is this?"

She didn't know, couldn't have told him if she did, because suddenly the creature reared back on its haunches and let out an earsplitting howl that drove her back and into his arms. She didn't want to cling, but she could only watch in terrified awe as fresh lightning split the sky, thunder pealed, and the clouds erupted, fragmenting into a dozen vapor trails. Twenty. Forty.

The cloudy shadows spun momentarily and then plummeted straight for the dome and then *through,* not deterred by the shield or the Nightkeepers' spells.

"Incoming!" Sebastian bellowed, and raised his machine gun.

"No!" Cara shouted, surging toward him even knowing she would be too late to stop it. "Hold your fire!" For a nanosecond his decision hung in the balance as a vapor trail beelined straight for him. He glanced at her. Didn't fire.

And the mist slammed into him and disappeared.

Sebastian yelled and staggered back, clutching his chest, then his forearm. "Son of a—" was all he got out before the fog erupted once more, streaming from where his fingers covered his bloodline mark. But it wasn't the same fog that had gone into him: As it emerged, it stretched and lengthened, growing wings and a body, gaining dark substance and form and a set of razor-sharp claws and a wickedly hooked beak.

The shadow creature—it was still a shadow, translucent despite the visible detail—flapped up and hovered above him while his face blanked with shock. "What? Who?"

"Whoo!" The huge owl was more streamlined than its real-world counterparts, with long, powerful legs and wings that cut through the air like scythe blades.

"Jesus, gods," Cara whispered, flashing back on the day of the funeral, when Sebastian had been nearly suicidal over having been marked by the magic. "It's his bloodline totem. The owl is his totem."

"The others too," Sven said, voice hushed.

She started to push away from him, but then her eyes went past Sebastian. And she froze at the sight of shadow creatures everywhere—felines, foxes, monkeys, reptiles, peccaries, and more. There was a totem shadow for each of the *winikin,* all bigger, stronger, and meaner-looking than their native cousins. The *winikin* themselves looked stronger and meaner too, as if they had been lit by a new inner power. And as they connected with their creatures, their shadow-familiars, their faces lit with fierce joy.

Magic, she thought, awestruck.

Shaking now, she turned back to the hellhound—so much bigger than the sleek coyote it had masqueraded as. The beast wasn't crouched down anymore; she was standing, her attention going from Cara to the outer perimeter and back again. Her body was quivering too, though with eagerness rather than shock, and a low whine sounded at the back of her throat.

Cara knew that sound from Mac. It meant, *Let me at 'em!*

Her pulse notched up. "Can you fight the *camazotz?*"

Enemy! Fight! Fightkillfight! The thought-glyphs came rapid-fire, almost unintelligible.

"Did you get that?" Sven asked.

"I got it," she said softly. She kept hold of his hand even though she didn't need the blood-link anymore—she could feel the magic inside her—but she let herself cling, just that tiny bit, as she approached the huge creature, reached up a hand, and stroked a massive shoulder. The female's fur was thick and coarse, and smelled of open skies and mossy hollows.

You're mine, she thought, and her throat closed when she got a wash of love, support, and acceptance in return.

"Cara!" It was Dez, his voice ragged. "Can they help?"

The *winikin* had gathered at the center of the dome, each with a huge shadow-animal nearby. Some lay prone or stood at attention; others flew in tight circles near the top of the shield, screeching battle cries.

At the sight, Sven hissed out a breath. "The cave painting."

She nodded, heart going *thudda-thudda* in her chest. "The coyote is their leader. That's what the painting means. She's in charge."

"Yeah." He squeezed her hand. "You are."

Pitching her voice to carry, she called to the others, "What do you think? Can we fight the *camazotz* now?"

There was a ragged chorus of assent, one that strengthened at its tail end.

"I can't hear you. Can we fight now?"

The chorus got deeper, stronger. "Yes."

"Can we kick ass now?"

"Yes!"

Her pulse was drumming, her palms going sweaty.

Don't overreach, she told herself. *Don't sacrifice anyone to make a point.* But her instincts said this was it; this was right. This was what she'd been brought here to do. "Our king has asked us to defend this place. Will you do it?"

It was a risk, but a calculated one, and it was rewarded with a resounding, "Yes!"

Grinning, Cara stripped off Natalie's wristband and tossed it to her. Then she pulled her combat knife, held it in the air, and shouted, "Then let's drop the shield and clear out the vermin!"

A huge shout rose up, coming from *winikin* and magi alike. Then the shield came down, and all hell broke loose.

Cara's hound bolted away from her, roaring a challenge, and the shadow-animals leaped to follow.

The *camazotz* screeched their unearthly cries and took to the air as the horde descended, leaving the lower-slung animals to howl in protest. Soon, though, they had work to do, as the airborne totems went to work shredding wing sails and sending the demons crashing to the ground. Or, like Cara's beast, leaping high in the air and snatching a bat demon midflight, then crunching and dropping it before lunging after another. Mac was right in the middle of the melee too, slashing at hamstrings and leaving the demons crippled and howling.

They would regenerate, though.

"Come on!" Sven tugged at Cara's hand, but she was already in motion, knife at the ready. She reached for her wristband, but he waved her off.

"I've got us covered." A shield spell—sleek and flexible, and like nothing she'd ever seen before—appeared in the air around her, molding to her body and creating lightweight, nearly invisible armor.

"Impressive." She hid the pinch of sadness. "I guess when your magic came back, it came all the way and then some."

He nodded. "I just needed to figure out my real priorities."

It hurt to know she wasn't one of those priorities, but she lunged into the fray, puffing one *camazotz* and then another to dust. The others had fanned out and were doing the same, working in twos and threes, often with *winikin* and magi mixed without issue, all watching one another's backs while the shadow-familiars knocked down their enemies.

"Look out!" Sven yanked her out of the way as a quick healer leaped up and made a grab for her. He launched a fireball that was so bright she had to close her eyes, then dispatched the thing with grim efficiency. When it was gone, he shot her a look she couldn't interpret.

"Sorry," she said. "And thanks."

There were other live ones, other close calls, but they worked their way through the slaughter, which was made far less macabre by the fact that the ichor vanished when the *camazotz* did. And all the while, she was aware of her creature—lithe and beautiful, violent and deadly—staying connected to her as the enemy ranks thinned, and—

"Incoming!" Sebastian bellowed as the opacity blocking the tunnel bulged and tore for a third time, letting more *camazotz* into the space. But they weren't like the others—these ones wore armor, and they had a plan.

Fast and fresh, they dodged the shadow-familiars and zeroed in on the Nightkeepers. Time seemed to slow for a second as Cara saw three of them catch sight of Sven and make a dive for him. She screamed and turned back, but she was farther away than she had realized, and the *camazotz* were lightning-fast.

"No!" She cried as the first one swooped down, un-furled its claws, and—

The hellhound appeared as if from nowhere and snatched it from the sky. Then she spit it out and grabbed the others. With the third still dangling from her jaws like a chew toy, she spun and bolted for the tunnel and the oily blackness of the torn barrier. Bat demons were still flowing out like water, and the opening was a nasty churn of shadows.

Stop enemies! The thought-glyphs appeared in Cara's mind, but it took her a second to translate, another to understand.

She surged toward the tunnel entrance. "No! Come back!"

"Cara, wait!" Sven caught her arm and dragged her back, launching a fireball in the same move and toasting the *camazotz* that had been aiming right for her. "What the hell are you doing?"

"Come back!" she cried again, her voice breaking on a sob, but the hound didn't hesitate. She gathered herself and launched straight into the roiling blackness of the tunnel mouth.

And disappeared.

"NO!" Cara pulled against Sven's grip, then clutched at him when the stone surface beneath their feet began to vibrate. The rattlesnake noise slashed through the space, growing louder and louder still.

"Cover your eyes!" he shouted, and pulled her into his arms and shielded them both just as the tunnel deto-nated with a huge roar of rock and dark magic.

Power blasted them, and shrapnel slammed into the shield. Cara clung to Sven, burying her face in his chest and trying to block out the sound of her familiar's demise, her sacrifice. "No." She didn't weep, not now. But she would. She might have known the creature for only a short time, but without realizing it, she'd been missing that part of herself for most of her life.

The noise died down, then faded to silence. She stayed pressed into him, though, not wanting to open her eyes and have it be time to move on.

"Cara." He eased her away. "Look. Look at what you've done."

She glanced around. The *camazotz* were all gone, vanished like they'd never been there. But they had left a disaster area in the wake of the fight. The beautiful cave was a shambles: The white sands were bloody red in places, warning that there had been injuries, maybe even more deaths than just Breece. The water was muddy, the tunnel a rubble-filled nonentity, and even the pretty green vines hanging down from above had burned, going withered and brown. "What a mess."

"No." Sven pointed to the others. "Look at them."

The others were picking themselves up and dusting off, talking in low tones. Nightkeeper, *winikin,* human . . . it didn't seem to matter anymore. There were handshakes and backslaps, and places where Nightkeepers had shielded *winikin,* and vice versa. And the shadow-creatures watched over it all, protecting the protectors.

A lump of emotion balled up in her throat. "We did it," she whispered past the tightness. "We won . . . and we did it as a team."

"You did it." He pressed a kiss to her temple. "You and your magic."

She sighed and let herself lean into him for one last moment, closing her eyes and savoring his solid strength, his kindness, his ... *Shit. Don't think about it.*

But if she couldn't think about Sven and she wasn't yet ready to think about the familiar she'd lost, what could she think about?

Whatever comes next, she decided. She would put one foot in front of the other, and not think about how she'd lost her man and her dog, and was one pickup truck short of a flipping country song.

Pulling away, she swiped at her eyes, took a deep breath, and faced Sven. "Well, I guess—"

Trapped!

The word was faint and pained, but she heard it loud and clear. And Mac must have too, because he let out a howl and bolted across the cavern to the tunnel. He sniffed and searched, racing from side to side and up the precarious rock slide, then gave an excited bark and looked back at Cara.

Heart kicking, she started toward him.

"Wait," Sven said from behind her. "Let me."

He must've sent some silent command, because Mac jumped down and sat on his haunches nearby, watching expectantly. Then warmth washed through her as Sven tapped into his magic. And the rocks began to move.

Huge gray slabs eased aside, boulders levered up, and smaller chunks floated as if on ghost wings while Cara stared in awe at the magic he could make.

"There!" Sven said. "I see her. Stay here." Without leaving room for discussion, he climbed up the rock slide and ducked into the hole he'd made.

Frowning, Cara started to follow. "What are you ..." She trailed off as he straightened and turned to her, carrying a dark-haired, normal-size coyote. "Oh." Her heart beat off rhythm as he carried his precious cargo down the slippery slope. "Be careful!"

"She'll need to see Sasha," he called, and got an, "On my way," from the healer. When he reached Cara, he nudged her back to a soft spot in the sand, and knelt to lay the coyote at her feet. And when she crouched down and cautiously touched the sable fur, she got a wash of love and support in return, along with a sighed thought-glyph of, *Found.*

Yes. She was found, all right. And she hadn't even known she was missing until now.

"She'll be okay," Sven said, looking at her across the coyote's furry bulk with eyes that seemed to be conveying a silent message she didn't understand. "I think she's mostly bruised and shaken up."

"She's not the only one." It was amazing how quickly things could change, she thought, and turned to Mac, who sat nearby. She threw her arms around the bigger coyote's ruff and buried her face in his dusty fur, choking out, "Thank you, thank you, thank you. I owe you. I owe both of you."

"No owesies," Sven said. "He loves you. He'd do anything for you." He paused. "And so would I. Because I love you too."

And just like that, everything changed again.

Stomach lurching, she let go of Mac and shot to her feet, hands balling to fists. "No," she said quickly. "You don't. That's adrenaline talking."

"No, it's me talking. I love you," he said, loud enough that the low murmur of conversation cut out and they became the center of attention.

A flush climbed up her throat and heated her face,

even as she wanted to weep. "Adding volume doesn't make it true." Softening her voice, she added, "Let it go, okay? Just . . . let it go." Because if he didn't, she was badly afraid she would do something really stupid. Like give him yet another chance.

"I can't let it go, because I love you. And I know how to prove it." There was something very determined in his eyes all of a sudden; the look brought a tremor of nerves and a quick, frantic thought that this was real. This was different.

But she'd thought that before, hadn't she?

She swallowed hard. "What proof? More promises that you'll take back when they get inconvenient?"

"Not exactly." Expression resolute, he reached into his pocket, pulled something out, and dropped down on one knee.

And all Cara could think was, *Oh, hell, no*.

For all that her inner seventeen-year-old—and maybe even parts of the woman that teenager had grown into—wanted to squeal, the rest of her, the smarter majority vote inside her, knew that this wasn't the right answer for either of them.

"Don't . . ." she began, but then trailed off and stared, shocked, at the piece of paper he was unfolding. Or not paper, really. An index card filled with Carlos's cramped writing done in pencil.

It was the *aj winikin* spell.

Cara gulped as Sven met her eyes. And started to read. "No. Stop." She took a step toward him. "Don't."

He didn't falter, just kept reading. Tension snapped into the air; she recognized it from when she got her mark, back beneath the wide-open Montana sky. It was the *winikin* magic. The servant's spell.

"Seriously, stop. I don't . . ."

He kept reading, but his eyes flicked to hers.

Panic gripped her. He couldn't do this. He couldn't! The king, the other Nightkeepers, her father . . . *Gods*. But he wouldn't stop. How could she . . . Then she knew. She hated it, but she knew how to make him stop. He was nearing the end and she was running out of time.

Planting herself squarely in front of him, she raised her voice to carry over the spell and said, "I don't love you."

He flinched. But he kept reading to the end of the card, and then locked his eyes with hers when, like magic—because that was what it was—a new mark appeared on his forearm: the image of a hand cupping the face of a sleeping child.

Cara looked down at her own wrist, where she wore the single coyote glyph with the double dot. "I don't feel any different."

"That's because it's a one-way street. It's my promise to you that I'll protect you, care for you, support you, and be there for you from now on. Period." He caught her hands and stood, and she suddenly realized they were back where their affair began, standing in the middle of Che'en Yaaxil, holding hands.

Only this time it was real. His commitment was real.

Her eyes flooded and she gripped his hands tightly. "I lied."

His shoulders eased. "About which part?"

"The part where I said I don't feel any different." She closed the distance between them. "I do feel different."

He brushed his lips across hers. "That's the only thing you lied about?"

"You mean the other part?"

"Yeah. That one."

And, with the Nightkeepers and their consorts, and the *winikin* and their shadow-creatures looking on, Cara smiled up into Sven's eyes and said, "I love you. I may have crushed on the boy you were and resented the adventurer you became, but I've fallen in love with the man you are today."

He exhaled a long, relieved breath. "So you'll give me one last chance to get it right?"

"You already did." She tapped his arm. "This is more of a sacrifice than I ever would have asked for."

"It's not even a fraction of what you deserve." He hooked an arm around her waist and lifted her to her toes to plant a real kiss on her, one that involved bending her back over his arm, elicited a few good-natured whistles, and lasted until Dez cleared his throat.

"If you two are finished . . ."

Sven let her go, grinning broadly. "I'd say we're just getting started."

"Then put it on hold for now. We've still got work to do." The king hefted the screaming skull in one hand and gestured toward the center of the cave. "If we could try this again . . . all of us this time?"

A few minutes later, distinctions forgotten, the endtime warriors—Mac and the nearly recovered sable coyote included—all linked together to form a double circle around the king, with the shadow-animals ringing the outer edge. And they set out to call the First Father back to earth.

This time the resurrection spell worked flawlessly. And Sven, with Cara—his mate, his love—at his side and their familiars at their heels, was in a perfect place to add his power to the whole and watch the magic unfold.

The *winikin* were the key, as Cara had predicted, along with their shadow totems. Dez had barely gotten past the second line of the spell when the animals began to move. They filtered through the double line of the blood-link and into the center of the space, where they started circling, moving ever inward and kicking up the sand, until there was a whirl of dust, shadow and light in the center of the circle. And all the while, Dez recited the resurrection spell and the magic amped from mage to *winikin* and back again, growing ever hotter, ever stronger.

The shadow-animals spun faster and faster; the power ratcheted up to a buzz and then a high-pitched whine that itched along Sven's jawbone, and then *boom!* There was a thunderclap and the shadows fled back to their *winikin,* went insubstantial, and disappeared into their holders. At each entry, the *winikin*'s eyes glowed briefly gold and then went normal again.

Cara smiled and said softly, "They'll be with us when we need them."

Sven nudged Mac with his toe. "Some more obviously than others."

Her smile went bright and brilliant, and made his heart turn over in his chest. He was so damn proud of her, proud to be with her, and proud to wear her mark, that he thought he might explode like the tunnel had. And he was psyched for her to have a familiar of her own, a thought-link of her own . . . and for neither him nor Mac to spend their nights alone anymore.

When the last of the shadow-animals disappeared, leaving only the coyotes behind, the storm clouds eased away and the sun finally shone through the overhead gap, chasing away the last of the mist . . . to reveal a brown-robed, hooded man kneeling in the center of the circle.

The resurrection was complete.

Despite not being much for religion, Sven got a shiver as the figure straightened.

Hands shot from the long sleeves of the brown robe, and marks flashed—too quick to be identified—as the man reached for his hood, pushed it back . . . and glared at the double circle with hard eyes.

Shock rattled through Sven. "What the fuck?" He was pretty sure everyone else was thinking it. He was just the first to say it. Because the sharp-featured man with the big hooked nose, heavy brow, and buzz-trimmed skull was no stranger. "Red-Boar?"

Because that was who it was. Rabbit's father, who had died in one of their earliest skirmishes, was back.

Gods help them all.

Cara's hand squeezed his and she pantomimed a *holy crap!* face that Sven returned

Red-Boar scowled. "Who the hell else did you expect?" His eyes went to Mac and the new coyote, and his eyebrows drew together. They nearly touched as he looked around, seeming to be counting up the new faces, only two of whom were full magi.

A low-level hum of whispers caught fire and spread, and headed quickly for hubbub territory.

"What are you doing here?" Strike asked, voice a little shaky, though Sven wasn't sure whether that was from shock or trying to suppress hysteria-tinged laughter.

The grizzled mage's scowl deepened. "Don't ask me. I wanted to stay dead. But the boar *nahwal* said my idiot kid got his ass in trouble again and I've got to bail him out if I want to get to the real afterlife rather than just the fucking in-between. So what's the deal?"

The air went tight as hell and everybody clammed up. Silence.

More silence.

Red-Boar zeroed in on Anna and stabbed a finger at her. "You. Start talking. Where is he?"

Something flashed in her eyes, but she said simply, "We don't know."

"Then why the hell did you summon me?"

"We didn't. We were trying to get . . ." She trailed off. "The Father. Oh."

More like, *Oh, shit,* Sven thought. But if Red-Boar had come back with a message about finding Rabbit, they must have summoned the right Father.

He hoped. Because if not, this was a serious fucking train wreck.

A little while later, once the sheer what-the-fuckery of Red-Boar's return had died down and Dez declared it time to head for home, Sven caught Cara's hand and tugged her to the sandy spit to steal another kiss.

She was smiling when they parted, but her eyes held worry. "I wonder if the gods knew what they were letting us in for, bringing Red-Boar back." She glanced to where groups started forming, mixing *winikin* with Nightkeepers to make sure the teleporters would have enough magic to get them home. "And how he's going to deal with everything that's changed since his time."

"He'll adjust," Sven predicted—though, remembering the irascible old mage, he wasn't so sure about that. He covered it, though, with another kiss. "All the changes have been good ones . . . especially this one." Another, deeper kiss.

"And this one." She dropped a hand to the top of the sable coyote's head in a gesture that was both proprietary and loving, and somehow sexy as well. All three tugged at his heart. He loved that she had a familiar, that she had magic of her own. And that she loved him back.

"What are you going to call her?" he asked with a nod to the sable female.

"Pearl." The answer was immediate and final. "I'm going to call her Pearl."

It took him a second before he got it. "As in 'Black Pearl'?" When she nodded, he made a face. "You're going with *Pirates of the Caribbean*? Really?"

"Says the guy who named his coyote after a character on *CSI: New York*."

He shrugged. "It's the eyes." When she rolled hers, the laugh that bubbled up out of him felt free and easy for the first time since . . . gods, since he didn't know when.

And, for the first time in just as long, he wasn't looking forward to the next adventure, the next destination. He was content right now, in this place and time, with the woman he loved. They would deal with whatever came next, and they would do it together.

That was a promise he would keep . . . or die trying.

EPILOGUE

September 24
Eighty-six days left until the zero date
Coyote Cave

Despite her sunglasses, Cara had to use her hand to shade her eyes from the sun's glare, trying to see across the rolling hills that surrounded the mouth of the empty cave. "He said for me to meet him out here."

Out. Pearl's tail whisked the hardpan, stirring little dust devils. Although she was adjusting to life inside the compound, she still preferred the wide-open spaces beyond the canyon. Risky or not, she liked being free.

"I don't see another Jeep, though, and he's not in the cave." And the flat, barren expanses between the hills weren't talking. "What gives?"

She was trying not to read too much into Sven's message—gods knew textspeak sucked at nuances—but he'd been gone since early that morning and he'd been furtive on the way out. She hadn't pressed, but she had definitely noticed. They were still feeling each other out in the relationship department, still figuring out how it was supposed to work. It wasn't like either of them had any practice at it.

He was trying, though; they both were. And her warrior's instincts—the gut feelings she had learned to trust even before she knew they were real—said they would get the balance right eventually. He would still need time alone and it would be a while before letting him in became second nature for her, but they would make it work.

There. Coming. Pearl rose to her feet with smooth, lethal grace and stood at alert, body quivering.

Cara didn't quite quiver, but it wasn't far off. Anticipation tightened her stomach as a big shadow came out from behind a nearby dune. "What the . . . ?" Then she burst out laughing at the sight of a contraption straight out of *Mad Max*, driven by the man she loved.

Sven, wearing surf trunks, wind goggles, and a huge grin, wrestled with a big wind sail set off-center on a two-person surfboard that rode on big, wide wheels. As he came around the corner and headed for her with Mac barking his fool head off and nipping at the tires, a gust caught the sail and sent the vehicle heeling over onto one set of wheels.

"Whooo!" Sven counterbalanced and rode the breeze right to her, then made a wide, braking turn that he managed to make look ridiculously elegant. Then again, he *was* ridiculously elegant, completely at home in an element that had nothing to do with magic or the war, and everything to do with him. With them.

Fun! Pearl sent. *Fun-fun-fun!*

Yes, it is, Cara thought, and went to meet her mate.

Love shone from his eyes as he dropped down from the wind sail and collected her for a sweaty, satisfying kiss that had her blood humming and tugged at the connection between them. When they parted, his eyes were dark with promises, and fully focused on her, on the moment.

"I like your new toy, sailor."

"*Our* new toy," he corrected. "Skywatch needs to remember how to have a little fun. Besides, I want to take you sailing, and thought this would be a good compromise for now." He was breathing lightly and grinning like a kid. "After the war we'll get ourselves back out to sea."

"It's perfect. And so are you."

"Can I quote you on that?"

"We'll see." Stepping away but linking their fingers to tug him along with her, in the easy contact that had become second nature, she went over to the contraption. "Take me with you?"

He moved past her to right the sail and turn the thing against the wind, but he looked back over his shoulder, met her eyes, and said quietly, "Always."

That one simple word lit her heart with joy. Things weren't perfect, but she wasn't waiting anymore; she was living in the moment with the man she loved, the one who stood there now, bare chested, tan, and laughing as he held out a hand to her in invitation with a quirked brow that said, *I dare you.*

And she dared. Oh, she dared. And as they sent the wind sail screaming across the desert, pressed together, laughing, kissing, and just being, with their familiars galloping behind, she couldn't imagine a more perfect moment, a more perfect man, a more perfect love. It was a world—and a life—worth saving.

Forever after.

Don't miss Rabbit's book,

Spellfire

Coming in November 2012 from Signet Eclipse!
Read on for a preview. . . .

Rabbit's father had always said that someday Rabbit would get what he deserved . . . and it turned out he'd been one hundred per-fricking-cent right. Shit, Rabbit could practically picture Red-Boar standing in the doorway, glaring at him from beyond the grave with a big-ass *See? I told you so* plastered on his mug, as leather whined through the air.

Then the brined lash cracked across Rabbit's back, laying open another bloody ribbon, and the image exploded into white-hot pain. He twisted against his shackles as if it were the first time he'd been whipped rather than the thousandth, and he might even have screamed.

Maybe not, though. He wasn't sure. He wasn't sure of much these days; his world had condensed down to the stone-block cell that had become his prison, and the golden-haired bitch who tormented him, tortured him, trying to make him give up something he'd already lost.

"Turn him around." At her order, talons scraped on stone and he was hit with a foul stench. Claws swung him on his chains, and he went from having his battered face pressed against the putrid wall to staring into the equally putrid visage of a *camazotz*.

Nearly eight feet tall, with the body of an overendowed man and a face cursed with ratlike red eyes, a smashed-in nose, and a triangular mouth that held way too many fangs, the bat demon was ugly from a distance, and really fucking gnarly up close. It kept its ragged wings and barbed tail curled near its body in the narrow confines of the cell, but the oily drool and the way its beady-ass eyes went over Rabbit's body said it was thinking about taking what little was left of his skin for wing patches.

A month ago, Rabbit would've told it to go fuck itself, and maybe even described the process in graphic detail. Now all he could do was groan as his spine grated against the sandpapery stone.

"Back off," his tormentor said from behind the creature, and the *camazotz* ducked its head and gave way, returning to its post beside the door with a hiss that was its version of *Yes, mistress, anything you say, mistress.* That left Rabbit with a view that—to him, at least—was worse than a chorus line of *camazotz* doing *Pirates of Penzance.*

He didn't know what the demon's natural form looked like—the *Banol Kax* could take on many shapes, from humans to three-story-tall winged monsters that breathed fire. This one appeared to be a woman in her twenties, with long, wavy hair, high cheekbones, and pale eyes that were unnervingly like his own. She wore a long red robe and had the trefoil mark on the inside of her right wrist, just as he did. All that was the same as it had been before, when he had known her in the world outside his cell. But where before she had come to him, slipping through the protective wards around Skywatch to speak to him in visions where she seemed ethereal and ghostly, now she was flesh and blood, or at least pretending to be.

It was all lies, after all.

As she approached, he forced a sardonic smile through split lips that hadn't even bothered swelling, as if his body had given up on any hope of repair, and said, "Hello, Mother."

She wasn't his mother, of course. She had played the hell out of the role, though, getting inside his head and offering him what he'd most wanted: a mother who had loved him and a reason to think that his old man had given a shit. She had sold him on the fantasy of having a real name—Rabbie—and a real family. She had cooed over him, coddled him . . . and then she had turned him, gradually and irrevocably, until he believed with every fiber of his twisted being that she was his only ally and all the others were his enemies, even the one person who had loved him unconditionally no matter what.

Myrinne. The word was a whisper in his soul, a cry of agony coming from the raw wounds of knowing what he'd done to her under the demon's influence.

"Rabbie . . ." The demon tutted sorrowfully. Even now, with him imprisoned and the charade unnecessary, she stayed in character. She might not be able to get inside his head anymore—his mental powers had vanished along with his magic—but she knew it was a bitter reminder to see her like this. Cruel enjoyment gleamed in her eyes as she leaned in close, brushed her fingertips along his swollen jaw, and whispered, "My poor, poor Rabbie. Why are you making me do this? You're hurting us both, you know."

His flesh quivered in muscle spasms that had him twisting away and then swinging back when he hit the ends of his chains. The scraping of the stone along his flayed back tore a groan from his throat.

Her eyes lit, though her voice stayed a purr. "Just give me what I want, and all of this stops and I set you free."

If he'd been another guy, in another place and time—some other Rabbit who lived in a parallel universe that wasn't a few weeks away from D-day—he probably would've taken the deal; anything had to be better than this, even death. But he knew that wouldn't put him out of the demon's reach. And he knew that if he couldn't escape from his shackles—been there, failed that—he could at least stall by pretending he still had what they wanted. Better for them to carve him up trying to gain access to Nightkeeper magic than have them go after one of the others.

It was his sacrifice, though they would never know about it. *He* did, though, and it brought him a spark of grim satisfaction to dredge up bloody saliva and spit in her face. "Kiss my ass, bitch. You want what's inside my head? Come and fucking get it."

She hissed, her eyes briefly flaring demon red as the air around them crackled with the oily rattle of dark magic. The magic was useless against him, though, at least for her purposes. She bit off a vicious curse and waved to the *camazotz*. "More. I don't care what it takes—I want him *broken*, damn you. We're running out of time."

Rabbit braced himself, knowing the first few blows were going to hurt like a bitch. He didn't close his eyes, though—he'd learned it was worse not knowing when the whip was going to hit. Instead, he glared at the demon bitch.

But as much as he hated her, he was far from innocent in his sins. She had whispered, suggested, seduced . . . but he was the one who had failed to tell his teammates about the visions. He was the one who had listened when she said Myrinne wanted him only for his power.

The lash cut through the air, then into his shoulder and chest. And it turned out this was one of the times when he welcomed the pain, baring his teeth and riding it out with a sick sort of relief, one that said, *Yeah, old man. I'm getting what I deserve*. Not that it made up for what he had done, but at least he was being paid back some.

By the tenth blow, the hot agony of each whip strike had turned cold and his body was shaking with chills. By the twentieth he was nearly numb, his eyes going unfocused as his consciousness threatened to take a hike.

And then the weirdest fucking thing happened. He saw his father.

It wasn't like he'd been imagining, either. It was more like Red-Boar was really there, planted in the doorway, wearing brown fatigues and a camo green T-shirt, with a machine pistol on one hip and a ceremonial knife on the other. He didn't register the blood or the beating, but instead scanned some distant horizon with a frustrated scowl on his battle-ax of a face. The vision was so real that even knowing his old man was dead and gone, Rabbit sucked in a ragged breath to call his name.

But then the image wavered and disappeared. Rabbit's struggles brought new pain searing as the shackles bit into his wrists and ankles, giving only slightly against the pins that held them in place. He wanted to roar and threaten. That would only please her more, though, so he just hung there, panting, while the nausea-inducing agony of the beating flooded back through him.

"There's no point. He's useless." The demoness waved away the lash. "Come. We're going after the girlfriend."

"No!" Rabbit bellowed, slamming to the end of his chains. "Don't you fucking touch her!"

Eyes gleaming red with excitement, the demon bitch shot a vicious look in Rabbit's direction. "Don't worry; she won't remember you by the time she gets back here. If she even makes it."

He roared incoherently, crashing at the ends of his chains as she left the cell, with the *camazotz* tossing the blood-soaked whip to the ground as it passed. Hatred pounded through him, would have consumed him if it hadn't been for the guilt and fear, the knowledge that they were going after Myrinne because of him. Even from there, he could still hurt her, it seemed. "No," he groaned, rattling the syllable up from the depths of his chest. "Please, gods, no!" But the gods didn't hear his prayers anymore, leaving it up to him to save her.

So, hooking his toes into the slimy stones for purchase and twining his numb, fumbling hands in his chains, he started climbing. He cursed when the rocks bit deep and then slid with blood, and again when pain made his stomach heave, but he kept going, pushing himself upward until he had a little slack in the chains. Before, he had found that it was just enough for him to get one hand near his face, and he had tried to tear the pin loose. Now he didn't bother with the pin. Instead, heart hammering a frantic beat of *Hur-ry, hur-ry, hur-ry,* he jammed his thumb into a link of the chain as high up as he could get it . . . and jumped.

There wasn't even enough free fall to register before the chains snapped tight and the full force of his body weight hit that thumb with a sickening *crack* that echoed inside his skull. He howled, jerked his mangled hand out of the chain and against its shackle. Pain hammered through him, hazing his vision, but by the gods his broken hand folded and went partway through the iron! His consciousness fought to waver, but he didn't let it; he couldn't—wouldn't—fail now.

He pictured Myrinne—not as he had last seen her, but back when things had been good and right between them, and he'd known for damn sure he was the luckiest bastard on earth to have her. He imagined her dark hair falling loose to her waist, mismatched stones glittering at her ears, and her brown eyes laughing up at him in challenge.

He didn't remember any smell or sound beyond those of his cell, didn't remember what it felt like to be touched with love rather than punishment, but he remembered that look. And it gave him the strength for another wrenching pull, one that dragged his hand the rest of the way free.

Gasping curses, he fumbled, struggling to get the pin free from his other wrist, then from his ankles. He tumbled to the floor, landed hard, lay there dazed and disoriented by pain and weakened by captivity. Maybe there was some part of his warrior self left inside him, though, because he somehow found the strength to force himself to his feet. Grabbing the fallen whip and holding it in his good hand, he stumbled through the door and into an unfamiliar tunnel lit by a string of bare bulbs. An echo of sound told him which way the demon bitch had gone, and he set off after her with murder in his heart.

He didn't have any magic, backup, or even a freaking clue where he was, but he knew one thing for damn sure: He was going to do whatever it took to reach Myrinne and protect her this time, or die trying.

JESSICA ANDERSEN

NIGHTKEEPERS
A NOVEL OF THE FINAL PROPHECY

In the first century A.D., the Mayans predicted the world would end on December 21, 2012. In these final years before the End Times, demons from the Mayan underworld have come to earth to trigger the apocalypse. But the modern descendants of the Mayan warrior-priests have decided to fight back.

"Raw passion, dark romance, and seat-of-your-pants suspense, all set in an astounding paranormal world."
—#1 *New York Times* bestselling author J. R. Ward

S0014